the Twisted Citadel

the Twisted Citadel

DarkGlass Mountain:
BOOK TWO

Sara Douglass

An Imprint of HarperCollins*Publishers*

THE TWISTED CITADEL. Copyright © 2008 by Sara Douglass Enterprises. All rights
reserved. Printed in the United States of America. No part of this book may be used
or reproduced in any manner whatsoever without written permission except in the
case of brief quotations embodied in critical articles and reviews. For information
address HarperCollins Publishers, 10 East 53rd Street, New York, NY 10022.

HarperCollins books may be purchased for educational, business, or sales pro-
motional use. For information please write: Special Markets Department, Harper-
Collins Publishers, 10 East 53rd Street, New York, NY 10022.

FIRST U.S. EDITION

Eos is a federally registered trademark of HarperCollins Publishers.

Map design © Sara Douglass Enterprises Pty Ltd 2006

Library of Congress Cataloging-in-Publication Data has been applied for.

ISBN 978-0-06-088215-0

08 09 10 11 12 WTC/RRD 10 9 8 7 6 5 4 3 2 1

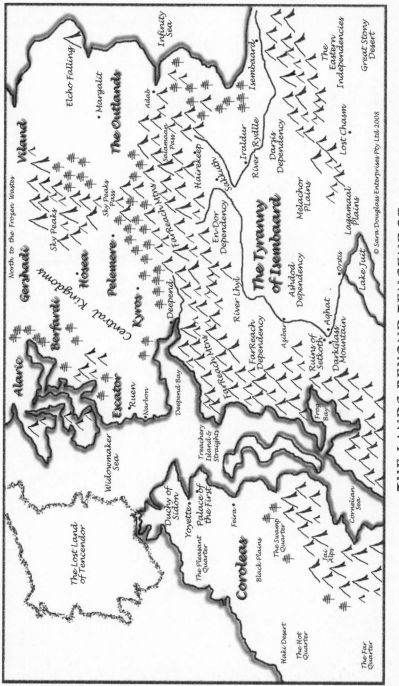

THE LANDS BEYOND TENCENDOR

© Sara Douglass Enterprises Pty. Ltd. 2008

PROLOGUE

Ancient Coroleas

The blade of the knife slid under the skin of his thigh, passing between skin and flesh sweetly and with exquisite gentleness, the heat of the blade cauterizing myriad tiny blood vessels. Every now and then the God Priest who wielded the knife paused, twisting his hand so that the skin lifted away a little from the underlying tissues.

Josia kept his eyes closed. The pain was bearable, just, but only if he did not allow himself to contemplate what the God Priest might do once he had completed making the long rents in Josia's thighs.

Or only if he did not allow himself to hear the gasps of anticipation among the crowd of hundreds within the packed chamber, or the smacking of their lips.

Josia lay as still as he might, his eyes tightly closed, ignoring the sounds about him, trying to keep his mind calm, and yet still he could not stop the tears sliding down his cheeks.

It had not been his choice to die in this manner.

The God Priest paused, contemplating the trembling and blood-streaked young man strapped naked to the top of the altar. The priest's mouth pursed in contemplation, then, decision made, he handed the knife back to his assistant, nodding at the query in the man's eyes.

Then he looked back to Josia.

The man was an extraordinary gift. Never before had anyone of such ability, of such *family*, been gifted to the God Priests. His soul would make a remarkable deity, and would sell for such a sum . . .

The God Priest licked his lips, anticipating the gold that would be his by day's end.

But first the young man had to die, and as badly as the God Priest could devise.

His assistant returned to the God Priest's side, and very carefully handed to his master the little pot of molten lead.

The God Priest bent down to Josia, the glow of the molten metal reflecting the avarice in the priest's eyes.

The assistant leaned forward, knife in hand, and lifted up the flap of skin on the nearest cut.

Josia smelled the metal, felt its warmth, felt the skin lift away from one of the cuts, and screamed.

He could not stop himself. He screamed and screamed, the breath wrenching in and out of his lungs, his body convulsing so badly he would have slid from the altar had not he been held tight with straps.

The God Priest poured the molten metal into the cut, taking great care now that the offering twitched so horribly, and wrinkled his nose in disgust at the smell that rose from Josia's burning flesh.

Then he moved to the next cut, pausing only so his assistant could refill the little pot of molten lead.

Josia escaped to the Twisted Tower. He ran down the path toward the corkscrew fortress, automatically counting out the eighty-six steps, and thudded against the wooden door, his hand closing about the doorknob.

He did not open it. He could, he knew he could, for the Twisted Tower would not prevent him entry, but if he entered while the Corolean God Priest was torturing him, then he might corrupt the tower and all its contents.

He huddled against the door, sobbing, wretched beyond imagining.

If he entered, then he would be safe, but he would corrupt the tower.

If he stayed outside then eventually the God Priest would have him, and his soul would be tortured into one of the Coroleans' cursed bronze deities.

Josia knew what he had to do.

He leaned his forehead against the door, trying to bring his weeping under control.

Inside the tower, his father and brother looked at each other, then both turned their backs on the door, closing their ears and hearts to the sound of Josia's horror.

The God Priest sighed.

After eight hours of the most exquisite of tortures, the offering was now in a wretched state. Both his life and his sanity hung by a very thin thread.

It would not be long.

As tired as he was, the God Priest managed a smile and a nod to the assembled mass of the Corolean First. He had saved the very best for last.

Once more he nodded to his assistant who brought forth a large gray rat, caged in a wickerwork basket. The God Priest lifted out the rat carefully—the very last thing he needed was a nip from the creature's sharp teeth—and held it down on Josia's belly while his assistant fetched a large copper bowl which had leather straps hanging from its rim. With both careful maneuvering and timing, the God Priest and his assistant trapped the rat under the upturned bowl, then strapped the bowl tightly to Josia's belly.

The crowd breathed in, almost as one, and every single man and woman of them leaned forward, their eyes wide with anticipation.

The God Priest looked about at the crowd, a slight smile on his tired face, reveling in the moment.

He took one of the two ladles his assistant held, paused, and then both he and the assistant beat at the copper bowl with all their strength, dancing about the altar in a maddened frenzy.

Josia couldn't let go. He couldn't die. All he wanted was to escape into death, even though he knew the God Priest would then trap his soul, but he couldn't let go.

His body was a mass of wounds. He had been beaten, tortured, agonized, teased, tormented. Every moment he existed was now spent in an ocean of pain.

Josia could not let himself take that final step into death.

He wanted to weep, but there were no more tears left.

He wanted the God Priest and his assistant to cease their infernal din on the bowl for it fractured his concentration, and if he wanted to die then he needed to concentrate or—

Oh gods, oh gods, oh gods!

The rat, driven into insanity by the noise and reverberation, desperate to escape, bit deeply into his belly.

Josia found he had, indeed, enough voice and breath remaining to scream.

The God Priest continued his beating on the bowl, but now it was slightly less frenzied.

He had seen from Josia's face the instant the rat had begun to chew into his belly—had seen the incredulous horror fill the man's eyes the moment before he had shrieked.

Then Josia convulsed.

The God Priest lowered the ladle, stepping away from the altar and indicated to his assistant to do likewise.

He was amazed that Josia still had the strength to move so violently.

He would make the most powerful deity the Coroleans had ever seen.

The God Priest watched intently, knowing that Josia's death was only heartbeats away . . . needing not to miss the moment.

A movement under Josia's rib cage caught the priest's eye, and he held his breath.

The rat was almost at Josia's heart . . . soon . . . soon . . . soon . . .

"Quick!" the God Priest hissed, and the assistant handed him a bronze statue, beautifully carved in exquisite detail into the perfect likeness of the man now lying dying on the altar.

Soon . . .

Josia's eyes remained wide open. He drew in a deep breath, readying for another shriek, when suddenly everything stopped.

Everything about him stilled.

The God Priest's own eyes widened; he held his breath, then he suddenly relaxed.

"Got you," he said, smiling in relief, and cradled the bronze statue against his body.

Josia existed. It was cold and heartless where he was now, but at least there was no pain.

There was nothing, save his existence, and a sense of what lay in the world about him.

A man, reaching for the receptacle which held Josia trapped.

A title, to go with the man. The Duke of Sidon.

Cold. Everything about Josia was cold.

He wept.

Within the chamber deep in the heart of the Palace of the First in Coroleas, all eyes were on the wondrous bronze deity that the God Priest now handed to the Duke of Sidon.

No one looked at the corpse lying on the altar, and thus no one saw the rat, wet with blood and shaking with effort, crawl from the corpse's mouth, drop from the altar, and scramble away into a dark corner.

No one saw it again, not for a very, very long time.

[Part One]

CHAPTER ONE

The Sky Peaks Pass, and DarkGlass Mountain, Isembaard

Ishbel Brunelle Persimius sank to her knees in the snow, watching Maximilian Persimius, the Lord of Elcho Falling, walk away from her into the night.

I'm so sorry, he said to her, over his shoulder. *So sorry.*

He vanished into the darkness, Ravenna at his side.

Very slowly Ishbel leaned over, her hands clutching into the snow, until her forehead touched the ground's icy surface. She stayed like that for four or five heartbeats, then her right fist beat once against the snow, then again, and she swore, very softly but very fiercely.

Ishbel straightened, sitting back on her heels, staring into the night.

She was furious. She had been kneeling in the snow, forehead to ground, for only a short space of time, but in that time she had journeyed from the absolute despair of Maximilian's rejection to a depth of rage that she'd never experienced previously.

Ishbel was not angry at Maximilian, nor even at Ravenna, but at herself. She could not believe that she, Archpriestess of the Coil, wife of the Lord of Elcho Falling, lover of the Tyrant of Isembaard, and a Persimius in her own right, had allowed herself to be outmaneuvered so easily. She could not believe that she, *Ishbel,* had allowed herself to be beaten into the snow, and so humiliated.

Even Maximilian's former lover, StarWeb, had not managed so easily what Ravenna had just accomplished with a few powerful words.

I carry his child, Ishbel. His heir. Maximilian Persimius will cleave to me now.

While Ishbel's current anger was directed at herself rather than at Ravenna, Ravenna *had* managed to earn herself Ishbel's enduring enmity—not merely for what Ravenna had said and done, but for the satisfaction with which she had delivered her triumph.

Ravenna's time would come.

Ishbel rose and brushed snow from her skirt and face with irritated, staccato movements. "Am I such a naive girl to be rendered so easily the fool?" she muttered. "I cannot believe I allowed Ravenna such an easy victory!"

Fool no longer, she thought, as she strode in the opposite direction from that which Maximilian and Ravenna had taken.

Ravenna need expect no goodwill from me in the future, and no more easy victories.

As she walked, her back straight, a hard glint in her eyes, Ishbel whispered into the night. *"Madarin! Madarin! Madarin!"*

Madarin was the soldier Ishbel had healed of a twisted bowel on the way down from the FarReach Mountains to Aqhat when Axis was escorting her to be Isaiah's new wife. She had no reason to believe that Madarin was still with that half of the enormous army which Isaiah had now brought as far as the Sky Peaks Pass, but somehow she *knew* he was here.

"Madarin," she whispered, every inch the priestess intent on her purpose. "Come, I have need of you."

Ten minutes later, as Ishbel stood shrouded by a line of dozing horses at the edge of the huge camp, a man emerged out of the night.

Kanubai stood in the Infinity Chamber in the center of DarkGlass Mountain and exulted. Far to the north the Lord of Elcho Falling vacillated, weak and indecisive, while here Kanubai stood fully fleshed and powerful, and with an army of gray wraiths at his command.

Moreover, here Kanubai stood, fully fleshed *from the flesh of the daughter of the Lord of Elcho Falling himself* and that would ensure Kanubai's success.

There was nothing the Lord of Elcho Falling could do against him.

Kanubai smiled.

There were a dozen or so Skraelings within the chamber, all crouched in various postures of servility and awe before their lord. They were loathsome creatures, but they would do.

Kanubai stretched his arms out and roared, knowing that roar would reverberate in the ears of the Lord of Elcho Falling and terrify him.

As he did so, one of his hands glanced against the blackened ruins of the once-beautiful golden glass of the Infinity Chamber.

And as his hand glanced against the ruined glass, so DarkGlass Mountain took him. More to the point, it absorbed him.

The pyramid had been waiting a very long time for just this moment.

Ravenna glanced at Maximilian, walking by her side. His face was set into a rigid, featureless expression which Ravenna knew meant he hid deep emotion.

She slid her arm through his, pulling their bodies together as they walked toward the tent they shared with Venetia, Ravenna's mother.

"I know it hurts," she said, "but it was the right thing to do."

Maximilian did not reply.

"Ishbel isn't the right—"

"Leave it be, Ravenna, I beg you."

Ravenna fell silent, torn between wanting to make certain that Maximilian understood the tragedy that Ishbel could make of his life, and knowing that pushing the issue could just as easily alienate him from herself.

His steps slowed, and Ravenna felt his body tense.

She panicked. "Maxel, it is done now. You can't go back."

Maximilian finally stopped, forcing Ravenna to halt as well. "I shouldn't have turned my back on her like that. Ever since her childhood, Ishbel has dreamed that eventually the Lord of Elcho Falling would destroy her life, and now—"

"Maxel, *she* is the one who will destroy *your* life."

Maximilian sighed, the reaction Ravenna dreaded the most. "I was too harsh, Ravenna. Too cruel. Ishbel didn't deserve what I just said to her."

Ravenna grabbed at one of his hands, bringing it to her breast. "She is weak, Maxel. Through that weakness she will destroy you. Ishbel will midwife nothing but sorrow into this land."

Maximilian regarded her, then leaned forward and kissed her cheek. "I know you mean only goodness, Ravenna, but I need to speak with Ishbel. I should not have walked away from her in that manner and I need to make sure she is all right."

"She will seduce you!"

He laughed, genuinely amused. "Not even Ishbel would think of that in this great chill! I treated her most badly, Ravenna. Let me go, I pray you, so that I may speak a little more gently to her. I will not linger, and I promise to you that I shall not allow myself to be seduced."

He started to pull back from Ravenna, but she clasped both her hands about his, tightening her grip. "There is something I should show you, Maxel."

"Not now, Ravenna."

"No. *Now!* Maxel, I know you think my aversion to Ishbel either a product of womanly jealousy or of blind bigotry—but it comes from a knowledge I have yet to share with you."

"Ravenna—"

"Let me share it now, Maxel."

He was still leaning away from her, but not so strongly now.

"Let me show you, Maxel," she whispered, and the snow about them vanished.

Maximilian pulled his hand from Ravenna's, but it was too late. The snowy ground about the army encampment disappeared and he found himself standing with Ravenna on a gravel path that wound through a misty marshland. Water festered in dank, black muddy pools to either side of the path, and thick mist drifted through stands of gray-green trees almost denuded of leaves, its tendrils becoming momentarily hooked on the trees' skeletal branches before twisting free and floating onwards.

It was very warm and Maximilian loosened his cloak.

"This is the Land of Dreams," Ravenna said. "*My* land."

"Why are we here?" Maximilian said. He was annoyed with Ravenna, but more so with himself. He wished, quite desperately, that he had not behaved so ungraciously toward Ishbel.

And he needed to find some solitude, so that he might wonder if he'd made the right decision . . . or not.

"I want to show you something," Ravenna said.

"Ravenna, I need to get back."

"No," she said, "you need to see this."

She waved a hand to her right, and the mists cleared.

Maximilian saw a roadway, winding its serpentine way toward a distant mountain, gleaming with gold at its top, set among the clouds.

Elcho Falling.

Bodies of men and horses littered the roadway. Icarii lay among the dead, and Emerald Guardsmen, and Maximilian could see Georgdi lying atop a heap of Outlanders to one side.

Look, whispered Ravenna.

An army now moved along the road toward Elcho Falling, pushing aside the bodies of the fallen as it went. The army consisted of creatures distorted into gruesome form, their eyes wide and starting—lost and hopeless. At their head strode a man of darkness.

This is what Ishbel shall generate, Ravenna said.

No, Maximilian said.

The army marched its way to the doors of Elcho Falling, and Maximilian and Ravenna saw, as if they stood only feet away, the man of darkness reach forth and pound his fist on the gates.

They will not open for him, said Maximilian.

They shall, said Ravenna.

The gates shrieked, and opened, and Maximilian saw Ishbel crawl forth on her hands and knees, weeping.

The man of darkness reached down to her and lifted her left hand, and Maximilian saw the Queen's ring gleaming on Ishbel's fourth finger.

"You have delivered to me Elcho Falling," said the man of darkness to Ishbel, *"and have sent its Lord into death. You have done well."*

"If you slide that ring onto her finger," said Ravenna, "you marry darkness to Elcho Falling and ensure your own death. Ishbel is your doom, Maximilian Persimius."

Maximilian could not speak. He continued to stare into the mist where the vision had appeared a moment ago.

"Ishbel will murder you and ruin this land," Ravenna said. "I know you love her, but she will bring you and Elcho Falling and this entire land nothing but sorrow."

"Enough!" Maximilian said. "For pity's sakes, Ravenna, don't you know when you have won? Don't you know when best to stop?"

Kanubai felt his hand slide into the glass and instantly knew what was happening.

All at once, the Lord of Elcho Falling seemed the very least of his problems.

The pyramid sucked him deep into its blackness where, for what seemed to Kanubai like an infinity of time, he and it did great battle.

Then, suddenly, the pyramid tired of its play, and it destroyed Kanubai, taking of the ancient creature only what it wanted.

Flesh. Breath.

"It is enough," Maximilian said, finally pulling his hand from Ravenna's grasp. He stepped back, his booted heel crunching into the snow.

"Don't go to her," Ravenna said. "*Don't.*"

"I—" Maximilian said, then he stopped, one hand half raised to his face as if his head ached.

"Maxel?" Ravenna said, putting a hand on his arm.

Maximilian said nothing, staring into the black night, snow catching at his dark hair. *Kanubai!* he thought. *What has happened?*

Ravenna didn't know what to do. She felt helpless in the face of his fatal fascination for Ishbel. What else could she say to Maximilian, what else could she show him, to bring him to his senses?

"Ravenna," he said, "I must go. There's something I—"

She grabbed his arm. "Don't go to her, Maxel!"

He tore himself loose, almost stumbling with the violence of his movement. "Just leave it be, Ravenna! Just for one hour, I beg you!"

Before Ravenna could say anything, he was gone, half jogging into the night.

The score or so of Skraelings who had watched Kanubai get sucked into the glass now cowered in a corner of the Infinity Chamber, terrified. Before them they could see Kanubai's form in the glass, twisting this way and that, being stretched first in one direction, then in another.

From time to time the glass walls bulged outward as Kanubai fought for his freedom, then they would snap back into rigidity as the Lord of Chaos weakened.

"What should we do?" whispered one of the Skraelings, its hand clutching at the shoulder of its nearest companion.

"Watch and wait," the other Skraeling replied. It grinned suddenly, its long pointed teeth glistening within the ambient light of the Infinity Chamber, its silvery orbed eyes bright with calculation.

"And *then?*" said the first Skraeling.

"Whatever necessity dictates," replied the second.

Some time passed—the Skraelings could not calculate how much—when suddenly the last vestige of Kanubai's form vanished.

The Infinity Chamber fell into stillness.

"What should we do?" hissed another of the Skraelings.

"Wait," whispered the pragmatist. "*Wait.*"

And so they waited and, eventually, something stepped forth from the glass.

It was the height and shape of a man, and with the head of a man, which was slightly less intimidating than the jackal head which Kanubai had assumed. In other respects, however, the creature was entirely un-manlike. Its flesh was not made of tissue and blood, but appeared to be formed of a pliable, and utterly beautiful, blue-green glass. Deep within the creature's chest a golden pyramid slowly rotated.

Its head was also glasslike, the creature's eyes great wells of darkness.

The Skraelings abased themselves upon the floor of the Infinity Chamber.

"Who are you, great lord?" asked the bravest among them.

"I am the One," the creature said. "I am perfection incarnate, for I am indivisible. I am Infinity, in its purest form."

"Then we are your servants," said the Skraelings, who, while understanding almost nothing of what the One had just said, were nothing if not realists.

As Maximilian strode into the night, and the Skraelings abased themselves before the One, Lister stood with three of the Lealfast atop a peak in the FarReach Mountains, looking southward toward Isembaard. Snow and icy wind coiled slowly about them, but none of the four paid the cold any mind.

At first sight seeming to be Icarii, with the same elegant human form and huge spreading wings, the Lealfast were at second glance something *else.* Their forms were not completely solid, but made up of shifting shades of gray and white and silver, and small drifts of frost clung to their features.

"Something bad has happened," Lister murmured, peering into the night as if he could physically see south to DarkGlass Mountain. "Kanubai has gone!"

Slightly to one side and behind him, the three Lealfast—Eleanon, Binga-leal, and Inardle—exchanged a quick glance.

What they felt could not be said before Lister.

Something perfect had just occurred.

CHAPTER TWO

The Sky Peaks Pass

Ravenna watched him walk away into the night. She tugged her cloak about herself, feeling her failure to keep Maximilian from Ishbel even more keenly than the cold. She had truly thought for a while that he realized the danger. He'd told Ishbel that Ravenna was carrying his child and that he would cleave to Ravenna, and then he'd allowed his guilt to overwhelm him and doubts to assail him.

He'd gone back to Ishbel. Not an hour had passed since he'd turned his back on Ishbel, and now he'd gone straight back to the woman.

Ravenna loved Maximilian, and she wanted the best for him, but his weakness as far as Ishbel was concerned drove her to despair. Maximilian had responsibilities and concerns far beyond Ishbel—far beyond anyone. He was Lord of Elcho Falling, and Elcho Falling should come first, otherwise this entire land would fall into ruin.

Maximilian needed to put Elcho Falling before Ishbel, and now Ravenna doubted very much that he could do that.

For months Ravenna had entertained doubts about Ishbel. In the past few weeks they'd firmed into certainty as she'd become more certain of the vision within the Land of Dreams. Ishbel had a weakness about her that would doom Maximilian—and through him this entire land—if he took her back as wife. But Maximilian resented it whenever Ravenna tried to talk to him about Ishbel. Even considering all the pain Ishbel had already brought into his life—her loss of their daughter, her affair with the Tyrant, Isaiah—Maximilian wouldn't hear anything said against her. Taking

Maximilian into the Land of Dreams tonight had been a calculated risk—Ravenna had dared it only as a last resort—and it had failed.

"Damn you, Maxel," Ravenna whispered; then she turned away and walked slowly deeper into the night.

Thank the gods, she thought, that she had conceived Maximilian's son. The child represented hope.

If not the father, then maybe the son.

Maximilian strode away from Ravenna, absolutely furious with her. This was not merely for her persistent harping about Ishbel, but because she had decided to harp just at the moment when he'd felt Kanubai vanish. All Maximilian wanted to do was to try and make some sense of what had happened to Kanubai, to *concentrate* on what might have happened to him, and all Ravenna could do was chirrup on and on about Ishbel.

Could she not leave well enough alone, for just one minute?

He had walked away, not daring to speak. He'd allowed Ravenna to think he was going back to Ishbel because he was so angry that he simply did not trust himself to open his mouth.

And he did not want to think about what Ravenna had showed him. Not right now. Not when something had just happened to make the entire world shift on its axis.

Maximilian walked through the camp, looking for Isaiah, hoping that he had also felt the surge of emptiness from the south and hoping that Isaiah might have been able to make some sense of it.

"Maxel."

Maximilian spun about. Isaiah was emerging from between a line of tents, his face strained.

Axis SunSoar was a step behind him.

"You felt it," Maximilian said to Isaiah.

Isaiah gave a curt nod. "Is there somewhere close we can speak? My tent is some distance."

"Not my tent," Maximilian said. He couldn't face Ravenna again this soon, and he also didn't want her to hear what might be said on this subject. "Axis?"

"Mine is close enough," Axis said, and led them a few minutes through the maze of horse lines and campfires to his tent, set close to that of

StarDrifter and Salome's. He held aside the flap, then indicated his father's tent. "Should I ask my father . . . ?"

Maximilian shook his head. "Not just yet."

Axis' tent, like that of all the main commanders, was commodious, high-ceilinged and well appointed. The three men pulled out chairs and sat at a large folding camp table. Axis' body servant, Yysell, set out a jug of ale and three beakers, then left the tent.

All three men ignored the ale.

"What's wrong?" said Axis. "Isaiah said something had happened."

Isaiah and Maximilian exchanged a glance.

"Something has happened to Kanubai," said Maximilian. "Very suddenly, within this past half hour. It felt to me as if all the threat associated with him suddenly dissipated."

Isaiah gave a nod. "I felt it, too."

"What do you mean," Axis said, "when you say that all the threat about Kanubai 'suddenly dissipated'?"

Maximilian and Isaiah exchanged another glance.

"Kanubai is gone," said Isaiah. "No more. Dead."

"Then why the long faces?" said Axis. "Surely, if Kanubai is dead, then . . ." He stopped, realizing the implications. "Oh gods . . . is it Dark-Glass Mountain? Has DarkGlass Mountain taken Kanubai?"

Maximilian gave a slight shrug. "I don't know." He rubbed at his forehead with one hand, looking exhausted. "Kanubai was so powerful . . . what *else* could have taken him save the glass mountain. Isaiah?"

"I think the pyramid might be even more dangerous than Kanubai," Isaiah said. "Lister," he continued, naming his ancient ally, "and I had wondered before if we'd been concentrating on the wrong enemy all this time."

"Oh, for all the gods' sakes," Maximilian muttered. "Why do I feel as if the ground is constantly shifting beneath my feet?" He paused. "Isaiah, where is Lister now? When will he be here?"

"He is flesh now, as I," said Isaiah. "He can only travel as flesh. He was most recently in the FarReach Mountains, and it may take him weeks to get here. We need to know what has happened, but I think that all of us are too tired. Maxel, have you been to bed at all? No? Neither have I. I think—"

"I want to talk to you about the pyramid, Isaiah," Maximilian said.

"Tomorrow, Maxel. Perhaps by then, refreshed, we will have gleaned more of what has happened. May I suggest we all meet in the afternoon? Axis, bring your father as well, and perhaps Malat and Georgdi. In the meantime—"

Isaiah stopped as the door of Axis' tent opened and Ishbel looked in.

She gave Maximilian an unreadable glance, then looked at Isaiah. "Isaiah," she said, "may I speak with you? It is important."

CHAPTER THREE

The Sky Peaks Pass

Maximilian tensed, looking away from Ishbel and down at his hands, and Isaiah did not miss his discomfort.

"Of course, Ishbel," Isaiah said. He rose, and joined her outside.

"Is there anything wrong?" he said, once the flap had fallen closed behind them.

"Not particularly," said Ishbel. "You have something I need. Where is your tent?"

Isaiah indicated a path through the sleeping encampment, and they walked quietly for a while.

"What is wrong with Maximilian?" Isaiah said eventually. "Something has happened."

Ishbel gave a slight shrug.

"*Something* has happened, Ishbel."

"I went to him tonight. I told him that I loved him, that I'd made a terrible mistake, and asked—well, begged—him if there was a chance we could remake our marriage. He, to be blunt, said that no, there wasn't." She paused. "Ravenna is pregnant."

"Oh, the *fool!*" Isaiah said.

To his amazement, Ishbel actually gave a small smile. "I was the fool, Isaiah. I cannot believe I made such a spectacle of myself, or that I allowed Ravenna to easily best me." Again, that slight shrug. "Well, no more."

"What do you mean?"

"It means that I have decided not to allow myself to be buffeted about by everyone else, Isaiah. Dear gods, I have more strength than that! I need to make my own way."

Now it was Isaiah who smiled. "Maybe Maximilian has done better tonight than I'd first thought. Well done, Ishbel. I have been waiting for this woman to emerge for some time. I don't suppose..."

As a test, he allowed his mind to linger over some memories of the time when they'd been lovers, wondering if Ishbel was now aware enough of her own power to pick up his mental images.

"Not tonight, Isaiah," she said, and he smiled again.

"What were you and Axis and Maxel doing so closely closeted?" she asked. "And all of you had great worry lines etched in your faces."

"Something has happened with Kanubai tonight," Isaiah said. "It feels almost as if he has vanished."

"DarkGlass Mountain," Ishbel said.

"More than likely. We decided we were all too tired to solve the problem tonight, and that we should sleep on it and meet later tomorrow to discuss it. Today, I suppose, as it must be close to dawn."

"I will attend, as well," Ishbel said.

"Of course."

They drew close to Isaiah's command tent, a great square scarlet extravagance of pennants and bells.

"What do you need from me, Ishbel?" Isaiah said, allowing her to pass through the doorway first.

She waited until they were both well inside the tent, and the doorflap closed behind them.

"The Goblet of the Frogs," she said, naming the magical goblet that Isaiah had shown Ishbel in his palace at Aqhat. "I assume you brought it with you."

Isaiah gave a nod. "And you want it because ...?"

"Because it is of my family," she said. "My ancestress Tirzah fashioned it. And I want it because I think it can teach me many things."

Isaiah studied her for a moment. All the time he had known her there had been an aura of fragility about her, or of worry, or of uncertainty. All of that had now gone.

"What happened tonight, Ishbel?" he said. "What *really* happened?"

"Maxel and I... everything between us was colored by my fear of the

Lord of Elcho Falling. The whispers I'd heard when I was a child in the house with the corpses of my family—"

Isaiah nodded. As an eight-year-old girl Ishbel had spent a month trapped in the charnel house of her family home, the corpses of her family rotting—and whispering—about her.

"—had taught me to fear the Lord of Elcho Falling, for he would bring nothing but bleakness and despair to my world. All through my girlhood and into my marriage with Maximilian, I had visions of how one day the Lord of Elcho Falling would turn his back on me and ruin my world. Maxel and I—" Ishbel made a helpless gesture with her hands. "I wanted to love him, but I feared what he would do to my life. He was the Lord of Elcho Falling and everything I had ever experienced had taught me to be terrified of him.

"Well, last night StarDrifter and Salome convinced me that I had to take the chance. That together Maxel and I could have something extraordinary. So I went to him and begged him, and he rejected me and presented me with his pregnant lover. Then he turned his back on me and walked away."

Ishbel took a deep breath. "And in the doing, he destroyed my world and fulfilled the visions I've experienced over all those years. An extraordinary blackness, a complete despair, overwhelmed me. It *crushed* me. I collapsed in the snow as he walked away. And then . . ."

"And then?"

"Fury consumed me. Not at Maxel, nor even at Ravenna—although, by the gods, I despise the woman and will surely have my revenge on her—but at myself. For being so stupid. For allowing myself to be so easily outmaneuvered. That fury was also a release. The worst *had* happened, and it was my fault, really, rather than that of Maxel, and now I was beyond it, and if I didn't want this to happen again, I needed to collect myself somewhat."

"That's quite a transformation for such a short period of time."

"It was almost instant, Isaiah. I was suddenly faced with the devastation I'd always feared . . . but it wasn't the Lord of Elcho Falling's fault, it was mine. It was . . ." Ishbel paused, trying to find the words to describe what she'd felt. "It was as if I'd experienced a gigantic release of pressure, I think. It was done, it was over, I didn't have to fear any more—not if I decided to take control and take back that strength I had lost."

"You don't still long for Maxel?"

"Not on his terms."

Isaiah stared at her, then he very slowly smiled. "Well, well. I have been waiting to meet this woman for a very long time. Maxel has an uncomfortable time ahead of him, I think."

She returned his smile. "Ravenna will have to cope with his black moods, not I. For the moment, she is welcome to them."

Isaiah walked over to a pack in one corner of the tent. He rummaged about in it, then withdrew a carefully wrapped parcel. "For you," he said. "For the Lady of Elcho Falling."

"What's happened?" Axis asked Maximilian once Ishbel and Isaiah had left.

"Oh gods . . ." Maximilian groaned and rested his head in his hands for a moment. "How did you manage it, Axis, Faraday and Azhure?"

Axis gave a short laugh, remembering that time so long ago when he had loved two women, and thought to have them both. "How did I manage it? Not well, Maxel. What happened tonight?"

"Ishbel came to me, told me she loved me, that she wanted us to remake our marriage."

"And you said?"

"Ravenna is pregnant, and I feel responsible for her—"

"Ah."

"—so I told Ishbel that it was impossible. Axis, you have no idea how guilty I felt walking away from Ishbel."

"You can still assume responsibility for Ravenna's child and take Ishbel back as your wife."

Maximilian stared at his hands and didn't say anything.

"Do you *want* to take Ishbel back as your wife, Maxel?" Axis asked softly.

"I don't know. Everything between us . . . there has always been such dishonesty and distrust, such—"

"Depth of emotion?"

"Such mismanagement, Axis. Do I love her? Once I thought I did, then when I found her with Isaiah, and our daughter dead, then I was certain I hated her. There is such distance between us. She has for years believed that the Lord of Elcho Falling would only ever bring her entire world to despair and dismay, and tonight . . . well, tonight I fulfilled that prophecy for her."

Now it was Axis who said nothing, watching Maximilian and allowing the man to talk it out.

"There is so much else I need to concentrate on, Axis. Elcho Falling, and whatever has happened to Kanubai. DarkGlass Mountain, and these damned Isembaardian generals who distrust me and doubtless plot against me. I do not need to be distracted by women just now."

Axis gave a slight shrug.

"Ravenna hates Ishbel," Maximilian continued. "For months she has spoken of her in nothing but dark terms and dismal tones. Her constant harping sets my teeth on edge. Tonight, as Ravenna and I walked away from Ishbel, Ravenna thought I was having second thoughts about rejecting Ishbel."

"Were you?"

Maximilian ignored the question. "Ravenna pulled me into the Land of Dreams, and there she showed me a vision."

"Of what?"

"Of Elcho Falling laid siege by an army of misshapen creatures, and with Icarii and human alike lying in piles of the dead. A creature, a dark nameless formless thing, walked to the gates of Elcho Falling, and they opened and Ishbel crawled forth and welcomed the creature into the citadel. It told her that it was glad she had done its bidding, not only in allowing it entry to Elcho Falling, but in my murder. Ravenna said that if I again took Ishbel as my wife, then the vision would become a reality. Ishbel will murder me and betray Elcho Falling. She may not mean to, but she will do it."

"Ravenna has a dark and bitter twist to her, Maxel."

"But what she showed me . . . I don't think she conjured that vision. It must be a true warning."

"I once thought that Azhure was my deadly enemy, too, Maxel, and I mistreated her so horrifically she almost died. If she *had* died . . ." Axis shook his head. "Maxel, I saw a truth, but I misinterpreted it so badly I almost lost the woman without whom . . . well, without whom I would have accomplished none of what later I managed. Trust your heart, Maxel."

"Hearts can be wrong."

Again Axis shrugged. "What are you going to do?"

"Raise Elcho Falling, one stone at a time."

Madarin was waiting for Ishbel when she left the tent, the bundle carefully held in her arms.

"I have arranged everything, my lady."

She smiled at him. "Really? Where?"

He led her back the way Isaiah had originally brought her. It was just on dawn now, and soft light permeated the crowded lines of horses and tents and equipment and campfires. Overhead, one of the Icarii drifted down toward a group crouched about one of the fires, while everywhere sleepy men emerged into the new day, yawning and stretching stiff, cold limbs.

"I am glad I can finally be of service to you, my lady," Madarin said as they walked. "Having saved my life, there is nothing I will not now do for you."

"I shall not ask anything too corrupt of you, Madarin, but whatever else you can give me, I shall be glad enough of. I think that . . . oh gods, Madarin, where did you find *that?*"

Madarin grinned as Ishbel stopped in her tracks and stared ahead. He was a middle-aged man, scarred and toughened by years in the military, and he had thought himself way past deriving pleasure from watching the wondering surprise of a lovely woman, but he supposed that perhaps he wasn't so hardened as he'd thought.

Ishbel was staring at the tent Madarin had sourced for her. Before she'd gone to find Isaiah, she had asked Madarin to find her a tent of her own. She was sick of sharing with others as if she were a stateless refugee, and she'd resolved that she would now house herself in a manner which befitted her new determination to be her own woman.

She'd imagined that Madarin would find for her one of the small, grayish canvas tents that soldiers used. It might be cramped and lowly, but it would be *hers.*

Instead, he had found for Ishbel a magnificence that was more beautiful even than Isaiah's scarlet extravagance.

The tent was of a similar size and shape to Isaiah's—full square, and large enough to hold within it a large canopied bed, a dining or conference table, and an area set about with cushions and low stools for more casual conversing—but instead of being scarlet it was of a vivid blue, picked out with gold and silver braiding, and hung about with tiny bells and golden tassels.

The tent itself was extraordinary enough, but the great pennant that fluttered from its pinnacle was almost miraculously lovely.

It had been sewn with cloth of a blue far more vivid than that of the tent. On this field of blue someone had stitched a device that left Ishbel momentarily speechless.

The device depicted an outstretched woman's arm, pale-skinned and delicately fingered. About the arm coiled a slim golden rope, its coils and knots intricate about the upper part of the woman's arm, but uncoiling to simplicity by the time it reached her wrist.

Behind the woman's hand was depicted the faint outline of a rising sun.

"I have been working on that pennant for many months," Madarin said softly, "and looking for the opportunity to give it to you for weeks now. I wanted to give you something, as you had given me my life—something that represented who and what you are."

"Madarin . . ." Ishbel didn't know what to say, or how to thank him.

"The tent," Madarin said, his voice a little choked at the tears gleaming in Ishbel's eyes, "is a spare tent that Isaiah carries with him on campaigns. It can be used by him if his usual scarlet tent is damaged, or it can be used for a visiting, or captured, king. I do not think he will mind that now you use it."

Ishbel wiped away a tear, then turned to Madarin and made a slight bow. "Thank you, Madarin. You have no idea what you have done for me this day."

The tent was simply but comfortably furnished. Ishbel washed, then unwrapped the goblet. She stood a while, staring at the beautifully caged glass, running a soft fingertip over the frogs gamboling about the reeds.

Then she lay down to sleep, curling her naked body about the goblet under the blanket.

She sighed, and drifted into sleep to the goblet's soft refrain.

Hold me, soothe me, love me.

Ishbel slept, and for the first time in many years, she did not dream.

An hour or two into sleep, Ishbel's arms relaxed enough that the Goblet of the Frogs rolled slightly away from her body. The goblet dislodged the covering blanket as it moved, exposing its rim to the night air.

For long minutes after that movement there was nothing but stillness, then something stirred within the yawning mouth of the goblet.

The darkness within the goblet bulged, then something emerged, jumped across Ishbel's white arm—causing her to stir a little, but not wake—and leaped down silently to the floor.

It was a large gray rat.

It paused a moment, looking about the tent, its dark eyes gleaming, then it scampered for the door and slid underneath its loose canvas bottom.

Minutes later it was moving about the boundary of the encampment, scurrying from shadow to shadow, until it reached open ground and was free to race southward across the snow-covered plains.

CHAPTER FOUR

The Sky Peaks Pass

Ravenna stood in the tent she shared with her mother and Maximilian. She had not returned immediately to this tent after Maximilian had left her, but had walked a while in the night, thinking.

"Maximilian acknowledged you before Ishbel?" Venetia said. She was a striking woman, in her dark coloring and beauty much like her daughter, but with more warmth about her eyes and mouth.

Ravenna folded a blanket from the bed she shared with Maximilian, then shook it out and began folding it over again. "Yes."

She glanced at her mother and gave a small smile. "You are surprised."

"Yes, I am."

"Well—I think he regrets it now. We argued over Ishbel, and he walked away from me, angry. I think he went back to her. Has he come here?"

Venetia shook her head. "Ravenna, you can't stand between those two, even with that child you are carrying."

"Mother, I have no choice. I—"

"Why? *Why?* Ravenna, I do not understand this desperate clinging to a man! No marsh witch needs a man the way you seem to want to cling to Maximilian!"

Venetia stopped, took a deep breath and moderated her tone. "Maximilian loves Ishbel and is uncomfortable with you as his lover—you must know this. None of this makes sense to me."

Ravenna took her mother's hand, and they sat down on the edge of the bed.

"When I first came back from the Land of Dreams, that night of the storm, I appeared on your doorstep with Maximilian and StarDrifter. Remember?"

Venetia nodded.

"We talked," Ravenna said. "I told you that I'd felt something darker coming, something from another world."

"Yes, I remember."

"I said I felt as if the world was about to pull apart."

"Yes."

"I was not entirely honest with you. I did not tell you *all* I had seen or come to understand."

Ravenna paused, choosing her words carefully. "Maximilian and Elcho Falling, and through them this land, are under dire threat, Mother. There *is* something coming, something vile, something which will wrench apart this entire world."

"Ravenna—"

"Ishbel is its servant. Not willingly, nor even consciously, but in some manner she is the catalyst of disaster. If Maximilian takes her back as wife . . . I am not sure *how*, nor even *why*, but if he does that, then he is lost, and Elcho Falling is lost, and all falls into catastrophe."

Ravenna gently stroked her mother's hand. "That is why I act as I do. That is why I fight to keep Maximilian away from Ishbel, and why, in the end, I conceived this child. I do not know if Maxel is strong enough to resist Ishbel's dangerous charm. Tonight he kept turning back to her, so I took him into the Land of Dreams and showed him what had been shown to me."

"And?"

"He was angry. I showed him what he did not want to know. He turned from me and walked away."

"Ravenna . . ." Venetia did not know how to put what she needed to say. "Maximilian is a powerful man, one who knows his own mind. You can't force him to do anything."

"I know, and that is why I am terrified he won't listen to me."

"Ravenna, you said the child . . . you conceived the child because you were afraid that you would not, in the end, be able to keep Maximilian from Ishbel. How does the child help?"

"How? This is a son I carry, Mother. Maximilian's heir. The next Lord of Elcho Falling should Maximilian fail. Or be tempted into ruination."

That pronouncement stunned Venetia into a momentary silence. Marsh women ensured they only ever conceived daughters. They had no use for male children, their world being an entirely feminine one, save for those occasions when they went to men to get with child.

"A *son?* What use do you have for a son, Ravenna?"

"Not for me, mother. For Elcho Falling. A new lord, should Maximilian fall."

Venetia stood up, pulling her hand from Ravenna's grasp. She moved to stand by the brazier and held out her hands, as if she were cold.

As indeed she was. Cold penetrated to the very depths of her soul, but Venetia did not think the heat from the brazier would help that chill.

What in the name of all gods was Ravenna doing? She thought to toy in something that was far, far beyond her, and Venetia did not like to think of the consequences.

Ravenna rose to her feet and moved to where Maximilian had left his pack. She rummaged within it for a moment, Venetia turning to watch her, then she straightened, a bundle in her hands.

"Ravenna! You cannot take the Weeper!"

"It is too dangerous to leave in Maximilian's hands. This bronze statue contains a great and powerful mystery, and may aid me to . . . oh!"

Venetia came over. "Ravenna? What happened?"

"The damn thing hissed at me!"

"Leave it, Ravenna! The Weeper is not yours, nor is Elcho Falling's destiny your concern. Why can't you see sense?"

Ravenna hugged the cloth-wrapped bronze statue close, even though its hissing was now distinctly audible. "I am going to do everything I can, Mother, to ensure that Elcho Falling—"

"Put that down."

Both women turned to face the tent entrance.

Maximilian stood there, one hand still holding back the flap of canvas that served as a door. "Put it down, Ravenna."

"Maxel," Ravenna said, "I was just—"

"*Put it down!*"

She held his eyes for a long moment, then very quietly and with great deliberation laid the Weeper on the bed.

Maximilian walked forward, retrieved the Weeper, then brushed past Ravenna to where his pack lay to one side of the bed.

"Did Ishbel take you back?" Ravenna said.

"I didn't go to Ishbel," he said, keeping the Weeper under one arm as he stuffed a few shirts that were draped over a chair into his pack. "I went to talk to Axis and Isaiah."

"About?" Ravenna said.

"About matters we needed to discuss!" Maximilian snapped, throwing the pack over his shoulder.

"Where are you going?" Ravenna said.

"I'm moving into my command tent. You and Venetia can keep this one. This camp is moving onto a war footing and I don't have time for—"

"Me?" Ravenna said.

Maximilian looked at her, very steadily, then allowed his eyes to drop deliberately slowly to the Weeper. "For disloyalty, Ravenna."

"It is Ishbel who—"

"It was not Ishbel who just tried to take the Weeper!" Maximilian moved toward the door. "Serge and Doyle will be tending me. One of them will collect the rest of my belongings."

He paused in the doorway, looked at Ravenna a moment, nodded at Venetia, and left.

"You pushed too hard," Venetia said, "and assumed too much. He's gone now."

Ravenna shot her a dark look before sitting abruptly on the bed.

Axis slept for four or five hours before he rose, washed perfunctorily, and dressed.

It had been a little over twenty-four hours since Maximilian had declared himself as the Lord of Elcho Falling to Isaiah's army and the tattered remnants of Georgdi and Malat's forces. A great deal had happened since and Axis wanted to scout the camp to get a sense of what the soldiers—and more particularly Isaiah's generals—thought and were doing. Loyalties continued to balance on a knife edge, and Axis needed to know which way they teetered.

The camp appeared fairly quiet, which reassured him. Men were going about the usual business of soldiers in camp; there were no tight groups of whispering men, no furtive eyes sliding away from Axis', no glaring gaps in the tent lines where men had decamped through the night.

He paused in amazement when he saw the blue tent with the pennant fluttering above it. He recognized the symbolism instantly—*Ishbel*—and he also recognized the man standing outside the entrance to the tent.

Madarin, the soldier Ishbel had healed of a twisted bowel when Axis had escorted Ishbel south from the FarReach Mountains. That occasion had been when Axis had become very aware that Ishbel had been far more than just a "ward" of the Coil.

"Madarin," Axis said amiably, strolling over, "I see you have found new duties."

"Lady Ishbel saved my life; it belongs to her. She called me to her service last night."

Axis nodded at the tent. "Ishbel is inside?"

"Asleep, my lord."

"I do not wish to disturb her, Madarin. Tell me, how does she?"

"Well, my lord."

"Hmmm." Axis stared at the tent again. "Where did this come from?"

Madarin explained how Isaiah carried a spare ceremonial tent with his military column.

"And the positioning of it?" Axis said. The tent was erected right at the edge of the main encampment, close to the tents of Maximilian, StarDrifter, Isaiah, and most of the other senior members of the army, as well as the large tent Isaiah—and now Maximilian—used for command briefings and meals. Yet Ishbel's tent was set slightly apart. Not much, but just enough to lend whoever inhabited it a certain eloquent and mysterious reserve . . . and command.

"I chose this location," Madarin said.

"Then you have done well for your lady," Axis said. "The pennant?"

"I stitched it for the lady myself," Madarin said.

Axis opened his mouth to comment, saw Madarin's face, and decided it better to leave doing so. He gave the soldier a nod of farewell.

As he moved through the encampment Axis paused and spoke briefly to several men, stopping to have a longer conversation with Insharah, the man with whom he'd ridden north from Aqhat to collect Ishbel. Insharah was now a senior commander within the Isembaardian force, having proved himself over this past year more than capable of promotion. He was still a good friend of Axis', however, and as such he was Axis' best conduit back into the heart and soul of the Isembaardian force.

"Tell me the mood," Axis said, once they had exchanged greetings.

"One of shock," Insharah said. "First this Maximilian, who had spent so many weeks trailing along with the column as a captured king, declaring himself lord of this or that and taking control of the army from Isaiah. Maximilian is a complete unknown, and what we'd seen of Isaiah had not suggested to us that he would just hand control of the entire army to Maximilian. No one quite knows what to make of it, Axis, or what to think.

"But worse was the news that Isembaard has been overrun by some army of...wraiths. Everyone is concerned about their families. Myself included."

Insharah paused to give Axis a sharp look. Insharah had a wife and children in Aqhat, just across the River Lhyl from DarkGlass Mountain where, apparently, this ghostly army gathered.

"I can give you no assurances," Axis said, "save this small hope. The Skraelings loathe water. It will take them days, if not weeks, to summon the courage to cross the Lhyl. I hope that will give people enough time to evacuate."

"Evacuate *where?*"

"Either up through the Salamaan Pass or down south, to the Eastern Independencies."

Insharah shook his head slightly. "If this Maximilian wants our loyalty, Axis, then he shall need to assure us that our families are safe. If we *don't* get that assurance, I cannot answer for how many men might decide to aid their families themselves."

Axis nodded, understanding. He rested a hand on Insharah's shoulder, thanked him for his honesty, and moved on. He walked down to the area where Isaiah's generals had their tents. There were the usual activities going on that he would have expected: some empty dishes being carried out of Kezial's tent, while Kezial's body servant was busy washing his master's linen in a tub to one side of Kezial's tent.

Axis moved toward Armat's tent—the youngest general was, in Axis' opinion, the most dangerous of them—when there came the sound of footsteps behind him. Axis turned about. It was a soldier that he recognized as one of Insharah's men, with a message that Axis was wanted at one of the horse lines.

Axis strode off, missing the look of sheer relief that crossed the face of the guard outside Armat's tent.

An hour after Axis had risen, Ravenna slipped quietly through the flap of Maximilian's command tent.

If Maximilian wouldn't, or couldn't, repudiate Ishbel completely, then Ravenna needed to know it—and be able to plan from there. As in taking Maximilian into the Land of Dreams to show him the vision which haunted her, Ravenna knew she was likely pushing too hard, but she needed to do this badly enough to risk the consequences.

Maximilian was asleep on a camp bed. Serge, one of the two Emerald Guardsmen who had accompanied Maximilian on his journey from Escator into Isembaard, rose from the stool where he'd been sitting by the brazier. Ravenna nodded toward the door.

Serge hesitated, then left.

She let out a small sigh. She still had enough influence for that, at least.

Ravenna pulled a chair over to where Maximilian continued to lie sleeping, then put a hand on his shoulder and shook gently.

"Ravenna?" Maximilian murmured, blinking sleepily and rising on one elbow.

"Why are you cutting me off, Maxel?"

Maximilian sat up, swinging his legs over the side of the bed. He rubbed his eyes and sighed. "Look, Ravenna—"

"What have I done wrong?" Ravenna knew as soon as the words were out that they were ill-advised. She wished futilely she could snatch them back.

"Apart from trying overhard to run my life for me? Apart from trying to steal the Weeper, probably in order to force me to your wishes?"

"Maxel, I know I shouldn't have tried to take the Weeper, but—"

"Ravenna, at the moment I need to concentrate fully on gaining complete control of this army. There are hundreds of thousands of men gathered about this tent, and as many in the provinces behind us, all weaponed and ready for war, none of whom trust me. I don't have time—"

"For me?" *Damn it!* Now she was acting like a hysterical tavern wench abandoned by her soldier lover.

"I don't have time for your games, Ravenna."

They stared at each other silently at that, and Ravenna wondered that such a distance could have opened between them in such a short time.

It was Ishbel's fault.

"I see Ishbel has found herself a bright new home," Ravenna said, referring to the tent she'd seen on her way to Maximilian's command tent. By the gods of dreams, such ostentation! "Did you give her that?"

Maximilian had noticed the tent earlier when he'd gone out just before dawn. "No, I did not procure that tent for Ishbel. But she has every right to it. She is a Persimius, and central to both the raising of Elcho Falling and the fight against . . . whatever it is we face."

Unlike myself, Ravenna thought. "You will need to make it clear to her that you will not take her back as your wife. You—"

"Oh, for gods' sakes, Ravenna, stay out of this! *Let it go!*"

"You know why I cannot do that."

Maximilian rose, pulling on a pair of trousers with sharp, angry movements. "You are doing yourself no favors."

"As neither are you." Ravenna stopped. "I'm sorry, Maxel. I shouldn't have said that."

"Ishbel doesn't concern you, Ravenna. Leave her alone."

Ravenna sat silently as Maximilian pulled on his boots and then a shirt and jerkin.

"She will kill you, Maximilian," she said eventually.

"Stay away from her. I can look after myself well enough." Maximilian sat back down on the bed. "Look, I am sorry if I have given you to understand that you and I . . . that we . . ." He stopped and sighed. "We should have talked about this a long time ago."

Ravenna gave a short, humorless laugh. "You do not need to put it into words, Maximilian Persimius. I can see the lie of the land well enough. All I want for you, Maxel, is a bright future. I did not save you from the Veins only to lose you to that witch, Ishbel."

Maximilian's eyes darkened at that last. "Is that what the child was for, then? Just another means to keep me from Ishbel? Another weapon to use against her?"

"This child," Ravenna said, "is Elcho Falling's future."

"Only if I recognize it as such," Maximilian said very quietly, then grabbed his cloak and left the tent.

CHAPTER FIVE

The River Lhyl, North of Aqhat, Isembaard

Hereward stood on the deck of the riverboat, arms wrapped about her upper body hugging her thin shoulders. Her dark hair blew into her eyes and across her face, obscuring her vision, but she made no move to tuck the strands behind her ears.

Her black eyes stared straight ahead, almost unblinking.

To the far bank.

Skraelings seethed there, staring back at her, globules of saliva dripping from their jackal-like jaws, although she thought their teeth both more numerous and larger than a jackal's. Their huge clawed hands clenched, desperate for her.

But they would not cross the water. They hated the water.

The River Lhyl was all that stood between Hereward and a tearing, agonizing death.

The Skraelings still panicked Hereward, still caused her stomach to clench in a twisted misery of fear and physical nausea, even though it had been weeks now since they had appeared on the riverbank opposite Isaiah's palace of Aqhat.

Weeks since her, and Isembaard's, world had disintegrated.

Hereward had lived a relatively good life within the palace. She was the result of a furtive, sweaty, and extremely hurried union between a slave girl and one of Isaiah's soldiers, but the *who* of that soldier meant Hereward had been freed at birth and had been given the chance at a responsible appointment within the palace in adulthood.

Her father was Ezekiel, now the most senior general to the Tyrant Isaiah.

Ezekiel had had very little to do with Hereward during her childhood. He'd been careful to ensure that she (and her mother) had adequate housing, and that Hereward had a good schooling. Ezekiel had taken greater interest in Hereward once she'd reached adulthood, and had secured her a position within the palace. By the time she'd reached her mid-twenties, Hereward had attained the position of kitchen steward, a pretentious title for the person who supervised the meals for the various departments of the palace: the Tyrant's private chambers; his wives' apartments (there were over eighty of them and Hereward could never remember all their names); the nursery where the Tyrant's many children were housed (Hereward didn't even try to count them, let alone memorize their names); the myriad governors, generals, guests, scribes, bureaucrats, servants, soldiers, and slaves who lived in and about the palace. It was an exhausting job, but Hereward took pride in it. She was free, she earned a good wage, and one day, she hoped, she might have saved enough to open a tavern . . . in Sakkuth, perhaps. Hereward had had enough of the rigidity and formality of palace life at Aqhat.

Then, everything had changed within the space of an hour or two.

Isaiah had left to undertake his northern invasion many months earlier, Ezekiel with him. Palace life had quieted to utter tedium as over ninety percent of the people who had inhabited the palace left to trail behind the Tyrant. Most of the wives had left for the eastern cities, their children with them. There was but a handful of soldiers left. Servants and slaves had enough time to enjoy a siesta during the hottest hours of the day.

And then one day . . .

Hereward had been in the palace's vast kitchens. She spent a large part of her day there, talking to the cooks, planning menus, supervising the cartage of food from the kitchens to wherever in the vast palace complex it was needed. It had been a strange day, for everyone had been unsettled without being able to pinpoint a reason. If a servant dropped a spoon, then everyone jumped at the clatter, shooting dark looks at the unfortunate offender. Hereward could not concentrate on the menus—and there were so few of them, by the gods, surely she could manage *this* small task!—and kept having to ask the cook with whom she spoke to repeat what he had just said.

For some reason, everyone kept looking to the windows.

Just before midday there had come a shout from the outside.

No. Not a shout. Hereward thought later that it had been a howl of sheer terror, the sound knifing into the bright midday sky.

For an instant everyone in the kitchen froze.

Then Hereward started to walk toward the door which led into the great courtyard beyond. Her legs felt leaden, every step an effort, and her chest felt as if a great hand had clenched about it.

Somehow, Hereward understood very clearly in that moment that her life was probably either about to end or to change so utterly that she would wish it *had* ended.

There was a great deal of commotion in the courtyard. People were grasping at the shoulders of others, asking them what had happened, what was wrong.

Others pointed to the gates which led to the river, and covered their faces with their hands and wailed.

Not wanting to, but unable to stop herself, Hereward walked toward the gates. She stepped through them, ignoring the people who brushed past her—either going in her direction to see what had gone wrong, or rushing back toward the palace, faces set in masks of horror.

Hereward stopped some twenty or so paces the other side of the gates. From this vantage point she had a clear view of the River Lhyl, and the far bank, where stood DarkGlass Mountain.

She stood and looked, unblinking.

Her mind could not process what she saw. It tried to present to Hereward various interpretations, all of which she knew were incorrect.

DarkGlass Mountain had not somehow become enveloped with every billowing white sheet hung out to dry in Isembaard.

DarkGlass Mountain was not covered in a sudden storm of snowy thistle flower.

DarkGlass Mountain was not burdened under a sudden and unexplainable invasion of white locusts.

Instead, the glass pyramid was covered—*crawled*—with an undulating, horrific tide of gray wraithlike creatures. They were coming from the north. Hereward was vaguely aware that the far riverbank was covered with the creatures as far north as she could see.

People were pushing and bustling about her. Hereward thought that some of them might be screaming, or shouting, or some such. She didn't really know or care. Right in this moment, all she could do was stare.

Then someone said: *What if they cross the river?*

Utter panic consumed Hereward. She racked in a huge breath, tried to expel it, and couldn't. She turned to run, but couldn't. Her legs just would not work.

Then came another shout (or perhaps a whisper, Hereward did not know). Skraelings!

Hereward knew of them. Every since the Tyrant Isaiah had brought Axis SunSoar back from the dead and into the palace, stories of Axis' life had circulated about the palace staff. Hereward had heard about the Skraelings. She knew of their horror.

Skraelings?

Somehow Hereward managed to force herself to breathe, and then she managed to take a step back toward the palace. Another breath, another step, and then she was running with everyone else, buffeted and bruised by the mass panic, her long black hair coming free of its pins and half blinding her.

She didn't care. All she wanted to do was to get inside the kitchens and *think*.

The kitchens were virtually deserted. Hereward sank down to her haunches behind the door, instinctively finding a hiding place. Her hands were buried in her hair, her eyes were staring, her chest heaved with her huge breaths.

She didn't know what to do. She still could not order a single thought, let alone decide on a course of action.

Jeqial, one of the cook apprentices, darted into the kitchen from outside. He ran into a side room where everyone stored their cloaks and outdoor sandals, then came out almost instantly, his cloak about his shoulders. He grabbed a hessian bag of root tubers that one of the gardeners had only brought in an hour previously, dumped the tubers onto the floor, then hurriedly filled the sack with a flask of wine, some bread, some fruit that was sitting on a serving platter to one side.

Then he saw Hereward.

"Hereward," he gasped, now twisting the neck of the sack closed and tying it with twine. "We have to get out of here."

Where? she thought, unable to articulate the word.

"We have to *go!*" Jeqial said. "Didn't you see what—"

He stopped. It was perfectly obvious that Hereward had seen.

"We have to go," he repeated more slowly, emphasizing each word.

"Where?" Hereward managed to say.

"I, ah . . . east. Far away."

East? Hereward thought. *East into the dry horror of the Melachor Plains?* "Perhaps Isaiah will be back," she said. "The army . . ."

"They are months gone, Hereward. Perhaps they are dead. We need to get away from here *now!* If we stay . . ."

If we stay . . . Hereward's stomach literally heaved at the thought of what would happen if they stayed.

"They won't cross the water," she said. "The Lhyl will protect us. They—"

"They will find a way to cross eventually," Jeqial said. "Stay here and die if you want, Hereward. I am going to live."

And with that he was off.

Gradually the kitchen staff returned. Some sat or stood like Hereward, stunned and unable to think or act. Others did as Jeqial, grabbing what they could and running . . . where, Hereward was not entirely sure, but running.

After what appeared to Hereward a very long time, she rose, clutching at a table for aid in getting to her feet.

She must have been crouched down for hours—her legs and back were stiff and cramped.

"We have to aid ourselves," she said to no one in particular. "No one will come to help us."

"Isaiah—" said one of the cooks, a man called Heddiah.

Hereward gave a small shake of her head. "Isaiah won't come."

"He has an army," said Ingruit, a vegetable preparer.

"He and they are either dead or they have forgotten us," said Hereward. "We must shift for ourselves."

"We need to leave, then," said Heddiah.

"Yes," Hereward said.

"East—" Heddiah began.

"*No,*" Hereward said. "Not east. Where in the east? Into the Melachor Plains? Into the mountains where live the bandits? In one we'd starve or die of thirst within a week, in the other we'd be murdered before the Skraelings had their chance at us. And in both, we'd stand no chance whatsoever once the Skraelings manage to get across the river. Have you *seen* how many of them there are? Millions! *Millions!*"

Hereward stopped, appalled at the note of hysteria in her voice.

"No," she continued, now controlling her voice and trying to inject as much persuasion into it as she could. "Not east. Even if we were left alone, or if we survived the Melachor Plains, it would take us many weeks before we reached any kind of safety."

"Where then?" said a woman called Odella.

"North," Hereward said. "North, up the River Lhyl."

"But the Skraelings are just across the river!" said Heddiah.

"They can't touch us," said Hereward. "Not on a boat. We just don't touch the western shore ... we *can't* touch the western shore, ever. Even if somehow, somewhere, the Skraelings manage to cross the river and surround us on both sides, they still can't reach us in the middle of the river. It is the safest place."

There was silence as people considered her arguments.

"We take a boat," Hereward continued, "and with the winds driving southwesterly we can tack upriver, many leagues each day. We can reach the north within ... what? Ten days?" She actually had no idea, but no one contradicted her.

"And then?" said Odella.

"And then we go wherever is safest. By the time we reach the north we will have a better idea of what is happening. There will be news." How they were going to gather news and information when they were stuck in the middle of the river Hereward did not know. But there would be news somewhere, somehow, surely. "We can make a choice then. But at least it is far away from *here*. We cannot stay *here*."

Now Hereward stood on the riverboat's deck, looking at the Skraelings hungering on the far bank. That terrible day in Aqhat seemed a year away now, although it had only been a matter of a few short weeks. The remaining kitchen staff had eventually agreed with Hereward that the boat north would be the safest and quickest, if the most terrifying, means of escape.

They had commandeered a riverboat large enough to hold their party—some twenty-eight, counting spouses and children—and had set sail northward. Five or six of the men had river experience, and they quickly taught the others how to steer and set the sails so they could tack into the wind and sail north against the Lhyl's gentle current.

The winds had not been as good as they'd hoped, and they had not traveled as fast as they had expected, but at least they had kept safe. They were careful to stay in the center of the river where the water was deepest and where the riverbanks were each some twenty paces away. Skraelings haunted the western bank, hordes of them, scores of tens of thousands of them, hungering for the *Tasty! Tasty! Tasty!* that the boat held. The Skraeling whispers pervaded the hull of the boat, and everyone had to grab what sleep they could while the terrifying whispers slid cold and malicious about them.

Hereward hardly slept. It was dusk now, and Odella had called her a while ago to come and eat with the others.

Hereward wasn't hungry. She felt that if she took her eyes off the Skraelings for just one moment then they would attack.

Somehow they would find their way over the water.

If she did sleep, Hereward had nightmares of waking to find them crawling over her, their terrible claws sinking into her flesh . . .

She'd come to hate Axis SunSoar and Isaiah. Somehow she'd managed to associate her current plight with these two men.

Whoever had heard of Skraelings before Axis arrived in Aqhat?

And why had Isaiah deserted them? Why had he taken everyone who could possibly have saved the people of Aqhat north into the lands above the FarReach Mountains?

Hereward had also come to loathe her father, Ezekiel, although she had never felt much affection for him. Ezekiel had always been so distant, and Hereward felt that he only concerned himself with her out of a sense of resigned duty. She was a bastard and had no place in his life. Ezekiel had a wife and legitimate children.

Those children, her half-brothers and sisters raised in luxury and privilege, lived in Sakkuth, well away from this place.

All of them had left her and her friends to manage as they may.

The Skraelings roiled and whispered on the far bank. Their long, thin arms reached out for her, their jaws drooled, their teeth caught the last of the light, and their tongues bulged obscenely from their mouths.

Hereward had never felt so alone and so hopeless in her life. She had never been able to even imagine feeling this way.

After a moment, she turned, and walked belowdecks to join the others in their evening meal.

CHAPTER SIX

The FarReach Mountains and
DarkGlass Mountain, Isembaard

It was almost dawn when Eleanon and Bingaleal heard Inardle approach their eyrie atop the mountain.

"Is Lister still asleep?" Eleanon said as Inardle crouched down beside them, and she nodded.

"He stayed awake for hours, wondering about the pyramid, sending his senses scrying south," she said.

"And?" Bingaleal asked.

"He felt nothing other than the fact of Kanubai's death," Inardle said. She paused, looking at the faces of the two birdmen, trying to read their expressions. "And you?"

Eleanon and Bingaleal glanced at each other.

"We've been waiting for you," Bingaleal said. "Three are more powerful than two."

Inardle nodded, relieved and pleased that they had waited. They must, like her, and like Lister, be desperate to discover precisely what had happened at DarkGlass Mountain.

"*Should* we do this?" she said.

"Are you having doubts?" Eleanon said.

Inardle gave a short laugh. "Of course! And you have no doubts? Don't tell me that."

"We need to know," said Bingaleal. "There is only one reason we have come on this adventure south with Lister. To grab some power and destiny for *ourselves*. Maybe this Lord of Elcho Falling will prove the road to our ultimate destiny, maybe there is some other path for us . . . we need to know, Inardle."

"Yes," said Inardle, now settling down cross-legged, as did her companions. "We need to know."

They sat facing one another in a small circle. Eleanon raised his hands before him, frowning in concentration. For a moment, nothing, then a tall glass pyramid appeared within the cup of his hands. In dimension and height it was the same as the glass spires the Lealfast had given Isaiah, Lister, and Ba'al'uz, but unlike those spires, this was of a dark, almost black, glass and was very slightly twisted, as if a hand had corkscrewed it while the glass was still hot from its making.

"Lister would panic if he knew we had this much power," Bingaleal said, looking at Inardle as he spoke.

"I shall not tell him," she responded. "He knows nothing about what we truly are."

"It is better the world does not know," Bingaleal said, "just what powers we do command."

"Shush!" Eleanon said. "*Concentrate!*"

Bingaleal shot him an irritated glance, but did as instructed, and all three gazed intently into the dark, twisted spire.

For several heartbeats nothing happened, then the spire glowed with light, cleared, and all three Lealfast found themselves looking directly into the Infinity Chamber.

Several Skraelings huddled in one corner, but the Lealfast's attention was completely absorbed by the man-shaped creature of blue-green glass who stood with his back to them. He was moving his hands very slowly over the tortured, blackened glass walls of the Infinity Chamber and, as his hands passed over the glass, so the glass was restored to its full golden beauty.

The creature paused, becoming aware of the intruders, and turned about unhurriedly.

"Who are you?" said the creature. "I know you somehow."

The three Lealfast glanced between themselves, then Eleanon took a deep breath and answered.

"We are the Lealfast," he said. "We traveled a while with the Skraelings. You are . . . ?"

The creature smiled, just a small uplifting of his mouth. "You do not know?"

Again the three Lealfast exchanged a glance, coming to a silent decision, then Bingaleal spoke. "You are the One, who the Magi once worshipped, and for whom they built the pyramid. You are perfection incarnate, and you are Infinity."

The One lowered his head in assent. "I am all of those things. You wish to speak with me? Why?"

"We do wish to speak with you," said Eleanon, "but we thought the Skraelings with you might like to be allowed to go hunt. I am sure our conversation would bore them."

The One's eyes narrowed, then he waved a hand in dismissal at the few Skraelings who remained within the Infinity Chamber. "Hunt," he said. "Now."

The One waited until the chamber was empty. "You wanted them gone," he said. He paused, considering. "I know you now. Lealfast you may call yourselves, but you hold within you the learning of the Magi who once honored me. How else could you have built that dark spire you use so effortlessly, or even the ones you gave about to others . . . yes, I know of them. And how is it you command the powers of the Magi?" His voice hardened, just slightly. "Come, tell me now, if you value my benevolence."

"You know of Boaz and his battle with the pyramid, Threshold?" Eleanon said.

The One bared his teeth slightly—they were curiously translucent—and they glimmered in the soft light of the Infinity Chamber. Two thousand years ago the renegade Magi, Boaz—a member of the Persimius family—had turned against his brethren and the One incarnate within the pyramid, seeking to destroy both the cult of the Magi and the pyramid. The One could not be destroyed—no one had the power for that—but the idea that Boaz even thought to make the effort had infuriated the One.

And made him wonder if the Persimius family might try again.

Like Kanubai, the One had no love for Elcho Falling or its master.

"Boaz caused the Magi to be disbanded," said Eleanon. "Many died, or killed themselves so that they might not have to endure a world which no longer permitted worship of the One . . . of yourself. But a few took what they could of the Magi's hoard of books and scrolls before their libraries were burned, and they traveled north, escaping the soldiers that Boaz's brother, Zabrze, sent after them. These few Magi arrived in the far north after years of travel and travail."

"They taught you," the One said.

"Yes. We welcomed them, for they brought a tantalizing glimpse of a future we had not considered, and power that we had never dreamed existed."

"Tell me," said the One after a considered pause, "are you loyal to the Lord of Elcho Falling?"

Inardle opened her mouth to speak, but Bingaleal forestalled her.

"Not necessarily," he said. "It would depend very much on what we might find at the end of the path the Magi showed to us."

The One's mouth curved upward in a wide smile. "We shall talk some more, I think," he said.

CHAPTER SEVEN

The Sky Peaks Pass

They met very late that afternoon for an early supper in the command tent. Maximilian had been out, and arrived in the tent once everyone had gathered. He looked tired and strained, and only nodded in greeting as he entered. Two serving men were still bringing in platters of food, setting them down before those already seated at the table. Maximilian ignored the table, and walked over to join the four men standing at the wine servery.

"Georgdi, Malat," Maximilian said. "Are you somewhat recovered? Have you slept? How are your peoples?"

"Most are well enough, Maxel," Malat said. "They are grateful for the shelter and opportunity to rest and eat after so many weeks on the run from the damned Skraelings. But within a day, I think, they shall be rested and fed enough to start worrying about what lies behind them—how much of their homeland remains, and if any of their families survived the Skraelings' horror. What I will say to them, I cannot think."

"We can send a scouting party to see what is left," Maximilian said. "I think—I *hope*—the Skraelings will stay south of the FarReach Mountains for the time being. *I* want to know what has happened to Escator. Georgdi?"

"I'd like to know what Isaiah's . . . sorry, *your* army has left of the Outlands, Maximilian," Georgdi said. "Once my men have rested sufficiently, I shall need to ride east to Margalit. I assume it still stands after Isaiah dragged almost a million soldiers and settlers through it."

"It still stands," Maximilian said, "but Isaiah left many thousands of his soldiers there to secure his rear. Wait," he said, as Georgdi opened his mouth to speak. "I know you want them gone, that you want *us* gone from the Outlands, but unfortunately this province is likely to become the first to feel the full force of the Skraelings' push north. I am not going to shift men from the Outlands until I know what is happening."

"Which is what we need to discuss tonight," Axis said, standing to Maximilian's right, with his father StarDrifter SunSoar at his elbow. He handed Maximilian a glass of wine, then nodded at the table. "Shall we sit? The serving men have left us in peace."

Salome, Ishbel, and Isaiah were already seated and had been conversing in soft tones. Now they fell into a watchful silence as the men approached the table, all eyes on Maximilian.

In his turn, Maximilian watched Ishbel out of the corner of his eye as he took his seat at the head of the table. Of all of them she looked the most rested, and certainly the most collected, and he wondered at the tranquillity she appeared to have acquired after his rejection of her.

He thought of the vision Ravenna had shown him of Ishbel crawling through the gates of Elcho Falling and opening the citadel to the dark invader.

Then he remembered what Axis had said the previous night: *I had seen a truth, but I had misinterpreted it, so badly I almost lost the woman without whom . . . well, without whom I would have accomplished none of what later I managed.*

Ishbel's chin rose slightly under Maximilian's regard. He thought she looked very lovely, with her blue robe and soft fair hair falling over one shoulder, and very noble, with her unexpectedly tranquil and collected demeanor.

She didn't look to him like a woman who would betray Elcho Falling, but then who was he to judge?

Maximilian gave her a brief nod, then acknowledged Salome and Isaiah.

"What has happened?" said StarDrifter. "Axis said something about Kanubai? That he has . . . vanished?"

"The sense of threat from Kanubai abruptly ceased late last night," said Maxel. "Both Isaiah and I, and I assume Lister, could sense Kanubai previously. That sense has vanished."

"DarkGlass Mountain," Ishbel said. "It has taken him."

"We think so," said Isaiah. "We think—"

"Who else?" said Ishbel.

"You have been in the pyramid, Ishbel," Maximilian said. "Do you truly think it capable of taking Kanubai?"

She looked at him without hesitation, or embarrassment. "Yes. It *hates*, Maxel, and that hate is a powerful force."

Again Maximilian contemplated her. Ishbel conversed easily with him, and he found that remarkable after the way he had treated her the previous night. He had been sure that she'd be awkward and embarrassed, and he had spent much of the time before this meeting trying to think of ways to put her at ease. Now all those strategies were very obviously redundant.

"The glass pyramid is a dangerous enemy," Ishbel continued. She glanced at Isaiah. "When Isaiah and I entered it . . . oh, I can't explain it, but it was almost as if the pyramid *lived*. It could reach out its walls and touch us. Kanubai might have been powerful, but was he powerful enough to best what he thought was an ally?" she concluded with an expressive shrug.

Maximilian gave her another nod, then looked at Isaiah. "No one knows DarkGlass Mountain as well as you," he said. "Talk to me. What is it capable of? What will it do?"

Isaiah sighed, rubbing at his eyes and using the movement to buy time to think. *What* was *the glass pyramid capable of?*

"It is hugely powerful," he said finally, "and hugely angry, as Ishbel said. That anger and hate stem from its ancient past, when one of the Magi, Boaz, Ishbel's ancestor and the nephew of the then Lord of Elcho Falling, caused it to be dismantled. I think, although I have no way of truly knowing, that it wants vengeance."

"Against whom?" said Maximilian.

"Anyone who stands in its way," Isaiah said, "but more particularly, against Boaz and Tirzah, who tried to destroy it, and so against all their descendants. Ishbel definitely, but also you, Maximilian, as you are of the same bloodlines and you are powerful enough to threaten it. It may have also inherited Kanubai's feud with Elcho Falling. I don't know. I just . . . I just don't think it is going to sit there and glow in the sun cheerfully. I think it will *act*. I think it *has* acted."

He paused, the fingers of one hand tapping slowly on the tabletop. "I think that the glass pyramid is the greater danger. Kanubai was known. The pyramid is utterly unknown. Not even the Magi completely understood it or its powers."

"So even though Kanubai may be dead I cannot go back to Escator, curl up in my bed, pull the covers over my head, and dream of happy hunting parties in the forests north of Ruen?" Maximilian said with a wry twist of his mouth.

Isaiah smiled. "No, Maxel. You cannot. There are still great trials ahead of us. None of us can afford to relax."

"And so what are you going to *do* about this?" said Georgdi. The Outlander general looked tense and frustrated. "My homeland has been invaded, and currently all you seem to propose is that your million soldiers and settlers just mill about in confusion. You don't even have any true or tight control over them! I—"

"I have in no manner proposed we do nothing," Maximilian snapped. "I am here to consult and to decide, not to dither."

Georgdi shot him a look, but said nothing.

"The world is torn apart, Maxel," Malat said. "If you want to ask for the loyalty of every man and woman north of the FarReach Mountains, then you shall need to stitch it back together again. Otherwise no one will fight for you."

"Malat makes a strong point," Axis said. "I talked to some of the Isembaardian soldiers today, and there is great restlessness. They may have owed Isaiah their loyalty, but they do not know you, Maxel. Moreover, they are terrified of what happens to their families in Isembaard. Rumors fly, and men talk of aiding their families by themselves if you cannot do it for them."

"And the generals?" Maximilian said.

"Quiet," said Axis. "I have seen Ezekiel, and the others rest in their tents. I will talk with them in the morning . . . but they will take instant advantage of any discontent within the army. We need to decide what to do with them."

Maximilian grunted. "Isaiah," he said, "do you know where Lister is?"

"I believe he is moving north from the FarReach Mountains," Isaiah said. "He will want to join you at Elcho Falling."

"What he wants is immaterial," said Maximilian, "particularly with what has happened over the past day. What are these glass pyramids, or spires, that you have used? Axis has told me of them. Do you have one with you?"

"In my pack," said Isaiah. "Not with me here."

"Fetch it, if you will," Maximilian said, and Isaiah rose and left the tent.

"Axis," Maximilian said, "what do you know of Lister? What did you learn about him while you lived and traveled with Isaiah?"

It was not Axis who answered, but StarDrifter. "If I may," he said, seeking permission from both Axis and Maximilian to speak, and at their nods continued. "Of Lister I know little, but Axis and I know something of the force that travels with him."

"Force?" Maximilian said. "I thought he traveled with the Skraelings."

"He did," StarDrifter said, "but also traveling with him, and still with him I assume, is a great force of winged people."

StarDrifter told the group around the table about the ancient history of the Icarii in Tencendor: how, when many generations ago they had escaped from persecution into the Icescarp Alps, a group of Icarii had continued traveling north into the frozen wastes.

"We thought them to have died," said StarDrifter, "but now Axis and I believe that they survived. They must have traveled deep into the frozen wastes and there, so we think, although we cannot explain *why* they did this, they interbred with the Skraelings to create a new race. They call themselves the Lealfast, and they command great magic through the Star Dance."

"I believed the Star Dance had been destroyed," said Maximilian.

"So did *I*," said StarDrifter, "but the glass pyramids that Isaiah and Lister use for communication were made by the Lealfast, and they tap into the power of the Star Dance, although anyone who commands power can use them. I don't know how, but the Lealfast still use the Star Dance."

"One of them flew down to Aqhat," said Axis, "to stage an attempted assassination of Isaiah in order to encourage his push north. He escaped before my eyes, using powerful enchantment. If the rest of the Lealfast command such power, then they may be powerful allies."

"Or powerful enemies," said Maximilian.

Isaiah reentered the tent at that moment, and sat down at the table. In one hand he held a glass spire, about the height of a man's hand, which pulsated with a rosy light. He placed it on the table, then gave it a gentle shove, sending it sliding down the table to Maximilian.

Every eye at the table followed its passage.

Maximilian stopped the spire with one hand. He studied it briefly, then picked it up.

"It is a thing of great beauty," he said softly. Then he lifted his eyes and looked again at Isaiah. "How does it work?"

"You cannot use it?" Isaiah said, his tone a little challenging.

Maximilian held Isaiah's gaze for a long moment, then looked back to the spire in his hand.

Everyone at the table watched him, and for several heartbeats nothing happened.

Then, suddenly, the glass glowed through the gaps of Maximilian's fingers. First pink, then red, then it flared suddenly into a deep gold before muting back to a soft yellow. The ascetic face of a middle-aged man appeared in its depths, his thin mouth curved in a slight smile.

"Lister," said Maximilian softly. "Well met, at last."

CHAPTER EIGHT

The Northern Borders of the FarReach Mountains, and the Sky Peaks Pass

Lister stared into his glass pyramid at the face of the man who looked out at him.

"My Lord of Elcho Falling," he said, and made a slight bow.

About him snowflakes fell from the sky, twisting lazily in myriad fantastic patterns. As each one hit the ground, it transformed into a birdman or birdwoman, their features and the line of their wings rimed with frost.

The Lealfast.

They gathered about the black-clad Lister in a circle, intensely watchful, their forms gradually solidifying. Three of them—Eleanon, Bingaleal, and Inardle—stood at Lister's shoulder, exchanging unreadable glances before they looked into the glass spire that Lister held.

"You have been a great trouble to my life," Maximilian said to Lister, "for I am led to believe that you were the one to orchestrate my seventeen years spent in the Veins."

"The path to greatness must necessarily be strewn with obstacles that—"

"Don't feed me such banalities, Lister. I am not in the mood for it this day." The focus of Maximilian's gaze changed slightly to take in Lister's companions. "Who are those who stand about you, and *where* are you?"

"My companions are the Lealfast," said Lister, "and they are your servants. As am I. As for our location, we stand at the foot of the FarReach Mountains where they meet the Sky Peaks."

"How soon will it take you to reach me?"

"The Lealfast could be with you within the day, two at most, should you ask it. I, like my companion Isaiah, am confined somewhat by the limitations of human flesh. Nonetheless, I do command some powers and could be with you within ten days."

"Then do it. Lister, what do you know of Kanubai? Something has happened."

"DarkGlass Mountain has eaten him, my lord," Lister said. "I ever thought the pyramid was the greater danger."

"Then you will do well to get here as quick as you may, Lister, that you may share with me the benefit of your infinite wisdom—as well as a plan of action that will see us all at home safe and sound before our hearths within the month. Now, step aside, that I may converse with whoever will speak for the Lealfast."

Lister raised his eyebrows at Maximilian's tart voice, but obediently stepped aside for one of the Lealfast, a man of handsome aspect and keen, frosty eye.

"Your name?" said Maximilian.

"My name is Eleanon," said the Lealfast male, "and I speak for the Lealfast."

"You are their commander?"

"*You* are our commander," said Eleanon, his voice heavy with sincerity, "but I speak on behalf of the Lealfast Nation."

"The entire 'nation' of the Lealfast is currently with Lister?"

"Yes, my lord," Eleanon said. "We number perhaps a quarter of a million. The larger majority are women with children and the older among us, but myself and my brother, Bingaleal, lead a fighting force of bowmen and women of some fifty thousand. We are experienced and able fighters, my lord, and we are at your command."

Maximilian did not reply for a moment. Then: "And you and yours can be here within two days?"

"If you desire it. Do you wish the entire Lealfast Nation to descend upon you?"

Maximilian's mouth curved in a wry smile. "I think not, Eleanon. Your fighting force, however, I shall be very glad to welcome. Where will the great number of your people stay?"

Eleanon leaned to one side and conferred with Bingaleal before turning back to Maximilian. "They will stay within the FarReach Mountains, my lord," he said. "It is safe enough for them at the moment, and provides good shelter. If needed, they can move. Quickly."

Bingaleal and Inardle exchanged a look and a secret thought: *The Nation can move from the FarReach Mountains as needed. Either way, north to Elcho Falling, or south to whatever the One might offer us.*

"Good," Maximilian said. "They can also act as sentinels should anyone, or thing, move north. Eleanon, do you have any reports of what is happening within Isembaard?"

"Many thousands, tens of thousands, of Isembaardians are fleeing north through the Salamaan Pass," Eleanon said. "Men, women, children."

Maximilian sighed. "We shall need to provide for them. Nothing pursues them as yet?"

"Nothing but rumor from Aqhat," Eleanon said. "We know nothing of any solid fact about what has happened in Isembaard."

"Very well. Should I expect you the day after tomorrow, then?"

"Yes, my lord."

"Eleanon, is there any way you can warn me of your arrival two hours in advance?"

Yes, said Eleanon, and Maximilian nodded.

Good. Eleanon, who do you serve? Me, or Lister?

If you tell us to tear Lister's head from his shoulders we shall do it, even though he has been a pleasant companion to us.

Maximilian raised an eyebrow. "Good," he said again, this time in his speaking voice. "I shall see you and your fighters soon." He gave a very small smile. "You shall be some good news from my south, and I have had little of that recently. Is Lister still close?"

Eleanon bowed, handing the pyramid back to Lister.

"My lord?" Lister said.

"I am assuming Vorstus is with you," Maximilian said, naming the man who had, for all his life, acted as Abbot of Persimius in Escator, and who had conspired with Lister to inter Maximilian in the Veins.

"Yes, my lord."

"With my crown."

"Of course, my lord."

"Then I will see you both within ten days."

"I shall look forward to meeting you, my lord," said Lister, "and also to renewing my acquaintance with Isaiah."

Maximilian gave a very small, tight smile, and the next moment the pyramid that Lister held dulled back into lifelessness.

"Just think, Eleanon," Lister said cheerfully, "within two days you meet the StarMan, Axis SunSoar himself."

Eleanon gave him a short look, then turned away.

Are you certain we should still profess loyalty to the Lord of Elcho Falling? Bingaleal said in Eleanon's mind as they walked away from the group.

Eleanon's stride did not falter and he gave no outward sign of Bingaleal's private communication.

For the moment, he replied, *while it suits our purpose.*

And the One? Bingaleal said.

When we know more, Eleanon said, *we can make our choice.*

Inardle watched Eleanon and Bingaleal walk away, feeling unsettled and disturbed. Her brothers were clearly attracted to the power the One offered, but Inardle preferred to keep a more open mind. The One was unknown, the Lord of Elcho Falling less so. The way of the Magi suited Eleanon and Bingaleal, but not so much Inardle, for the Magi had despised women and offered them little power.

Still...the way of the Magi, and the One, offered such rewards that it could well be that the One was what the Lealfast needed.

"I hope you have no weakness, Maximilian Persimius," Inardle muttered, "for otherwise you and your world are dead if the Lealfast should turn our backs to you."

CHAPTER NINE

The Infinity Chamber,
DarkGlass Mountain

The One could feel the use of the spires. The Lealfast had constructed the glass spires with Magi knowledge (*with the power of the One*) and their use always touched the One's soul.

He moved slowly about the Infinity Chamber, running his hands over the ruined glass, restoring it to its full beauty and power. Within a day or two the Infinity Chamber would once again be whole, and would once again connect the pyramid with Infinity.

Then would the One be at full power.

He hummed as he worked, and occasionally sang snatches of song he could recall the Magi singing to him in reverence as they built the pyramid. He was trying out his voice, seeking the perfect pitch and timbre, endeavoring to make it as perfect and as beautiful as was the caged golden glass and the dimensions of this chamber. The One also appreciated deeply the ability to speak and sing. So long he had been nothing but an entity which had existed first in the abstract and then as a glass pyramid. Now he was flesh incarnate, and he could move and speak and act in a manner he'd never been able to previously. Physical form brought its own challenges, but the One enjoyed challenges.

He always won.

As he worked and sang, the One thought about the Lealfast. It was no accident that some of the Magi had escaped so far north when the traitor Boaz sought to destroy the pyramid two thousand years previously. The One had ensured that their knowledge did not die, but lived on within the Lealfast.

They would be his new Magi.

They might hesitate for the moment, but the One knew that eventually they would bow before him.

Servants.

"All my servants," the One whispered, his hands continuing their slow purposeful movement over the blackened glass, "all working my will."

He paused a moment, amused as he recalled that he had come to flesh at that very same moment Ravenna had shown Maximilian Persimius the vision within the Land of Dreams.

"Dear Ravenna," the One whispered, one of his fingers now stroking a piece of glass that once more glowed golden. "Sweet Ravenna, believing everything I show you. So malleable."

The One's hands resumed their slow dance over the glass. The Persimius family had tried to destroy him through the renegade Magi, Boaz, who was a prince of the Persimius blood. They would not get the chance again. When the One moved against Maximilian Persimius and his erstwhile bride, Ishbel, the death strike would come from any one of four or five directions.

Maximilian would never be able to anticipate or counter all of them.

The One smiled, then resumed his singing, perfecting the pitch of his voice until the Infinity Chamber rang with its glory.

CHAPTER TEN

The Sky Peaks Pass

If I'd had to listen to a single more 'my lord' from Lister," Maximilian muttered, "I swear I would have shattered this damn glass."

He looked up at the table. "It shall be most interesting for you, Axis, StarDrifter, and Salome, meeting your long-lost cousins."

"I have only just got used to my new immediate family," Salome said. "Now you say there are fifty thousand more arriving the morning after next? And a quarter million more lurking in the mountains? I shall *never* remember all their birthdays."

The group about the table laughed, then chatted about inconsequential things for a few minutes as they ate and drank.

"Maxel," Axis said eventually, "we need to talk about the army. It is—"

"I know," said Maximilian. "We can speak tomorrow. For now I am weary, and can think clearly of nothing but my bed."

"Before you think too longingly of bed," Isaiah said, "there is something I need to talk to you about. I would also ask that Ishbel stays with us. This concerns both of you. It is a personal matter. Axis, would you stay, too?"

The group broke up with that, leaving Maximilian, Isaiah, Ishbel, and Axis sitting about the remains of the meal. Serge and Doyle shepherded in some servants to clear the table and to set out fruit and cheese, and then the group was left alone.

"If I can take a moment," Maximilian said to Isaiah, "before you speak? Thank you. The Isembaardian soldiers worry about their families. Who can blame them? And *I* worry about what is happening down south, what is happening at DarkGlass Mountain and with the Skraelings. Isaiah," he said, leaning forward a little, "I am going to test our newfound trust."

"You want me to go there," Isaiah said.

"Yes. I want you to go into Isembaard, do what you can for your people, and discover for me what that cursed glass pyramid is about, what it is *doing*, and what it has *become*. We know too little about it. Can you do that for me?"

Ishbel answered before Isaiah could speak. "Maxel! That is too dangerous! Isaiah is a man apart from many others, and with powers that few can command, but even so you are surely sending him to his—"

"I want to send some of Eleanon's Lealfast fighters with Isaiah," said Maximilian quietly. "They can move quickly, and they are of great power. They command the Star Dance, and, from what I have heard of the assassination attempt on your life, Isaiah, they are handy enough with their bows. Isaiah, I will give you half of Eleanon's force—twenty-five thousand. Will you go?"

"Yes," Isaiah said, "if the Lealfast agree. I cannot travel as fast as they, Maxel, but I can move faster than ordinary men. Once I reach the river, I can travel faster."

"We will discuss the details later," said Maximilian. "Axis, what do you think? If I send their Tyrant into Isembaard to rescue what he can, and with a strange, magical, powerful force at his back, will it ease some of the men's fears?"

"It will surely surprise them," said Axis. "But, yes, it will allay their fears, for a while. At least you are being seen to do something, and they trust Isaiah. Mostly. But . . . are you sure about the Lealfast? We know so little about them. To trust them with such a mission is—"

"Foolish?" said Maximilian. "Perhaps, but neither can I afford *not* to use them. I can't sit about for a year trying to gauge the Lealfast and their potential for treachery. I'll risk it, Axis. Isaiah knows how to look after himself, and how to command men."

"Be careful, Isaiah," Ishbel said, meeting his eyes. "Please."

Maximilian hesitated as he looked between them, then spoke. "Once the Lealfast are here we can hash out the details, but I needed to speak to you first, Isaiah."

Then he looked at Ishbel. "Ishbel, I shouldn't have treated you the way I did last night. I—"

"It doesn't matter, Maxel," she said. "You have chosen Ravenna."

"Ishbel—" Maximilian said.

"It is over now, Maxel," Ishbel continued, her tone even and calm, her posture relaxed. "That is the best for both of us, I think. I'm sick of harboring fears and grudges, and it is time we forgot what lies behind us and just concentrate on what waits ahead. We both need to get to Elcho Falling." She paused. "What lies between you and Ravenna doesn't bother me, Maxel. Truly. I wish you the best."

"Ishbel—" Maximilian said again, his voice tight.

"There was something you wanted to say to myself and Maxel?" Ishbel said to Isaiah, and Maximilian bit his tongue and looked away.

Axis looked at Ishbel, his eyes narrowed. A pretty speech and, even better, one that sounded relaxed and sincere. Had she *truly* turned her back on Maximilian?

Isaiah took a deep breath, and now Axis looked at him. *That had been a breath of sheer nerves. Stars, what was Isaiah going to say?*

"I need to talk to you about your child," Isaiah said to Maximilian and Ishbel. "Particularly now I won't be here much longer."

"The child is dead," Ishbel said. "She no longer matters. There's nothing you need say. Please don't drag up the past, Isaiah."

"She does matter, Ishbel," Isaiah said. He took another deep breath. "Kanubai rose into flesh in that moment when Ba'al'uz killed your daughter, and I took Ba'al'uz's head and that of the dog."

Isaiah stopped there, wanting Maximilian and Ishbel to understand what he was trying to say without him actually having to say it.

There was silence, everyone looking at Isaiah.

"Maxel, Ishbel," Isaiah said softly, dragging each word out, "Kanubai took flesh and was born of the sacrifice of your daughter. That was his plan. He wanted to take the flesh and blood of his enemy. He was born of both of you. And now... whatever has taken him also has that blood coursing through its veins."

Again a silence, save that this one was rigid with shock and horror.

"I'm sorry," Isaiah whispered, looking at Ishbel. "I should have taken better care of you."

Ishbel left after that. She could not bear to stay another moment, nor could she bear to see Maximilian's face.

That child had been so important to him. It was bad enough that the baby girl had died, but now to hear this foulness . . . to hear that Kanubai, and whatever had taken him, had Maximilian's and Ishbel's blood coursing through it . . . that the girl had died to create flesh for Kanubai . . . No. That was too much.

Ishbel could not have looked at Maximilian's face at that point.

So she just rose and left.

Maximilian caught up with her within six or seven paces, catching at her arm with his hand, forcing her to stop and face him.

"Ishbel, I'm sorry."

"Stop apologizing to me, Maxel. And just let me be for a while, please."

"We need to speak at some point. Tonight or tomorrow."

"Yes, very well. But not now, *please*, Maxel."

"Not now," he said softly, letting his hand slide from her arm. "Ishbel . . ."

She stared at him, clearly wanting to get away.

"Ishbel, if you need me, you can find me in the command tent." He nodded at the tent they'd both just left. "I'm no longer sharing a tent with Ravenna and Venetia."

Then he left her staring after him as he ducked inside the tent.

Ravenna stood in the shadow of a tent as Ishbel passed. She had watched the command tent for a half hour or more, knowing Maximilian and his commanders *and Ishbel* were inside, and not surprised at, yet resenting, the fact she had not been asked to attend.

She felt physically and emotionally exhausted. She could not understand why Maximilian kept Ishbel close after she had lost the child he'd wanted so much, and then treated him so vilely by flaunting Isaiah as her lover. She could not even comprehend why Maximilian could still consider Ishbel an ally after Ravenna had shown him the vision, the *truth*, for the Land of Dreams did not lie.

But Maximilian wanted Ishbel as much more than an ally, didn't he? No matter what he had said to Ishbel last night in the snow, Maximilian still wanted her. Ravenna had watched as Ishbel emerged from the tent, clearly upset about something (had one of the others justly questioned her apparent good faith?), and then Maximilian had followed her, not a breath later, catching at Ishbel's arm and pulling her close for a quiet conversation.

Ravenna had been sure Maximilian would lean down to kiss Ishbel, but he did not, and that likely due, Ravenna thought, to Ishbel's determination to tease him and make him beg for her after he'd humiliated her before Ravenna.

Ishbel would have her way with him eventually. She would cajole Maximilian into her bed and his ring onto her finger.

Ravenna was now certain of that. There was nothing left that she could do or say to make Maximilian see *sense*, and realize that Ishbel would bring catastrophe to his life, and to Elcho Falling and the entire land.

She felt ill at the thought, and wished that Maximilian had been a stronger man.

Ravenna watched as Ishbel walked away toward her tent, then she moved away quietly into the night.

Ishbel stood twenty or so paces from her tent, not yet willing to enter it. She needed the night air, needed it to clear her mind and heart and restore some peace to her soul.

She wished Maximilian had not followed her out once she'd walked away from him.

"Are you all right?" Axis said softly, stepping up behind her.

"Not particularly," she replied, not looking at him.

He stood with her silently for a little while, his eyes wandering over the stars in the sky.

"Did you mean what you said to Maxel," he said finally, "that what lay between you is over?"

"Yes," Ishbel said. "There is a freedom, you know, in not loving him as once I did, and in not yearning for him. It is more peaceful."

As once I did . . . Axis wondered what she meant by that.

"Will you be my lover?" he said.

She looked at him, momentarily startled. "You waste no time, Axis SunSoar."

"I mean to be first in line."

Ishbel laughed softly. "My answer is no, Axis. I have had enough of lovers for the moment. The gods alone know my last was ill-timed enough." She hesitated. "Did you mean it?"

He gave a small smile, his eyes reflecting the starshine. "No."

"Azhure is a lucky woman," Ishbel said.

Axis shrugged slightly. "Not so lucky, if you think that she rests still in the Otherworld while her husband lives untouchable in this."

"Do you miss her?"

"Not as much as first I did. When Isaiah pulled me from the Otherworld, from death back into life, my yearning for her was a throbbing pain. Here." He tapped his chest. "I used to write her letters every night. I think Isaiah had a servant steal them from my bedchamber so that I would think they had been spirited by magic into the Otherworld."

Ishbel smiled.

"Then Isaiah sent me north, to fetch you from Ba'al'uz," Axis continued, "and my yearning for Azhure dulled. I no longer write her letters. I think of her most days . . . but I do not yearn for her." He sighed. "She has lost me, I think, to the adventures of life."

"Do you think you will ever love again? As you did Azhure?"

"Not as I loved Azhure, no. Not that, not ever again. But love, in a different manner, shape, and form?" Axis paused. "I hope so, Ishbel. I could not bear to live this new life completely without love."

When Axis left Ishbel he thought to stroll past the tents of the generals, to see if all was peaceful. But as he turned to go, he saw that StarDrifter and Salome's tent was still lit, and he decided to speak with them.

The generals could wait until morning.

StarDrifter and Salome were sitting up on their bed, quite naked, Salome leaning against StarDrifter's chest, one of his hands resting on her distended belly. Salome was now some seven months pregnant, glowing with satisfaction at the place in life she had unexpectedly found herself, and somewhat amused as she saw Axis' slight discomfort at finding his father and her in such intimacy.

But he pulled up a stool, sat down, and nodded at Salome's belly. "What do you think, StarDrifter?" he asked his father. "What kind of son are you breeding this time?"

"A peaceful one," said StarDrifter, watching his son a little carefully. He was not sure how Axis would react to this child—for so long Axis had been the favored, and then the only, son.

Now he would have a brother.

Axis gave a slight smile at StarDrifter's words. "Neither Gorgrael nor I had ever been 'peaceful' sons," he said, referring to his half-brother and one-time Lord of the Skraelings whom Axis had eventually killed in battle. "And Salome, if you forgive me for saying this, is a considerably less 'peaceful' woman than either my mother or Gorgrael's."

"Then feel your brother," said StarDrifter. "Place your hand on Salome's belly and feel him."

Axis hesitated. It was not simply the familiarity, and the amusement in both Salome's and StarDrifter's eyes at his uncertainty, but the fact that he would be able to intimately sense the baby. All Icarii could sense and communicate with unborn children, and it was not an ability they had lost with the Star Dance.

Axis was not sure if he wanted to meet his new brother just yet.

"Axis?" Salome said.

He leaned forward, sliding his hand over the mound of Salome's belly as his father withdrew his.

Her skin was very warm, very soft, and very tight over her womb.

Axis could literally feel the curve of his brother's body and two very slight bumps, either of hands or of feet.

And he could feel more. The rapid thrum of his brother's heart . . . and his brother's interest, the movement of his tiny body as he shifted within the womb so that more of his body was exposed to the gentle pressure of Axis' hand.

"What do you sense?" StarDrifter said.

"Curiosity," said Axis. "You had not told him about me. He did not know he had an elder brother."

"There has been so little time . . ." StarDrifter said, waving a hand languidly, and Axis shot him a sharp look, then looked back to his hand, which he shifted gently this way and that.

"He *is* gentle and peaceful," Axis said. "You are right." His mouth quirked. "That is unexpected in a SunSoar. He wants to learn, he is *so* curious."

Then Axis blinked, leaning back from Salome's body and removing his hand from where it rested.

"He will be a great singer," he said. "A beautiful voice. StarDrifter, what have you named him?"

Salome and StarDrifter glanced at each other.

"StarDancer," said StarDrifter.

"And how shall he do that," Axis said softly, holding his father's eyes, "when none of us have access to the Star Dance?"

"The Lealfast arrive soon," StarDrifter said. "They shall tell us how to touch the Star Dance again. They can touch it, and they will tell us."

Axis doubted very much that the Lealfast would just "tell" anyone, but StarDrifter had now broached the subject Axis wanted to speak to him about.

"How do you feel about them, StarDrifter?" he asked. "They number so many, a quarter of a million, and shall be so strange to us. From my brief glimpse of the one who staged the assassination attempt on Isaiah, they are an alien people. They are—"

"They are Icarii," StarDrifter said.

Axis shook his head slowly. "I don't know, StarDrifter. They have the outward shape of an Icarii, but they are still so strange. They have Skraeling blood in them—and abilities that are beyond us, and beyond even what we commanded when we had the Star Dance and were at the full height of our powers."

He paused. "And they give their loyalty to Maximilian, to the Lord of Elcho Falling. Not to you as Talon."

"There will come a time," StarDrifter said, "when both the Lealfast and the Icarii shall be one nation again. They came from us, Axis. They shall return to us."

Axis grew more uncomfortable by the moment. Almost everything about this visit had disturbed him, just slightly, and he felt a distance between himself and his father that he hadn't felt previously.

He really didn't think the Lealfast would prove firm and fast and immediate friends to the Icarii, and he suspected that StarDrifter expected them to accept him as their Talon.

"Perhaps," Axis answered, then he took his leave of Salome and StarDrifter.

CHAPTER ELEVEN

The Sky Peaks Pass

I shbel?"

Ishbel twisted about on the stool, caught in the act of brushing out her hair before she dressed it for the day, irritated that Maximilian had found her at such an intimate moment.

"May I sit?" Maximilian said, coming further into the tent and nodding at the chair to one side of Ishbel's mirror. "I'm sorry to disturb you before your breakfast."

"Of course." Ishbel set her brush to one side, keeping her movements slow and ordered and her expression carefully neutral as she regarded Maximilian.

"Ishbel, I do need to speak to you about what happened the other night in the snow."

"There is no need to—"

"I should not have treated you in the manner I did. You did not deserve it."

"You have done nothing these past months but allow me to believe that *was* how I should be treated."

"We have both said things hurtful, and done things that—"

"Maximilian, leave this, please. I meant what I said earlier. Our past is now past. It is gone. I realized that after you'd left. There is no point in either of us trying to resurrect a relationship that has caused us nothing but pain."

Maximilian regarded her steadily for a long moment, and Ishbel had to drop her eyes. *That little speech had sounded ridiculous.*

"You always said that the Lord of Elcho Falling would bring you nothing but pain and grief, Ishbel. I cannot believe I fulfilled that prophecy so readily."

"It *is* gone, Maximilian. You have Ravenna now, and her child, and—"

"Did you not hear what I said about the command tent, Ishbel?"

"You can't possibly want me to believe that not an hour after you turned your back on me, you then did the same to Ravenna." Ishbel paused. "*Can* you?"

Maximilian shifted his eyes away from her as she had so recently averted hers.

"You amaze me," Ishbel said. "I can't believe it. You were willing to grind me into the snow with your heel and—"

"Ishbel—"

"And for what? For *what*? To then do the same to Ravenna not an hour later? I cannot believe you have the *nerve*, Maximilian, to sit there and . . . and expect me to fall about with gratefulness and dewy-eyed radiance and hold out my arms to you!"

"That is not why I came here!"

"Of *course* not. Oh, I am well rid of you, Maximilian Persimius! Do you know what I felt as you walked away from me in the snow? Do you know? It was anger, not at you or Ravenna, but at myself for having allowed myself to be so foolish as to love you!"

Ishbel closed her eyes briefly as she took a deep breath and damped down her anger. "Maximilian, I harbor no ill will toward you. I will do anything I can to aid you. But I will not love you. You need to understand that *very* clearly. I want control of my life back, and I want never again to find myself so hideously vulnerable as when I loved you. You were right all along. The marriage is over. The love is over."

"You have abandoned love in short order, it seems."

"As you abandoned love, and two women, in short order."

He said nothing, looking down at his hands, the muscles in one cheek working.

Finally, he looked at Ishbel. "May I ask something?"

She sighed. "Why not?"

"Have you ever had any other visions or dreams than those which you told me about—myself, in the snow, destroying your world?"

She looked at him quizzically. "What kind of visions?"

"You, on your knees, opening the door of Elcho Falling to a lord of darkness."

Now Ishbel looked very steadily at him for a long moment before answering. "No. The only nightmares I ever had were about you, Maxel."

He looked at her sharply at that, but Ishbel continued straight on. "Where did you get that little gem from?"

He gave a slight shrug of his shoulders, again not meeting her eyes.

"Ravenna?" she said, and Maximilian's mouth tugged upward in a small smile.

"Yes," he said. "She tells me that you will bring nothing but sorrow, and destroy me, Elcho Falling, and the entire land in the process."

Ishbel laughed hollowly. "Oh, that I had that much power, Maxel." She paused. "Do you believe her?"

"She showed me the vision. I saw it."

"Well then, believe it if you must. Malat is talking of riding to the Central Kingdoms. I can go with him. I believe he is wifeless now the Skraelings ate his—"

"Ishbel!" Maximilian took a deep breath. "Don't."

"But you have *seen* this vision."

"Don't taunt me, Ishbel. Visions can be misinterpreted."

"I hope you didn't say that to Ravenna. It might have made her very cross."

Another smile tugged at Maximilian's mouth. "Do you mean me treachery, Ishbel?"

"No. But I am assuming that what Ravenna deduced from the vision was that I am weak-willed and prone to disasters of monumental proportions."

"Your vision of me destroying your world . . . did it eventuate as you had thought?"

"Very close, but not quite, perhaps. I am still here, breathing, and my world is not shattered. Only my fear and doubt were destroyed." She paused. "I allowed you to create such misery in my life, Maxel, because I loved you, and I won't—"

"Allow that to happen again?" he said. "Yes, so you have said."

Their eyes met, and both almost smiled.

"You have not come here to ask me to leave, Maxel?"

"No. I want you to stay."

"And Ravenna's vision . . ."

He shrugged, thinking of what Ishbel had said: *Only my fear and doubt were destroyed.* "Maybe it is truth, maybe not."

Ishbel hesitated, then spoke. "Thank you for telling me about it, Maxel."

He nodded. *"Will* you stay with my column?"

"You are going to Elcho Falling?"

"Yes."

"Then I will stay with you. Elcho Falling is my home, too, Maximilian."

"I know that."

"Good."

He rose, walking to the tent door. "Ishbel, be careful of Ravenna."

She cannot possibly do me the harm that you have done, Ishbel thought, but was too tired to put those words to voice. She gave a nod.

"We need to talk again," Maximilian said. "About Elcho Falling."

She gave another nod.

He looked at her, then turned and left the tent.

CHAPTER TWELVE

The Sky Peaks Pass

Maximilian spent the morning with Axis and Ezekiel, inspecting some of the Isembaardian units and talking with the soldiers. He had a brief lunch, then, feeling restless, he waved away Serge and Doyle, took his cloak, and walked out into the countryside.

There was a hill about three or four hundred paces from the northern border of the camp, and he made for it at a brisk rate, enjoying the exercise.

The hill was perhaps fifty paces high and he climbed it easily. By the time he reached the summit he was sweating gently, thoroughly warmed by the exercise. He circled about the summit, taking deep breaths of the chilly air, enjoying its invigoration.

His breath steamed, and he clapped and rubbed his hands together as he took in the view. It was still late winter, but spring could not be far away, and on the summit, where the rocks were warmed by the sun, the snow had melted away.

The great Isembaardian army, swelled now by Georgdi's and Malat's ragged column and a few Icarii, stretched away to the south and east almost as far as Maximilian could see.

What was he going to do with such a mass? And how was he going to keep it together?

He did not fool himself that the shout of loyalty in that instant after Isaiah had so stunningly handed command to Maximilian, meant much at all. The men had done as they were told, but their hearts had not been behind their voices. Maximilian was not surprised at what Axis had told him, that the men murmured about their families and worried.

He, too, would worry and murmur.

He turned slightly, catching sight of Ishbel's blue tent with the pennant fluttering in the breeze.

A smile tugged at the corner of his mouth.

She amazed Maximilian, almost as much as she disconcerted him. He had been so sure that he had devastated her world with his coldness and denial two nights ago in the snow. But instead Ishbel had straightened her back, tossed her head, and emerged from it the stronger.

So much stronger.

Maximilian was not entirely sure why he'd gone to talk to her earlier in the day. Yes, he had needed to sound her out about Ravenna's vision, because it worried him. But Maximilian thought also he had gone to make sure she hadn't been pretending when she'd said, so calmly and assuredly, that what had once been between them was now past.

His smile faded as he remembered how he'd rushed after her, and made himself look like a foolish youth by telling her that he'd now moved into the command tent.

Without Ravenna.

Well, it had left Ishbel unmoved. He had truly destroyed whatever had once been between them with his ill-thought guilt over Ravenna's pregnancy.

A movement below caught his eye.

It was Ishbel, leaving her tent. She stopped outside to talk with the Isembaardian soldier—Madarin, Maximilian thought his name was—who guarded it, then Madarin was turning to the hill and pointing.

Ishbel turned to look, her hands shading her eyes in the bright sunlight, and then she started for the hill.

Maximilian felt a flutter of nerves in his stomach.

He sat down on a patch of exposed, dry rock, his eyes following Ishbel's progress toward the hill. She walked and then climbed smoothly, without any hint of breathlessness.

All the months in the saddle had strengthened her, Maximilian thought, and then had to fight to stop himself wondering just how strong and supple her body—always slender and lithe—might be now.

"I thought you would have seen enough of me for the day," he said as she reached the summit and sat herself down beside him.

"You just happen to be occupying the top of the hill," she said, "where I thought to sit and digest my lunch."

He smiled. "Who is that soldier—Madarin? He seems devoted to you."

"You haven't heard of him?"

Maximilian shook his head.

"Well, you'll need to ask Axis for the details," Ishbel said, "but he is devoted to me because many, many months ago, when he was part of the detail accompanying Axis to bring me to Isaiah, I healed him of a twisted bowel. My skills as the Archpriestess of the Coil did not only encompass death."

"I keep finding ever more hidden depths within you, Ishbel."

She made a noncommittal movement of her shoulders, and they sat in silence for a little while.

Maximilian's attention was eventually caught by a movement to the west. There was something in the sky . . .

"Icarii," Ishbel said, who had caught his look and frown of concern. "Can you see? One of them has such pink feathers!"

Maximilian smiled, relaxing. "Yes. I can see. There must be fifteen or sixteen of them. Where have they come from, do you think?"

"Perhaps they have heard that they have a new Talon, and that he travels with you."

Maximilian nodded slowly. "Word must be filtering out into the eastern lands."

"StarDrifter will be happy to gather his people about him."

Maximilian nodded again.

Ishbel drew a deep breath. "I came up here because I wanted to apologize for the way I spoke to you this morning."

"I deserved it."

Another small silence.

"Surely we must be done apologizing to each other now," Ishbel said, and Maximilian laughed softly.

"If you say so."

Now the silence was a little more awkward.

"I don't want to hurt you, Maxel," Ishbel said. "If Ravenna has shown you a vision where I—"

"Don't . . ." Maximilian said. "Come with me to Elcho Falling. You are a

Persimius, and it is your home as much as mine. Whatever happens, happens."

He picked up a small fragment of rock where the frost had splintered it from the greater one, and turned it over and over in his hand. It struck him, once more, just how different were Ravenna and Ishbel. Ravenna had not once stopped trying to persuade him that Ishbel was a nightmare just waiting to wake, while, contrariwise, Ishbel had not once, in all the months she'd had the opportunity, said a single thing against a woman she had every cause to loathe.

Ravenna would hate it that Ishbel had offered to stay behind, and he had refused.

"All Persimians must be true fatalists," Ishbel said, and Maximilian laughed out loud.

"Grim fatalists," he agreed, still smiling.

"I wish our baby had lived," Ishbel said.

Maximilian hesitated, wondering where this would lead. "So do I," he said.

Ishbel didn't take it any further, and Maximilian thought that somehow they had, in those two simple statements, probably encompassed as much—and as well—as if they'd spent hours beating their breasts about the tragedy.

Ishbel took a deep breath. "Are you looking forward to Elcho Falling?"

"Yes," Maximilian said. "How long have I been on the road now? Eighteen months? Longer? You almost as long. I left Escator to find a bride . . . and here I still am, on the road. So, yes, I am longing for Elcho Falling—longing for a home. Longing for an end to this journeying."

"And Elcho Falling is home, not Escator?"

"I think so. Escator seems so far behind me. I don't think I could go back there and be happy. I would always be restless. I *was* always restless there, I think, perhaps knowing that it would not be where I ended my days."

"You should not talk so about ending your days."

He shrugged.

Ishbel chewed her lip, looking over the vast encampment. "Do you worry about this army?"

"Yes. I have no idea what I can do to hold it together. Isaiah could barely do it, and I am not Isaiah."

"Perhaps you need to allow it to fracture apart."

He looked at her, frowning. "What do you mean?"

"Look at us, Maxel. Here we sit, talking comfortably, and when have we ever done that? Neither of us keeping any secrets . . . and when before have we had such truth between us? What did it take, Maxel, for us to reach this moment where we could trust each other and be friends?"

She rose, and Maximilian had to squint into the sun in order to look up at her. He thought she smiled at him just before she turned to walk down the hill, but was not sure.

He watched her all the way back to her tent, thinking about what she had said.

Perhaps you need to allow it to fracture apart.

What did it take, Maxel, for us to reach this moment where we could trust each other and be friends?

The frown smoothed from Maximilian's face, and he smiled, tossing the fragment of rock high into the air before catching it again.

Suddenly he could see the road ahead to Elcho Falling clear and straight.

"Thank you, Ishbel," he murmured, then rose and made his own way down the hill.

CHAPTER THIRTEEN

The Sky Peaks Pass

Ishbel sat in her tent, the Goblet of the Frogs in her hands. It was late at night. Madarin had long settled down in his bedding in a small shelter built into the back of the tent, and Ishbel supposed that she, too, should go to bed. The Lealfast were due to arrive in the morning, and it would be a day partly of excitement, partly of nerves. No one truly knew how the Isembaardians would react to the arrival of such a supernatural force—or even how the Lealfast themselves might behave.

She turned the goblet over and over. It felt wonderful in her hands: the glass was smooth and warm, and even when it did not whisper to her the goblet managed to convey such love and warmth that Ishbel found it difficult to pack it away.

It was so beautiful. Ishbel thought that her ancestor, Tirzah, must have been extraordinary to have created something this beautiful.

It was because she loved the man for whom she created me, the goblet said.

"Boaz," Ishbel murmured, so relaxed by the goblet's soothing presence that the fact it spoke to her did not mar her serenity in the slightest.

Love can do many amazing things.

Ishbel smiled, just slightly. "You think that Maximilian and I . . ."

It is a possibility only.

"I don't think so," said Ishbel. "I am the stronger without him."

Possibly.

"I can't think that—"

"Talking to yourself, Ishbel?"

Ishbel looked up, startled.

Salome was standing just inside the door of the tent, looking at her quizzically.

"Talking to myself only," Ishbel said, folding the goblet away in a piece of cloth. She smiled. "I find it helps, sometimes."

Salome smiled back, sitting down on a stool and arranging her robe and wings to her satisfaction.

"The baby?" Ishbel said.

Salome rested a hand on her growing belly. "He is doing well, but I am almost at that point where I will be happier with him outside of me than inside. StarDrifter will not allow me to fly. He says I still am too ungainly in the air—" Salome made a moue "—and my flight muscles not yet strong enough to bear us both. I might harm his precious son should I topple from the sky."

"I am sure he is just as worried for you, Salome."

"Well, perhaps."

"Maxel and I saw some Icarii flying in today. What do you know of them?"

"Ah! StarDrifter is so pleased! Apparently BroadWing sent word back with several Icarii when first he realized StarDrifter was heading north with Isaiah's force. Now Icarii are heading to join with their Talon." Salome smiled. "Many are coming, including a goodly number, BroadWing told me this afternoon, who were once with Axis' vaunted Strike Force. All I can hope for, my dear, is that StarDrifter's entire family does not reappear. I simply could not manage."

Ishbel laughed.

"Now," Salome continued, "you must tell me all about you and Maximilian. You told me yesterday what transpired when you went to declare your love for him, but now it appears that Ravenna has been left to mope alone with her mother, and Maximilian is all of a sudden casting hooded looks your way!" Salome smiled in genuine warmth. "And now you tell me that you and he met earlier? Ha! Do you remember that day when first we became friends, and I said how I admired you for the fact that you so carelessly manipulated the love of kings and tyrants—without even being aware of it?"

"Yes."

"Any other woman would have crumpled with despair at Maximilian's rejection, Ishbel. I know of no one who could have managed such a disaster with aplomb and dignity. And now look at you! You wear your clothes with such . . . difference. Two days ago that gown would have hung dispirited on you. Now you wear it as though it were a vestment fit for the most powerful empress. As though *you* were the most powerful empress. What is your secret?"

"You asked me that on the first day we met, as I recall," Ishbel said.

"Tell me what happened once Maxel had walked away from you, Ishbel."

Ishbel gave a little shrug. "I became angry—at myself. I couldn't believe I'd allowed myself to sink so low. So, Salome, that is my only secret."

Salome's eyes drifted to the cloth-wrapped goblet, and she slid Ishbel a sly glance, but did not comment on it.

"How do you feel for Maxel?" she asked.

"Exhausted," Ishbel said, then gave a soft laugh. "I am exhausted with loving him, and am enjoying not having to do so."

"Well, then, you are finally your own woman," Salome said, rising to her feet with admirable grace considering her advanced pregnancy. "Ravenna is angry."

"She thinks I will ruin Maximilian's life, and the entire world besides."

"Venetia had a talk with me this morning," Salome said. "She worries about her daughter."

"I do not," Ishbel said.

"Perhaps you should," Salome said, then leaned down to give Ishbel a good-night kiss, and departed.

Maximilian was fast asleep in his tent when he was startled awake by a hand on his shoulder.

"Doyle?" he said, rising onto one elbow.

"My lord," Doyle said, his voice tight, "there is something I need to tell you."

Far distant, the Lealfast fighters glided through the night. They journeyed in their magical form, almost transparent crystals of snow that sliced through the air against the wind. At night they were invisible; during the day they could be seen only in numbers, and only then as a filmy gray cloud high in the sky.

As they flew, Eleanon, Bingaleal, and Inardle talked, traveling far enough away from the others that they could not be overheard.

"The One is extraordinary," Bingaleal said, as he had said many times on their journey north toward Maximilian.

"He is dangerous, too," Inardle said.

"He promises more for us than Maximilian," said Eleanon.

"But at what price?" Inardle said. "What shall he ask of us?"

"We have always thought that only the Lord of Elcho Falling had the power to achieve what we needed," said Eleanon.

For a moment the three Lealfast shared the dream to which all Lealfast aspired. Wholeness. Freedom from their half-and-half nature—half Skraeling, half Icarii. The Lealfast despised both Skraeling and Icarii and yearned for their own future, their own identity.

Wholeness.

Formerly they had thought only the Lord of Elcho Falling had the power to strip them of both their Skraeling and Icarii blood, but now . . .

"Now, there is the One," Bingaleal said, "and suddenly we have a choice. Inardle, we must consider that choice, and we must keep our choices open. The nation depends on the decisions the three of us make."

"But we must not be hasty," Inardle said.

"Indeed not," said Eleanon. "We fly to Maximilian, we consider him, and then we learn as much as we can about the One and what he offers, and then we consider him as well. We shall not be hasty. But we *shall* do whatever is needed to better the Lealfast. But for the moment, our loyalty shall be publicly with Maximilian. Until . . ."

"We find a better choice," said Bingaleal, "and are certain in that choice."

Far below them a tiny dot scampered south.

It was the rat which had crawled from the Goblet of the Frogs, and it was moving supernaturally fast.

CHAPTER FOURTEEN

The Sky Peaks Pass

Maximilian drew the razor down the side of his cheek, then flicked off the soap and bristles into a dish of water at his feet. He drew the razor down his other cheek, and then again, flicking away the soap and bristles after each pass, and then over his chin.

Axis sat on a chair in the command tent, watching the Lord of Elcho Falling as he shaved in the predawn. Maximilian looked more relaxed than Axis had seen him in a while, and he wondered at it. Axis had spoken to Insharah very early this morning, and the soldiers were more edgy than ever. They didn't know why they were sitting here in the snow when back home their land was, for all they knew, being torn apart and their families slaughtered.

Maximilian would somehow need to pull a miracle down from the sky if he wanted to retain control of the army.

The Lealfast.

"What will happen today, Maxel?" Axis said. "Tens of thousands of Lealfast are, presumably, going to descend from the sky. It might not do much for the mood of the camp, which is already restless. Do you have any . . ." Axis stopped, searching for the word.

Maximilian wiped the razor on a cloth, then set it to one side. "Plans?" He picked up a towel and wiped his face and neck clean of soap, then handed the towel to Serge, who cleared away the shaving paraphernalia. "Yes, of a kind. Axis, I need you to assemble as much of the army as you can manage by midafternoon, in the space surrounding that small hill about four hundred paces away to the north. You know it?"

Axis nodded. It was a good place for one man to address a huge crowd.
It was also a good place for one man to be obliterated by an angry mob.

"I can't protect you there, Maxel," Axis said softly.

"I know. I live or die by my words and actions today."

"You seem very calm about it."

Maximilian gave a slight shrug.

"Have you heard from Eleanon?"

"Yes. He and his fighters are close, gathered about an hour's flight from
here. They know when to arrive, and where. Don't worry, Axis. I will be
careful with the introductions."

"What do you want me to do with the generals?"

Maximilian didn't answer immediately, considering Axis. "The generals?" he said after a moment. "At the front again, as they were when we met
Malat and Georgdi. Now, Axis, you have a couple of hundred thousand men
to organize. Best get to it."

Axis gave Maximilian a measured look—the man was keeping something
from him—but in the end he just nodded a farewell as he rose and left.

It had been a very long time since Axis had command of an army, and never
one of quite this size. He had yet to feel out his chain of command through
all of the units, and still depended very greatly on Insharah to relay his orders through the mass of men.

Still, Axis had spent a goodly portion of the nights on the long trail sitting about campfires talking, and entertaining with his harp and voice, and
although there was initial disquiet and muttering, by noon most of the army
was moving, as asked, north toward the hill where Maximilian would address them.

They took no gear with them and only hand weapons—Axis had thought
about ordering they take no weapons at all, but knew that, firstly, he'd
never be able to enforce such an order and, secondly, weaponless men were
even more likely to be moved to anger and action when faced with a
strange and unnerving situation than those who at least had a sword or
knife to hand.

Once the bulk of the men were moving, Axis and Insharah walked toward the generals' tents. Axis wasn't looking forward to talking to them,
and even less to persuading them to attend this gathering.

"They've been too quiet these past days," he said to Insharah as they approached Lamiah's tent. "I should have spoken to them earlier."

Insharah shrugged. "No doubt they've been plotting and planning," he said, and then there was no more time for words as they halted before the sentry at Lamiah's tent.

"Your master is in?" Axis said to the man.

"Washing, my lord," the guard said. "He would not wish to be disturbed before he is fully garbed."

"Lamiah is a laggard indeed," Axis said, "if he still wanders undressed at this time of day."

He stepped forward, meaning to enter the tent, but the sentry grabbed at his arm. "My lord—"

The sentry got no further, for Insharah wrenched him back.

"Watch what you do, man!" Insharah barked, and Axis sent the sentry a hard look before he lifted the tent flap and stepped inside.

It was empty. Empty, that is, save for a stripped camp bed and dirty dishes with congealed and mouldy scraps stuck to their surfaces.

There was no man, let alone a general, washing.

Axis froze to the spot, then suddenly he was outside, running for the tents of Armat and Kezial.

CHAPTER FIFTEEN

The Sky Peaks Pass

Ravenna wandered the rapidly emptying camp. No one paid her any attention, which suited her purpose yet still managed to annoy her.

She wasn't sure what to do. Over the past day and night—mostly spent wandering, walking, thinking—she'd tried to think of what she could do to negate Ishbel's danger. It was obvious that Maximilian would take Ishbel back and would heed no warning, no matter how clear, of the risk about Ishbel.

But what to do about it?

Ravenna had no friends, no allies. Once she could have counted on her mother, but now even Venetia was set against her.

I do not understand you, Venetia had said to Ravenna over and over during these past days and nights. *Why cling to Maximilian? Why cling to a man?*

In vain would Ravenna try to explain that it was not so much the man as everything he represented that she fought for. She could not just leave and walk home to the marshes.

But Venetia would only shake her head and turn away.

Ravenna sighed, looking about, feeling lost and unsure. Maximilian had called a great meeting at a hill to the north. The rapidly growing emptiness of the camp was starting to unnerve her, and Ravenna thought she might as well follow the last of the columns winding north. Just as she was about to turn and do so, she caught a glimpse of Axis running through the tent lines.

Ravenna stopped, her heart pounding at the look on Axis' face.

He was heading toward Maximilian's command tent.

Quickly Ravenna moved through the tent lines. She masked herself in darkness, so that neither Axis, nor Serge or Doyle standing guard outside the tent, could see her approach, and reached the tent just as Axis pushed his way through the flap.

Ravenna positioned herself directly behind the tent, leaning against the canvas as close as she dared, listening.

"The generals have gone," Axis said to Maximilian, who Ravenna could hear rising to his feet. "They've likely been gone since the first night after you took control. *I* haven't seen them, and no one else has either."

"*All* the generals?" Ravenna heard Maximilian say.

"Ezekiel remains," Axis said, "but Kezial, Lamiah, and Armat have gone. They have at least two days' start on us, Maximilian."

Ravenna heard Maximilian breathe in sharply. For a moment he didn't say anything, and Ravenna leaned both her body and senses closer to the canvas. She wanted to use a little of her power to actually *see* inside, but was worried that Maximilian might detect it.

She would use her ears only.

Inside the tent, Maximilian put a finger to his lips, and leaned his head close to Axis'.

"Ravenna is outside," he murmured in Axis' ear. "Take your lead from what I say."

Axis' eyes darted to the canvas wall of the tent, then he gave a tight nod.

"Gone," Maximilian said. "This is ill luck, indeed. How is it you did not realize they were gone, Axis? Gods, they have the power to utterly undo me!"

"I'm sorry, Maxel," Axis said.

Maximilian gave a grunt, as if reluctantly accepting the apology. "If you were them," he said, "what would you do, Axis? Where would you go? How would you eventually move against me?"

Again Axis' eyes shifted briefly to the tent wall. "Isaiah has left half his army scattered about the eastern and southern Outlands. I'd be making for those units—stars, Maxel, that's at least two hundred thousand men. That's not counting all the settlers who came with the army—another half a million people scattering about the southern Outlands. The generals may well garner more fighting men from them."

"And once the generals have their two hundred thousand, at least?" Maximilian said.

"They have two choices. They head back south through the Salamaan Pass into Isembaard. But that's only if they're feeling particularly suicidal, and I think they're anything but that. Or they may come after you. You have some pretty magics, Maxel, but those generals, once they have a substantial force behind them, could defeat you easily . . . particularly as you have not yet cemented your hold over the army you have here."

There was another silence, and Ravenna leaned so close to the canvas her ear now rested against it.

"They have perhaps three days' start on us, Axis. Can we catch them? Can *you* catch them if I send you after them?"

"Perhaps. With the Lealfast, almost certainly. Their magic and their wings can do what a thousand men on horseback could not. Maxel, this is my fault. I should have had them placed under guard. I should have *watched* them closer."

The Lealfast. Ravenna had heard of them from her mother, who had been told of them by StarDrifter.

Axis sighed. "There's something else. I *did* go to check on them two days ago—but I was called away before I managed to get too close. But I saw their men about, washing the general's clothes, carrying empty dishes out of one of their tents . . . Maxel, their men were disguising the fact the generals had gone. We can't ignore the fact that many already know the generals have fled and are likely to be rallying a force against you to the east or south, and we can't ignore the fact that soldiers among what is now your army conspired to hide the fact they had gone. What you need to do today, my friend, is to buy yourself enough time that I can catch the generals before too great a damage is done."

Maximilian paced about with short, angry steps. "I can't send you now," he said. "We will need to wait until after the Lealfast have arrived, until after I have addressed the army. Then I can send you, and the Lealfast, after the generals."

"I pray the Lealfast are everything you hope," Axis said softly.

"As do I," said Maximilian, "for if they cannot catch those generals then I am lost."

Ravenna drew back from the tent, moving quickly through the close-struck tents until she was far enough away from Maximilian that she could risk her power.

She was shaking, knowing that she had been handed a golden opportunity.

Those generals could save Elcho Falling for her.

But should she dare it? Should she?

"Oh, Maxel," she whispered, "if only you had chosen to believe me."

Then she moved.

She had, she thought, some two hours to accomplish what she needed.

The One paused in his continuing task of restoring the glass of the Infinity Chamber. He looked closely into one newly refurbished piece of golden glass, and saw Ravenna walk away from her eavesdropping.

He smiled, then returned to his work.

So malleable. So predictable. And who knew, she might even prove useful.

Maximilian stilled, every sense trained on the back wall of the tent.

Then he relaxed slightly. "She's gone," he said.

"How much of that was theater," Axis said, "and how much truth?"

"Some theater and a little truth. But . . . I knew they'd gone, Axis. Doyle told me last night."

Axis wished the earth would open up and swallow him. He slumped down into a chair. "Oh stars, Maxel. I am sorry. I am useless to you."

Maximilian shrugged and walked away, fussing with some gear on a folding table to one side. "They have gone . . . and to some extent that suits my purpose. Once Isaiah and half of the Lealfast fighters have departed for Isembaard, I will be sending you and the other half on a hunt for the generals."

"Then we will find them for you."

Maximilian turned back to look at Axis, a half smile on his face at the determination in Axis' voice. "Maybe, maybe not, but at the least it will give you a chance to test out these Lealfast, and see just how good, or not, they are."

"Why do you say the generals' betrayal suits your purpose?" Axis said.

"You know I have worried about this army, how I can keep it together."

"Yes."

"Ishbel said something to me yesterday that made me think. She said that sometimes a group needs to fracture apart before it can ever solidify into a unified force."

Axis leaned forward, frowning. "And so . . . you are going to let this force just tear asunder? Maxel, are you sure that is a good idea?"

Maximilian gave a short laugh. "I am not so sure it is a good idea, Axis, but I do know that to try artificial means—whether promises or fear—to keep this eclectic combination of forces together is a far worse mistake. I could perhaps hold it together for a few months . . . and then what? Have it fall apart just when I need it most? Have one among it stab me in the back just when I thought I had his true loyalty?"

Maximilian sat down in a chair opposite Axis. "I want to know just who is loyal to me, Axis, and I think I am going to find that out within the next few weeks. I am not going to fight to keep this army together or under my control. If it wants to fracture, then so be it. I would rather enter Elcho Falling with a tiny fraction of what I have now if it means that fraction is utterly loyal. Tell me, Axis, you welded once-enemies together under the single banner of Tencendor. How did that fare?"

Axis dropped his eyes.

It had failed.

"Ishbel suggested, and I agree with her," Maximilian said, "that by allowing the army to fracture now, then I will ultimately control a far stronger force. People will come home eventually, Axis." He smiled, just slightly. "I hope."

"This is a dangerous path to tread, Maxel."

"All paths are dangerous."

When Axis had left, Maximilian went to Ishbel's tent. She was standing just outside, looking toward the mass of men gathering about the northern hill.

Madarin melted away from her side for a few paces as Maximilian approached.

"Ishbel," Maximilian said. "You will attend this gathering at the hill?"

Ishbel looked at him, her eyes worried. "If you wish, yes. What are you going to do?"

He answered only with a gentle smile. "You told me once that you could 'unwind' the memories of the scars on my body."

"Yes."

"Are you a powerful enough Archpriestess of the Coil, Ishbel, that you could share such a memory with this entire gathering?"

Ishbel took a deep breath, her eyes huge. "Yes."

"Will you, if I ask it?"

"Yes."

"Thank you. Madarin? Will you escort your mistress to the hill, and ensure that she is safe and comfortable at the inner edge of the gathering?"

CHAPTER SIXTEEN

The Plains of the Central Outlands

Kezial, Lamiah, and Armat had moved swiftly once Maximilian had taken control of the Isembaardian army. The man's murder of Morfah had demonstrated that he had hitherto unsuspected powers, and that they would need to be careful about him while in close proximity.

But Maximilian was still a man, and he could still be assassinated... preferably with a buffer of ten thousand men wielding swords and spears between him and the three generals.

And ten thousand men, at the very minimum, could easily be arranged.

Isaiah had managed to keep his generals under control. Just. But whatever fragile loyalty the generals owed to Isaiah did not in any manner transfer to Maximilian. In fact, like Morfah, the three generals were aghast that Isaiah had just so casually handed control of close to a million soldiers and settlers, a million *Isembaardians*, to a foreigner no one knew and who was hitherto nothing more than the king of a tiny poverty-ridden kingdom. Maximilian's talk of Elcho Falling did not impress the generals in the least.

The generals were damned if they were going to allow Maximilian to take a command they considered their right.

An army of half a million men, half a million more loyal settlers, and a land waiting to be conquered. The Skraelings could keep Isembaard.

They'd crept out of the encampment by the Sky Peaks Pass as soon as it had fallen dark on the day Maximilian had taken control of the army. There was little loyalty—make that next to none—to Maximilian within the Isembaardian army, and there were scores of soldiers who had conspired with the generals to see them safely and quietly out of the camp, and who had promised to make it appear as if the generals still kept to their tents within the camp.

Neither Kezial, Lamiah, nor Armat had approached the senior general, Ezekiel, to come with them. He was an old man, and set in his ways, and they suspected his friendship with Axis SunSoar.

In the new order of things, Ezekiel would play no part.

Now, several days after they had crept out of camp, the generals and a small band of intensely loyal (and ambitious) soldiers rode as hard as they could for the east. Isaiah had left hundreds of thousands of soldiers scattered at stations from the Sky Peaks to Margalit, and then further south to Adab and the entrance to the Salamaan Pass. The generals barely slept. They commandeered food and fresh horses from the supply stations Isaiah had established along his rear, and in the brief time they spent at each station they infused enough doubt into the minds of the soldiers stationed there that they would never give Maximilian their loyalty.

We will return, the generals told the men, *and we will bring a mighty force with us.*

It was midmorning, and Lamiah called for a brief halt to blow the horses and to eat a small meal themselves. They did not dismount, but allowed their horses long rein in order to stretch their necks and backs, and passed food and water from man to man.

"This is a bleak land," Armat muttered about a mouthful of bread and cheese. "Few trees."

"Nowhere to *hide*," Kezial said.

Everyone, whether general or one of the ten men who rode with them, looked about uneasily. There was indeed nowhere to hide, and they dreaded seeing either a cloud of dust further back along the road they had traveled, or one of the damned flying creatures who had arrived with the ragtag column commanded by Georgdi and Malat. They had discussed traveling separately in order to increase the chances that at least one of them would reach the large forces stationed to the east, but none of the three generals trusted the others enough to allow them out of his sight.

It was a race against time, they knew it. To be honest, none among their group could believe they'd made it this far without hearing a hue and cry on the road behind them.

"This Maximilian will be easy prey," Lamiah said, "if he has managed to allow us this far." He grunted. "What commander of any worth could fail to notice that those most dedicated to his downfall have slipped away in the night?"

"And Axis," said Armat. "The great legendary war leader. Ha! I doubt he can even piss in a straight line."

The group laughed.

"We should reach Margalit within a week if we continue to travel this fast," said Kezial. "And then . . ."

And then . . .

"And then this land is ours," said Armat. "The Skraelings have emptied it for us. All we need do is bury Maximilian and Axis and take it for ours."

"And perhaps not," said a woman's voice to one side, "for Maximilian and Axis know you are gone and, within the day, mean to throw at you a magical force that will see your murdered flesh scattered for a league along this forsaken track."

Men dropped food, grabbed for reins, and drew their swords. They swung their horses about to where the voice had sounded, and saw standing a few paces away an ethereal woman.

Armat recognized her instantly. "You are Ravenna," he said, "Maximilian's lover. And a witch, I can see, from your wraithlike appearance."

Ravenna—or rather, the glamour that represented her—laughed. "Indeed, a witch-woman, but Maximilian's *former* lover. He has abandoned me." She rested her hand on her belly. "And his heir."

"A foolish mistake," Lamiah said, watching the glamour warily and hefting his sword. He knew the sword was of no use against this enchantment, but he felt better with it in his hand. "What do you here, witch-woman?"

"I come to warn you, and aid you," said Ravenna.

"Why?" Armat said.

Kezial gave a short laugh. "She said she was Maximilian's *former* lover. He has slighted you, eh, Ravenna? You want revenge."

Ravenna hesitated, then nodded. "Yes. And I want power, just like you."

"We may not want to share it," Lamiah said.

"You will be *dead* without me," Ravenna snapped. "And all I want is one single mountain at the edge of the world. Nothing more. You can take whatever else you want. Just one mountain."

"It must be a very powerful mountain," Kezial said.

"And it will be *mine*," Ravenna said. Her glamour took one step forward, and such was the menace she imparted that every single man reined his horse back a pace or two.

Armat waved a hand airily. "A single mountain, then. And for that, what do you offer us?"

"A glamour," said Ravenna, "more powerful even than the one I use now. One that will mask you from the sight of the creatures that Maximilian sends after you. And once you have made your escape and gathered your forces about you, I shall offer you information from within Maximilian's camp."

Lamiah gave a small shrug, as if indifferent.

"You are a stupid man, Lamiah," Ravenna said. "Without me you will be dead by the end of the day."

"We can outfight anything that—"

"Not these," said Ravenna. "Not the Lealfast. They traveled with the Skraelings, and are a blood combination of Skraeling and Icarii. They are deeply magical and dangerous creatures, far more so than the Icarii."

Lamiah locked eyes with Kezial, then with Armat. A decision made, he then gave a single nod to Ravenna. "If you give us this glamour enabling us to escape these Lealfast, and then feed us information from within Maximilian's camp—providing you can get it now you no longer share his bed—then what precisely do you want in return?"

"The mountain. And that you live to defeat Maximilian," said Ravenna.

Again, a nod from Lamiah. "Then hide us within your glamour, witchwoman Ravenna, and we shall do as you wish."

Ravenna let her glamour fade, and came to her conscious self, hidden deep within Maximilian's army encampment.

Her eyes were glassy with tears, but otherwise Ravenna had her expression under tight control.

What she had just done was the most heart-wrenching action of her life. *Betraying Maximilian.*

She had started on a path that might, if she were not careful, lead to Maximilian's death...but was that death not assured anyway, if he took Ishbel back to his bed?

Ravenna brought her emotions under control. She had said to the generals what they had wanted to hear, in words they would understand.

"It doesn't need to be this way, Maxel," she murmured, "if only you would listen to me."

"Ravenna?"

Ravenna jerked about.

Her mother was approaching, her face creased with anxiety. "Ravenna? Where have you been? I have been looking everywhere for you this past hour."

"Just wandering, Mother."

Venetia stood a moment looking at her daughter. "I felt the touch of a marsh witch's power, Ravenna. What were you doing?"

"Nothing," Ravenna said, too sharply, and pushed past her mother.

CHAPTER SEVENTEEN

The Sky Peaks Pass

Axis SunSoar climbed to the top of the rocky hill, pausing there to take a breath. He had once more assumed the all-black clothing of the BattleAxe, lacking only the twin axe emblem on the chest of his tunic jacket.

Outwardly very calm and confident, Axis was in fact extremely nervous. If matters got out of hand here, there was not a thing he could do to protect Maximilian.

He rested one foot on a rock, relaxing his body, and looked about.

To the south, a great bank of low, gray snow cloud was rolling in.

The Lealfast. Axis had no idea how Maximilian was going to manage their introduction, and was still highly concerned that the sudden apparition of the ghostly Lealfast descending from the sky might provoke the Isembaardian soldiers into panicked action.

He looked down at the throng of men about him.

The Isembaardian army surrounded the hill, stretching back many hundreds of paces on all sides. The sea of faces moved gently, constantly, as men shifted on their feet, bent close to a neighbor to murmur a few words, and turned this way and that to gauge the emotions and reactions of those about them.

They were on edge. Unsure.

But at least they were here, and they were prepared to listen.

Axis wondered what Maximilian would say to them.

He looked to the front ranks of the mass. Here in the inner circle, perhaps four or five paces down the hill, stood anyone who had any seniority at all.

StarDrifter and Salome, very watchful and tense.

BroadWing EvenBeat, the senior of the Icarii below StarDrifter and Salome, as well as several other of the Icarii who had traveled with Georgdi and Malat, were nearby. They would meet their long-lost cousins today, if all went well.

Axis hoped that StarDrifter would behave himself.

Georgdi and Malat sat a little further about the circle. They were looking much better than when Axis had first met them a few days earlier. Rest and food had banished the grayness and gauntness from their faces, but they looked as uneasy as Axis felt—surrounded as they were by so many armed men.

Like StarDrifter, they had a few of their closest retainers standing just behind them.

A little further on stood Ishbel. She looked impossibly lovely, clothed now in a rose-colored heavy silken gown (*Where does she get such gowns?* Axis wondered. *Madarin?*), her fair hair coiled in an intricate knot over one shoulder. Amid all these tense-faced men, amid all the uncertainty and nerves, Ishbel was an oasis of serenity and surety.

Axis wondered how she did it.

There was something else about her. Axis remembered how she had been after she'd healed Madarin—every inch the archpriestess, a little haughty, very sure of herself, ready to face down the entire world if need be. She had that air about her again this day.

Axis almost smiled as he imagined her single-handedly gutting every soldier who might step forward to challenge Maximilian.

She saw the glint of humor in his eyes, and her own mouth curled upward. They shared amusement a moment, then Axis inclined his head, glanced at the soldier Madarin, standing guard behind Ishbel's chair, then allowed his eyes to roam further.

Venetia stood just along from Ishbel, and two or three paces from her stood Ravenna.

Axis studied Ravenna a moment. He did not trust her now, not at all.

Why had she been listening to his conversation with Maximilian? What would she do with the information?

She looked calm enough, and completely unthreatening, but still . . .

Of everyone who was someone within this gathering, the only notable absentee was Isaiah. Axis knew he was here somewhere, and that Maximilian would require him later. But for the moment the stage was Axis', and then Maximilian's.

Axis stood straight, taking a deep breath.

His was the task of introducing Maximilian formally to this army.

Ishbel tensed as Axis prepared to speak, feeling very nervous about what Maximilian might want her to do later, and looked around at the great gathering of soldiers.

They were all watchful. Most were silent, but here and there Ishbel could see men lean close, muttering.

Their eyes were flat and unsympathetic.

Ishbel could understand their concerns and their disinclination to give Maximilian anything but the most cursory of respect.

Did they know, she wondered, that three of the generals had absconded? Yes, they likely did.

Then Axis lifted his head and spoke, and, like everyone else gathered here, she had eyes for no one else.

"My friends," Axis said in an easy voice which nonetheless carried a great distance, "do you know who I am?"

Silence, and Ishbel looked about, concerned.

Axis looked completely relaxed, and not at all disconcerted by the lack of response.

"Who am I?" he repeated, his voice as calm and as even as previously.

"You are Axis," came a voice, and Ishbel looked its way, recognizing one of the soldiers who had ridden with Axis when he'd rescued her from Ba'al'uz's men.

Then, from a man that Ishbel did not recognize, another response.

"You are a legend."

Axis laughed, soft and easy. "Aye, I am a legend. A man, a battle leader, a general. An Enchanter, a god, a ghost. I have ridden with the stars and walked the halls of the Underworld."

He smiled, just a little, just enough to charm every man and woman who saw it, and Ishbel thought that had he smiled at her like that when he'd asked her to be his lover, she would not have refused.

"I am the Skraelings' nemesis," he said, and at that his face hardened and his eyes glittered.

There was a marked response among the ranks. Tens of thousands of men shifted, and their regard became keener, their interest sharper.

"I know where the Skraelings are now," Axis said, turning in slow circles so he could gaze upon each section of the army in turn. "They are in Isembaard, where are so many of your families. Soon," he said, his tone now very strong, implacable, "we shall have to do something about that."

Now there was a cheer, then another, and then ten thousand more, and Axis had to hold up a hand to silence the army.

"I am a great battle leader," he said. "A legend. But do you know why I am here, this day?"

Silence, watching.

"I have come back from death, struggled back from the Otherworld, to introduce to you a legend both ancient and new. A legend to whom even *I* bow my head."

"I had not thought Axis so great the flatterer," muttered a dry voice just behind Ishbel, and she turned her head very slightly.

Maximilian stood there. So great had Ishbel's attention—as everyone else's—been on Axis that she had not heard him approach.

"Are you ready, Ishbel?" he murmured, and she inclined her head.

He gave her a small smile, and then Ishbel turned back to Axis.

"I have come here," Axis went on, "to introduce to you this legend. This place, this day, this moment, witnesses the rebirth of the greatest legend this world has ever seen.

"My friends, I commend to you my Lord of Elcho Falling."

Axis turned about in one last full circle atop the hill, catching every eye in the mass below him, then he stepped down, passing Maximilian, who now stepped up to take his place.

Good luck, Maxel. I have done all I can for you.

Axis moved to stand beside Ishbel, and she exchanged a small smile with him.

Axis wondered if his face looked as strained as hers. He looked up. The skies were gray now, and clouds still billowed to the south. There was a step behind him, and Axis turned his head to see BroadWing, one of the Icarii who had aided Maximilian to cross the FarReach Mountains, and who had then fought with Malat and Georgdi as the Skraelings seethed through the Central Kingdoms.

BroadWing looked to the gathering clouds. "The ghosts arrive," he muttered.

The Lealfast. Gods, Axis hoped so, and then fresh nerves set his stomach roiling.

Maximilian stood as easily as had Axis, likewise turning in slow circles so he could meet the eye of each rank in turn.

"You may know something of me," Maximilian began, his own voice carrying as well as had Axis'. "A king of a small eastern kingdom called Escator, a king of an amiable people, and who had little else to do save supervise the weekly bean market.

"But I came to my throne strangely, and from a strange place—and I go from the throne of Escator strangely, and to an even stranger place. Perhaps you know something of my early manhood—trapped in a gloam mine for seventeen years, and with no memories of my early life beyond the hanging wall, because to remember would have been to go mad."

He stopped, as if thinking, and Axis frowned slightly. *He had to do something more than this . . .*

"Ah," Maximilian said, "but what are words? Any man could stand before you and spend half his life describing *who* he was in words without any of them truly showing you *what* he was. You need to know me before you can trust me, or before you can choose to lend to me your lives. Ishbel, if you please."

Ishbel drew a deep breath and walked toward Maximilian.

He took her hand briefly as she reached him.

Thank you, Axis saw him mouth, then Maximilian let go of Ishbel's hand and addressed the massed soldiers once more.

"Allow me to present to you Ishbel Brunelle Persimius, Archpriestess of the Coil, my former wife, and a woman more powerful than perhaps you can imagine."

Axis looked at Ravenna at that.

Her face was a rigid mask of impassivity, but Axis could see that the tendons of her neck were tight, and he thought she must be angry. She would hate it that Maximilian had called Ishbel to him, and not her.

Axis looked back to Maximilian, who had unbuttoned his jacket and tossed it across a nearby rock, and was now rolling up the sleeve of his left arm.

Axis frowned. *What in the stars' name was he doing?*

Maximilian held Ishbel's gaze, then he raised his bared arm, and turned in a slow circle so that all could see it.

"I have scars all over my body from my years in the Veins," Maximilian said. "Scars caused by the vengeful swords of guards, and scars caused by the collapse of the uncaring rock face. This one here," he tapped his arm just above the elbow, where ran a livid, twisted scar, "I will ask the Lady Ishbel to uncoil for you, so that you may see and understand from whence I came." He hesitated, then spoke again. "Whatever happens next, my friends, do not fear. It will pass."

Now he held out his arm to Ishbel.

She hesitated, then stepped close and wrapped both hands lightly around his arm over the scar.

She bowed her head, Maximilian doing likewise so that their foreheads almost touched.

For a minute . . . silence, then . . .

Axis found himself existing in nothing but blackness. He had no name, and he had no identity, save that of his number: Lot No. 859. If he had ever had a name, he did not know it.

There was nothing in his existence save the rhythmic raising of the pick above his shoulder and burying it in the rock face before him, over and over. Five swings over his left shoulder and five over his right before swinging back to his left shoulder.

There was nothing but the black tarry gloam collecting around his naked feet, nothing save the grunts of the anonymous man chained to his left ankle, and those of the seven other anonymous men in the chained gang.

Raise the pick, swing it, bury it. Breathe. Raise the pick, swing it, bury it. Breathe.

Keep doing that, day after day, week after week, year after year.

"This was my life." Maximilian's quiet voice intruded, and Axis managed to pull himself out of the vision sufficiently to understand that it was only vision, and not reality.

"This," said Maximilian, "was my entire world—for *seventeen years.*"

This was the entire sum of existence, nothing else. Occasionally when someone in the line of chained men died, and another was brought to fill his place, the new man would babble about sun and wind and children and happiness beyond the hanging wall—the rock face that hung over their heads.

But Lot No. 859 knew there was nothing beyond the hanging wall, just a greater blackness, extending into infinity. Sometimes he thought he dreamed of something—an echoing memory, a glimpse of a rolling green sea, the scent of something called apple blossom—but Lot No. 859 knew these were figments of his imagination. Lies created by hopelessness to torment him.

He raised the pick, swung it, buried it in the rock face, feeling pain ripple throughout his body, but ignoring it because pain was such a constant companion that it had ceased to have any meaning.

Every so often men came, and demanded they stop, and gave them food and water, and told them to sleep.

Lot No. 859 did not ever sleep, or, at least, if he did, then he did not know the difference between dream and waking.

"One night," Maximilian's voice intruded again, "the guards thought they needed some amusement."

"Jack and I," said one of the guards, "can't decide whether or not you feel pain. You never complain. You never moan. I've seen you standing with blood running thick down your body and never a single whimper. Why is that then, eh? Do you have some magical ability to withstand agony?"

Lot No. 859 did not answer.

The guard grabbed at him, shaking him a little. "Why is that?"

Lot No. 859 did not answer. It was of no interest to him. If they did not require him to wield the pick at the moment, then he would just stand here, and breathe.

Just . . . breathe.

The guard cursed, angry that the prisoner ignored him, and grabbed something from one of the other guards. It was a piece of wire, and the guard wound it tight about Lot No. 859's left arm just above his elbow.

"D'you feel this, then?" the guard said, and twisted the wire with a knife, tightening it.

Lot No. 859 felt it. The wire cut into his flesh, slicing through skin and muscle. It did hurt, it agonized, but the pain did not disturb Lot No. 859. He set it to one side. It was of no matter.

All that mattered was that he raise the pick, swing it, bury it in the rock face. Breathe. Rest. Then raise the pick once again.

"The guard screamed at me," said Maximilian. "He tightened that wire until it cut down to the very bone. But I did nothing. Nothing mattered to me then, save that I continue to breathe.

"That—the constant tightening of the wire—was my life, my entire existence, for seventeen years."

Axis blinked, and suddenly he was standing once more in the hollow. All about him men were blinking, coming back to their senses.

Ishbel and Maximilian still stood close in the center of the hollow, then Ishbel slowly pulled her hands away from Maximilian's arm, gave him a long look, and stepped back a pace.

"That was his life, his entire life," she said, echoing Maximilian's own words. "For seventeen years. You have seen and you have *felt* what he endured. Could *you* have survived that? Could *you* have emerged sane at the other end of it? Maximilian Persimius is not Isaiah the Tyrant. He is not a battle leader."

She waved a hand briefly toward Axis. "You have Axis SunSoar for that.

"What you have in Maximilian," Ishbel continued, once more looking about at the crowd of soldiers, "is a man to whom you can entrust your hearts and souls, and not fear that he will destroy them. Maximilian is endurance, and he is understanding. If you find yourself lost amid blackness, my friends, then he is the man to lead you forth from it."

Axis had his mouth slightly open at the end of Ishbel's speech. *By the stars, if that was something she could do for a man when she professed not to love him, then what could she do when she admitted love?*

There was a gentle snow falling about them now, and Axis suddenly realized its presence. He glanced up at the sky: it was leaden gray, low-hung with clouds. Here and there . . . no, in myriad places, individual snowflakes did not fall, but hovered within the air.

The Lealfast fighters.

Axis shivered.

Ishbel had returned to her place in the front ranks of the soldiers, and Maximilian was once again left alone in the center of the hollow.

"That is my past," he said to the crowd, then smiled suddenly. "Thank the gods!"

Axis grinned, as did most people he could see. Maximilian had certainly managed to create some empathy.

"This," Maximilian said, raising a hand into the sky, "is my future."

Axis, as everyone else, looked up and gasped in wonder.

The snowflakes—both those snowflakes that were Lealfast fighters, as well as every normal snowflake, which Axis assumed the Lealfast were somehow controlling—were arranging themselves in the sky in patterns. They changed every heartbeat or so, swirling into new and even more fantastical arrangements of coils and whirls that twisted far into the sky until they vanished into the clouds.

Axis stared, his initial wonderment being replaced now by an urgent sense that he should understand something about what he was seeing . . . something about the patterns . . . *something so important about the patterns* . . .

"This," said Maximilian, "is where I am going and what I will become. This is Elcho Falling."

Once more the snowflakes rearranged themselves, but now instead of forming abstract patterns, they formed the outline of a citadel, an incredible fortress of twisted spires and great peaks that reared far into the sky.

A massive crown of three entwined rings enclosed the peak of the very highest tower.

The citadel hung over the entire army, revolving very slowly so that all could see every aspect

It was stunning, awe-inspiring.

Axis stared. The sense that there was something he should be understanding about what he was seeing—apart from the skill of the Lealfast in forming this representation—was now so all-consuming that he could barely breathe.

There was something . . . something . . .

"Oh gods . . ." Axis muttered, staggering a little on his feet with the depth of his emotion.

Oh gods . . . he understood suddenly just how it was that the Lealfast could touch the Star Dance.

Almost frantically he looked about, this way and that, Ishbel watching him carefully as if she thought he had been caught in a sudden fit of insanity.

Axis didn't care. He turned, his eyes almost starting from his head, as if searching out a ghost within the air.

And then, with incredible sweetness, the Star Dance filtered through his body, and Axis was whole once more.

CHAPTER EIGHTEEN

The Sky Peaks Pass

Maximilian knew. He stared at Axis, and gave him the ghost of a smile, then raised his hand in the air to attract the attention of the massed soldiers.

"Behold," he said, and he waved his hand.

Then, before the startled eyes of the watching tens of thousands, the representation of Elcho Falling blurred, then fell apart. Most of the snow-flakes tumbled to the ground, coating the heads and shoulders of the army below, but many thousands of them remained hovering in the air.

There was a long moment when they just hung there, quivering slightly in the faint wind, and then the snowflakes transformed into the indescribably beautiful frosted outlines of winged men and women.

Axis had never seen anything like it; the sight eclipsed, for the moment, his joy at being able to once again touch the Star Dance. The sky filled with the creatures, light glinting and shimmering off their wings and the outline of their bodies. They rose into the air, higher and higher, a great cloud of glimmering lights, a tangle of wings and outflung arms and the curve here and there of a back, or a shoulder, or a cheek.

Axis dragged his eyes away to look at his father. StarDrifter was staring upward, transfixed, his mouth open.

It was a similar reaction all about. Men stood, utterly still, staring up-ward, mouths hanging open.

"These are the Lealfast," said Maximilian, his even voice carrying across the entire assembly. "You do not need to fear them. They have pledged themselves to me, the first to do so with their entire hearts and loyalties."

Maximilian opened both arms, his face now looking up at the Lealfast hanging in the sky far above him.

"My friends!" he called. "Will you inhabit the winds for a time, while I speak to this great crowd?"

As one, every Lealfast in the sky bowed—with exquisite gracefulness— then wheeled away to the north.

In five heartbeats they were gone, and Axis felt a breath go through the mass, as if of disappointment.

"The Lealfast," Maximilian said again, "are the first peoples to pledge themselves to me. Others may follow." He paused. "I do not command you by any right, nor by any heritage. I am the Lord of Elcho Falling only, not of the world. But the doors of Elcho Falling are open to any who wish to join with me, or have like cause with me. Isaiah has handed command of you into my hands, but I cannot command the same loyalty that you owed Isaiah, nor should I try to do so.

"That loyalty is something you must give me freely."

Again Maximilian paused. "Some among you have chosen a different path to mine. Kezial, Lamiah, and Armat, three of Isaiah's generals, as well as some of their confidantes, have fled, preferring lonelier campfires to those here."

Stars, thought Axis, *be careful with this, Maxel.* He wondered if he should use the Star Dance somehow, to aid Maximilian, then realized that Maximilian would hate that.

Axis almost smiled. He was looking for an excuse now, any excuse, to use the Star Dance.

Despite his concern, Axis was glad that Maximilian had mentioned the generals' desertion openly. The fact of that desertion would be widely known within the Isembaardian army.

"Many of you are worried about what has happened to your homes and families in Isembaard," Maximilian continued. "I know that, and I sympathize with it.

"I can do a little about it. Tomorrow I am sending your once-Tyrant, Isaiah, back to Isembaard. Accompanying him shall be twenty thousand or so of the Lealfast fighters."

Axis hoped that Maximilian had already mentioned this to Eleanon.

"Your loyalty," Maximilian said to the Isembaardians, "you need to give to me freely. I shall not seek to force it."

He took a deep breath and gave a nod, and dismissed the gathering with that simple action.

Maximilian turned to step down from the top of the hill, but as he did so three Lealfast materialized above his head, and descended before him. As they landed, they attained full flesh, although their forms still shimmered with a semitransparency and frost still rimed the ridges of their features.

They bowed to Maximilian, spreading their wings out behind them in the same manner as the Icarii when paying someone their respects.

"Lord of Elcho Falling," said one of them, a bold, handsome man, "my name is Eleanon, and I speak for all the Lealfast. We have waited thousands of years for you, Maximilian Persimius, and our lives are now yours to command as you will."

Then Eleanon rose and, just before Maximilian addressed him, shot Axis a look of chilling triumph.

[Part Two]

CHAPTER ONE

DarkGlass Mountain

By the end of the third day, the One had completed his restoration work within the Infinity Chamber. Once more it glowed with light, and once more the power of Infinity powered the One's soul.

He exulted, then left the pyramid.

This was an adventure for the One, and a revelation.

He strode along the internal corridors of the pyramid, his green glassy form reflecting shadows from the fused black glass which lined the corridors, and gloried in the physicality of *movement*.

Then he emerged from the pyramid, and discovered the warmth of the sun, and color, sound, scent, and wind. For a moment all these different sensations threatened to overwhelm the One, but he took a deep breath (*feel the warm, scented air fill his lungs!*) and he absorbed these varied sensations, and they became at one with him.

He turned slightly, enough so he could see the pyramid rising high above him. This was a strange feeling, to look back on that which had contained him, which had literally *been* him, for so many thousands of years. He reached out a hand, touching a plate of green glass.

His hand blended with it (*into it*) perfectly.

Feel how smooth, how warm.

"Master?"

The One blinked, momentarily angered by the intrusion. He blinked again, and saw that it was a Skraeling.

He didn't like the Skraelings. But they were necessary, and they would prove useful.

Behind this single Skraeling the One could see many of the creatures, almost an infinity of them, stretching along the riverbank beyond the pyramid.

"Master?" the Skraeling said again.

"Yes?"

"It is good to see you again. We thought you had forgotten us, crouched so deep within your glass mountain."

The One thought this was presumptuous of the Skraeling, and did not deign to answer.

"Have you been talking with the Lealfast?" the Skraeling said.

"And if I have?" the One said.

"You should not trust them," said the Skraeling. "We are their fathers, yet they affect to despise us."

The One did not find that very surprising. He would expect nothing less than that his Magi should despise creatures such as these.

"One day," said the Skraeling, "they may affect to despise you, too. They have no great sense of loyalty. Unlike us. *We* are your true servants."

"And you have my gratitude for that," the One said, loathing them, and hoping that they did not intend to whine at him for hours. He waited, expecting the Skraeling to drift away, but it still stood there, clasping its claws in anxiety and looking at him with those disconcerting watery silver orbs.

By Infinity, they were disgusting!

"Was there anything else?" said the One.

"We are hungry."

"Hungry." The One pondered this. *What was hunger?*

"We need to eat, please. We've come a long way. You said you'd feed us."

"Kanubai said he would feed you. I am the One. I am not Kanubai. I am perfection incarnate."

"We still need to eat."

"You may not eat me!" the One roared.

"Of course not!" said the Skraeling, springing back to what it hoped was a safe distance. "We'd like to eat flesh, please."

"That is such a weakness, your need for flesh."

"Nonetheless . . ."

"Well," said the One, trying to work out what the Skraeling wanted him to do about this apparently overwhelming hunger—by Infinity itself, the whole horde of them appeared to be slavering! "Can't you find some flesh around and about to sate your hunger?" He waved a glassy hand about vaguely. "Does not flesh populate this land? I have been aware of much flesh these past few thousand years. Much and very annoying flesh."

Like Boaz, who had once worshipped him, but who had then presumed to plot to destroy him.

"Yes," said the Skraeling, who had now crept back a little closer, "once flesh did walk this land. But the land on this side of the river," the Skraeling's face twisted with fear as it said the word "river," "has curiously little flesh about it. We think the man Isaiah—"

Now the One's thoughts coalesced about the man who had spent hours sitting in the Infinity Chamber—*Isaiah*—and some of the hate that the One felt for Boaz managed to transfer itself to Isaiah.

Isaiah was trouble, too, and Isaiah was still alive, which was worse.

"—emptied the land this side of the river before we came," the Skraeling continued. "Nasty man. Now we're hungry, and we think that there is much flesh, much *vulnerable* flesh, waiting over the river."

As if to underscore the point, the Skraeling turned its head and looked longingly over the River Lhyl where stood the palace of Aqhat.

"It looks fairly empty to me," said the One.

"It was full when first we arrived," said the Skraeling, "but it has been *days* now, days and days and days since we arrived, and in that time people have been escaping east and north and south *and we haven't been able to chase them!*"

"Why not?"

The Skraeling hung its head. "We're afraid of water."

The One smiled. "What water?"

The Skraeling frowned, then looked again at the river.

It was gone, replaced by a glassy surface, rippled in patches where the water had struggled against its death.

The Skraeling drew a deep breath, then moved so fast its form almost blurred.

As it moved, so did its millions of comrades, and within a heartbeat the rigid river was lost beneath an undulating tide of gray wraiths.

The destruction of Isembaard had begun.

The One crossed the glassy Lhyl several hours later, once the initial fuss was over. The Skraelings had mobbed the palace of Aqhat, finding little save one old bedridden man whom the fleeing servants had forgotten, rats, a score of dogs, and a few cats.

From Aqhat they swarmed eastward, fanning out over the countryside, the leaders running with their noses close to the ground, sniffing out the trails of the people who had fled as soon as they'd seen the Skraelings appear on the other side of the river.

The One knew he'd have to call them back eventually, but he was coming to understand the need to feed, and so for the time being he would let them roam.

It wouldn't do any harm.

There were still a few score Skraelings snuffling around the reed beds of the Lhyl, perhaps hoping for a river lizard or two, and for a time the One stopped and watched them.

They were truly horrid creatures, but they would serve his purpose well.

There was a sudden commotion within the reeds, and the One strolled over to see what was happening. Had the Skraelings found a water lizard after all?

No, as it transpired. They had found a cat with a litter of kittens.

The mother cat had tried desperately to defend her litter, but in vain. She was now dead, torn between two of the Skraelings and ingested. The litter had consisted of seven kittens, but in the moments it had taken the One to walk over, the Skraelings had devoured six of them, leaving only one blood-spattered corpse which, just as the One stopped, one of the Skraelings reached for.

"Stop," said the One. He was curious about this creature, and picked up the bloodied corpse himself.

It lay in the palm of his hand, limp, damp with blood . . . and then it suddenly moved, and sank its teeth (or at least, it attempted to sink its teeth) into the meaty flesh at the base of the One's thumb.

The One jumped in surprise, almost dropping the kitten. He steadied, raising his hand so that he might study the creature more carefully.

Skraelings surrounded the One, wailing in frustration at the scent of blood and flesh so close.

The kitten rose on its paws, hissing at the One.

The One hissed back instinctively, but there was no malice in it. Instead he found himself confused by a strange sensation that began in his belly and rose into his chest.

It was . . . emotion, he realized, but he could not identify it.

"I might keep it," the One said of the kitten. "It requires further study."

As one, the Skraelings hissed in frustration.

"It was not dead at all," said the One, "merely covered with the blood of its siblings. Now all that remains from the litter is the one." His mouth curved and his eyes glinted as he realized the significance. "The one . . ."

The One studied the kitten more closely and noticed, as it flattened its ears and hissed at him again, that its teeth were tiny replicas of the ones the Skraeling had crowding their mouths.

"It must eat flesh, too," said the One. He lifted his free hand, pointed it at one of the Skraelings, and the next instant the Skraeling dissolved into finely shredded strips of meat.

The One bent down, retrieved a strip, and dangled it over the kitten.

The kitten's ears quivered, then pricked forward, and it reached for the meat.

The One smiled.

CHAPTER TWO

The Sky Peaks Pass

Maximilian walked toward his command tent. Behind him came Axis, Ezekiel, Ishbel, and three of the Lealfast: Eleanon, another male Lealfast, and a lovely woman, whom Axis found himself glancing at far more frequently than the two males. They had come here straight from the gathering about the hill, Maximilian asking that StarDrifter, Georgdi, and Malat meet him in the morning.

StarDrifter had not been pleased. He had wanted to speak with the Lealfast, but had eventually acquiesced to Maximilian's suggestion that that be left for the next day.

The walk from the hill had not been accomplished without some tension between the Lealfast and Axis. The Lealfast walked to one side of Maximilian, Axis a few paces to the other side with Ishbel and Ezekiel, and Maximilian thought he would have been skewered a thousand times had the looks they'd shot each other been daggers.

He repressed a sigh. More Icarii could be expected to fly in to join StarDrifter now that word was filtering out that once again there was a Talon of their people, and Maximilian had no idea how well the two winged peoples would get on.

Badly, if this was any indication.

He was glad he'd asked StarDrifter to stay away.

Serge was waiting by the tent flap and opened it as Maximilian approached.

"Isaiah is inside," Serge murmured. "And with bad news, I think."

Maximilian nodded. "Isaiah?" he said as he stepped into the tent.

"Maxel," Isaiah said, rising from his chair, "I am sorry I did not attend your gathering. There is more bad news from Isembaard."

Maximilian wished now that Ezekiel wasn't with him, but the Isembaardian general was already inside the tent, together with the others, and would have heard what Isaiah had said.

"Then just tell it to me, Isaiah," Maximilian said.

"The River Lhyl is dead," Isaiah said. "Murdered by whatever that damned pyramid has become."

Eleanon and Bingaleal exchanged the briefest of glances.

"Oh no!" Ishbel said, sinking into a chair. "Not that magical river. Isaiah, I am so sorry."

"If the River Lhyl is no more," Axis observed, "then the Skraelings have full access to Isembaard. The waters had held them back. Now . . ."

"All the more reason, then, for you to go back, Isaiah," said Maximilian.

"And how much," said Ezekiel, "do you think these frosted sprites and Isaiah can do, Maximilian?"

Maximilian sent him a level look, but did not respond. Instead he turned to the three Lealfast. "Eleanon," he said, offering his hand, and finding himself somewhat surprised to discover that the Lealfast man's hand was warm. "Will you introduce your fellows?"

"My brood brother Bingaleal," said Eleanon, indicating the other Lealfast male. Maximilian thought that Bingaleal had a harder, more experienced air about him than Eleanon. His entire manner had a cold edge to it, and, like Eleanon, he was watchful and alert.

Axis had recognized him instantly as the man who had tried to assassinate Isaiah in the great audience chamber of Aqhat, and he locked eyes significantly with Isaiah.

Maximilian shook Bingaleal's hand, then looked at the woman. She was very lovely, but radiated a sense of distance that reminded Maximilian of Ishbel when first they had met. Of a height with Eleanon and Bingaleal, the woman was slim and elegant, every turn of her head or lift of her shoulder the movement of a dancer. Her long pale hair was braided so that it ran in two twists from the center of her forehead to either side of her head, curving together again behind her head to meet at the nape of her neck. The twists glittered with rime and framed her lovely face as would a crown.

Maximilian glanced sideways, and saw that Axis was staring at her.

"My brood sister, Inardle," said Eleanon. "She was Lister's companion for a while, but now is not."

"An interesting manner of putting it," Axis murmured.

"Axis SunSoar," said Maximilian, deciding to move into his own introductions before Axis could say anything else, "of whom you must have heard. Isaiah, of Isembaard, likewise; Ishbel Persimius, again likewise; and Ezekiel, the senior of Isembaard's generals."

Cautious nods were exchanged all about.

"The rest of the social niceties shall have to wait," said Maximilian. "As Isaiah has pointed out, Isembaard is in crisis." He looked at the Lealfast. "Do all three of you command your fighting group?"

"Eleanon and myself," Bingaleal said. "Inardle fights among us, but does not command."

"Then why is she here?" said Axis.

Bingaleal looked at Axis, his entire manner chilly and aloof. "Because she stands for the rest of the Lealfast, StarMan. And because she has always stood among the elite, and in Lister's inner circle."

"Definitely within Lister's inner circle," Axis murmured, "if she was sleeping with him."

"Axis," Maximilian said, and Axis gave a shrug and turned aside a little, as if distancing himself from the conversation.

"I need your help," Maximilian said to Eleanon and Bingaleal. "I want to send perhaps twenty-five thousand of your fighters, with Isaiah, to aid the Isembaardians to escape." He gave a little smile. "I may have preempted your agreement a little with my announcement to the army earlier."

"You are our commander, my Lord of Elcho Falling," said Bingaleal. "You do not need either Eleanon's or my permission to use our force as you need." A slight hesitation. "We shall be glad to aid in Isembaard in any manner we are able."

"Why?" said Axis, now turning back into the conversation. "*Why* so loyal to Maximilian? There is no history between you, so far as I am aware."

He looked at Maximilian at this, and Maximilian gave a slight shake of his head.

"As there is none between you and he," said Eleanon, "and yet, here we all stand."

"We have heard of Elcho Falling whispered in the winds of the frozen northern wastes for all the centuries of our existence, StarMan," said Inardle. It was the first time she had spoken, and all the non-Lealfast studied her curiously. Her voice was very low, husky, but clearly audible and underscored with strength.

"We yearn for Elcho Falling," Inardle continued, "more than you can understand. We *know* it, which is why we could describe it in the sky above you this day. Its lord is our lord."

It was a brief but powerful speech, and it was followed by a momentary silence.

"Thank you," Ishbel said. She rose from her chair and inclined her head at Inardle. "That was beautifully spoken. I think there must be much we can learn from each other."

Beautifully spoken, perhaps, Axis thought, *but did it truly answer my question?*

"Eleanon, Bingaleal," Maximilian said, "how long do your fighters need to rest? You have already had a long journey to reach me."

"We travel effortlessly in our snow form," Bingaleal said, "and can return south again in the morning." Bingaleal slid a glance toward Isaiah. "Is it your wish that this man command us?"

"You will operate under his direction, yes." Maximilian paused, looking between Isaiah and Bingaleal carefully. He recognized the tension between them, but did not yet understand it. "Is there a problem with this, Bingaleal? Isaiah knows both the land and the enemy well; you do not."

Bingaleal gave an expressive shrug. "I have no problems, my lord. I just thought that perhaps Isaiah might feel uncomfortable about it."

"Why—" Maximilian began.

"Bingaleal was the Lealfast that Lister sent to Aqhat to stage the assassination attempt on Isaiah," Axis said. "That was the attempt that created the chaos that allowed Ishbel to be attacked and her child murdered."

"And for that tragedy," Bingaleal said, "I hold myself fully responsible." He stepped forward to Ishbel, bowing before her in the Icarii manner, wings spread out behind him in deference. "My lady, I cannot tell you how badly I wish I could undo that action. The last thing I wanted was for you to lose such a precious child, and with such horrific results."

"It would have happened either way, Bingaleal," Ishbel said. "It was no one's fault. Fate, only."

The tent door opened, and Ishbel, who had been going to say something else, looked over.

Ravenna had entered.

She smiled pleasantly, apologized for disturbing them, then looked at Maximilian. "Should I go, Maxel?" she said. "Am I intruding?"

Yes, she was, Axis thought, watching Maximilian. The man was obviously irritated with her presence.

He glanced at Ishbel.

She had turned very slightly, presenting her shoulder to Ravenna.

It was a clear but elegant rebuff, and Axis' mouth twitched with humor that the woman who had to all intents and purposes been utterly rejected a few nights ago now held such a strong advantage. He wished he'd witnessed the scene in the snow. It had patently been a turning point in all three participants' lives, but in ways that none of them could have predicted.

He looked about the room.

Everyone, including the Lealfast, was watching with interest.

"I thought you might have need of my counsel," Ravenna said to Maximilian.

Axis almost winced. *That had been a bad move.* If Maximilian had needed Ravenna's counsel, he would have ensured her presence.

Before Maximilian could respond, Ravenna turned to Eleanon, Bingaleal, and Inardle. "Greetings," she said, moving over and extending her hand. "My name is Ravenna, and—"

"Ravenna aided in my rescue from the Veins some years ago," Maximilian said to the Lealfast, taking Ravenna's elbow just before she reached the Lealfast, "and she has been a good companion in my efforts to find Ishbel. Ravenna, this is but a war council and would bore you. I think—"

She looked him directly in the eye. "I have ever been ready at your side, Maxel. I have risked my life for you. May I not have the courtesy of your ear?"

"Ravenna," Maximilian said, his voice gentle, "this really has nothing to do with you."

"And this child?" Ravenna said, her hand on her belly.

Maximilian's expression hardened. She had pushed too far with that question.

Axis folded his arms and leaned back against one of the tent's internal support poles, more intrigued than ever.

"You should go back to your mother," Ishbel said, "and your dreams of dark misshapen creatures and betrayal."

Axis could hardly believe he'd heard that. *Maximilian had told Ishbel about Ravenna's vision?* He looked to Maximilian to see if he looked surprised, but he continued to regard Ravenna calmly.

Ravenna had gone white. She stared at Ishbel, then at Maximilian. "You have made your choice, then," Ravenna said, and she turned her back and left the tent with, Axis thought, more dignity than he thought he'd be able to muster under the circumstances.

Ravenna's brief interruption had left Axis astonished. Whether he had admitted it to himself or not, Maximilian had indeed very clearly made his choice. Officially very much apart so few days ago, Ishbel and Maximilian had just now presented a united front against Ravenna.

Ishbel turned then, catching Axis' eye, and she gave him a very slight smile.

He gave her a small nod in return. *Your victory, Ishbel.*

Then he looked at Isaiah, and saw that his eyes gleamed with amusement and not a little pride.

"I apologize for that interruption," Maximilian said, very much collected. "Bingaleal, if we may take up where we left . . . you are certain you can work with Isaiah?"

Bingaleal looked at Isaiah and raised an eyebrow.

"We can work together," Isaiah said, his voice quiet and even. "I am grateful for whatever aid Isembaard may have."

"Good," Maximilian said. "You have fifty thousand among your force here, Bingaleal?"

"Give or take a few thousand," said Bingaleal.

"And you travel light, no supplies?"

"What you see before you is all that we are," Bingaleal said. "We eat food and drink wine such as you when it is available, but otherwise we may exist on what we gather within the air itself."

At that point Bingaleal glanced at Axis, who gave the Lealfast man a small smile.

They feed from the Star Dance.

"We travel light and fast," Bingaleal finished.

"Then take twenty-five thousand south, Bingaleal," Maximilian said. "The rest, together with Eleanon and Inardle, can remain here with me."

Bingaleal inclined his head and then, as Maximilian looked away, sent his brother an intense glance.

"Isaiah," Maximilian continued, "how fast can you travel? I know the speed at which the Lealfast can move, but—"

"We can take Isaiah with us," said Bingaleal. "We have the means. We can all reach Isembaard within a day, two at most."

Maximilian looked surprised at that. "You can do that for Isaiah, but you left Lister to travel at his own pace to reach me?"

"Lister and Isaiah are different propositions," Bingaleal said, and with that oblique answer Maximilian had to be content.

"My other purpose in calling you here," said Maximilian, "is to discuss the three missing generals. Ezekiel, what do you know of this?"

"I knew the night they'd fled," Ezekiel said. "That first night, Maximilian, after you'd taken 'control.'" His mouth quirked. "They did not approach me to accompany them. They thought me too much Axis' friend. I was not 'safe.'"

"If you knew the night they'd fled, Ezekiel," Axis snapped, "then why not tell us?"

"Because I thought that if you were as good as the legends said, Axis, you would have discovered their absence within hours."

Eleanon and Bingaleal looked away, repressing smiles.

"You are right," Axis said, "I should have known. Tell me, Ezekiel, you know these men better than any here. Where will they be going?"

"Riding as hard as they can for the soldiers Isaiah left stationed along his route to this point," Ezekiel said. "Seize command of them—two hundred thousand and more, if I am not mistaken."

"Will they try to return to Isembaard?" Maximilian said.

Ezekiel shook his head. "No. They can see vast territories here waiting to be seized. The Outlands and Central Kingdoms are in disarray because of civil war and the Skraelings' invasion. The generals will see an opportunity."

"But there is Maximilian," said Axis.

"Of course," said Ezekiel, the too heavy irony in his voice making Axis' eyes narrow.

"They will know that I cannot be certain of the Isembaardian soldiers here," said Maximilian. "The generals will certainly have supporters here to spread their word."

"You could have done more today," said Ezekiel, "to rally the Isembaard-ians to your cause. By the gods, Maximilian, you sounded almost as if you were giving them permission to follow in the generals' footsteps!"

Maximilian gave a little shrug of his shoulders.

"If you cannot retrieve those three generals," Ezekiel said, "then there will be war across the Outlands. Maximilian, you face a greater and nearer crisis than whatever waits below the FarReach Mountains, I think."

"Then I shall need *your* help," said Maximilian. "Do I have it?"

Ezekiel did not immediately respond. Then, finally, he gave a terse nod. "Save what you can from Isembaard, Maximilian, and I will give you both my help and my loyalty."

"Good," said Maximilian. "Eleanon, if your brother flies down with half of the Lealfast fighting force to Isembaard, then I shall need *your* help, and the rest of the Lealfast's, to discover these generals before they can do much harm. It has been three days. They cannot have got far."

"Maxel," Axis said, "perhaps I can ride after them, too. Their escape is the result of my negligence, and—"

"We can find them faster, StarMan," Eleanon said, and Axis jumped a little at the use of his old title.

"We have no need of Axis," Eleanon said, looking at Maximilian. "All we need is a description, and the direction which they were most likely to take, and we shall have them for you within a day."

Goodness, thought Axis, *if this lot are as good as they think they are, then I could have secured Tencendor against Gorgrael within a week, and relegated the Timekeeper Demons to the dustbin within two.*

"A description..." Maximilian said. "Ezekiel? You knew them better than anyone."

Ezekiel was about to answer, but Axis forestalled him.

"I can do far better than a description," he said quietly, and ran the Song of Recall through his mind. It was one of the first Songs he had learned dur-ing his training as an Enchanter, and it returned to him easily now.

Instantly the space within the center of the tent filled with a vision.

Axis and Isaiah, standing in Isaiah's private chamber within the palace of Aqhat. Ezekiel, white-haired but fit and hard, stood slightly to one side of the other four generals, Morfah, Lamiah, Kezial, and Armat.

"Morfah," said Axis, pointing him out, "is now dead, thanks to one of

Maximilian's tricks. That," Axis now pointed to a balding man with a deeply wrinkled face, "is Lamiah. The taller, thinner man next to him is Kezial, and the youngest man Armat."

"And *that*," said Maximilian, "is one mighty surprise, Axis. I thought you had lost your Enchanter powers?"

"Lost," said Axis, looking between Eleanon and Bingaleal, "but now regained. Eleanon, you have your men, now hunt them down."

There was a slight challenge in his voice at the last, and Eleanon responded to it with a sardonic tilt of his head.

"It is late," said Maximilian, "and we are all weary. Isaiah, may I see you in the morning before you leave? Eleanon, Bingaleal, and Inardle, do you need sleeping arrangements made for you? No? Then I shall see you in the morning as well. Ishbel, Axis, can you stay a few moments, please? I need to talk to you."

A little later, as Eleanon, Bingaleal, and Inardle stood talking at the edge of camp, Ravenna slid out of the shadows and approached them.

"I am sorry I did not make my acquaintance with you fully in Maximilian's tent," she said, noting how the faces of all three Lealfast closed over as she approached, and how swiftly they silenced their words.

Eleanon gave a little tip of his head and a lift of his eyebrows.

It could have meant anything.

"I heard, before I entered," Ravenna continued, "your explanation to Axis regarding your remarkable loyalty to Maxel."

"Maximilian Persimius commands the loyalty of many people," Inardle said.

"So truly he does," Ravenna said, "if somewhat falsely."

"Explain your 'falsely,'" Bingaleal said.

Ravenna gave a slight shrug of her shoulders "Once," she said, "the Lords of Elcho Falling were great and powerful."

"Once?" Bingaleal said, and his attitude, as that of Eleanon and Inardle, was now very watchful indeed.

"Once," Ravenna said. "But now ... ah, my friends, so much has been forgotten. Maximilian himself has lost fully two-thirds of the lore needed to wield the power of Elcho Falling. Do you know of the Twisted Tower?"

The Lealfast exchanged a wary look, then Eleanon managed a nod. "We have heard of it."

"The Twisted Tower is almost empty," Ravenna said. "Maximilian can no longer access the knowledge he needs. His is but an empty title, my friends ... unless he can somehow, magically, find all those lost objects on the muddy road to the east. He means well, but ..."

She gave an expressive shrug, then turned and left them watching her as she walked away.

"I think it just as well, brother," Eleanon said in a low voice, "that you shall be journeying into Isembaard. Discover what you can before we must commit ourselves fully."

Then he looked at Inardle. "Are you still so sure, sister, that the Lord of Elcho Falling represents our only path to salvation?"

"I have only ever said that we need to be careful," Inardle said, "and not leap into the new and exciting at our later cost. We must be cautious."

"As we shall," Eleanon said. Then his manner relaxed and he grinned. "Did you see, sister, how Axis StarMan looked at you?"

Inardle laughed, low and lovely. "His sharp tongue revealed his interest."

"He has a weakness for women," Bingaleal said. "The more distant they be with him, I think, the greater his interest."

"Then perhaps you can affect some distance, Inardle," Eleanon said. "Can you imagine what we might learn—perhaps what knowledge we can offer the One—if you are in Axis' bed?"

Inardle shrugged, much as Ravenna had just shrugged. "Perhaps," she said.

CHAPTER THREE

The River Lhyl, North of Azibar, Isembaard

Hereward was just sitting down to her evening meal in the cramped cabin of the riverboat when suddenly the entire boat tipped slightly to one side. She grabbed at a bulkhead to stop herself falling over; then, before anyone could speak, there came the frightful sound of grinding and splintering and the boat tilted even more alarmingly.

Everyone in the cabin was now grabbing for handholds.

"What's happening?" cried Heddiah the cook.

"I don't—" Odella began to say, then fell silent as something smooth and shiny and very, very sharp splintered through the hull of the boat, through her back, and then out her abdomen.

It was a huge shard of glass.

Hereward, as everyone else, was so shocked that for a long moment she could do nothing but stare. Then she opened her mouth and moved slightly, but before she could even reach out a hand to Odella, a score more shards of glass splintered through the hull, skewering two more people.

Suddenly it was all noise and movement as people leapt away from the hull and climbed onto the central table. Hereward picked up a small toddling boy and clambered onto the table, keeping him locked in her arms.

There was something wrong.

Something *other* than the fact that the boat had been inexplicably pierced by great shards of glass.

Something other . . .

"Oh gods..." Hereward whispered as she realized what it was. "Shush!" she yelled. "*Quiet!*"

The boat was no longer moving. It was stuck fast, canted over to one side, as if it was caught in...a river of glass.

"Quiet," Hereward whispered, now holding the boy so tightly against her chest he whimpered.

"Listen," she said.

There was the sound of something outside, scampering over the glass river. Something soft and heavy, something that moved on clawed feet.

Something...

"*A tasty, tasty!*" came a whisper from outside, and in that instant Hereward's world turned to hell.

Skraelings poured down the ladder into the cabin. People screamed, trying desperately to find somewhere, *anywhere*, to escape.

There was no escape. As Hereward twisted about she saw two men try to attack the Skraelings, only to be torn to shreds before her eyes. Another man tried to evade them, but impaled himself on a wicked shard of glass sticking through the hull.

Hereward had never felt panic like she felt now. Her terror on the banks of the Lhyl when first she'd seen the Skraelings crawling over DarkGlass Mountain could not compare to the sheer depth of her current fright. She thought her heart would burst; she *hoped* it would burst, because it would be a better death than that which must only be heartbeats away.

A Skraeling grabbed a woman just in front of her, and tore her head off with one bite.

Then Hereward saw its eyes lock on her.

She shrieked, scrabbling back along the table, dragging the boy with her.

The Skraeling swiped at her, but she managed to evade it with a desperate lunge to one side that saw her slide completely off the table.

She clambered to get to her feet, but tripped over a body as she did so, and slammed into the decking boards again.

There was a whisper behind her, and she knew it was the Skraelings.

She rolled over, trying to get under the end of the table, but the creature's hand grabbed into her hair and dragged her half upright.

Blood poured down her face and neck from the wounds the Skraeling's claws caused in her scalp.

In her arms the little boy shrieked, and the silver orbs in the Skraeling's jackal face slid down to the child.

The Skraeling's tongue flopped out one side of its jaws, and Hereward saw it literally slaver in delight.

Then, suddenly, the creature's grip in her hair was gone and it seized one of the boy's arms.

Hereward scrabbled backward desperately, trying to hold onto the boy, who was now screaming in terror while the Skraeling tugged at the boy's arm.

It tore off, making the Skraeling stagger backward.

Blood spattered over Hereward—not only from the boy, but also from one of her kitchen companions, Ingruit, who had just been opened up from breast to belly by a Skraeling claw.

Ingruit fell to the floor beside Hereward, and three Skraelings leapt on her, burying their heads in the body of the still-breathing woman.

Hereward continued to scrabble backward. The movement was automatic, for Hereward was now in such deep shock she was incapable of coherent thought.

The boy was still moving in her arms, still shrieking—and then he was gone, torn from her grip by the Skraeling who had taken his arm, now recovered in its balance.

Hereward was covered in blood. She could feel it soaking through her hair, her clothes, into every crevice and pore of her skin.

And the stink—the cabin was crowded with Skraelings and with the corpses they fed on, and the air was thick with the stench of hot blood and split bowels. Hereward could not believe she was not yet dead, and could not believe she could be forced to go through so much suffering while waiting to die.

She continued to move backward, finally shuffling up against the bulkhead.

Two Skraelings advanced on her. Their jaws and bodies were red with blood, and, having already eaten, they approached slowly, enjoying her terror.

Feeding on her fear, as they would shortly feed on her body.

Hereward tried to stand, forcing her legs to work, sliding further and further up the bulkhead.

One of the Skraelings feinted toward her, and she shrieked and jerked upright...

...and hit her head on a shelf.

She slumped to the floor again, and then something toppled off the shelf and hit her on the head and shoulder.

Hereward cried out, grabbing at the thing as the two Skraelings, now tired of their play and wanting only to eat, lunged at her.

Whatever the object was, it was large and very heavy, and Hereward meant to try and throw it at the Skraelings... but it was far too heavy for her fear-weakened arms and she could only wave it ineffectually about before dropping it in her lap.

Hereward had her eyes tightly closed, sure that at any instant Skraeling claws would shred into her flesh.

Nothing.

Quiet.

She sat there, breath wheezing in and out of her lungs, eyes tightly closed, and wished they would just *do* it, get it over with, just *kill* her, please, gods, just kill her...

Nothing.

Quiet.

Then the faintest of whispers.

"A nasty, nasty."

Hereward managed to open one eye, just a slit. It was an effort, as blood had gummed it shut, and for a moment she thought that the blood smearing her vision must be making her see wrongly.

"A nasty, nasty," repeated one of the Skraelings, hand partly lifted to point a claw at the object in her lap.

Then, unbelievably, the Skraelings turned as one and filed out of the cabin.

Hereward heard their footpads on the deck above, then heard them retreating across the glassed river.

Very slowly she looked down at her lap.

Resting there was a huge leatherbound book.

CHAPTER FOUR

The Sky Peaks Pass

W hy hunt down the generals, Maxel?" said Axis. "From what you have said to me about your and," he glanced at Ishbel, "Ishbel's policy of allowing everything to break apart, as well as what you intimated to the army earlier, the generals' lack should not bother you overmuch. So why send the Lealfast after them?"

"Because I need to gauge the Lealfast's usefulness," said Maximilian. "The Lealfast say they have vast experience as fighters, but how do I know that? But I also send them because I *do* need to know what the generals are doing—as Ezekiel pointed out, they will undoubtedly come after me at some point, and whatever you may think, I have no suicide wish. Use this time to evaluate the Lealfast, Axis."

"That was a pretty spell you performed for us just then, Axis," Ishbel said. "How did you do that, if your Enchanter abilities are as dead as you have said?"

Axis grinned. "I'd known the Lealfast could access the Star Dance, but I had no idea *how* until this afternoon. When they did that trick for you, Maxel, forming an image of Elcho Falling in the sky, I suddenly remembered something I'd been taught when first I'd started out as an Enchanter."

He gave a soft laugh. "By the stars, the Icarii are known for their blind arrogant stupidity, and our inability to use the Star Dance over these past years is evidence of that."

"What do you mean?" Ishbel said.

"We'd always assumed that the only way to use the Star Dance," Axis said, "was to *hear* it. But that isn't the only way . . ."

He grinned at the puzzlement on Maximilian's and Ishbel's faces. "I will explain to you, but do you mind if it is tomorrow? This is something I'd like to share with my father, and then with the other Enchanters among the Icarii."

Maximilian gave a nod and a smile. "At a later time, then. I'll bid you good night, Axis. We can talk again in the morning."

Axis said good night and moved to the door. Just as he reached it, Maximilian spoke again. "Axis? Congratulations. You must feel as if half the world has been returned to you."

"I feel," Axis said softly, "as if the entire world has been returned to me, Maxel."

With that, he was gone, and Maximilian turned to Ishbel.

Isaiah was standing in the shadow of an equipment tent when Axis left Maximilian's tent and came up to him.

"Be careful in Isembaard, my friend," Axis said. "I like you too much to be speaking the address at your memorial service anytime soon."

Isaiah inclined his head, accepting Axis' concern. "I had thought you were off to see your father."

"I shall be, in a moment. Isaiah . . . be careful of the Lealfast, eh?"

Isaiah gave a short laugh. "I shall not trust them overly, if that eases your concern."

"Aye, it does. Isaiah . . ." Axis paused. "Ravenna has shown Maxel a vision."

Isaiah's attention sharpened. "Yes?"

"Apparently it shows Ishbel opening the doors of Elcho Falling to doom. Ravenna says Ishbel will deliver sorrow throughout the entire land." Axis gave a small shrug. "The maddened jealousies of a bitter woman, no doubt."

"Perhaps," Isaiah said. *Perhaps.*

Axis was grinning to himself, not noticing Isaiah's introspection. "I asked Ishbel to be my lover."

"And she refused," Isaiah said, bringing his attention once more to the conversation. "You do not need to tell me that. Now, let us say good-bye,

Axis. I think we shall both have some adventures to relate to each other when next we meet."

They gripped hands, then hugged each other fiercely.

"Go see your father, Axis, and tell him how to open his eyes to the Star Dance once more."

"Ishbel, I know it is late, and you are tired. I won't keep you long."

She sat down in a chair, arranging her skirts carefully. "It is of no matter, Maxel. What did you want to talk to me about?"

"Do you remember me asking you about the Twisted Tower? It was a long time ago, on our way to Escator."

She frowned, thinking, then her face cleared. "Yes. It was on the way from Pelemere to Kyros."

"You did not know what it was."

"No. Maxel... will you tell me now?"

"The crown of Elcho Falling carries with it countless mysteries... and the heir to the crown needs to learn them. Many, many generations ago one of the Lords of Elcho Falling constructed the Twisted Tower in which to store the mysteries and secrets of Elcho Falling. It is a memory palace."

"A memory palace?"

"A memory palace is an imagined building, filled with objects—for us it is a great twisted tower with ninety levels. Each level contains one chamber, and each chamber is crowded with objects. Each object contains a memory."

"And as a child... you had to learn each single object?"

Maximilian smiled at the horror in her voice. "Yes... although it wasn't as bad as you might think. The Twisted Tower was closely linked to the Persimius bloodline. It was simple for every Persimius heir to know an object. We merely had to pick it up and we could 'recall' the knowledge it contained." He sighed. "But... there's a problem."

Now it was Ishbel who smiled, a soft, gentle thing. "Of course there is."

"Knowledge of the Twisted Tower has been handed down through scores of generations. The problem is that every generation seemed to forget a few of the objects." Maximilian's mouth twisted slightly. "Maybe some of my forebears thought there was little point in remembering. Elcho Falling had been unneeded for so long that there was little likelihood it would ever need to rise again. What harm if one heir forgot the blue vase under the window of level nineteen, and his son the contents of the third drawer in the chest on level forty?"

"How much has been lost, Maxel?"

"About two-thirds of it. From the thirty-sixth level the chambers begin to progressively empty, so that by the time I reach the top of the tower, each chamber is utterly bare. So much has been forgotten."

Now his mouth curved again, this time with more humor. "I had hoped that somehow you held some miraculous key to recalling the empty space of the Twisted Tower. I had thought that was perhaps why you were sent to me . . . that somehow, in your forgotten Persimius line, the lost objects could be remembered."

"And I know nothing. Maxel, I'm sorry. Perhaps Elcho Falling has the answers."

"Perhaps. Oh gods, I *hope* so. Without the knowledge that has been lost, Ishbel, then I am helpless. I can raise Elcho Falling . . . but I can do little else. You have no idea how desperately I hope that Elcho Falling has the answers. Ishbel . . . I just wanted to explain to you about the Twisted Tower. I should have done so before."

He'd also just wanted to talk his worry out, Ishbel realized, and was mildly surprised to discover herself glad that he'd wanted to talk to her about it.

"There's something else I wanted to mention," Maximilian said. "Have you heard of the Weeper? The bronze deity that StarDrifter brought with him out of Coroleas?"

"Yes. He and Salome told me something of its history. StarDrifter also said that you and he thought it was responsible for the regrowth of his and Salome's wings. It is a very powerful object."

"You know the damn thing talks."

She gave a small smile. "Yes. It is metal. I am sure that it talks."

They looked at each other. Both were Elementals, born with the ability to hear the chatter of the elements within metals and glass. Ishbel had repressed her ability to hear them for many years after her terrible experience as a child, when the jewelry on her dead parents had whispered to her to expect the rise of the Lord of Elcho Falling. Now, although she had accepted her ability, Maximiljan thought she remained just a little wary of it.

"What does it say?" Ishbel asked after a moment.

"For the longest time, it said very little. It chatted to my ring—" Maximilian held up his right hand which bore the Persimius ring "—a great deal, but to me . . . very little. It just wanted to be near me. But in the past few days it has been whispering your name, Ishbel. It wants to speak to you."

Ishbel's face went very still.

"I think it is harmless enough, Ishbel."

"Ha. I doubt that very much. But if you want, I will see it."

She paused. "Maxel . . ."

"Yes?"

"I am of Persimius blood, too. Can I see the Twisted Tower? Can you show it to me?" *Will you trust me that far?*

CHAPTER FIVE

The River Lhyl, North of Azibar, Isembaard

Hereward sat for what felt like hours, staring either at the book or at the horrific scene in the cabin before her. Bodies, or the remains of bodies, lay strewn about, and there did not appear to be a single space that was not coated in blood.

One thing in particular caught her eye. It was the remnant of a body stuck on one of the shards of glass that had pierced the hull. Hereward couldn't quite decide *what* part of a body it was, though. Part of an abdomen? A shoulder? A buttock? The Skraelings had obviously chewed the person while still attached to the glass, and Hereward found herself wondering if they left that remaining fragment because they didn't want to cut their tongues on the sharp glass.

It was a very meaty fragment. Hereward thought it must have been difficult for the Skraelings to abandon.

Maybe they'd left it because of the book.

Hereward looked down at it once more. It looked like any ordinary book. It was very large, almost an arm's length in height, and half as wide, and as deep as the length of her hand. It was covered in fine-grained calfskin with an elegant tooled gilt edging about the front cover.

It didn't look dangerous, and Hereward could not think why it should have scared the Skraelings so greatly. With its covering of calfskin, she thought they would have thought it a tasty, tasty, not a nasty, nasty.

. Hereward sat there until she felt her back and legs start to cramp. She was very cold, still in deep shock, and could not understand why the Skraelings did not come back for her.

Were they waiting outside? Were they tormenting her?

Why this delay in death?

Should she go find them, offer herself to them?

Or should she try to live instead?

In the end Hereward shoved the book to one side and, with great effort, managed to get to her feet. She stood for a few minutes, swaying slightly, then took a step or two toward the door at the far end of the cabin.

Then she stopped, looked behind her, and stepped back to pick up the book.

She almost dropped the thing, it was so heavy, then she steadied it in her arms and began the gruesome walk to the door, stepping over the body parts as she went and taking care not to slip in the pools of blood.

It was night outside, and a gentle breeze blew in from the east. Hereward stood on the slanting deck, hugging the book to her chest, looking about.

Everything looked so calm, so peaceful.

There was a band of Skraelings some fifty or sixty paces away on the east bank, outlined in the moonlight. They were moving slowly, their snouts snuffling along the ground.

One of them looked up and saw her, then they all raised their heads, stared, and as one moved off further to the east.

"What are you?" Hereward whispered to the book. She thought about opening it—there was a lamp still burning on the prow of the boat and she could easily read by its light—but for the moment all Hereward wanted to do was to strip off her blood-soaked clothes. She put the book carefully down on the deck, then looked around.

The river was useless. As far as she could see, it was nothing but green glass.

The same color as DarkGlass Mountain.

Hereward had heard rumors about the evil nature of the pyramid all her life, and had loathed it intuitively.

Now that same intuition told her that the pyramid, or whatever inhabited it, was responsible for this.

Hereward sighed. She could not bathe in the river, but there was a barrel of rainwater wedged against one of the boat's railings, and so she stripped away her blood-stiffened clothes and washed herself down, scrubbing at her long dark hair to get the blood out, and not caring about the sting of the cuts in her scalp.

She also did not worry about the Skraelings. Surely, if she was fated to die, then the Skraelings would have taken her before this.

There was a chest tied in close against the cabin, and from it Hereward retrieved a linen robe—it was Odella's, and a little too big for Hereward's slim body, but she belted it in tightly.

At least her sandals could be washed clean of the blood and slipped back on.

Hereward knew she had to make a decision about what to do, but delayed it by deciding to examine the book.

She hefted it, wandered over to the lamp burning in the prow, and sat down with a thump on the deck.

Another band of Skraelings drifted past on the river, but they gave the boat a wide berth.

Hereward opened the cover to a blank, creamy page. She turned it over and came to what was obviously a table of contents.

She frowned at it—the writing was unfamiliar, foreign, and she couldn't—

The writing shimmered, and suddenly both script and language were familiar, and she could read.

The page listed in order a series of stories . . . save that all the stories were the same.

One: The story of the woman Hereward who waited on the riverbank with the book.

Two: The story of the woman Hereward who waited on the riverbank with the book.

Three: The story of the woman Hereward . . .

And so on for thirty stories.

"Wait," Hereward muttered. "On the riverbank."

Far to the south, the One raised his head from the kitten in his hands and looked northward.

"What is this that rises?" he whispered. "What ghost from the past be this?"

The book stank of Boaz, and the One instinctively hated it.

CHAPTER SIX

The Sky Peaks Pass

C an you show me the Twisted Tower, Maxel?"

"You want to see the Twisted Tower?"

"Will you trust me that far?"

Maximilian breathed in deeply. Distrust and uncertainty had been the twin pillars of their relationship before even they'd met. But now that that relationship had been utterly torn apart, it appeared to be progressing in leaps and bounds.

Now that it had been fractured . . . Ishbel's mouth moved in the hint of a smile.

"If you wish, then certainly." Maximilian fell silent, thinking. "But for this first time, I will need to touch you. It is the only way."

"I don't mind, Maxel."

Nonetheless, Ishbel took a big breath as Maximilian pulled his chair close, hesitated, then lifted his hands and slid his right about the back of her neck, cradling her head, and lay the other against her cheek.

"Now it is you who will need to trust me," Maximilian said softly. "I need to take your consciousness and turn it in a slightly different direction. You can stop anytime you want."

"I trust you, Maxel."

"Close your eyes."

She did so.

"Relax your neck and shoulders. Let me cradle your head."

She did this, too, though with some effort, as the intimacy reminded her so much of their brief period of almost happiness.

How long had that lasted? A week? Two? But even that brief time had been founded on lies and had collapsed at the first test.

"Ishbel, trust me."

Trust me.

Ishbel's mouth opened on a small, silent gasp. It felt as if Maximilian's fingers had suddenly intruded right into her mind and were gently twisting it, just a little, very quietly, almost tenderly.

"Do you feel what I am doing with your consciousness, Ishbel? Do you think you could turn your mind so, on your own, later?"

His fingers were still so gently turning her mind. Their pressure felt very curious, but not uncomfortable or unsettling, and Ishbel could understand what he was doing.

He was turning her consciousness so that it altered her perception of her surroundings and of the world she inhabited.

"Yes," she whispered.

She felt him smile, felt the alteration in the warmth that radiated out from his face.

"Good. Right about now, Ishbel, you should see a path before you. Do you see it? Do you *feel* it, beneath your feet?"

"Yes. Yes!"

And Ishbel did. She stood with Maximilian on a paved pathway that wound through a garden of low flowers and shrubs toward the most extraordinary structure she had ever seen. A tower rose before her, twisting in a corkscrew manner so high into the blue sky that she had to crane her head to look at it.

"Ninety levels," said Maximilian. "One chamber per level, and one window only, at the highest level." He smiled. "I have never seen this garden on either side of the pathway, Ishbel, nor have I seen the sky so blue. You brought that with you."

She looked at him. He was smiling, and she thought he looked very relaxed.

"Now look to the pathway," said Maximilian. "There are eighty-six steps to reach the door. You always need to take eighty-six steps, and you must learn to count them as you approach. Soon the eighty-six will become second nature."

"Why eighty-six?"

"The tower is a thing of order. It is also a thing of immense memory . . . ordered memory. If you approach it in a disordered manner, then that disorder will reverberate throughout the entire tower. Come. Let us begin these eighty-six steps."

He took her hand, and led her toward the tower. They stopped before the door, and Maximilian paused in the act of reaching out to grasp the doorknob.

"You open it," he said. "Only someone of Persimius blood can open it."

"Are you testing me?"

"No. I'm allowing you to do some of the work for a change."

Ishbel bit back a smile, and laid her hand on the round brass knob.

Hello, Ishbel Persimius. Never before have I had a queen of the blood visit.

Ishbel's fingers trembled a little, then they firmed and she twisted her hand so that the door clicked open.

She stopped, one foot inside the door, astounded at the clutter and crowd of objects in the room.

Maximilian put a warm hand in the center of her back, gently encouraging her inside a step or two.

"Welcome to the Twisted Tower, Ishbel Persimius."

Maximilian led Ishbel through the lower chambers of the Twisted Tower. He showed her a few objects, and watched her face as she picked them up.

"I know what memory this plate contains," she said. "It holds a memory to do with the opening, or raising, of Elcho Falling. Yes?"

"Yes." He explained to her precisely what the memory meant, and what was its message, and the small frown cleared from Ishbel's brow.

"How did I know that?" she said. "I knew the general gist of it, but not the particulars, which you needed to explain. But now that you have explained . . ." she turned the plate over, then returned it to its place on a table. "I know I will never forget it. But how did I have the basic knowledge, anyway?"

"That's your Persimius blood," said Maximilian. "We all have the basic understanding—we just need to have someone guide us through and restore to us a full and clear understanding of the memory of each object."

"Ah," she said. "I was being tested again."

"Not at all. I knew you would know each object, and that you had the memories within you." Maximilian hesitated. "In the same way that you knew the basic memory in that plate, so I knew the instant I touched you that you were of strong Persimius blood."

They looked at each other, remembering that night when Maximilian had first come to Ishbel, and had seduced her.

"It is *why* I wanted you so badly that night, Ishbel," he said. "I had come merely to say hello." His mouth quirked. "I ended up doing far more."

Now Ishbel felt uncomfortable, and a little irritated at the idea that he might now be trying to seduce her all over again. "I'm tired, Maximilian. It has been a long day. Perhaps we can go now?"

"Of course. Do you know how to leave?"

"Yes, I think so. I just need to twist my consciousness back the way it has come and—"

Ishbel's head jerked in Maximilian's hands and she opened her eyes with a start.

"Oh," she said, staring at the inside of the tent.

Maximilian smiled. "Very good."

He was very close, and Ishbel again felt deeply uncomfortable. She tensed her head, ready to pull it out of his hands, but he moved them first.

His left hand dropped away completely, but his right . . . the fingers of his right hand trailed down behind her left ear, then continued in soft, lilting movement down her jaw until they, too, finally dropped away.

Ishbel froze, staring at Maximilian.

That had been a signature movement of his when they had made love, a tender conclusion that he had almost always employed.

Ishbel had loved it, and always turned her face into it.

Now she sat rigid, unable to think or move.

Maximilian sat back. "You can find your own way into the Twisted Tower now," he said. "You may go whenever you like."

Ishbel ran her tongue about her mouth, trying to will some moisture into it, and finally managed to find her voice. "You don't mind?"

"Not at all. I might join you sometimes, and show you the meaning of more of the objects."

"Why would you do that?"

"Because it doesn't hurt to have two of us with the knowledge."

"Oh. Maxel, if you have the basic memories of all the objects already within you, then why can you not remember the ones that were lost?"

"Because we need to touch the object, *see* it, to spark the memory carried deep within us. Did you know of that segment of the raising ritual of Elcho Falling before you touched the plate?"

"Oh," Ishbel said again, and felt foolish. "I think I will say good night now, Maxel."

"I have kept you far too late. I'm sorry."

Ishbel rose, but Maximilian spoke once more as she reached the door.

"Ishbel, you may go whenever you wish into the Twisted Tower, but I shall demand a price from you."

She turned back to him, her expression wary.

He grinned. "A flower. Give me a flower for every time you visit."

"A *flower?*"

He gave a little shrug.

Ishbel looked at him, let out her breath in exasperation, then left.

After Ishbel had gone, Maximilian remembered that he should have reminded her of the Weeper. It was growing more insistent now, calling Ishbel's name many times while Maximilian was about.

Maximilian sighed. Never mind. Doubtless he would find time soon.

CHAPTER SEVEN

The Sky Peaks Pass

Axis paused just outside his father and Salome's tent. Very gently he used a little of the Star Dance to sense inside.

He smiled.

StarDrifter lurched up from Salome's body as Axis entered the tent.

"By the stars, Axis, did you not think to announce yourself before your entry?"

Axis sat down in a chair and stretched out his long legs. He smiled lazily. "I thought you'd be interested in what I know about the Lealfast. Forgive me, is this a poor time?"

StarDrifter muttered a curse and sat up in bed. Salome stretched languidly, not caring that the sheet only covered to her thighs, and gave StarDrifter an amused glance as he tugged the sheet higher.

Axis narrowed his eyes a little, watching Salome. She was as desirable heavily pregnant as she had been when first he'd met her. *That SunSoar blood.* He turned over in his mind the thought that he need not tell his father about the Star Dance, and instead could use it to win Salome to his side.

She would be drawn to it irresistibly. StarDrifter could do nothing to hold her.

He could have a SunSoar woman back in his bed once more . . .

"Axis?" said StarDrifter. "Why are you here?"

Axis dragged his eyes back to his father. "May I tell you a story?"

"Oh, for the gods' sakes," StarDrifter muttered.

"Shall it amuse us?" Salome said.

"Assuredly," said Axis.

"Then go ahead," said Salome, turning languidly over on her side to face Axis and allowing the sheet to fall away from her breasts.

Their eyes met.

All he would need do was to keep the secret of the Star Dance to himself, and he could have her.

Salome smiled. She was not able to read his thoughts, but she understood the expression in his eyes.

"Axis?" StarDrifter said.

"When I was a young man," Axis said, "learning the ways of the Star Dance and the powers of the Enchanter, I spent some time with Orr, the Charonite Ferryman, who guarded the waterways of the Underworld."

"I know this," said StarDrifter. "I don't know why—"

"Salome has not heard this tale," Axis said.

StarDrifter muttered another curse and cast his eyes up to the roof of the tent as if it cradled salvation.

"I spent time with Orr, the Ferryman," Axis continued. "He was a man, a being, of great power and wisdom. He told me something about the waterways—I'm not sure if ever I told you—"

StarDrifter made an impatient gesture with one hand.

"Well," Axis said, "he told me that, as the Icarii Enchanters used music to mirror and then manipulate the patterns of the Star Dance, the Charonites used the waterways in the same way."

StarDrifter suddenly shifted his gaze to Axis.

"Whenever the Charonites wanted to use the Star Dance for a purpose, to create an enchantment, instead of singing a Song, they traveled a particular waterway. They used movement—*dance*, if you like—to create the same effect."

"The Star Dance was lost when the Timekeeper Demons destroyed the Star Gate," StarDrifter said.

"That is a myth," Axis said, holding his father's eyes. "We both know the Lealfast still use it. We just lost the ability to hear it."

"Axis," said StarDrifter, now so tense he was almost rigid, "have the Lealfast told you how to access the Star Dance?"

"No," said Axis. "I think they rather hate us, StarDrifter. They wouldn't give me the time of day, let alone their secret to the Star Dance."

StarDrifter's body slumped once more against the pillows.

"Nonetheless," Salome said, her eyes narrowed, "you are telling us this delightful little tale about Orr the Ferryman for a reason, are you not?"

"Indeed," said Axis. "StarDrifter, all we lost was the ability to *hear* the Star Dance. Look, the Icarii were used to hearing the music of the Star Dance, yes? It filtered through the Star Gate from the heavens and into our daily lives. It surrounded us always. But what if we were so used to hearing it this way that we'd been blinded—and I use that word deliberately—to other means of recognizing or of allowing the Star Dance to filter through us?"

"Axis," said StarDrifter, "have you regained your connection to the Star Dance?"

"Yes," said Axis.

StarDrifter literally leaped over Salome and crouched before Axis, his hands on his son's arms. "*Tell me!*"

"You can't see it yet?" said Axis.

StarDrifter's grip tightened until his fingers dug into Axis' flesh. "*Tell me!*"

"We can *see* it, StarDrifter," Axis said, pulling his arms away from his father's grip. "The Lealfast can *see* it. And once you can *see* it, then suddenly you can hear it again—not as loudly as we were once used to, but hear it none-theless. Salome."

She jumped a little, surprised at being addressed. "Yes?"

"You have not been corrupted by a lifetime of Icarii blindness," Axis said. "Maybe you will understand. What has StarDrifter told you of the Star Dance?"

She glanced at her husband, then looked back to Axis. "The Star Dance is the music made by the stars as they weave their way through the heavens."

"Yes," said Axis. "Good stock answer. Carry on."

Salome gave him a black look, but continued. "The music made by the stars filtered through the Star Gate—"

"Tell me, Salome," Axis said, "was that the only way to *see* the stars, through the Star Gate?"

She sent StarDrifter another glance. "Well, no, we can see them in the night sky. But I have been told that the stars in the night sky are but a pale reflection of what was visible through the Star Gate."

Axis sat and waited, regarding Salome steadily, and StarDrifter turned away from his son and stared at Salome also.

She narrowed her eyes, thinking. "The stars in the night sky are but a pale reflection of what you could see through the Star Gate . . . but they are still there."

Axis' mouth curved in a small smile.

"Ergo," she said, "the Star Dance is still here, too, but a paler reflection of what you could once hear via the Star Gate."

Now Axis was grinning, and looked between his father and Salome. "The Star Dance *is* still here. It falls to earth gently about us, day and night. It drifts down from the heavens. It isn't as concentrated nor as loud as what we heard via the Star Gate, *but it is still around us.* We just need to open our senses to it. Listen, when I watched the Lealfast do their pretty snowflake thing in the sky above Maximilian, my mind was screaming at me to make some connection, and I just couldn't."

"They were making patterns," said Salome.

"Yes," said Axis. "They were making patterns. And as that thought came into my head I remembered what Orr had told me about the waterways making patterns so the Charonites could manipulate the Star Dance . . . and suddenly it just clicked."

"What just clicked?" StarDrifter said.

"It would have been better to do this during the day," said Axis, "as our sight would be clearer then, but there is a light snow falling and it will do better than nothing." He stood, and picked up a lamp. "Come with me. Oh, and toss on some clothes. It will be cold outside."

StarDrifter cursed, and grabbed at his breeches.

Axis led StarDrifter and Salome outside and held up the lamp. "The Star Dance is drifting down gently from the heavens," he said. "Look at the pattern of the snowflakes as they fall."

StarDrifter and Salome stared, their brows furrowed.

"Would it help," Axis said softly, "if I said that you can see music as well as hear it? That you can write music, and understand it? That the—"

"Star Dance is twisting the snow as it falls!" said StarDrifter. "The twists and cadences of the snow as it falls show us the music of the Star—"

He stopped, his face going completely blank.

Axis watched him, then saw the instant the Star Dance filled his father's consciousness. StarDrifter's entire body sagged and his eyes filled with tears.

"Everything about us is affected to some extent by the gentle fall of the

Star Dance from the heavens," Axis said. "Everything. All we have to do is open our eyes to it. The motes of dust dancing in the air, the tilt of a bird's wing in the sky, the clouds as they bubble and tumble across the sky. And once you can *see* it, once you *understand* that the Star Dance is all about us— albeit in a more subtle form than we were used to hearing it previously— then the music fills our souls again. Salome, can you feel it? See it?"

"Yes," she said, and gave Axis a lovely smile, "I think that I can. You know, I used to hear this as a child, and then I thought it a figment of my imagination. It used to fill my dreams at night."

They stood in silence for several long minutes, wonder transfixing Salome's face, thankfulness StarDrifter's.

"But what I don't understand," Salome said eventually to Axis, "is that if the Star Dance was all about you anyway, why could the Icarii Enchanters not use it anymore when the Star Gate was destroyed?"

"Because we were so blind," said StarDrifter. "Because we were so used to hearing the harmony of sound from the Star Gate that we were utterly blinded to the subtlety of this gentler music. Because it takes, on average, a thousand years for the damned Icarii to comprehend the easiest of secrets!"

Axis looked at his father and laughed, the sound one of pure joy.

They stayed up most of the night, sitting in StarDrifter and Salome's tent, laughing with their joy and playing with the Star Dance. Axis and StarDrifter found their control of the music weaker than it had been when they'd heard the full thunder of it through the Star Gate, but even in the few hours that they had toyed with the Star Dance, they felt their use of it becoming firmer.

Toward dawn there came a murmur at the tent flap. It was StarHeaven, one of the Icarii who had arrived the day Maximilian and Ishbel had talked atop the hill.

"StarMan?" she said as she entered. "Talon? What is happening? Myself and several other Enchanters," she indicated that they waited outside, "have felt as if . . . as if . . ."

"The Star Dance has been rediscovered," said Axis. "Come in, Star-Heaven, and your fellows, too, and rediscover yourselves."

CHAPTER EIGHT

On the Road to Serpent's Nest

The morning was very cold. The snow had ceased falling before dawn, and now a heavy frost lay over everything in camp. Winter was having its final, cruel stab before spring's warmer breezes.

Despite the cold, everyone in camp was moving. Tents collapsed ungracefully into the snow, sending puffs of white powder about knees and hips; horses moved restlessly as saddles were thrown across their backs; cooks shouted irritably as hooves and boots kicked dirty snow into their fires.

Maximilian was breaking camp and making for Elcho Falling.

Ishbel, tired after a restless night of little sleep, made her way carefully through the ranks, Madarin trailing a few steps behind her. She was looking for Isaiah, and found him, eventually, standing with Eleanon and Bingaleal.

"Isaiah," she said, "may I have a brief word?"

The Lealfast bowed, then faded—quite literally—away.

Ishbel rubbed her hands together, trying to restore some circulation into them. "Isaiah, be careful. Please."

"I will, Ishbel. I didn't think you would be so concerned."

"Well, I am. You can consider it a triumph."

He tilted her chin up with a gentle finger. "I need to get back to my river, Ishbel. I cannot stay away from it too long."

"I know. Be careful."

"You and your lord must come visit me one day."

Ishbel ignored the "your lord" for the moment. "You're not coming back?"

"My work here is done. My work in Isembaard awaits."

"Isaiah, you don't know *what* awaits you there!"

"I have a good idea. And I *will* be careful. Ishbel . . . look after that goblet. Listen to it. And listen to your heart."

Then he leant down to her, kissed her softly, and was gone.

Eleanon and Bingaleal stood apart, unseen in their magical state, watching Isaiah and Ishbel.

"I wish you luck in Isembaard, brother," Eleanon said.

Bingaleal gave a nod. "I hope I may discover hopeful news. The more I hear about Maximilian, and the more I talk with him, the more I feel that the One may offer us a better pathway. Eleanon . . ."

"Yes?"

"It might be worth considering fooling Maximilian and Axis into thinking we are poor fighters. It might do us good if they underestimate us."

"And our powers. They only know of our command of the Star Dance. Not of . . ."

"Not of the power we learned from the Magi," said Bingaleal. "Not of the power of the One."

He stopped and exchanged a small, secretive smile with Eleanon.

"Then they shall think us useless," said Eleanon. "I will talk to Inardle about this, too, and make certain she tells Axis only what we want him— and Maximilian—to know. You are right. It is best for us, and best for our hopes, if they underestimate us completely."

Isaiah walked to a snowy space some distance from the bustling encampment. One of the Lealfast stood there, waiting for him.

Bingaleal, Isaiah's erstwhile assassin.

About him drifted clouds and banners of snow, and from the corner of his eye Isaiah could see a glimmer of faces and wings and hands within—the Lealfast who were to accompany them south.

"Off to save Isembaard, then," said Bingaleal.

"What we can of it," Isaiah said. He studied the Lealfast, trying to see past the exterior reserve to the being within. He didn't entirely trust the Lealfast. He wasn't too sure of their allegiance to Lister, nor was he sure of their apparent willingness to abandon Lister on a whim. What did they want? What master did they truly serve?

Would they aid or hinder in Isembaard?

"I would like Maxel's army to see us depart," said Isaiah. "It will—"

"Help Maximilian?" said Bingaleal. "Perhaps. We can make a showing for him."

"Good." Isaiah hesitated. "How—"

"—will we carry you?" said Bingaleal.

Isaiah thought that if Bingaleal kept interrupting his every utterance to finish it for him then their nascent friendship might come under severe strain.

"With great ease, Isaiah, river god," Bingaleal continued. He reached out a hand, frost trailing from the tip of his index finger along his arm to the point of his muscular shoulder. "You are of the water, we are of the snow. We are brothers, you and I."

He hesitated, then took a step closer and rested the palm of his hand against Isaiah's forehead. "Welcome to the flow, brother."

For a heartbeat nothing happened, then Isaiah's body faded, replaced just for an instant with lines of frost, and then he and Bingaleal were gone.

Another heartbeat, and every head in the encampment lifted and stared into the sky as tens of thousands of ghostly wings beat once, twice, and then a third time, before the sky, suddenly, strangely, was clear.

Axis rode his horse up and down the lines, talking, smiling, giving encouragement, barking orders. After only a few hours' sleep he was tired and fractious, but kept his irritation buried, using it only sparingly, and only when needed.

Elsewhere Ezekiel and Insharah were doing much the same thing, and Maximilian, too. Could four of them get this massive encampment moving? Axis had seen Isaiah do it, but Isaiah was here no longer, three of his damned generals were here no longer, and the army needed, *somehow*, to get used to a new commander and a new mission. At least the mutterings about going home to aid their families was now far more muted. Isaiah and many thousands of Lealfast had departed hours earlier in a showing that had left even Axis wide-eyed with admiration.

Axis hoped they'd be able to do something. If rumors kept reaching this army about devastation back in Isembaard, Axis did not think Maximilian could keep control of them for very long.

As for the three renegade generals, Kezial, Lamiah, and Armat, Eleanon and a large contingent of the Lealfast remaining with Maximilian had gone during the night to fan out across the vast spaces of the Outlands. He had not had a chance to speak with Eleanon save for a very brief word as the Lealfast departed. Axis would have liked nothing more than to gallop his horse out across the plains in search of the generals himself, but he had to concede the Lealfast could do a far better, and far faster, task of it.

He hoped that by the evening Eleanon would return with good news.

As for everyone else . . .

Ishbel was packed and riding well forward in the column (well, that part of it which was moving), Madarin having proved a little better at getting his mistress on the road than Axis was at getting the rest of the army marching. Axis had caught a brief glimpse of her, enough to see that she'd apparently had little more sleep than had he.

StarDrifter and Salome, together with what Icarii had arrived in the camp, were grouped together to one side of the chaotic encampment. The Icarii looked well rested, and from what he'd seen of them Axis knew they were impatient to be up into the thermals. He didn't know if they'd had any interaction with the Lealfast yet. He knew his father hadn't, but determined to speak to BroadWing as soon as he could to discover if any of the other Icarii had spoken to their cousins. Axis had no idea how, or if, the two groups would get along. Both were as arrogant as the other, and from the little he'd seen of the Lealfast they didn't appear overly eager to renew their acquaintance with their long-lost relatives.

He hoped his father wouldn't try to reimpose his authority as Talon over the Lealfast. From what Axis *had* seen of the Lealfast, that would not be well received.

The column was a little smaller than it had been yesterday. Although he had not seen Malat, Axis had been told by Georgdi, an hour or so earlier, that Malat had spoken to Maximilian at dawn and requested that he be allowed to travel west into the Central Kingdoms. Malat wanted to go home, to see what was left of his kingdom of Kyros, and for that Axis could not blame or fault him. Maximilian had sent a contingent of two thousand Isembaardian soldiers with Malat's own men to help with . . . well, with whatever Malat found.

Axis hoped they would do well for Malat.

"My lord?"

Axis broke from his reverie and turned his horse around.

It was Insharah.

"My lord," Insharah said, "there's a problem with the horses of the fiftieth contingent."

Axis sighed, and went back to the task of getting this great lurching beast onto its feet.

By late afternoon he was exhausted, but at least the entire army was now on the move. He'd left Ezekiel in charge of keeping the rear of the great column in some order. Axis thought he could trust Ezekiel . . . in the end, though, he had no choice. Senior commanders were somewhat thin on the ground in this army, and Axis thought he'd speak to Maximilian about promoting some of the better Isembaardian middle-ranking officers. Insharah, for one. The man was more than capable, and was liked and trusted both by the Isembaardians and Axis.

Maximilian had spent the day riding up and down the column, speaking to the men, pausing now and again to ride his horse a while alongside one of them as he chatted at length. It was a good thing to do, and Axis was pleased to see Maximilian taking the initiative. Now Maximilian had ridden closer to the front of the column, perhaps prepatory to making camp for the night.

Axis pulled his horse to a halt about fifty paces from the main column and let it rest awhile. He'd barely stopped all day, and the horse must be exhausted. He let the reins hang loose, allowing the horse room to stretch his neck and blow out.

Where were the Lealfast? Axis had not heard from them all day, and now his imagination was running riot. All the scenarios that vivid imagination came up with had one source: Axis simply did not know, nor trust, the Lealfast.

Who were they, really? Why their apparent devotion to Maximilian? And what did they want? What was their purpose?

And *why* hadn't they come back with news of their hunt for the generals?

"Damn you, Eleanon," Axis muttered.

"Unkind words," Eleanon said behind him, "for one who has exhausted himself in the hunt to right your wrong."

Axis closed his eyes for a fraction of a moment, cursing silently, then opened them again and swiveled about in the saddle.

Eleanon stood two or three paces away, behind and to one side of the horse, arms folded, regarding Axis with his habitual unreadable expression. His wings trailed behind him, frost glittering along their ridges and riming their ivory feathers.

"Will you dismount?" said Eleanon. "I find it difficult to crane my neck to address you."

Axis wondered when he'd ever found himself at such a disadvantage. He tried not to allow it to show on his face, however, and swung one leg casually over the horse's wither and slid to the ground, his boots crunching into the snow.

"I had expected to hear of your success before now," said Axis.

"Success being all that you know, of course," said Eleanon.

Axis allowed his mouth to curve in a small smile. "Success being something I am only rarely good at," he said. "I am sorry, Eleanon. I am tired and ill-tempered and thoughtless. I would rather have been riding with you in the wind today than driving this grudging army forward. Tell me, what news?"

"Not what you were hoping for," Eleanon said, finally unfolding his arms. "We have scoured most of the Outlands save for the area directly about and below Adab. We have seen no sign of your generals."

Axis opened his mouth, but Eleanon forestalled him. "They could not have ridden further than Margalit in the time since they left this army, Axis, and even that city would have required phenomenal—or enchanted—effort. That we could not find them . . ." He gave an expressive shrug.

"They have gone to ground somewhere?"

Another shrug. "Perhaps. But there is more. Axis, there is the stink and trail of a gloomy enchantment along the trail leading to Margalit."

"A 'gloomy' enchantment?"

"An enchantment meant to disguise, hide, conceal. Gloomy. Worse, when flying back to this column we detected some of it here as well. I think that someone within this column has aided the generals in their escape. Concealed them with enchantment. Who might that be, do you think?"

Ravenna, Axis thought immediately, remembering StarDrifter's stories about how Ravenna had used her powers to help Maximilian and his party move unseen through the vast bulk of Isaiah's army on their way to Sak-kuth.

"*Who?*" said Eleanon.

Axis hesitated, and Eleanon nodded.

"The woman who interrupted Maximilian in his command tent," he said. "Ravenna was her name, yes?"

"I don't know, Eleanon. I know she has the power, as does her mother, Venetia, who is with us."

But Venetia would never have done this.

"I'll talk to Maximilian about it," Axis said, and Eleanon nodded, ac-cepting it.

"Eleanon," Axis said, "can you see through the enchantment?"

Eleanon gave a slow shake of his head. "It is something we cannot under-stand. We cannot see through it. If your generals are still out there, Axis, and I suspect they are, then they are disguised from both you and me, I think." He paused. "Until they decide to attack."

"They would think twice about attacking a column this size."

"I don't think so. *I* think they might feel they'd stand a good chance that most of this column might join them rather than fight."

Axis did not immediately reply. Eleanon was likely right. Whatever Maximilian had said and done to this point had merely delayed the inevi-table test of loyalty.

"I hope to the stars above that Isaiah and Bingaleal and your comrades with them manage to help in Isembaard," Axis said finally.

Another shrug from Eleanon. "They will do what they can. The Lealfast will help the Isembaardians to escape, Axis, wherever they can. But they will not fight the Skraelings."

"*What?*"

"Did you think Bingaleal was leading the Lealfast down there as an avenging army, Axis? We will do many things for the Lord of Elcho Falling, but we will not lay hand or sword to the Skraelings."

Axis tried very hard to control his temper. "Have you told Maximilian that?"

"He has not asked."

"I am damned sure he *thinks* that you will one day aid him against the Skraelings! How can you—"

"You know why we cannot," Eleanon said quietly.

Axis fell silent.

"They are our blood," Eleanon said. "We hate them, but we pity them, too. We cannot touch them. Whatever harm we do to them, we do to ourselves."

Axis took a deep breath, turning away and looking back toward the column. It snaked very slowly forward, a huge dark stain on the snowy landscape, although here and there Axis saw units peeling off to right and left to make camp for the night.

"Would you like to know who we are, Axis SunSoar? Would you like to hear precisely *what* happened to those Icarii who were so long ago lost to the snowy wastes?"

Axis turned back to him. "Yes," he said. "Yes, I would like to know."

CHAPTER NINE

On the Road to Serpent's Nest

What do you know of our origins?" Eleanon asked. He had led Axis some distance from the now dozing horse, and they stood in the midst of a vast snowy expanse, both horse and army appearing as if far away.

Axis realized that Eleanon was using a little of the Star Dance to create this effect (and using it in such a strange, strange way) but was not perturbed by it.

Anything to know better Eleanon and the Lealfast.

"My father told me that during the Wars of the Axe in Tencendor, thousands of years past, the Icarii were driven north into the Icescarp Alps," Axis said. "There the majority decided to make their home, but a small group, numbering some fifty or sixty, believed that the Icescarp Alps were not safe enough, and decided to push even further north."

"Seventy-two Icarii, to be precise," said Eleanon. "My forebears. Look."

He waved a hand, and Axis repressed a gasp. In the middle distance, between where they stood and the Isembaardian army struggled west, a group of several score Icarii had appeared. They struggled forward through deep snow, several of their number falling occasionally and having to be helped to their feet by their comrades.

"They were exhausted," said Eleanon, so softly that his words did not intrude upon the scene before them. "They could no longer fly. They'd been traveling north, north, north for weeks."

"What kept driving them? They must have known they were traveling into hell."

"Arrogance. Pride. A disinclination to return home to say they were wrong. Who knows? But look, see now, help came."

The group struggled forward, but now they glanced over shoulders and to each side with anxious eyes.

There was a light snow falling about them, and in it Axis could see . . .

"Skraelings!" he hissed.

"Aye, Skraelings," said Eleanon. "But the Icarii were in luck, for this year there was a glut of snow rabbits, and the Skraelings were well fed. And see, the Skraelings left them food, that they might survive."

The Icarii had come upon a small pile of headless snow rabbits. There was hesitation, and discussion, but soon they fell to their meal, tearing the rabbits apart and eating them raw.

Axis winced. The Icarii must have been desperate indeed to resort to such barbarity.

"The Skraelings do have some kindness in them, Axis," said a new voice, and Axis turned to look at Inardle, who had appeared at Eleanon's shoulder.

He thought again how striking she looked. He noted also that whereas Eleanon's expression radiated distance and haughtiness, Inardle's was softened by the faintest hint of vulnerability.

She was . . . hypnotic, and while Axis realized he was staring, he could not move his eyes from her.

Inardle gave Axis a half-shy smile, and he wondered at it: genuine or ingenuous?

He inclined his head in greeting, then returned to the conversation. "Kindness is not a quality I have ever associated with Skraelings."

"Nonetheless," Inardle said, and she nodded back to the vision, "they left them food, day in and out, and even helped the Icarii build shelters."

Axis could hardly believe what he saw. Skraelings emerged from the freezing mists, some bearing rocks, some bearing blocks of ice. With these, and the snow about them, they helped the Icarii build low rounded shelters. The Icarii were obviously wary in the extreme, but they accepted the help, and were glad of it.

Without Skraeling assistance they would have died.

Time passed. Axis could see it in the way the snow moved about the collection of low shelters, built up against one aspect then drifted away again.

"There was talk among the Icarii about returning to the Icescarp Alps," Eleanon said, "but the general consensus was that the Acharites, with their axes, would have murdered their fellows left behind. They felt it was too dangerous to return."

"Besides," Inardle said, "they were getting used to the frozen wastes. And..."

Axis looked at her. She was gazing at the tableau before them with an expression that was part grief, part yearning.

"Besides?" he said.

"Besides," Inardle said, "one of the Icarii, a young enchantress called SummerStar—"

She looked at Axis now, and she smiled, the expression so warm and glorious that Axis' breath caught in his throat.

"Imagine a name like that," she said, "amid an existence like *this*!" She waved a hand back at the group of icy shelters. "Imagine... well, Summer-Star formed an attachment to the Skraelings. She pitied them, and believed that good could come of them. She befriended those that she might."

Axis was now looking back at the tableau before him. He knew where this story would go, and he felt sick to his stomach. He didn't want to hear it—*see it*—but knew that he must.

A young Icarii woman had emerged from one of the shelters. She was very lovely, and Axis could see a sweet expression on her face.

"She was very naive," said Eleanon, "but good-hearted and well-meaning."

"And have not half the disasters of our worlds, Axis," Inardle said, her tone now bitter, "been caused by the naive and well-meaning and good-hearted?"

Again he glanced at her, and saw embittered grief clearly in her eyes.

"Look, Axis," Eleanon said. "Look."

SummerStar was now sitting with a group of Skraelings. Just seeing her sitting so calmly there, with the terrible ice wraiths with their over-sized heads and slavering jaws and great silvery orbs for eyes, deepened Axis' nausea.

Gradually the Skraelings rose and drifted away, until there was only one remaining with SummerStar.

She reached out and laid a hand to its cheek.

Axis literally gagged. For a moment he stood, half bent over, hands on thighs, trying hard not to retch.

He felt a soft hand on his shoulder.

Inardle.

"She only meant well," Inardle said, very softly. "SummerStar only ever meant well."

Axis took a deep breath, wiped his mouth with the back of his hand, and straightened. Inardle kept her hand on his shoulder, standing close to him, for which Axis was grateful. He did not think he'd be able to get through what he knew he was about to witness without her support.

The Skraeling leapt onto SummerStar. She tried to scream, but one of its massive clawed hands covered her mouth, and she was helpless.

"Oh gods . . ." Axis whispered.

"A Skraeling mating is never pleasant," Eleanon said, somewhat conversationally. "It is also very painful. Sometimes at night, when we were in the north, we would hear them—"

"*Enough!*" Axis hissed. He could not tear his eyes away from what was happening before him, although he wished he had the courage and will to do so.

SummerStar was desperate. She tried everything she could, but the Skraeling had her pinned, and was far too strong for her. It tore the clothes from her body, pried her legs apart—causing deep wounds in her flesh with its claws—and then mounted her with a great curved and barbed phallus.

SummerStar could not scream, not audibly, but Axis heard it through every fiber of his body. She was using the Star Dance, using it to call and plead for help, using it to articulate her horror, her agony, and her inarticulate shrieks for aid reverberated through Axis' being.

Inardle's hand tightened on Axis' shoulder.

Icarii tumbled out of the shelters. They tore the Skraeling from SummerStar's body, but it was too late.

"At least the Skraeling mating is brief," said Eleanon. "Once they're in, they're done."

"Have you *no* compassion at all?" hissed Axis.

"We have lived with this for eons," Inardle said. "We have learned to come to terms with it."

The Icarii were now carrying SummerStar's battered body into one of the shelters.

"Time passed," said Eleanon.

Again the snow shifted about the ice shelters.

SummerStar emerged once more, and this time her belly was large and rounded. She squatted down in the snow, and Axis saw her body shudder and contract.

Within moments, she had given birth—a tiny, squalling infant that looked like any Icarii infant, save for its strange transparent nature and the rime of frost about its skull.

"What do you know of the Skraeling breeding habits?" Eleanon asked Axis.

"Not a great deal," Axis said, still feeling ill, but thinking that at least the worst had now passed. So this was how the first of the Lealfast had been born—but why were others born? How was it there was now a great nation of them?

"I know they make nests and lay eggs," Axis said, remembering coming upon an underground chamber once, filled with Skraeling eggs and hatchlings.

At least SummerStar had not laid an egg.

"The Skraeling mating may be short and brutal," said Eleanon, "but at least they only do it once. A pair meet, mate, and then mate no more."

"But," Inardle said, "the female continues to lay eggs through her life."

"No . . ." Axis whispered.

"The male's seed remains within its mate's body all her life, continually fertilizing her," Eleanon said. "Once she had given birth, SummerStar fell pregnant again."

Before them, SummerStar rose from her childbirth, only to lay a hand to her belly once again and wail. Her belly grew and swelled before Axis' eyes, and once again SummerStar squatted down in the snow to give birth.

"Icarii live such long lives," Eleanon said, "and SummerStar was only in her thirties when she was mated by the Skraeling."

"She had two hundred and eighty-six children," said Inardle, "before she died of exhaustion during her two hundred and eighty-seventh pregnancy."

"And so you see why we are," said Eleanon. "We all come from the one mother and the one father."

"The other Icarii," Axis said, not surprised to discover his voice hoarse with horror. "What became of them?"

"The Skraelings ate them, the year after SummerStar gave birth to her first child," said Inardle. "It was a bad year for snow rabbits, that year."

"But SummerStar . . ." Axis said.

"Oh, her they kept alive," said Eleanon. "They adored her children, and nurtured them. SummerStar herself . . . well, for many years she distanced herself from the children, existing in a fugue of self-loathing and pain, but she was a creature of love and compassion, and eventually she called her children to her and taught them the way of the Star Dance."

"They were all Enchanters," said Inardle. "All the Lealfast are. We are all magic."

Eleanon waved a hand and to Axis's great relief the vision before them vanished, replaced once again by the view of the Isembaardian army struggling east.

"Once SummerStar was gone," Eleanon said, "the Lealfast continued to breed among themselves."

Inardle saw the expression on Axis' face and she gave a sad smile. "Oh, in all manner of things we are Icarii, Axis, save in some aspects of our mysterious and magical selves. We do not breed like the Skraelings. We make love as any other."

There was a little bit of a challenge in her eyes now, but Axis ignored it. "You remained close to the Skraelings?" he said.

Eleanon shook his head. "Part of us despises them, Axis. They, too, came to partly despise us. We were all they could not be; they were all we never wanted to be. We tolerate each other."

They stood silently a moment, Axis still caught by the horror of the vision that Eleanon and Inardle had shown him.

"You use the Star Dance differently," Axis said.

"Yes," Eleanon said. "One day, if I decide I like you, I may explain it to you."

"Perhaps Inardle can explain it to me," Axis said, returning in his own glance a little of the challenge he had seen in her eyes earlier.

Inardle dropped her hand from his shoulder. "You have discovered the Star Dance again, Axis StarMan."

Her voice had lost its earlier warmth, and Axis was surprised—and a little perturbed—to find himself disappointed at that lack.

"I have been blind," he said, "and am now a little less so."

"It is late, Axis, and you are exhausted," Eleanon said. "My brothers and sisters will spend the night abroad, gleaning what they can about the generals. I will speak to you in the morning."

With that, he and Inardle simply faded from view—their strange gray frosted eyes being the last thing to vanish into the gloom of dusk.

"That was well done, Inardle," Eleanon said as they drifted away unseen through the air.

"I do not like it," she said.

"You do not like Axis?" Eleanon said. "I thought few women could resist him."

"That is not what I meant."

"You did this with Lister," Eleanon said, his tone hardening slightly. "Do it, also, with Axis. The future of the entire Lealfast Nation rests on our shoulders, Inardle. Now is not the time to develop coyness."

"It is not coyness," she muttered, "but perhaps a little conscience."

CHAPTER TEN

On the Road to Serpent's Nest

Axis was exhausted by the time camp was made and wanted nothing but a meal, his sleeping roll, and time to think before he could finally drift into a gratifying sleep.

But first he needed to speak to Maximilian.

He finally got to Maximilian's tent, where Serge and Doyle crouched outside over a game of dice by their fire, late at night.

"Anyone else inside?" Axis asked the two men.

"No one yet," said Serge, "but StarDrifter and Georgdi are expected."

Axis nodded his thanks, and stepped inside the tent.

Maximilian was seated at his table eating a meal of bread and cheese, and gestured Axis to join him. Axis sat, poured himself a glass of warm ale, then bit hungrily into a piece of bread and cheese himself.

"Eleanon brought news," Axis said once he'd swallowed his first mouthful.

"Yes," Maximilian said, "he told me, as well. The generals' escape and persons are hidden by some gloomy enchantment."

Axis sent him a significant look as he took another bite of his meal.

Maximilian sighed. "Ravenna?"

"My father told me how she and you hid your party with such a gloomy enchantment when traversing northern Isembaard," Axis said. "Maxel . . . do you think it is her?"

Maximilian sighed and rubbed at his eyes wearily with one hand. "I don't know. I'd like to think not . . . but . . ."

"She is going to prove a dangerous enemy, Maxel."

Maximilian grunted.

"What will you do?" Axis said.

"I will speak to her."

"And will she reply truthfully?"

Maximilian hesitated, and in that silent moment there was a noise at the tent door and StarDrifter and Georgdi entered. StarDrifter was looking cheerful, Georgdi looked almost as tired as Axis.

Both pulled out stools and sat down at the table, and Axis poured them some ale.

"Fifteen more Icarii arrived with the convoy today," StarDrifter said. "Five Enchanters among them. They have told me that hundreds, *thousands*, are flying to join me."

Axis exchanged an amused glance with Maximilian. StarDrifter's joy was infectious and lightened both their moods.

"You may well have a goodly portion of your Strike Force back, Axis," StarDrifter said.

"Not my Strike Force any longer," Axis said. "They are yours, but..."

"But...?" StarDrifter said.

"BroadWing is a good man to place as Strike Leader, StarDrifter. If you were looking."

StarDrifter smiled, and gave his son a nod. *BroadWing had a new job.*

"Georgdi," Maximilian said, "I know you have been chafing at the bit to take your soldiers and do what you can for the Outlands."

"A million Isembaardians have invaded my homelands, Maxel," Georgdi said, "and refugees must be continuing to pour through the Salamaan Pass. Yes, I am chafing."

"I think that every sword shall be needed over the coming months," Maximilian said. "I know you want to leave..." He paused. "Georgdi, do you have trusted and capable lieutenants among your men?"

"All my men are trusted and capable," Georgdi said. "It is our strength."

"Good," said Maximilian. "Leaving aside for the moment the problem of the half a million or so Isembaardian soldiers, there is something we can do about the settlers and refugees. Georgdi, can you spare men enough to start to organize the Isembaardian civilians into convoys west?"

Georgdi nodded, but raised his eyebrows. "West?"

"I do not think the Outlands is going to be the safest place for them," Maximilian said. "The Central Kingdoms can absorb them—if you will excuse my bluntness—far better now that the Skraelings have emptied half of their populations."

"You might also like to think about evacuating the Outlanders," Axis said quietly. "Whatever comes up from the south is almost certain to come through the Salamaan Pass, and—"

"The Outlanders will stay to protect their land," Georgdi said. "We are all born with swords in our hands." He drained the last of his ale, then poured himself some more. "I'll send men out in the morning to do what they can with the Isembaardian settlers and refugees, Maximilian. They will do what you need."

Maximilian bowed his head in thanks.

"And me?" Georgdi said. "My family are in Margalit, and—"

"You will prove more useful to me here," Maximilian said, very quietly. "I beg you to stay, Georgdi."

"Doing what?" Georgdi said. "Shepherding ever more resentful Isembaardian soldiers along the road to Elcho Falling? Frankly, Maxel, you could have done more yesterday to rally them to your cause."

Axis sent Maximilian another significant glance.

"I decided not to try and force them to my cause," Maximilian said, then told Georgdi and StarDrifter about his policy of allowing the gigantic force to fracture along its fault lines.

"I can never hold it together," Maximilian said, "and it would be foolish of me to try. What I wanted them to see yesterday was who I am, and where I go. Maybe one day they will remember it, when they are cold and dark and hopeless."

"That's a risky policy," StarDrifter said. "If this force does fracture, then it may turn to bite you."

"But not as hard as it might had I tried to force it to stay with me," Maximilian said.

Georgdi was looking at Maximilian and grinning.

"What?" said Maximilian.

"I smell Outlander cunning about this," said Georgdi.

Maximilian laughed. "And you are right. It was Ishbel who suggested the strategy to me."

Georgdi was still smiling, but it had faded somewhat, and he regarded Maximilian with a keen eye. "I hadn't been very impressed with you, Maximilian Persimius, until this very moment. That is a courageous course you plan . . . and a subtly brilliant one. What can *I* do for you?"

"Join Axis in running a small errand for me," Maximilian said.

"And that is?" Axis asked.

"The Lealfast are all over me," said Maximilian, "professing loyalty and a long-held desire to reside at Elcho Falling. But I don't trust them, and I don't yet believe in them. Axis, Georgdi, I want you to test them a little. Take Eleanon and the twenty or so thousand he has with him, and roam the plains of the Central Outlands. Look for the generals. I don't think you'll find them, but I want you to test out the Lealfast. Give them some rope, and see what they do with it."

Axis nodded. "Good. They are full of themselves and their fighting experience, but *what* experience? *Who* have they fought before?"

"The Skraelings—" StarDrifter began.

"No. Not the Skraelings," Axis said. "Eleanon told me this afternoon they have never, and will never, raise sword nor fire arrow against the Skraelings."

"Why not?" said StarDrifter as everyone else gaped at Axis.

"Because," Axis said, "the Lealfast are half Skraeling, as we surmised. They loathe the Skraelings and their connection to them, but they pity them, too. Eleanon said that the Lealfast cannot touch the Skraelings."

"Oh, for mercy's sake," StarDrifter murmured. "Of what use are they?"

"Did you believe that explanation, Axis?" Maximilian said.

Axis gave a small shrug.

"That's what we need to discover," said Maximilian. "Axis, Georgdi, will you ride out in the morning?"

Axis and Georgdi exchanged a glance, and then both grinned and nodded. "It will be good to ride out a-hunting again," said Axis. "Georgdi, how many of your men can you bring?"

"A few hundred," Georgdi said.

"With Axis gone," said Maximilian, "I will need someone to act in his stead."

"Ezekiel?" StarDrifter said, but Maximilian shook his head.

"No. Ezekiel is of little use to me. I think he is largely finished as someone who has any influence within the Isembaardian army. Axis, who can I raise up from among the Isembaardians to act as one of my senior lieutenants and as my conduit back into the Isembaardian army?"

"Insharah," Axis said without hesitation. "He is relatively young, but he is respected. He is also experienced, and, perhaps more importantly, he has a clear head atop his shoulders. Insharah also had family who were left at Aqhat. The Isembaardians will know that, and will trust him for it. Maxel, I do not know quite what you want from Insharah, but I think you will find him a good advisor, and an honest one."

"Thank you, Axis," Maximilian said. "Insharah it shall be, then. Arrange for him to attend me at dawn."

When Axis finally left, he caught up with StarDrifter, who was almost back at his and Salome's tent.

"StarDrifter," Axis said, "can I have a few minutes?"

StarDrifter nodded. "What is it?"

"This afternoon Eleanon showed me the origins of the Lealfast. I think you need to know."

StarDrifter looked into his son's eyes and saw the pain there.

He nodded. "Come inside, then."

CHAPTER ELEVEN

On the Road to Serpent's Nest

Ravenna?"

Maximilian walked a bit further into the night, away from the column. She was here. He could feel it.

Ravenna?

He turned slightly to his left, sensing her in the night.

"Ravenna, talk to me."

"Why? I had thought you tired of me. Embarrassed, perhaps. Have you taken Ishbel back to your bed? Have you been that foolish?"

Maximilian walked very carefully toward her. She stood a little distance away, all wrapped in blackness and reserve, only her pale face and gray eyes clearly visible in the night.

"Ishbel has nothing to do with this, Ravenna."

"She has *everything* to do with it! Maxel, she will destroy you, and—"

"And Elcho Falling and this land. Yes, I have heard it all before, Ravenna."

"And yet you ignore it. Dear gods, Maxel, what *else* can I say? What can I do to make you understand?"

"Are you aiding the generals, Ravenna?"

Everything about her closed off from him. Maximilian could almost feel her shrink back into the night.

"It is not me, Maximilian."

"It stinks of your power, Ravenna."

She didn't say anything.

"How did we come to this, Ravenna?"

Again she did not reply.

"Ravenna," Maximilian said, "don't turn me into your enemy. Please, you saved my life once. You were my friend. Don't now turn against me."

"I am carrying your child, Maximilian."

"Don't use that to manipulate me!" Maximilian said. He took a deep breath, quelling his anger. "Damn it, Ravenna, that child is the only thing keeping you safe in this column right now!"

"This child," Ravenna said, "is the only thing keeping Elcho Falling safe right now."

"That child," Maximilian ground out, "was a mistake. Everything about us and between us was a mistake, Ravenna."

As soon as the words were out Maximilian wished he had not said them. It was, he thought, too stark a truth for either of them to bear right now.

But he had no chance to take the words back, or to moderate them. Ravenna sent him a hard, brilliant-eyed look and then she was gone.

"Do you remember, Maximilian Persimius, what happened in the mine that day you battled Cavor?"

Maximilian whipped about. He'd stood a few minutes after Ravenna had left, wondering what she might do after those words he'd said to her.

A tall, well-built man stood a few paces away. Thick cobalt hair fell down over his brow and his eyes sparked with blue fire. His fine, beautiful features were almost ethereal.

Maximilian gave a small bow. "My Lord of Dreams. Drava."

The Lord of Dreams gave a small smile. "No need to bow to me, Maximilian. Tell me, do you remember that day?"

How could Maximilian forget it? He'd fought with Cavor in the dark mine of the Veins, battling for the right to regain the Escatorian throne. At first they'd fought with swords, but then the Lord of Dreams had set them a test of compassion and laughter, in which Cavor failed and Maximilian triumphed.

"Yes," Maximilian said, "I remember it."

"And do you remember what happened once I appeared?"

Maximilian gave a short bark of grim laughter. "Ravenna turned from me in a moment, and revered you."

"Aye, that she did. And when I asked her to step into the realm of dreams with me, she did so without hesitation. Maximilian, do not allow guilt over Ravenna to allow her to manipulate you. One day you will need to act."

"Are you warning me against her?"

"In a manner, yes. Ravenna is one of the very few marsh witches who has been able to tread the Land of Nightmares beyond the Land of Dreams. Even I dare not tread into the realm of Nightmare. She is very, very powerful."

"She carries my child."

Drava shrugged.

Maximilian sighed. "Have you seen the vision that she showed me in the Land of Dreams?"

"Yes. It is likely something that Ravenna found in the Land of Nightmares. I cannot find any other way to explain it, for this vision is foreign to me, and to the Land of Dreams."

"Is it truth?"

"Who knows, Maximilian. All I can say is that dreams are too often misinterpreted or misunderstood."

"That is what Axis SunSoar told me."

"Then he is a wise man. Maximilian, perhaps the vision shows a possibility, even a probability, but not a reality that cannot be changed. That is why Ravenna acts as she does. She wants to change that future for you."

"But there could be other ways to alter the future."

"There always are."

Maximilian stood quiet awhile, comfortable in the silence between himself and the Lord of Dreams.

"Everyone, so it seems, has warned me at one time or another against Ishbel."

"But you always believed in her."

"Until I began to listen to her detractors."

"Elcho Falling is a great prize, Maximilian."

"What is that supposed to mean, Drava?"

"That there are many who will confuse your path toward it."

Maximilian took a deep breath. "Thank you, Drava."

Drava gave a very small smile, and then he disappeared, and Maximilian was left alone, the snow swirling about him.

* * *

That night, a terrible dream gripped many of the Isembaardian soldiers. They dreamed that the Skraelings had seethed over the River Lhyl and were eating their way through the people Isaiah had left behind.

Each sleeper saw members of his own family being slaughtered.

They saw also Isaiah and the Lealfast—standing to one side, too terrified of the Skraelings to intervene.

In the morning, just after dawn, Insharah stood in Maximilian's command tent, trying very hard to hide his incredulity.

"You mean me to take Axis' command position, my lord?"

"Of the Isembaardian portion of my force, yes," Maximilian said.

Insharah looked to Axis, standing to one side. "You suggested this?"

Axis gave a nod, watching Insharah carefully.

"I don't have the seniority," Insharah said.

"You do now," Maximilian replied.

"Of course, I do expect you to give it back," said Axis with a small smile, "when I return from my foray into the wilds of the Outlands."

"Can you do this?" Maximilian said.

Insharah gave a nod. "To my best ability, my lord."

"Good," Maximilian said, then turned away, signifying an end to the conversation.

"My lord?"

Maximilian half turned around, an eyebrow raised.

"Have you any news from Isaiah?" Insharah said. "The soldiers ask."

"He has only just left, Insharah."

"We are anxious, my lord." Insharah hesitated. "The Lealfast *can* save our families from the Skraelings?"

Maximilian and Axis exchanged a look.

"My lord?" Insharah asked, his voice tight.

"They will do their best to aid your people," Maximilian said, "but unfortunately the Lealfast will not do anything to harm the Skraelings. They are close kin and . . ."

Maximilian drifted to a close, seeing the horror on Insharah's face.

"I am sorry, Insharah."

CHAPTER TWELVE

The Salamaan Pass

Isaiah was a being many millennia old, and he had witnessed more things than most who had lived, but he'd never before experienced anything like being carried a-wind with the Lealfast.

He decided later, once he'd had some time to think about it, that it was very much like flowing in a river, save that the river the Lealfast used was air rather than water. He could feel all about him the strange, mysterious souls of the Lealfast riding the air currents beside him, and feel deep within him the tug of their strange magic. Isaiah knew the Lealfast used the Star Dance as the source of their power, but this . . .

This, he thought, *is going to cause Axis some troubles.*

They arrived at the southern end of the Salamaan Pass by late afternoon of the day they'd set out. The speed of their travel was extraordinary. Nonetheless, Isaiah could see from the gray lines on Bingaleal's face that it had also been exhausting—the Lealfast had been traveling here and there for many weeks, and had covered an astonishing amount of territory within only the past few days.

There was a moment when Isaiah could feel the transition from whatever state the Lealfast had put him into back into his fleshed form, and then he was standing on pebbly, sandy ground, and he could feel the soft breeze wrap about him, and smell his land, stretching away south before him.

There was a soft sound at his side and Bingaleal appeared.

"Thank you," Isaiah said simply. He and Bingaleal were standing just inside the entrance to the Salamaan Pass, against the western wall, and Isaiah turned to look south.

"Oh my gods . . ." he whispered.

Before them the pass was filled with a jumble of disordered people, children, animals, carts—the panicked flotsam and jetsam of a population fleeing rumor and terror. Even though the gloom of dusk had enveloped the Pass, Isaiah could see that hundreds of thousands were abandoning Isembaard.

On the one hand he was glad that so many *had* escaped; on the other the thought of what might be happening further into the land appalled him.

"Where are the other Lealfast fighters, Bingaleal?"

"On the ridges of the pass where the gloom shall, for the moment, disguise them. I thought it best that they not land within the pass itself and panic the refugees. Isaiah, what do you want of us?"

"To rescue as many of the Isembaardians as you can. There are two escape routes—north, through the Salamaan Pass, and south, through the Lagamaal Plains, to something called the Lost Chasm."

Bingaleal raised his eyebrows. "The Lost Chasm?"

"It lies on the borders of the Eastern Independencies, and is where the mortal Isaiah met his fate," said Isaiah. He grinned. "It is an abyss, Bingaleal, and likely to be a mystery that even you have yet to know about."

"And a chasm can somehow shelter," Bingaleal waved a hand at the mass of people moving north, "a crowd *this* size?"

"Even more," said Isaiah, "although I think there will be few left alive in the south of Isembaard." He paused, staring at the mass of people trudging north. "Gods, where do we start?"

Bingaleal sighed. "In the morning, Isaiah. If we start now we will just create panic."

In the end, the fleeing refugees accepted the Lealfast more easily than Isaiah had imagined. It was likely, he thought, that the Lealfast were a great deal less terrifying than what was at the refugees' backs.

They started early the next morning. Isaiah commandeered a horse from someone, then rode up and down the lines of refugees as they approached the pass, waving overhead at the Lealfast in the skies and saying simply that they were here to help the Isembaardians escape the Skraelings.

At midmorning Isaiah waved Bingaleal down.

"Any signs of Skraelings?" he asked.

Bingaleal shook his head. "I believe they are still very far to the west, although I have no doubts they will be moving this way swiftly. Currently, it is rumor and fear more than anything else driving these people."

Isaiah thought a moment. "Your fighters are all still here? In the Salamaan Pass area?"

Bingaleal nodded.

"Then divide them up. Send ten thousand to the southeast. I am certain there will be refugees moving to the south, as these here move to the north. The ten thousand sent south need to help them reach the Lost Chasm."

Isaiah spent a few minutes giving Bingaleal some idea of the route the refugees would be taking, and the path they'd need to take to reach the Lost Chasm.

"I wish your Lealfast great luck down south," Isaiah finished. "The Skraelings will be thick on the ground there, and your comrades shall need to be careful not to be outnumbered if they get into battle."

"That won't happen," Bingaleal said.

Isaiah frowned, not understanding. "They won't be outnumbered?"

"The Lealfast will never attack the Skraelings," said Bingaleal. "Not under any circumstances."

"*What?* For all the gods' sakes, Bingaleal, why can't you—"

"They are our kin. We will not harm them."

"Then what good are you? My people need the aid of *swords!*"

Bingaleal gave Isaiah an inscrutable look at that, but did not otherwise answer.

"*Shetzah!*" Isaiah muttered, turning aside in order to quell his frustration.

"We will do what we can," said Bingaleal, "but we will not attack our kin."

"Then if you can perhaps ask them nicely to stand aside," Isaiah ground out, "and allow my people passage to safety, then I would be most profoundly grateful."

"We will do what we can," Bingaleal repeated.

"Does Maximilian know this piece of information?"

Bingaleal shrugged.

Isaiah barely restrained himself from hitting the birdman. He gave Bingaleal a long stare, then walked away, fuming.

The next day, Isaiah took a small bag of supplies and a sword and set off by himself for the west. There was little he could do for the refugees, and he was still so angry with the Lealfast he wanted to spend as little time with them as possible. Once he reached the River Lhyl (or whatever was left of it) he would follow it south to DarkGlass Mountain.

Perhaps *he* could do something, if not the cursed Lealfast.

CHAPTER THIRTEEN

On the Road to Serpent's Nest

Several days passed. The great convoy continued to inch its way toward Elcho Falling. Maximilian called to him five senior Isembaardian officers and made them commanders within the force, answerable only to Insharah and himself.

The men seemed pleased and gratified at Maximilian's trust, but he could still sense their disquiet beneath their smiles, and he wondered what they found to talk about at night, around their fires.

At night, the dreams continued for the Isembaardians.

Ishbel had kept mainly to herself since the convoy had begun its journey east. Some hours each day she rode with Salome, who insisted on keeping to horseback despite her advanced pregnancy. Ishbel enjoyed Salome's company, but she also spent much of the day riding alone, slightly apart from everyone else. She used the time to think: about going home to Serpent's Nest, or, as it soon would be called, Elcho Falling, and what might await her there; about Isaiah, and what was happening to him in Isembaard; and about Maximilian, and the Twisted Tower.

She had not seen Maximilian privately since that night he'd taken her into the Twisted Tower. They sometimes passed on horseback during the day, and exchanged a nod or a few words. Ishbel had on two occasions shared an evening meal with Maximilian and his commanders in his tent, but had left for her own tent without speaking to him alone. Although either brief, or in the company of others, the time they had spent together had been marked by a new easiness in the other's presence.

It was indeed, Ishbel mused, as if that terrible scene in the snow where Maximilian had turned his back on her had been so cathartic that it had been a cleansing—if terribly painful—experience for them both.

Twice in the evening, once more alone in her tent, she had sat in a chair close by the brazier and had traveled back to the Twisted Tower. The first time, Ishbel had been nervous that she either would not be able to reach the Twisted Tower, or that she would not find her way home. But she found recalling how to twist her consciousness into the Twisted Tower's reality easy, almost as if, like the memories contained within each of the objects within the tower, it was already a part of her blood.

Ishbel had not spent long either time within the Twisted Tower. She'd felt a little as if she were intruding, and she kept turning about, half expecting to see Maximilian.

But he was never there.

Ishbel spent a fair bit of her time thinking about Maximilian. It still angered her that he had set Ravenna to one side not an hour after he'd told her that *he had to cleave to Ravenna, now.* All that pain, all those tears, and he'd walked into the night with Ravenna and said, *I am not so sure I really want you, either.*

What did Maximilian want from her? She wasn't sure, and that unsettled Ishbel.

She wasn't sure what *she* wanted, either, and that unsettled her even further.

It might have been better, she thought, *easier,* had they remained utterly estranged.

Ishbel went to Maximilian's command tent on the fourth night of their march. She had waited until Madarin told her he was alone, and then gathered her courage and her cloak and set off, winding her way through the horse lines and rows of tents until she reached Maximilian's tent.

Serge and Doyle were standing outside, talking, and both nodded her through when Ishbel raised her eyebrows at them.

"Ishbel." Maximilian had been sitting at a side table, reading some reports, and he rose as she walked into the tent.

"I owe you these." Ishbel placed on the table two tiny clover flowers. "It was all I could find. I am sorry."

Maximilian picked them up, held them a moment, then slid them into the inside upper pocket of his jacket. "You did not stay long, either time."

"You could feel me inside the Twisted Tower? I have no secrets from you."

Maximilian gave a small smile. "You still have a few. How far did you go inside the tower?"

"No higher than the third chamber. I still feel as if I am intruding."

"You are not intruding. How many objects did you pick up?"

"Only a few each time."

"And their memories?"

"One or two I found easy to retrieve, others more difficult."

"Maybe you need me with you."

"Maybe."

"Ishbel, sit down, there are a couple of things I need to talk about with you."

He nodded at two chairs by the brazier, and they sat down. Doyle entered, bearing a tray with two steaming mugs on it.

"My lady," Doyle said, presenting the tray to Ishbel, "my lord usually has some hot tea at this time of the evening, and I thought that you, too, might like a mug."

Ishbel thanked him and took a mug, and they both waited silently until Doyle left the tent.

"The army is splintering," Maximilian said, smiling a little as he looked into his steaming mug. "It will not hold together."

"You do not sound very worried."

He gave a little laugh. "Oh, I worry. I worry if I am doing the right thing. I worry that I might create a nightmare that will turn and bite me. I worry . . ."

"Maxel?"

Maximilian sighed. "Ravenna is aiding the generals with her magics. She denies it, but I am almost certain."

Ishbel didn't know what to say. This conversation had very suddenly skidded onto thin ice, and she was terrified that she'd fall through as soon as she opened her mouth.

"Ravenna has been a great mistake on my part," Maximilian said.

Ishbel carefully slid her mug of tea onto the table. She didn't trust herself to hold it anymore.

The silence strung out, and eventually Ishbel had to speak. "What do you want me to say, Maxel?"

He made a helpless gesture with a hand. "I just wanted to tell you."

"Why?"

Maximilian avoided the question. "Do you see Ravenna about the camp?"

"From time to time. She and her mother travel much further back in the column. You can understand, perhaps, that I would wish to avoid her."

"Yes. I can understand that. Ishbel, a few nights ago Drava, who is the Lord of Dreams and Ravenna's former lover, appeared to me. He warned me about her."

"He left it a little late."

Maximilian chuckled. "Yes. He did at that."

"And did he warn you about me?"

"No. He is, indeed, one of the few who have not."

Now it was Ishbel's turn to smile.

"Ishbel," Maximilian said, "you and I—"

"Don't."

"Our lives, yours and mine, have become such a mess, Ishbel."

"They are perfectly delineated to me at the moment, Maximilian."

He chuckled again, although not with such amusement this time. "Very well, Ishbel. As you wish."

He rose, and Ishbel looked at him a little warily.

"There is something you need to see, Ishbel."

"Oh, the Weeper. I almost forgot."

Maximilian, who had been reaching into his pack, looked up and almost smiled at the relief in her voice. "Yes, the Weeper."

He drew the cloth-swathed bundle from the pack and unwrapped it.

"This has caused so many people so much trouble," he said. "What do you know of it, Ishbel?"

"That in Coroleas it was revered as the most powerful deity their god priests had ever made. That the soul of a very powerful man had gone into its creation. That it moved heaven and earth, and created a few storms along the way, to get to you. That people have died to lay their hands on it."

"Aye." Maximilian had uncovered the Weeper now, and it lay in his hands, a beautifully formed bronze likeness of a man. "It has been whispering your name for a while now, Ishbel." He held it out to her. "Beware, if you touch it, for it may speak to you."

Ishbel ignored his last comment and took the Weeper into her hands.

Ishbel, the Weeper said to her as soon as she took its full weight. *I have waited so long for you. So long . . .*

Maximilian sat watching Ishbel in silence. He was grateful to the Weeper if only for the reason that her study of it gave him the opportunity to watch her.

Of all the things he had got wrong, how could he have mismanaged Ishbel so badly?

She looked up, eventually.

"Maxel?"

"Yes?"

She hesitated. "There is a dark and very complex sorcery that has bound this man's soul deep within the statue."

"But . . ."

"I can unwind it. If you like."

Maximilian's heart suddenly pounded so hard he thought it literally had broken out of his chest cavity and into his throat. "You can unwind it?"

"Yes. I can free the man's soul. Do you want me to do it?"

"Yes, oh gods, *yes!*"

"Now?"

Maximilian almost said *Yes!* again, but stopped just as the word leapt into his throat.

"Ishbel," he said, "how much danger will that cause you?"

She took a deep breath. "Some. The workings of the Corolean God Priests are intricate, and I am certain they have left traps. I am certain, however, that I can evade them."

"It will be dangerous."

"Yes."

Maximilian sat thinking a few moments. "Perhaps we can leave it until we get to Elcho Falling . . . you would be safer there. Elcho Falling can itself grant you some protection."

"As you wish."

"Ishbel?"

"Yes?"

"Can you tell who the Weeper is? *What* he might be?"

Ishbel gave a soft shake of her head. "I'm sorry, Maxel. That I will only know when I reach out my hand to touch his soul."

CHAPTER FOURTEEN

On the Road to Serpent's Nest

On the sixth day since he had been named as Axis' replacement, Insharah was riding about midway down the column when several men rode to join him. They were longtime friends and comrades, and Insharah greeted them with a smile and a nod for each man.

"How should we call you now, Insharah," joked a man named Rimmert. "My lord? Sir? Excellency?"

Insharah grinned. "Insharah will suffice as well as before, Rimmert."

The men laughed, and for a few minutes there was jocular chatter.

Then the mood sobered.

"There has been talk," said a man called Olam.

"There is always talk," Insharah said.

"Many among the men," Rimmert said, "have been voicing their concerns about the dreams that we have *all* been having. Don't deny it, Insharah. I have no doubt that you have been tossing and mumbling in your sleep."

Insharah said nothing, keeping his eyes ahead on the trail.

"They are but dreams," Rimmert continued, "but they do reflect the men's inner fears. What is happening to our families? *Is* Isaiah and this army of winged ghost men actually going to help?"

Insharah's face went expressionless.

"Moreover," said another man, Glimpel, "a man standing guard outside Maximilian's command tent heard Isaiah say that the River Lhyl had been turned to stone, or some such. The water is no more. We all know what that means."

Again Insharah did not respond, but, yes, he knew what that meant.

The refugees from the Central Kingdoms had been with the Isembaard-ians long enough to tell the southerners what they knew about the Skrael-ings.

How they butchered every person they came upon, and ate them.

How there was only one thing that held them back—water.

And how there was only one person who'd ever had any success against them, and that was Axis SunSoar.

But Axis SunSoar was still in the Outlands, not south in Isembaard, where he might be saving their families.

"Damn it," Glimpel said quietly, edging his horse closer to Insharah's. "Everyone likes this Maximilian. He's a good man. I'm sure he's been very nice to you. But what in all the gods' names are we doing trudging along this slushy trail toward some mountain called Elcho Falling when *our families are dying down south*?"

"Insharah," said Olam, who had been watching his commander's face carefully, "what do you know?"

Insharah did not reply, staring ahead.

"Insharah?" Rimmert hissed.

"The Lealfast will do nothing against the Skraelings," Insharah said. "They will not fight them. They are *kin*."

"*Shetzah!*" Rimmert and Olam exclaimed together.

"But Maximilian said they would help!" Olam said. "Gods, Insharah . . . this is unbelievable! What the fuck are we still doing *here*?"

"What are you suggesting, Glimpel?" Insharah said.

Glimpel exchanged a glance with Rimmert, Olam, and the others.

"We would do better south, Insharah," Glimpel said. "Tell me, where did you leave your wife and children?"

Insharah sent him a stricken look.

"Ah," said Glimpel, "they're in Aqhat, aren't they? So is my wife, as also Rimmert's."

"And if they're in Aqhat," said Olam, "then they're already—"

"Silence!" Insharah said. "Enough of this talk, you understand? Do you really suggest that *we* ride south? We'd not get there for weeks at best, and in that time . . ."

"Better that than sitting on our arses trailing along behind some man to whom we owe no allegiance, with whom we share no common cause," snapped Rimmert, "and who has sent uselessness to 'save' our families!"

With that, he jerked his horse's head to the side, peeling away from Insharah, the others following him within a heartbeat.

Insharah rode in silence for some time, brooding over what he'd heard from his companions and how he felt about it. He was jerked from his reverie by the galloping hooves of a horse and rider coming from the rear of the column.

He pulled his own horse out to intercept the rider.

"What is it?" he barked.

"There are soldiers approaching from the rear," the man said.

CHAPTER FIFTEEN

Isembaard

Isaiah moved rapidly through the north of Isembaard. He had his own methods of speeding travel; none so impressive as that used by the Lealfast, but good enough that he covered more territory per day than other men could.

He met no one. By this point anyone who had been in the extreme north of Isembaard had already traveled into the Salamaan Pass. In any case, this part of his tyranny had always been sparsely populated.

The soil was poor this close to the FarReach Mountains, unable to sustain any farming communities, and the only inhabitants had been goat herders and peddlers, traders and soldiers moving through in order to reach somewhere else.

Isaiah could feel a presence to the south. He couldn't define it any more than that, but it was very keen and he knew that it knew he was here.

It wasn't Kanubai, although Isaiah could sense some shadow of Kanubai hanging about it.

Kanubai was dead. Eaten.

On the third day after he left Bingaleal and the Lealfast, Isaiah came upon what was left of the River Lhyl.

His feet slowed as he approached, his heart thumping. Its wrongness leapt out at him, even from a great distance, and that sense grew stronger as he approached.

The river suffered. It still lived, but under such a burden of powerful and dark enchantment that its entire existence had become a torment. Here, where the Lhyl emerged from the FarReach Mountains, it should have been a narrow torrent of foam and joy, but all Isaiah could see was a jumbled morass of dulled, fractured glass.

He dropped to his knees on the riverbank, staring.

There was nothing but the glass. Isaiah had wondered if only the surface had been affected by the enchantment, and had hoped that beneath this horror the water still flowed, but every single drop of water down to the riverbed had been turned to glass.

Glass. The pyramid.

A tiny green frog crept from Isaiah's hand and inched its way to the river's edge. It reached out a pad and touched a glassy wave hesitantly.

It sprang back immediately, and hid once more within Isaiah's flesh.

Isaiah stood, and turned south.

He could feel the presence in the south watching him ever more closely.

"What do you want?" whispered Isaiah.

The One stared north. About him Skraelings milled, begging favors, but he ignored them. For the moment he wanted nothing to do with them—they could roam as far through Isembaard as they liked, eating what they wanted. Later they would be useful, but not now.

But north . . .

Isaiah the river god was back.

The One smiled sardonically. Come to release his beloved river? Come to save Isembaard from the Skraelings?

"What do I want, Isaiah?" he whispered. "For the moment, I want you, I want what that foolish girl holds so close to her heart, and I might as well take this opportunity to begin some amusing diversionary tactic to keep you and Maximilian occupied and your eyes away from the Lealfast."

Maximilian would be expecting something, some move on the One's part, and the One was ready to oblige.

He started walking north, taking great strides that ate up the distance, and he walked directly up the center of the glassy surface of the River Lhyl.

Isaiah walked south along the riverbank. Occasionally he saw Skraelings roaming in small bands. The first band he saw, just after he'd started south, had moved toward him, patently thinking him an easy meal.

But when they were about twenty or thirty paces away they'd pulled up in their tracks, hissing, their terrible jackal faces twisting in disappointment, and backed off. They'd shadowed Isaiah for an hour or two, but eventually drifted away.

They'd been warned away from him.

In the afternoon, after he'd traveled nonstop for almost nine hours, Isaiah stopped suddenly, peering ahead.

At the very limits of his vision he could see the figure of a woman standing on the riverbank, her arms wrapped about something she clutched to her chest.

She was looking directly at him.

It took Isaiah another half hour to reach her. He approached slowly, not knowing who or what she was, nor why she would be standing out here so vulnerable.

Yet so intact.

The Skraelings had left her as alone as himself.

As Isaiah came close, he wondered if he knew the woman. She looked somewhat familiar. She was pretty—or could be if she had some decent clothes, if her hair was combed and neatly arranged, and if she didn't look so worried—but a little too thin for Isaiah's liking. She also had the demeanor of a servant. She clearly recognized Isaiah, and he saw her arms tremble slightly as she held the book to her chest.

He stopped a pace or so away from her. The woman was very anxious now, and Isaiah suspected it took all her courage to stand her ground.

He supposed she was fighting the instinct to abase herself.

Isaiah gave a nod of greeting, holding her eyes with hers. "Do I know you?" he said.

The skin across her cheekbones tightened, and Isaiah thought she might be angry. Gods alone knew why. Surely she didn't expect him to remember the name of every one of the hundreds of servants who had attended him?

"My name is Hereward," she said. "I was your kitchen steward at Aqhat. You'll remember Aqhat. It was a big, sprawling palace. Very beautiful. Not anymore. It is covered in blood now."

"Hereward—"

"You arrogant bastard," Hereward said. She stepped forward, lifted the book, and with all her strength slammed it into the side of his head.

CHAPTER SIXTEEN

On the Road to Serpent's Nest

Maximilian heard the pounding of the approaching horse, and wheeled his own about to meet the rider.

"Yes?" he said, wishing his voice wasn't so curt, but hoping also that the man didn't bring bad news.

"There is a column of soldiers approaching, my lord. They are not far behind the end of our column. They've come from the west."

"Malat and his men?"

The soldier shook his head. "No. They are well uniformed and weaponed. There are at rough estimate some four thousand, with supply and cooks' wagons bringing up the rear."

"And the manner of their uniforms?"

"I could not see too closely, my lord, but their jacket coats are a brilliant emerald, and—"

The soldier stopped, his mouth open.

Maximilian had gone, his horse booted into a gallop.

He rode like a madman, reining in his mount only as he approached Ishbel on her horse.

"Maxel?"

"Come with me, Ishbel. Come, please. You can ride that horse at a gallop?"

"Yes, but—"

"Come."

He was gone, and Ishbel, uncertain, waited a moment or two before she, too, turned her horse and rode after him.

"Egalion! Garth! Gods, *gods*, it is good to see you!" Maximilian pulled his horse to a halt and dismounted in one movement, hugging to him first Egalion, Captain of the Emerald Guard, and then Garth Baxtor, his old friend and court physician, as they also dismounted. "You are well? You *look* well! And you have bought the entire Emerald Guard? Ah, thank you, thank you! Escator—how is it? Did the Skraelings..."

Egalion and Garth were laughing.

"It is good to see you as well," Garth said, more than a little relieved at Maximilian's obvious joy. He had not been entirely sure of his reception. When Maximilian had left Escator to rescue Ishbel so long ago, they had not parted on the best of terms.

He took a moment to study Maximilian. The man looked overjoyed to see them, but Garth could see lines of strain and sadness about his eyes and mouth.

And this army ahead of them! What was Maximilian doing with such an army? It stretched into tomorrow's sunrise, so far as Garth could see.

"Escator escaped virtually unscathed," Egalion said. "Lixel is still in charge, and enjoying his duties as king too much, I think. Serge and Doyle? Are they are still with you? Are they well?"

"Yes," Maximilian said. "Serge and Doyle are with me, and are well, and will no doubt relish the chance to tell their comrades of their adventures these past months." He sobered. "As do I. There are...many things of which I need to tell you."

Just then there came the sound of a horse approaching, and Garth looked up.

It was Ishbel, looking wary at the approaching reunion.

"And I see you found your wife," Garth said, softly. He thought she looked very different than when he had first met her at Pelemere. She looked more open, stronger, far more confident.

And mildly unhappy at seeing Garth again.

Maximilian glanced behind him. "Yes. I found Ishbel." He paused. "As I said, there is much I have to tell you. You didn't see Malat and his men on your way? You didn't talk to them?"

"We saw Malat briefly," said Egalion. "He told us only that you were ahead and that you headed for Serpent's Nest. When we pressed him for more, he said it was your story to tell."

"He wanted to ride for Kyros as fast as he could," Garth said. "We told him that it had been attacked by the Skraelings, but had not suffered too much damage as they'd seethed south before they'd had time to get their claws too deep into the city. Malat's wife and children are well."

"Thank the gods," Maximilian muttered.

Ishbel had drawn her horse to a halt two paces away, and she dipped her head at Egalion and Garth. "Well met again," she said. "I am happy to see you."

"Not too happy, I think," said Garth, "and for that I must apologize . . . ah, there I go again, Ishbel, I am always apologizing to you!"

He injected as much lightness and humor into his voice as he could, and was rewarded with a slight thawing in Ishbel's manner to the extent that they almost managed to share a smile.

But then she glanced behind Garth and Egalion to where the Emerald Guard waited, and her face shut down.

"Maxel," she said, very softly, "see who rides with your men."

Maximilian had his hand on Garth's shoulder as he looked back into the column of men, and Garth felt it suddenly tighten.

"Lister and Vorstus," Maximilian said, looking at the two men who sat horses four or five paces away. "You've finally managed to find me."

"They joined us two days ago," Egalion said. He was looking at Maximilian, clearly worried by the barely concealed hostility in Maximilian's face and voice. "Vorstus said you'd know who Lister was. He said that—"

"You never asked Vorstus for an explanation as to why he'd deserted Ruen?" Maximilian asked Egalion.

Egalion looked uncomfortable. "I didn't have any reason to distrust him, Maximilian."

"Lister and, to a slightly lesser extent, Vorstus," said Maximilian, "are the two men primarily responsible for most of the ills of my life. If you want to know who truly imprisoned me in the Veins, and then kept me there for seventeen years, then look no further than those two. They suggested the entire idea to Cavor, and kept me there until it suited them to 'rescue' me. If you want to know who destroyed Ishbel's life as a child, then look no further than those two. They took two lives and ruined them in order to further their own ambitions."

Egalion and Garth were now staring at him with their mouths agape.

"Vorstus?" said Garth. "*Vorstus* was responsible for your horror in the Veins?" He couldn't understand it . . . Vorstus had been the one who had set Garth on the path to being able to release Maximilian.

"Vorstus is far more than the amiable Abbot of Persimius he appears to be," Maximilian said.

"Vorstus," said the man himself, "has only ever been concerned for your welfare, Maximilian."

Maximilian took two strides toward the two mounted men. "And now I suppose I should be pleased that you have finally found me."

"We can help you, Maximilian," Lister said. "Try to believe that."

Maximilian stared at him a long, silent moment. "Frankly, that is something I find rather *hard* to believe."

He switched his gaze to Vorstus. "Tell me, Vorstus, do you have something of mine in your pack?"

Vorstus reached behind him and untied a satchel from the back of his saddle. He held it out to Maximilian. "Your crown, my Lord of Elcho Falling."

Elcho Falling? Garth thought.

Maximilian turned his head very slightly. "Ishbel? Will you take that for me, and keep it safe?"

She looked puzzled, but did as Maximilian asked, pushing her horse forward and taking the satchel from Vorstus.

"Well met, my lady," Vorstus murmured.

Ishbel ignored him, looking instead at Lister, the man who for most of her life she had worshipped as the Great Serpent.

"How dare you think yourself worthy of continued breath," she said, "when you have destroyed so many lives?"

Then she turned her horse and rode away.

CHAPTER SEVENTEEN

Isembaard

Isaiah lay on the ground, barely conscious, his head ringing with the force of the blow.

"That was for all the people you left behind," Hereward said. "If my point hasn't quite been made, I don't mind hitting you again."

Isaiah managed to raise a hand to ward her off. It trembled badly, and that made him furious.

"Did you think I *wanted* to leave everyone behind?" he said, trying to sit up, only to slump to the ground again as he almost blacked out with the movement. He fought unconsciousness, and only barely won. "Did you think I wanted to leave a single person behind? I had no way to get everyone out. All I could do was to evacuate as many people as—"

She hit him again, this time with her open hand. Isaiah's head snapped back, and his neck cracked, but at least this time he didn't end up in the dust.

"Have I made my point sufficiently *now*?" Hereward said.

Isaiah opened his mouth to hiss at her that he was doing all he could, had done all he could, then thought better of it. Gods, the woman was mad.

"Yes," he said.

She sank down into the dirt beside him, crossing her legs, arranging her skirts modestly, and laying the book in her lap. Isaiah peered at it, sure he would see his blood smeared across it—the woman might have been thin, but she was well muscled—but the leather cover was unmarked.

Isaiah very carefully managed to sit upright without having to lean on one or both of his hands, and tried to regain control of the situation. "Why are you here?" he said. "Why—"

"Why am I here, Excellency?" Her voice cracked with sarcasm on that last word. "Oh, the small matter of Aqhat being overrun with horror. The desire to escape. The desire to *live*. The desire to—"

"Hereward, please, I am truly sorry for what has happened and, yes, I bear responsibility for every person who was lost. I cannot even begin to imagine the nightmare that you, as everyone left behind, has had to endure. How is it you have ended here, on this deserted stretch of the Lhyl? And how is it that the Skraelings leave you be?"

Isaiah watched the emotion play over Hereward's face, and knew she was battling the desire to berate him yet more. But she didn't, and for that Isaiah was grateful. Very slowly, and with a fair degree of prompting, Hereward told of her escape from Aqhat on the riverboat, and of the subsequent slaughter of her companions when the river turned to glass and the Skraelings surged onto the vessel.

She paused at that point, and Isaiah saw in her eyes and across her face a partial reflection of the terror, the horror, that she must have endured.

"I knew I was dead," she said, clutching the book in her lap with white-knuckled hands. "There was nowhere for me to run. I had backed up against the bulkhead, and in my terror dislodged this book from a shelf above me."

She glanced at it. "I had never seen it there previously."

Hereward looked at Isaiah. "The book knocked me to the deck . . . and when I managed to regain my senses I saw the Skraelings standing about me in a semicircle, pointing at the book and whispering, 'A nasty, nasty.' Then they turned and filed out. They haven't bothered me since."

"A 'nasty, nasty'? Hereward, can I see the book?"

Hereward's hands tightened on the book, and Isaiah could see she struggled with herself. Finally, after a long moment, she lifted it and gave it to him.

He knew as soon as he took it in his hands that it was an object of great power, and he knew as soon as he opened the leather binding and looked at the chapter page what it was.

It was the *Book of the Soulenai*, lost now for many hundreds of years.

Lost, or merely biding its time?

"What is it, Isaiah?"

"This book . . . I know of it. It is many thousands of years old, and originally came from the north . . . from a place called Elcho Falling. It came to this land in the possession of a man called Avaldamon, who passed it to his son, Boaz, and his wife, Tirzah. The woman who came to Aqhat, my new wife, Ishbel . . . you remember her?"

"Yes."

"Ishbel is the descendant of Boaz and Tirzah."

"The book is *mine*, now."

Isaiah gave her a gentle smile. "The book is its own, and chooses who it stays with. For the moment, yes, it has chosen you."

He ran his fingers down the list of chapter titles.

The One walks north.

Prepare for confrontation.

Isaiah and Hereward meet with the glass man.

Feed the pretty kitten.

Those four chapter titles were repeated down the page. The first three Isaiah could understand, but . . . feed the pretty kitten?

He closed the book and handed it back to Hereward. "A visitor comes, Hereward. I fear he may not be very pleasant."

"A visitor?"

The One. Isaiah knew instinctively who that must be.

"The pyramid walks north, Hereward. It wants to talk with me. It wants *me*. I'm sorry, my dear, but I think your life is about to get immeasurably worse, and that is, again, all my fault."

CHAPTER EIGHTEEN

On the Road to Serpent's Nest

Ishbel sat in her blue tent, staring at the satchel which lay unopened on the camp table before her. To one side a brazier glowed, warming the interior of the tent, while the remains of a meal lay on another small table. Ishbel had not joined Maximilian, Egalion, and Garth this evening. Maximilian had a great deal to tell them, and she had thought it best she not be there.

Why had Maximilian given *her* the crown of Elcho Falling?

Ishbel had turned and ridden away from Lister as soon as she'd insulted him. Partly this was because she simply could not bear to stay in the company of the man who had cold-bloodedly caused her and Maximilian so much misery, partly it was to escape an already uncomfortable meeting, and partly because Ishbel could not trust herself to remain in the man's company without causing him some bodily harm.

How could she have devoted twenty years of her life to him?

She took a deep breath, staring at the satchel as she tried to distract herself from Lister. She had not touched it other than to drop it on the table on her return. Hours had passed as she ate, bathed, dressed in her nightclothes, and then brushed out her long blond hair—listening as Maximilian and the Emerald Guard arrived back in camp, and half hoping that Maximilian would drop by to see his crown—but now she could not put the moment off any longer.

The satchel *throbbed* at her.

Indeed, the crown had been whispering to her from the moment she took the satchel from Vorstus.

Ishbel supposed she had grown up a little, because the crown's whispering had not bothered her to anywhere near the same extent as she'd been bothered by Maximilian's whispering rings. She'd managed to put its voice and words out of her mind, aware of its whispering, but not disturbed by it.

But now there were no more delaying tactics available to her. Ishbel took a deep breath and slid the satchel close. She undid the straps and folded back the leather flap. Then she took an even deeper breath, slid in her hand, and grasped the crown of Elcho Falling.

She froze, staring down at the satchel and her wrist as it vanished under the flap.

The crown was alive.

It was all Ishbel could do to keep her hand on its cool metal.

Ishbel, the crown of Elcho Falling said, *do you remember what Isaiah said to you when first you met?*

"No," Ishbel muttered.

He said that you were the priestess of the Lord of Elcho Falling. That *is why Maximilian gave me to you to keep for the moment.*

"Oh," Ishbel said, as she realized the meaning of what Isaiah had said to her, and the reason Maximilian had wanted her to have the crown.

"You should be the one to crown him," said a voice behind her, and Ishbel whipped about, pulling her hand from the satchel.

Lister stood there.

Ishbel stared at him, for the moment so angry at his intrusion that she could find nothing to say.

He gave a little smile. "May I sit?"

"No."

"Once you were pleased to see me. You hung off my every word."

"You deceived me. You murdered my family in order to manipulate me into what you wanted. Had you never thought to merely *ask*, Lister?"

"Don't be so angry, Ishbel. I did what was needed, and I can still aid and advise you. Besides, do not forget that you owe all your power to me—"

No, the crown said, and Ishbel understood that Lister could not hear it. *You have far more power than what he gave you. Far more. The blood of Elcho Falling runs in your veins, and he envies it.*

Then it hissed, again inaudible to Lister, and Ishbel involuntarily gave a small smile.

Lister mistook the reason for her smile. He relaxed, and reached for the back of a wooden chair, meaning to lift it close and sit down. "It is all behind us now, Ishbel. Between us, you and I can make of Maximilian what we need—"

"Get out."

Lister froze in the act of sitting. "Ishbel—"

"Get out. You are nothing to me now, Lister. Meaningless. I suspect you are now very meaningless to Maximilian and to Elcho Falling as well. Go. Find some other poor soul to manipulate if you must, but leave us alone."

"You will need me, Ishbel. Both you and Maximilian."

"I can't imagine the circumstances under which either of us would voluntarily call for your aid, Lister. You have delivered the crown. I'm sure Maximilian is grateful. Now . . . just *go*."

Lister stared at her for a long moment, then he turned on his heel and left.

Ishbel closed her eyes and forced the muscles of her shoulders and neck to relax. The very sight of him made her feel nauseated.

All the people who had suffered and died due to his meddling.

And why? Would Maximilian have been any less the man he was now for *not* having spent seventeen years existing in hell? Would she have been any less the woman had she been allowed to grow within her loving family instead of living among their corpses?

Who was the greater fool? Lister for his meddling, or herself for perhaps alienating a man, a *god*, who could aid Maximilian?

"Maxel," Ishbel murmured, rolling her head a little to stretch her neck and shoulders, "I hope I haven't ruined this for you, too."

Then she opened her eyes and looked at the satchel. Slowly, but now without any hesitation, she slid her hand in once more, took hold of the crown of Elcho Falling, and drew it forth.

For a long minute Ishbel held it in her hands, then she placed it atop the satchel on the table.

Ishbel knew its shape and proportions from holding it in her hands: three heavy rolled bands, probably of gold from the occasional glimpse she caught of them, twisted around each other to create a simple yet elegant crown. But she could barely see the golden bands. The entire crown was almost completely obscured by a roiling cloud of darkness.

"Why are you so dark?" she said. "Why the gloom?"

"Perhaps it sees you for what you are," said another voice behind her.

Oh, for all the gods' sakes! Ishbel turned about on her chair, hardly able to believe the fact of another intruder.

Ravenna stood in the center of the tent, very dark, very still.

"Ishbel," Ravenna said, "do you not know how dangerous you are to Maximilian? Can you not see how—"

"Get out," Ishbel said.

"Leave him," Ravenna said. "Let him live."

Ishbel rose from her chair and walked up to Ravenna. "Do you have nothing better to do than rail against me?"

"You will destroy him."

Ishbel's hand twitched, and she kept it by her side only with the greatest effort. "I must be a terrible threat to you, Ravenna. You hated me from the first moment you heard my name, I think."

To Ishbel's surprise, Ravenna's eyes gleamed with tears. "You think this is about you, Ishbel? Only incidentally. All I want is Maximilian's happiness and success. But you stand in the way. Step aside, Ishbel."

"If you cared this much then you should have stayed at Maximilian's side, Ravenna. Not abandoned him the moment you thought you'd found someone a little more powerful. What a mistake Drava was, eh?"

"You think you love Maximilian, Ishbel, but you will inevitably betray him, and Elcho Falling, and this land besides."

"And this you have seen."

"And this I have seen."

"You are truly tedious," Ishbel said. "Get out."

This time Ravenna went.

"Ravenna."

She turned about. A man approached her through the night.

"Lister," she said, and gave a small bow of her head.

"Ishbel appears to have fallen out with both of us," Lister said.

"Apparently."

"You are being cautious," said Lister, "but I wonder if we might talk. Your tent, perhaps?"

"I share my tent with my mother, and she is more Maximilian's ally than mine."

"Then we shall speak here, and I shall be brief, that neither of us perish from the cold. There is a rumor about this camp, Ravenna, that you aid the three Isembaardian generals against Maximilian."

"Many people are too willing to speak ill of me."

Lister waited.

"I do not know what you want," Ravenna said. "You have been Ishbel's ally and mentor for many years."

Lister's mouth curved in a sardonic smile. "Ishbel has not proved the loyal acolyte, I fear. You seem somewhat . . . disenchanted with her yourself."

"I fear that she will bring Maximilian nothing but sorrow."

"In what way?"

Ravenna hesitated. She sensed that Lister was not antagonistic to her, and that he entertained doubts, either about Maximilian or Ishbel.

"For months," Ravenna said, "I have been troubled with a vision."

"Can you share it?" Lister said.

Again Ravenna hesitated, but not so long this time. "Yes," she said, and led Lister into the Land of Dreams.

When the vision had faded, and Lister and Ravenna once more stood in the snow, Lister spoke softly.

"Have you shown this vision to Maximilian?"

"Yes."

"And?"

"He prefers to ignore its clear warning. He is weak, and I worry."

"He loves her."

"A love you engineered."

Lister chuckled. "Am I being blamed?"

"I want to know why you are here talking to me."

"Are you aiding the generals?"

"Why do you wish to know?"

Lister did not answer immediately. "If Maximilian makes one misstep," he said eventually, "Elcho Falling will be destroyed. Ravenna, marsh witch, do you know what Elcho Falling really is?"

"I have a good idea."

Again Lister chuckled. "You do not allow your secrets to slip easily, Ravenna, and that is a commendable quality."

"We are both proving equally adept at this sidestepping dance, Lister. *What do you want from me?*"

"I think I may need an ally," he said, leaning so close that his breath frosted in her face, "as I think also do you. Tell me, Ravenna, is that a child you carry in your belly?"

"Yes."

"Maximilian's child?"

"Yes."

"A son."

"Yes."

Lister smiled. "Have you met my friend and helper, Vorstus? No? Then perhaps we can track him down, and find ourselves a fire, and talk some more."

CHAPTER NINETEEN

On the Road to Serpent's Nest

Ravenna and Venetia packed away their night things, ready for the day's march. They worked in silence, each avoiding touching the other or catching the other's eye. It was a well-worn ritual, enacted as it had been every morning over the past week.

Whatever closeness had once bound them was now long dead.

Soldiers were standing about outside, stamping their feet and blowing on their hands, waiting for the two women to leave the tent so they could pack it away for the day's march. There was a murmur of voices, a movement, and the tent flap lifted back.

"Venetia? Ravenna?"

Both women turned about, startled.

Garth Baxtor entered the tent, looking unsure of himself. "Is this a bad moment?"

Venetia and Ravenna exchanged a glance, then Venetia smiled, set aside the blanket she had been folding, and walked forward to hug Garth.

"No, it is not a bad time. Garth, it is so good to see you."

Garth hugged her back, relieved at the warmth of her welcome. He had seen Venetia on several occasions over the past few years, stopping by her hut in the marshes to exchange news and information about herbal remedies, but it was strange to see her here, and under these circumstances.

Then Venetia stepped back, and Garth looked at Ravenna.

The moment stretched out awkwardly. She was so different from the girl he remembered. She had grown into a beautiful woman, but there was a hardness about her, and a singular determination that Garth found unsettling.

But perhaps his discomfort was too much influenced by the tale Maximilian had told him and Egalion last night.

"Ah," said Ravenna, very softly. "I see by your eyes, Garth, that Maxel has been chatting to you."

Garth tried to inject a little more warmth into his smile. He stepped forward and kissed Ravenna lightly on the cheek, his hands on her shoulders.

Maximilian's son, he thought, sending his Touch through Ravenna's body, *and healthy.*

"I could have told you that," Ravenna murmured, pulling herself away from Garth's touch, and his smile slipped a little.

Why was it that he was always making an ass of himself with Maximilian and his women?

"Garth," said Venetia, "I'll let you and Ravenna talk. I'll ride a little with you later, yes? We can talk then."

"That would be good, Venetia," Garth said, then turned back to Ravenna as Venetia left the tent. "It has been a long time. We've all changed. Maxel . . . I had no idea that he should inherit another, and stranger, crown and I wager you didn't either, Ravenna, when you helped rescue him from the Veins. As for Vorstus . . ." Garth shook his head. "I trusted him with my life, as Maxel did, and he was our friend for these past eight years. To now find that he helped imprison Maxel . . . it is difficult."

"These are difficult times, Garth." Ravenna stuffed the last of her things into a pack, then picked up her cloak.

"Ravenna—"

She turned to face him. "Do you speak for Ishbel now, Garth? Am I no longer your friend?"

"Ishbel and I do not have a history of friendship, Ravenna. When I first met her I instinctively distrusted her. I never truly liked her as Maxel's wife."

Ravenna visibly relaxed. "She is a hound from hell, Garth. Maximilian is fixated by her, to his shame."

"He loves her, I think, despite the distance currently between them."

Ravenna waved a hand dismissively. "So he may, but Ishbel will murder him, and spread disaster throughout this land. She will ally with evil, Garth, and betray everything for which you and I have ever worked. You must speak to Maximilian, make him see sense where I have failed. He must put Ishbel aside."

Garth's sense of discomfort grew more intense. "I do not think Maxel is a man who takes well to being told what he must or must not do."

Ravenna gave a soft, bitter laugh. "As I have discovered. Why does he not see reason, Garth? Why?"

"Ravenna . . . you and he . . ." He stopped, not knowing how to say gently what he thought best.

"What?" Ravenna said. "He and I . . . not suited to each other? Is that what you want to say?"

"I think he has only ever wanted to be your friend, Ravenna."

"Then he should *be* my friend and listen to what I say to him."

"He feels trapped by the baby. He thinks that—"

"That *I* trapped him? That I conceived this child to bind him to my side? No marsh woman does that, Garth. I conceived this child not to win Maximilian to my side, but to save Elcho Falling, should he refuse to see Ishbel for what she is."

She threw the cloak about her shoulders, tying it closed with angry jerks. "Enjoy your ride with my mother, Garth. I am sure she, too, will speak nothing but poison against me."

Garth stood looking at the tent flap for a long time once Ravenna had gone. He could barely believe the woman she'd become. It was as if Ravenna the girl had been the promise, and Ravenna the woman the . . .

"What, Garth?" he murmured. "What?"

He thought about what Ravenna had said to him just as she left the tent. She had conceived the child to save Elcho Falling.

What did that say about her loyalty to Maximilian?

What if Ravenna ever came to believe that *Maximilian* threatened Elcho Falling?

Garth shivered, and, hearing the soldiers outside move impatiently, went to mount his horse.

CHAPTER TWENTY

Outside Margalit, the Outlands

A rmat stood in the doorway of his command tent, studying the scene before him. Men scurried about the encampment, readying for a sortie west; horses were being brushed and saddled; weapons cleaned and sharpened.

He wasn't concerned about being seen from the air—by either a passing Icarii or the Lealfast which Ravenna had told him about—as Ravenna's sorcery still kept him concealed from any eye not belonging to a friend or ally.

Armat, as Kezial and Lamiah, had managed virtual miracles since they had abandoned Maximilian's camp—such miracles aided, of course, by a little more of Ravenna's sorcery. Armat had taken the leadership role within the group of three generals. He was the youngest, but he was the more decisive, and Kezial and Lamiah had made no murmur as Armat began to take an ever more commanding role.

Armat knew they would be easy to manage when the time came. And if not, then they could be killed as easily.

Armat currently controlled almost eighty thousand soldiers, all grouped just beyond the city of Margalit. This number was composed of the forces Isaiah had left at Margalit itself, as well as several Rivers of ten thousand men that the Tyrant had left stationed in the Central Outlands and within a few day's march south of Margalit.

There were many tens of thousands more soldiers to the south, and Lamiah and Kezial had ridden south many days ago to gather them together.

Kezial had the task of combining the forces about Adab; Lamiah, the forces stationed between Adab and the Salamaan Pass.

Armat expected them to consolidate the forces, certainly, but did not truly expect them to rush back to his aid. Out on their own, with armies of their own, both generals were likely to succumb to their own personal ambitions.

Armat didn't care very much. He could outgeneral both Lamiah and Kezial and, in the end, he would likely control the much larger army. Not right at the moment . . . but soon. Armat's eyes lost their focus as he looked further to the west. Maxel was leading some two hundred thousand Isembaardian soldiers east toward Elcho Falling, but Armat didn't expect Maximilian to have two hundred thousand for very much longer. He had his own men among Maximilian's army, and he knew that they'd be spreading the soft word of treachery: *Ride for Armat. He can give you what you need—safety for your families and land on which to prosper.*

Lamiah was supposed to also discover as much news as he could about Isembaard, but Armat didn't care one way or the other what he discovered. Isembaard was the past, Elcho Falling the future.

And Armat didn't intend to allow the witch-woman Ravenna to control the mountain and all its riches and power.

Elcho Falling was going to be his.

But for now, Armat thanked Ravenna every time she appeared to him— which was every second day or so—and promised that the army he gathered would be used to destroy Maximilian and take Elcho Falling for Ravenna's baby son.

Armat did not care that Ravenna would discover his duplicity eventually. In the end, witch-women were as vulnerable to the sword as any other man or woman.

"But that joy is in the future," Armat murmured to himself, one hand checking that his sword lay correctly in its scabbard. "For now, there are more entertaining amusements to be had."

Axis and the Lealfast.

Ravenna had told Armat all she knew about the Lealfast, which proved to be an extraordinary amount. On the face of it the Lealfast were terrifying, with powers which would render them almost unbeatable in any military confrontation.

After all, Armat had been there when one of them had made the assassination attempt on Isaiah, and had seen for himself just how easily the Lealfast assassin had escaped Isaiah's soldiers.

Imagine what a force of twenty thousand or more would be like, attacking from the sky.

And now such a force was sent to hunt him down, with the great Star-Man Axis SunSoar at its head.

Armat despised Axis. He'd had his day, and if he had won some impressive battles, then they were long in the past. All Axis had done at Isaiah's court was wander about and play at being Isaiah's lapdog. If it had been *him* . . . well then, Armat would have murdered Isaiah and taken control within his first half day back from death.

Axis hadn't done a single thing to impress since he'd returned from death. He was a useless legend.

Armat was similarly unimpressed with the Lealfast. They had wings and they had magic, but they were as vulnerable to the blade as Ravenna would one day prove to be.

Armat had come away from Isaiah's assassination attempt with one important lesson learned. The Lealfast might travel virtually invisibly, but in order to act they needed to take fleshly form, and that instantly put them back on a par with human soldiers. Armat also wondered if they might be just as vulnerable when they were less visible.

Just a hunch, but Armat was good with hunches. It was why he'd attained a generalship at such a relatively young age.

A day previously he had sent out a small party to test his hunch. They were due back today, and thus he waited in the sheltered doorway of his tent.

Waiting for confirmation that he could destroy any Lealfast sent against him.

Armat smiled in anticipation. Once the Lealfast were taken out, then Axis . . .

The armed party of nine men came back just before noon. Their leader rode directly to Armat's tent, dismounted and saluted.

"Well?" said Armat.

"It was as you said, my lord."

Armat took a deep breath, his eyes bright, then stepped inside the tent, gesturing the man to follow him. "Tell me," he said.

"We rode two hours to the gully you spoke of," said the soldier, Habal.

Armat nodded. They'd known the Lealfast were in their area, and no matter how magical the Lealfast were in large numbers they could be spotted—a gray snowy cloud drifting through the air. A good man could easily differentiate between a cloud of true snow and a cloud of Lealfast.

"Bruen peeled off before we arrived at the gully," Habal said, "and took up a concealed position within the rocks at the top of the gully."

"Yes, yes," said Armat. "Get on with it."

"The eight of us remaining rode into the gully, making no effort to conceal ourselves, and flying your standard. Within minutes the cloud of Lealfast drifted closer for a look."

Habal took a deep breath. "Bruen readied his slingshot, took good aim, and slung his stone into the cloud. The Lealfast hadn't seen him and hadn't tried to avoid the spot where he was concealed."

"*And?*" Armat was ready to murder the man for drawing it out.

"One of them fell from the sky. Not far, not all the way to the ground, for he recovered twenty paces before he hit, but he fell, clutching at a thigh where the stone had struck. My lord, the instant he was injured—"

"He became visible. Good, Habal. *Good!*"

Habal grinned, relieved to have made Armat happy.

"Do you think he knew what had hit him?" Armat said.

"I doubt it, my lord. He would only have felt the sting of the impact. The Lealfast must still be wondering what it was. If I may say so, my lord, your idea to use the slingshot rather than the arrow was brilliant."

Armat didn't say anything. He stared at Habal, his eyes glittering, then he very slowly smiled. "You are a good man, Habal. You bring me good news. Thank you."

He clapped the man on the shoulder, then dismissed him.

Good news. The best.

The Lealfast were vulnerable, even when traveling in their magical form.

"I'm going to slaughter them," Armat said, then laughed.

CHAPTER TWENTY-ONE

On the Road to Serpent's Nest

Ishbel sat relaxed on her horse, allowing the animal to amble at its own pace beside the great convoy of soldiers and equipment. She rode ten paces or so to one side of the convoy, slightly distanced from it not only physically, but emotionally as well (Madarin, riding five paces behind her, was such an easy and accepted part of her life that she didn't consider his silent presence an intrusion). Partly this was because she wanted to think over the visits of Lister and Ravenna, and partly it was because she was a little unsettled by the arrival of Garth and Egalion. She hadn't spoken to either of them since their brief, initial meeting, yet knew that by now Maximilian must have told them all that had happened.

The loss of their daughter.

Her affair with Isaiah.

His with Ravenna.

Ishbel's hidden identity as Archpriestess of the Coil, and her tie by blood to the Persimius family.

Elcho Falling.

Ravenna was a troubling element in the mix. Ishbel knew that Garth and Ravenna had worked together to free Maximilian from the Veins eight or nine years ago, and that they had been very good friends. Given Ravenna's own hatred of Ishbel, and Garth's previous dislike of her, Ishbel did not think Garth would think much more of her now, particularly not once Maximilian had done with his tale.

It was a shame, because Ishbel was tired of disliking him, and thought that he could well be a good friend.

"Wake up, my lady. You are about to fall off your horse."

Startled, Ishbel snapped out of her reverie. Garth Baxtor had ridden his horse up alongside her, and was now regarding her with a mix of careful friendliness and anxious uncertainty.

"Garth," Ishbel said, not knowing how else to continue.

"I should retract my words about the falling off," Garth said. "You have gained some fine horsewoman's skills since last I saw you, my lady."

Ishbel managed a small smile. When first she'd left Serpent's Nest to travel west with Maximilian she'd barely been able to sit a horse without falling to an ungracious heap on the ground.

"I have had many months' practice since then, Garth." Ishbel paused. "And, please, call me Ishbel. I am sorry I ever snapped at you for being too familiar."

The wariness in Garth's eyes relaxed fractionally. "Ishbel, then."

He lapsed into silence, and for a few minutes they rode in an increasingly awkward quiet.

"Has Maximilian told you—" Ishbel began.

"Yes. He spent last night with Egalion and myself. Ishbel, what a tale. I . . . had no idea . . ."

"You must think poorly of me."

"No. Not at all. Not now having heard so much of who Maxel is and will be, and of who you are and were, and of how the both of you were manipulated by so many around you. Vorstus . . . I had no idea . . . I cannot believe how Maxel has not taken a knife to him. And Lister, and what he did to you . . . Ishbel, it has been a tragedy." He thought a moment. "And the greater tragedy is that you and Maxel are now estranged."

Estranged, thought Ishbel. *Such a stiff word for what has happened between us.*

And how inappropriate, she thought, with a little start of self-realization. Currently she and Maximilian were at their least "estranged." They'd been far more estranged when they'd shared a bed and a marriage.

She gave a shrug as her only answer.

"You know that once I was opposed to your marriage," Garth said.

Ishbel gave a nod.

"I wish..." Garth said, then trailed off. "This is very awkward," he finished.

Ishbel looked at him at that. "I had thought you would dislike me even more once Maxel had told his tale."

"No," he said. "It has made me see, made me *wish*, that you and Maxel—"

"It won't happen, Garth. Too much has gone wrong between us. There has been too much tragedy. No one survives that."

"You and he should—"

"No, Garth. *No*. It is better the way it is now." Ishbel smiled wryly. "We have never got on so well, or so honestly, as when we are good friends working together toward a single cause rather than lovers or spouses. At least we can be at peace this way."

Garth thought that "at peace" didn't quite manage to describe either Ishbel or Maximilian right now, but he let it pass. He did not want to interfere. Whatever happened was up to the gods.

"I spoke with Ravenna this morning," Garth said.

"Ah."

"I thought at the time that she has changed so much, but then, after some reflection, I wondered if she had changed at all. I don't know. She was so unknowable even as a girl, and so determined always to get her own way." He fell silent again. "Whatever friendship that once was between us has gone, I think."

Ishbel didn't respond to that.

"I feel for Venetia," said Garth. "She is a woman I admire greatly."

"I have had little to do with her," said Ishbel, "but from my few brief meetings, yes, I think I would like her, too. I cannot believe she could have a daughter like Ravenna. Who on earth did she choose as the father?"

Garth gave a funny half smile. "I think Ravenna's father is my father. We're half-brother and sister."

Ishbel stared at him. She opened her mouth to say something, then shut it again.

"I cannot be sure," said Garth, "but my father has always been awkward and secretive about Venetia—and she about him. I think that when he was younger, he must have gone to Venetia to talk with her about her herbal cures, and she seduced him, perhaps, much as Ravenna seduced Maxel, but without the ulterior motive."

"Ulterior motive?" Ishbel said.

"Ishbel . . . Ravenna said something to me this morning. She said that she had conceived the child not to trap Maxel, but to save Elcho Falling." *Should Maximilian refuse to see Ishbel for what she truly was,* but this Garth did not say.

Ishbel sighed. "Garth, I do not wish to speak about Ravenna's child."

"I'm sorry, Ishbel." Garth thought of the child Ishbel had lost, and both her and Maximilian's distress over it. Ravenna's pregnancy could not be easy for Ishbel. "I feel I should also apologize for Ravenna."

"You have no need to apologize for her, Garth!"

"Nonetheless, someone has to, and it was I who involved her in Maximilian's life in the first instance. Oh gods, Ishbel, I can't believe he slept with her!"

Ishbel laughed at the affront in his voice. "I had thought that you'd sympathize with her."

Garth shook his head. "Ravenna has ever been her own person." He glanced at Ishbel. "I was quite desperately in love with her myself, you know, when we were young."

"Then you had a lucky escape. Particularly if she is, as you think, your half-sister."

He laughed, and they looked at each other.

"I think we might be friends, Ishbel," Garth said.

"That would be a relief, Garth. You are too likeable for me to be bothered trying to maintain a dislike of you."

They shared a smile, then looked around at the sound of hoofbeats behind them. Maximilian rode up, pulling his horse in on the other side of Ishbel's.

"No knives?" he said.

"No knives," Garth and Ishbel said as one, and they shared another smile.

They chatted about inconsequential things, before Ishbel finally asked Maximilian where Lister and Vorstus were within the column.

"Far enough away that I cannot see them," Maximilian said, somewhat shortly.

"Lister came to see me last night," Ishbel said. "To make friends, I think. I don't know. Maybe to gauge my residual loyalty. Perhaps to tell me what he thought I ought to be doing."

"More likely the latter," Maximilian said. He glanced at the satchel tied to the back of Ishbel's saddle. "Have you touched the crown?"

"Yes," said Ishbel. "It is a grim thing." She shot him a look, and a brief smile. "It had a talk with me."

"I don't want to know what it said," said Maximilian. Then he, too, smiled. "Strange. I didn't hear you run screaming from your tent at the sound of its voice."

"We all change, Maxel."

"Aye, we all change." Now Maximilian looked at Garth. "And what think you of Vorstus, my friend? You were close, once."

"A long time ago, Maxel," Garth said. "As once Ravenna and I were. As you said, we all change." He paused, thinking. "I am almost not surprised to hear he has been so duplicitous and so manipulative. Frankly, Maxel, I'd set the pair of them to digging out the latrine ditches each night when we make camp."

All three smiled, and the shared amusement gave Garth the encouragement to ask something that had been feeding his curiosity ever since Maximilian had told him Ishbel was, in fact, the Archpriestess of the Coil.

"Ishbel," he said, "when first Maximilian received news of the Coil's offer of a new bride, no one truly knew what to think about you."

"I am sure you are being very diplomatic, Garth," said Ishbel.

"We all advised Maxel against you," said Garth. "We thought you'd be nothing but trouble. But Vorstus argued that Maxel would know if you were a priestess of the Coil, because you were sure to be marked. But . . . Maxel has mentioned no mark . . . and he said he did not know for certain that you were a member of the Coil—let alone its archpriestess—until he found you in Sakkuth."

He left the question unasked, but dangling in the air between them.

"I can assure you," said Ishbel, "that Maxel looked for it. Very diligently."

She paused, enjoying the moment, keeping her eyes ahead.

"He just didn't look in quite the right place," she said eventually, a smile taking any sting out of her words. "And he's lost his chance now."

Further up the column, the soldier Rimmert rode his horse up to join Insharah's.

"There is deep unhappiness, my lord," Rimmert said to Insharah. "Every man among us wonders why we continue on this road to Elcho Falling, when we'd be doing more good further south."

"Enough, Rimmert."

Rimmert studied Insharah. The man's voice had lacked conviction, and Rimmert noted that there were deep lines of worry and sleeplessness about his eyes.

"What are we *doing* here, Insharah?" Rimmert said, lapsing back into old familiarity. "There is word that Armat has consolidated his forces to the east, and even now prepares to march south to Isembaard."

"Rimmert—"

"That word, Insharah, has spread like wildfire throughout the troops. Armat is acting, while . . . *here?*" Rimmert spat to one side. "We are merely riding toward some vague glory. I don't know. I just don't *know*, Insharah. Elcho Falling has nothing to do with us, while the fate of Isembaard and our families has *everything* to do with us. Everyone believes we would be better south than—"

"*Enough*, Rimmert!"

Rimmert gave Insharah a long, hard look. "Tonight fully one hundred thousand men are going to desert . . . if 'desert' is the right term to abandon a man and cause to which we owe no loyalty. I will be with them. It is your choice, Insharah, whether you allow us to go, whether you alert Axis . . .

"Or whether you join us."

CHAPTER TWENTY-TWO

Isembaard

Isaiah stood, stretching out his muscles and looking around him. It had been two days now since he'd discovered Hereward and the *Book of the Soulenai*.

Both had complicated everything.

He'd wanted to continue further south, surveying the damage that had been done to Isembaard (*and to his river*), and discovering what had happened to Kanubai and to the pyramid.

In the latter case, Isaiah now had a very clear idea of what had happened to Kanubai, and had no need to travel south to investigate what had happened to the pyramid.

It was coming north with supernatural strides, coming to talk to him.

Isaiah could not have moved in any case. Shortly after he handed the *Book of the Soulenai* back to Hereward, Skraelings had begun to congregate nearby.

Not close, perhaps fifty paces away, but within hours thousands upon thousands of the wraiths had encircled them. Still, silent, hunched on the ground staring with their great silvered orbs hanging from their dog faces.

They allowed Isaiah and Hereward to visit the riverboat on two occasions to retrieve some supplies, but would not allow them to move any greater distance from their small camp by the side of the glassed river.

Isaiah knew their purpose was to keep him there for the One's visit.

The One. The physical manifestation of mathematical perfection, as once worshipped by the Magi?

The wait was troublesome, not merely because Isaiah was highly wary of any confrontation between himself and the One—did it want to negotiate with him or destroy him?—but also because of Hereward.

Isaiah did not like her very much, and she, so far as he understood, loathed him. She also perplexed him, for he did not know how to treat her. His life as a Tyrant had been spent dealing with generals and soldiers, with nobles, with legends and heroes. The slaves and servants at his palace of Aqhat had been all but invisible to him. Isaiah had dealt with his palace chamberlain—he knew the man's name, and he knew some of the man's life beyond his role as chamberlain—but as for the others who served him, and who slipped in and out of the shadows of the palace . . . he had no idea.

He'd recognized Hereward's face when first he'd seen her, so Isaiah *knew* he'd seen her about the palace—she'd very likely served both him and Ishbel within his private chambers—but she'd made no impression.

Kitchen steward?

He stretched the muscles in his back, then decided to sit down, and perhaps engage the woman in some conversation.

Anything to relieve the tension of waiting for the One.

"You worked directly under the palace chamberlain?" Isaiah said, trying to keep his mild dislike for the woman out of his voice.

Hereward, who had been looking at the book in her lap, now raised her gaze to his. "Yes. I reported to him. I organized all the meals in the palace, from what appeared on your breakfast platter to what the slaves scavenged in the stables, and supervised the kitchens."

"An important role then. I must thank you."

"If you must. I care not."

Isaiah sighed. "Hereward. I can apologize again if you like. I am sorry that—"

"Oh for gods' sakes, Isaiah. You're just uncomfortable talking to someone who is so far beneath you. Leave it."

Isaiah was sorely tempted to "just leave it," but Hereward was by now becoming a serious irritation.

"Not everyone has time to take every slave under their wing and offer them endless kindness and compassion, Hereward."

"I was *not* a slave!"

"My mistake." No mistake at all. If she'd held such an important role within the palace then she could never have been a slave, but, as irritated and apprehensive as he was, Isaiah couldn't resist taking the time to needle her.

They sat silently for some minutes, each careful not to look at the other, before Hereward finally spoke.

"What is happening, Isaiah? Our world is destroyed—do you not owe me some explanation?"

"Ancient demons and gods are risen, Hereward. I'm sorry, it is probably too much for you to take in, so I'll—"

"Oh, you are a true bastard, aren't you! Everyone not of your own nobility is a dimwitted ass whom you can safely either ignore or pity. None of you care one jot for anyone beneath you!"

"That's not true, Hereward. We—"

"Don't lie to me. Tell me, did Ezekiel take his family north with him? With your invasion?"

Isaiah was disorientated by the sudden question. "Ezekiel? Ah . . . yes, his three sons were with the invasion and I believe his wife and daughters traveled with the convoy as well."

"Not all his daughters, Isaiah."

"Sorry?"

"I am Ezekiel's daughter, got on a slave one drunken night . . . and left to die while those born of a noble mother were taken north to revel in the glories and riches of victorious invasion."

"By the gods, your well of bitterness is bottomless!"

Hereward's jaw clenched and she looked away. "All I want to do is get away from you," she said. "All I want is to get to some kind of safety, and live some kind of life. If I can't have that, then all I want is to die. Damn it. *Damn* it! Take this book, Isaiah, and do with it what you want! Just let me go."

She got to her feet and threw the book at Isaiah, who caught it awkwardly. "Let me go," she said again.

"It is not I keeping you here, Hereward."

Hereward stared about at the distant circle of Skraelings. Eventually she lowered her face into her hands and turned her back to Isaiah.

He sighed, and looked down the river.

CHAPTER TWENTY-THREE

On the Road to Serpent's Nest

My lord, Commander Insharah wishes to speak with you."
Maximilian paused with the razor halfway down his cheek, looking up at Doyle.

The man had a somewhat cynical smile on his face.

"Send him in, Doyle. Thank you."

As soon as Doyle had turned away, Maximilian looked back to the mirror, staring at his reflection.

He was amazed Insharah had stayed as long as he had.

Insharah ducked inside the tent, and Maximilian resumed his careful
shaving. "Yes?"

"My lord," Insharah began, then stopped.

"Sit down, Insharah. There is no need to—"

"I would prefer to remain standing, my lord."

Maximilian gave a slight shrug.

"I have been speaking with some of the men," Insharah said. "There is
trouble."

"There is always trouble," said Maximilian, putting the razor down and
wiping his face clean of soap with a towel. "Define this particular trouble, if
you please."

Insharah took a deep breath. "Many of the men are going to desert tonight, my lord. Tens of thousands, but there may well be more."

Maximilian quirked an eyebrow at him, but did not speak.

"They are so worried about their families," said Insharah. "And about what is happening back in Isembaard. We—"

"I know, Insharah," Maximilian said.

"My lord," Insharah said, "many of the men, myself included, have been having nightmares. Dreams that are not true dreams, showing us our families in terrible plight—"

"They are dreams sent by a witch," Maximilian said.

"They are reflections of our troubled consciences," said Insharah.

"You want to join those leaving," Maximilian said.

Insharah hesitated, then gave a terse nod. "I have a wife and children in Isembaard. At Aqhat." Again he paused. "Not everyone wants to leave, my lord," Insharah said. "Many will stay, and follow you to Elcho Falling."

"Really? *How* many?"

"Perhaps ten thousand," Insharah said, very quietly.

"Out of what? A quarter of a million?"

"I am sorry, my lord. I don't know what I can say to—"

"You don't need to make me feel better, Insharah." Maximilian paused, thinking, the fingers of one hand tapping on the top of his shaving table. "Insharah, move among the army and tell the men that whoever wants to is free to leave to follow his conscience. They can take what stores they need— I ask only that you leave enough stores and spare horses for myself and my party, my Emerald Guard, and whoever decides to remain with me. I ask also that you respect the land and the peoples you move through once you do leave. The Outlanders have done you no wrong, and I would not have you wrong them."

"You are just going to let us go?" said Insharah. "Just like that?"

"Yes, I am."

"Maximilian's forces abandon him," Ravenna said. "What is he doing, to so let them go?"

She sat with Lister and Vorstus in the tent they used. It was small, but it had a good brazier, and they all sat about it, staring into its warmth.

"Ishbel is the canker," Ravenna said.

Lister tipped his head as if agreeing, but he wasn't ready to heap all the blame on Ishbel's head. He thought Maximilian deserved to shoulder a fair weight of it, too.

What was the man doing *to allow the majority of his army to defect? Did he not know that sooner or later an army of horror was going to seethe up from the south?*

"What should we do?" Ravenna said.

"Watch," said Lister, "and wait. Yes, yes, I know you want to act, but I would prefer to hear news of Isaiah and what awaits us from the south first."

Ravenna looked between Vorstus and Lister. "How much faith do you have remaining in Maximilian?"

"Not a great deal," Vorstus said. "We think that Ishbel may have been a vast error on our part."

Then, as one, both Lister and Vorstus looked at Ravenna.

CHAPTER TWENTY-FOUR

Isembaard

Isaiah sat and watched Hereward sleeping. She was deeply asleep, her entire body relaxed, her mouth slightly open, her face so tranquil Isaiah thought it almost looked pretty.

The book lay at her side.

Isaiah looked at it for a very long time before he leaned over and gently slid it away from her.

He more than thought Hereward would have sprung awake as he took the book, but she slept on, and Isaiah settled himself with the book in his lap.

They'd lit a small fire earlier, and it still flickered enough that he could read the list of chapters.

They were all the same.

What the river god needed to do to save the land.

Isaiah sat with his eyes on the book for some time, then he raised his face to look around.

There must be, he thought, a hundred thousand Skraelings encircling them now. They were hunkered down on the ground, their silvery eyes noting his and Hereward's every movement, their tongues lolling from their mouths. From time to time one of them would whisper, or whine, but they made no move in their direction.

Isaiah looked to the south. He could feel the One moving closer. He would arrive within the day, and Isaiah felt his stomach turn over with the nausea of fear.

What did the One want? To kill him? To chat?

Even if Isaiah had wanted to, there was no escape.

He returned his attention to the book, and turned the page to the first (and only) story: *What the river god needed to do to save the land.*

It was not very long, and Isaiah read it in only a few minutes.

He closed the book, his face expressionless, his thoughts in turmoil.

Finally, after almost an hour of sitting completely still, he slid a finger under the cover, opening a very slight gap into the pages, then he whispered a phrase in a strange guttural language.

For a moment, nothing. Then there was a movement among the black braids that hung about his shoulders, and a small green frog crept down his arm, hesitated on his hand, then slipped inside the book.

Another one followed, then another, and soon score after score of frogs were emerging from Isaiah's braids and moving over his shoulder and down his arm to vanish into the book.

Eventually, it was done. Isaiah closed the book and slid it back close to Hereward.

It was very dark by now, and he did not think that the Skraelings had seen the frogs crawling over his arm and hand into the book.

He hoped not.

Isaiah and Hereward slept.

There was a movement at the edge of the river. A rat, unbelievably, crawled out from the glass river as if it had been mere water. He crept close to the sleeping couple, his eyes keeping careful watch on the encircling hordes of Skraelings, even though he was certain they could not see nor otherwise perceive him.

The rat did not pause to study either Isaiah or Hereward. Instead he moved straight to the *Book of the Soulenai.* The rat paused as he reached the book, then reached out a forefoot and touched the cover gently.

A moment passed, then the rat edged up the cover and, with a wriggle, slipped inside the book.

The cover of the book sank back down flat, and all was still.

To the south the One strode out, drawing closer to Isaiah and Hereward.

His face was set directly north, but his thoughts were elsewhere—to the northeast, where he could sense the Lealfast aiding Isembaardians to flee through the Salamaan Pass.

Bingaleal. It was Bingaleal who led the Lealfast contingent at the Salamaan Pass.

Good. The One knew that Bingaleal was the most committed to the idea of abandoning the Lealfast's loyalty to the Lord of Elcho Falling. Whatever Bingaleal decided, the rest of the Lealfast would accept, sooner or later.

Once he'd had his fun with Isaiah, then Bingaleal awaited and the trap for Maximilian Persimius could be set.

How long did the last of the Persimius mages have to live? A few weeks at the most.

And then . . . then everything on this land—every animal, every flower, every soul—could be absorbed into Infinity.

The One began to sing, his rich voice echoing over the landscape, and he sang of the nightmare of Infinity.

[Part Three]

CHAPTER ONE

The Central Outlands

D o you know what I believe, Axis?" Georgdi said as they rode their horses eastward in an easy loose-reined amble. "I think you are enjoying this freedom so much that you are secretly pleased the Lealfast haven't spotted so much as a general's whisker in the days since we've left Maximilian."

Axis grinned. "As are you, Georgdi. You Outlanders are never happier than when roaming your country's vast plains with no destination in sight."

"It would be better," said Georgdi, "if there were no Isembaardians in sight, either."

He suddenly realized what he'd said, and looked at their companion in some consternation. "Present company excepted, of course, Zeboath."

"No offense taken," said Zeboath. The young physician had been traveling with the Isembaardian army ever since it had left Sakkuth so many months previously. He'd not had much to do, apart from splint the occasional broken bone from campfire brawls, and now reveled in the chance to travel in a much smaller unit with Axis—as once they had when they'd escorted Ishbel from the FarReach Mountains down to Aqhat.

"It cannot be easy for you," Zeboath continued, "to see such vast numbers of foreigners suddenly move through your land."

"I don't have much say in the matter," Georgdi said.

The conversation lagged, and the three men rode in silence for a while. Their men rode in a loose column behind them, relaxing in the late winter sunshine.

The Lealfast had seen nothing of the generals in the days since Axis had left the main army. There had been a single incident a few days previously, one of the Lealfast being slightly injured by a collision with a bird while investigating a small column of Isembaardian soldiers, but no sign of the generals.

Well, no physical sign, but there were signs that they were active. The Lealfast had reported to Axis that troops were massing near Margalit, which was almost certainly due to one or more of the generals' influence. Axis had sent word back to Maximilian, but until he could see for himself—and he was at least a week away from the larger troop congregations—he wanted to take no action.

Axis was also having some doubt about the Lealfast.

He'd had gnawing doubts ever since Eleanon and Inardle had shown him the origin of their people, mainly centered about the *why* of the Lealfast's apparent devotion to Maximilian. Added to these doubts were now grave reservations about their fighting ability. He'd tried to talk to Eleanon about the Lealfast's experience, with no luck. He'd tried to draw out the Lealfast man on tactics.

With no luck.

Whatever Axis tried to discuss, Eleanon evaded. Axis thought that evasion was what the man was best at.

Axis felt as if his hands were tied. If he pushed, he was afraid he might alienate the prickly Lealfast so greatly that they would abandon Maximilian altogether, and Axis was not sure Maximilian could afford to lose them.

Well, at least he was riding with them now, if a day or two behind their forward units.

At least he was closer, if something should go awry.

Eleanon drifted with his fighters, looking for Armat, although in truth his heart was not in the search. As each day, almost each hour, passed, Eleanon grew more resentful at Axis' attitude, even though it was little more than he had expected from the StarMan. Axis kept probing and jibing, and Eleanon just withdrew deeper into his defensive arrogance.

He communicated a little with Bingaleal. As yet Bingaleal had heard nothing from the One, but he had met some of the roving parties of Skraelings who told him that the One was a great god who thought the Skraelings his true servants and would reward them, once he had consolidated his power over all lands, by making them his favored counselors. Naturally riches and much free meat also featured in the Skraelings' tales of just how the One would eventually reward them.

It irritated Eleanon that the Skraelings had such contact with the One and the Lealfast as yet did not. The dark spire was too dangerous to use while Axis watched Eleanon so closely and while the marsh witch Ravenna was out scrying for power to fuel her own ambitions.

The One surely understood that the Skraelings were vile creatures, useful only for the mass terror they could generate, while the Lealfast could be much better partners in the One's quest for power.

Surely.

Eleanon wished he were in Isembaard. This entire journey north to Maximilian Persimius had been all but useless. Maximilian was weak and could not give the Lealfast what they needed.

He should be south.

South was almost certainly where lay the Lealfast's future.

CHAPTER TWO

Isembaard, and the Outlands

"I saiah?"

He woke, springing almost instantly into full wakefulness. How had he slept so long? It was midmorning already.

"What is it?" he asked.

"The Skraelings aren't looking at us anymore."

He blinked at her, not understanding, then looked at the Skraelings.

They were all staring south.

"*Shetzah!*" Isaiah muttered.

"What is it?"

"The One comes. The pyramid made . . . well, made of whatever flesh it is, I suppose. Hereward, I don't know what will happen. I will do my best for you."

Hereward's eyes welled with tears, surprising Isaiah.

He hesitated, then rested a hand on her shoulder, only to have her shrug it off.

"I just want to get *out* of here, Isaiah. I just want . . ."

She didn't finish, but she didn't need to.

I just want to live.

"I will do my best for you," Isaiah repeated, wishing he had something better to say.

Hereward wiped her eyes, then nodded at the Skraelings. "Look."

The Skraeling throng was slowly shuffling apart by the glassed river, opening up an avenue to the south.

Isaiah glanced at the book—it was lying by Hereward's feet—then looked down the newly formed avenue.

Something was coming.

It was still a few hundred paces away, but Isaiah could just make it out.

A man-shaped figure, but one formed by what appeared to be gleaming blue-green glass.

Hereward took a step closer to Isaiah, and he thought she must truly be scared to want to stand so close.

Strangely, given their mutual dislike, he was very glad of her presence. Hereward would be useless in any confrontation between the One and himself, but at least she was *there*, providing the comfort of another warm, living person.

The Skraelings had begun to whisper, a low, hissing, undulating mumble of adulation.

A shiver ran down Isaiah's spine.

The One drew closer, and Isaiah could make out its features. It had assumed the form of a handsome man with a strong nose and piercing eyes, and Isaiah recognized its features instantly.

The pyramid had taken the physical aspect of Boaz, the Magus who had once thought to destroy it.

Boaz, Maximilian's kinsman and Ishbel's ancestor.

Then Isaiah's eyes were caught by something trailing a pace or two behind the One, and his eyes widened in shock.

It was a small, red kitten, gamboling along as if it didn't have a care in the world.

Feed the pretty kitten, the *Book of the Soulenai* had said.

The kitten was so incongruous, and so bizarre, that Isaiah had difficulty dragging his eyes away from it. It darted this way and that, enjoying itself hugely, chasing an insect here, an airborne speck of dust there.

Then it suddenly realized its master had walked too far ahead, and it sped forward, batting at the One's ankles with its paws.

Isaiah managed to drag his eyes back to the One, who was ignoring the kitten. He was very close now, and Isaiah could see the glow of the pulsating golden pyramid within the creature's translucent breast: *he had the Infinity Chamber for a heart.*

"Well met, Isaiah," said the One, coming to a halt a few paces away. His voice was strong and rich, surprising Isaiah, who had expected something uglier.

Instead, his voice was almost hypnotic in its beauty.

Hereward had by now crept so close to Isaiah that she was pressed against his side, and he put an arm about her shoulders.

Isaiah doubted very much that either of them were going to get out of this alive.

"I'm not going to kill you," said the One. "Not if you do as I wish. Shall we sit?"

"I know who and what you are," the One said to Isaiah, once they sat in an awkward little circle on the riverbank.

The kitten was playing a few paces distant, just at the corner of Isaiah's vision, and he found it irritatingly distracting.

He wondered what its purpose was.

"Water or river god, tyrant, meddler, call yourself what you will," the One said. "It is of no matter to me. All I need from you is to deliver a message for me."

A message. Not death, then.

"And you?" said Isaiah. "What should I call you? Kanubai?"

"I am not Kanubai, as well you know," said the One. "Kanubai is dead. Used and useful, but very dead. Now *I* walk. I am the One. I have no name save for the indivisible.

"Now," the One continued, not giving Isaiah a chance to respond, "you will deliver a message to Maximilian Persimius."

"As you will," said Isaiah. "A message is easy enough. But will you not tell me of your purpose? Why it is that you have chosen to wake from your pyramid and walk? Why you have chosen to murder this land and river?"

The One smiled. His teeth were completely translucent, and Isaiah could see the green swell of the creature's tongue through them. "*My* land and river now. No longer yours, in any measure. And how have I murdered it? I have merely turned it to my own will."

The One's tone changed as he spoke, becoming infinitely more threatening, and so Isaiah inclined his head, deciding to deflect the creature's anger. "As you will. Will you tell us the message you wish Hereward and myself to deliver to Maximilian?"

"*You* are going to deliver the message to Maximilian Persimius for me, Isaiah. Hereward's fate is not yours to decide."

Isaiah saw Hereward turn her head and stare at him, terrified, and he hoped she would keep silent.

Hereward said nothing. She dropped her eyes to her hands clasped in her lap, and Isaiah now found himself irritated that she *had* kept her silence.

"Maximilian and Ishbel," said the One, "are committed to my destruction. It is in their blood. So I need you to deliver to them this message."

The One took a deep breath, and Isaiah found himself fascinated by the movement of the glass of his chest. It looked very pliable, almost soft, and Isaiah wondered if it was warm to the touch.

"Maximilian Persimius," said the One, "and Ishbel Brunelle Persimius are to bring to me, at Sakkuth—"

Isaiah kept his face impassive, but the choice of meeting place puzzled him. Sakkuth?

"—three objects. They are to bring the Weeper. They are to bring to me the Goblet of the Frogs. And they are to bring to me the crown of Elcho Falling."

"Or...?" Isaiah said.

The One smiled, very tight, very cold, and there was a brief gleam in his black eyes. "Ah, in the 'or' lies the rub, does it not?"

Bingaleal stood on the plains between Hairekeep and the entrance to the Salamaan Pass. Thousands upon thousands of Isembaardians continued to stream into the Pass, hoping to escape from the destruction of their homeland. Some of his companions had reported to Bingaleal earlier in the day that there was a massive wave of Skraelings sweeping through Sakkuth. Soon they would be moving northeast toward the Salamaan Pass.

The reports had also said that there was not much left of Sakkuth.

The Isembaardians had generally accepted the Lealfast's attempts to aid them. The Lealfast were, after all, better than what lay behind them. Most of the refugees were completely benumbed. All they could think of was that they needed to get beyond the FarReach Mountains into safety.

Bingaleal did not know how "safe" the Outlands would prove. He was not sure if the Skraelings would stop at the Salamaan Pass, or if they'd just continue to surge through.

And if they did? What then?

In the end, Bingaleal did not care overmuch. What he was truly interested in lay much further south.

All he wanted was the chance to explore it. He wondered, not for the first time, if he should abandon the Isembaardians and fly down to DarkGlass Mountain.

But every time this thought crossed his mind, something stopped him. Some deep instinct told him that flying south to the pyramid was a useless exercise.

It was coming north to meet him.

Far to the north, in the Central Outlands, Bingaleal's brother, Eleanon, led a large sortie of Lealfast toward a column of soldiers some five thousand strong marching northwestward.

The Isembaardian column was led by the renegade general Armat, in full view of the forward-flying Lealfast scouts.

"If Maximilian and Ishbel do not bring me these objects," said the One, "I will invade their lands with such horror that—"

"They will resist you," said Isaiah.

"Ah, I was so afraid that you would say that," the One said. "It might get very messy, yes?"

Again, that frightful, cold smile and the brief gleam in his obsidian eyes.

"They will not refuse," said the One. "I am, Isaiah, going to build a curse on their future. It is not a 'might be' curse, it is a reality. The instant I build it, their future has altered. Watch, Isaiah, and see what Infinity can do when it is roused."

The One lifted a hand. "Watch," he said, "the power of the One."

"Armat!" the scout reported back to Eleanon. "*Armat!*"

"Where?" Eleanon said. He, and the other Lealfast with him, were traveling on the air, almost invisible.

"A half hour's flight to the east," said the scout. "He's leading a column of some five thousand men to the northwest, perhaps to try to intercept Maximilian's force."

"Perhaps." Eleanon wondered why Armat had chosen to show his hand now.

"I'll fly on to the StarMan," the scout said, "and tell him what we've seen."

"No," said Eleanon. "Wait."

He stopped, thinking. Was it a trap on Armat's part? And if it was, what should he do? If he was sensible, Eleanon should tell the scouts to keep an eye on the column while he relayed the intelligence to Axis.

If he was sensible . . .

But "being sensible" stuck in Eleanon's craw. Axis didn't think much of him, and neither did Maximilian, who, Eleanon was only too well aware, had sent Axis on this mission to test the Lealfast.

Why *not* do what Axis and Maximilian assumed he would? Something foolish. It was what Bingaleal had counseled—deceive Maximilian and Axis into thinking that the Lealfast truly were nothing but arrogant foolishness. This would be the perfect opportunity, but, oh, how it irritated Eleanon that for the moment Maximilian and Axis should have their egotistical suspicions confirmed.

Still . . . it would position the Lealfast splendidly for the future.

Eleanon's thoughts churned; he was aware that the scout waited impatiently. *If* he did what Maximilian and Axis expected, then he would have the freedom to journey south without raising their suspicions *and* confirm in their minds that the Lealfast were useless as fighters—but, oh, the price . . .

"Eleanon? Should I fly on to Axis StarMan?"

"We can handle this," Eleanon said, the bottom of his stomach almost falling out of his belly as he made his decision. "We are tens of thousand strong, and far superior to five thousand Isembaardian soldiers. We have the advantage of near invisibility and of height. They'll never know what hit them. We'll capture Armat, *then* tell the StarMan."

The scout regarded Eleanon for a brief moment, then nodded his head. "As you will."

"Then lead on. Show us this general."

This decision would kill hundreds of Lealfast, perhaps thousands, but Eleanon justified it to himself on the grounds that it would position the Lealfast the better to ultimately betray Elcho Falling. He also promised himself that he would personally murder Axis for what this day would bring.

Today's blood would be Axis' fault, not Eleanon's, and Axis would one day pay for it.

The One traced his finger through the air, green trails of light following in its wake. Within moments he had drawn a perfect outline of a pyramid that stood about the third of the height of a man. Once it was completed, he laid his hands upon the pyramid, drew it before his face, and closed his eyes.

Light flared briefly, then the One guided the pyramid down to the ground in the center of their circle. It was now clothed in blue-green glass, capped with gold—a perfect representation of DarkGlass Mountain.

"Rather more beautiful than the spires you used to contact your friend Lister, eh?" said the One.

Isaiah was feeling progressively more uneasy. He glanced at Hereward. Her face was white and drawn, and Isaiah wondered if his own looked much better.

The One was toying with them, and Isaiah sensed that very soon the One would grow tired of the game and move straight into horrifying practicalities.

"There is no longer a question of what will happen *if* Maximilian and Ishbel refuse to bring me the objects I desire," the One said. "The curse I am about to build shall be a reality. It *will* happen. The only question is whether or not I can be persuaded to destroy the curse before it does too much damage. But see, I have not yet finished."

His voice strengthened, became harsh and sharp, like the sound of the cold wind whistling over the striking sword.

"Do you feel the power I now wield, Isaiah? Can you recognize it?"

Isaiah jerked his head in assent, so overwhelmed by the power that now throbbed about the circle that he dared not speak.

"Name it!" hissed the One.

"The..." Isaiah swallowed and tried again. "It is a power made of the blood of Maximilian and Ishbel's daughter, of the blood of her death, and of the power of Infinity, which you touch."

"Very good, Isaiah. I needed you to recognize the power I use so that you can later vouch for the veracity of this curse."

The One lifted his hands and ran them lightly down two sides of the pyramid, from cap to base.

Isaiah and Hereward both gasped. As the One's hands traveled down the glass, so it became translucent and they could see within.

A man and a woman lay on a great bed. They were naked.

"Maximilian," said the One, looking at Isaiah. "And Ishbel. Yes?"

"Yes," Isaiah said reluctantly.

The One waved a hand at the pyramid and what it contained. "This *will* be, Isaiah. Understand that."

"Maxel and Ishbel no longer—"

"This will be, Isaiah! *Understand that!*"

Isaiah gave a jerk of his head.

"Good. Then witness herewith my curse on Ishbel," said the One. "When Maximilian Persimius succumbs to her blandishments and beauty and once more slides the ring of the Queen of Elcho Falling on her finger, and slides his own flesh into her body, then so shall sorrow and despair envelop Elcho Falling and all it touches."

The One's voice became increasingly stronger and harsher as he spoke, his words falling over themselves, and Isaiah could *feel* the One's power binding the curse to Ishbel.

Within the pyramid, Maximilian slid the ring onto Ishbel's outstretched finger, and then rose over her body.

"When Maximilian slides that ring on her finger," the One continued, "and once he bears her down to his bed, then so shall he marry the One to Elcho Falling. I shall become its lord, and when I arrive at the gates of Elcho Falling, so shall Ishbel crawl forth and surrender to me all the power and might of the citadel of Elcho Falling."

Ishbel cried out as Maximilian entered her, and clung to his shoulders.

She rolled her head to one side on the pillow, and for an instant her eyes met those of Isaiah's.

"And so shall Ishbel be sorrow's midwife," Isaiah murmured, almost unaware he spoke aloud. "As Ravenna foretold."

The One suppressed a smile. *Ravenna. She had been so useful.* "Do you recognize the power with which I have made this curse, Isaiah?"

"Yes."

"Do you recognize its reality?"

"Yes."

"Shall I make a fine Lord of Elcho Falling, do you think?"

Isaiah could not answer.

"Do you think I shall make a fine Lord of—"

"Yes. Yes!"

"Maximilian will succumb to Ishbel's beauty," the One said, his voice almost soft now. "You know this. I can see it in your eyes. And when he does . . ."

The One waved his hand and the pyramid once more turned green, hiding the sight of Maximilian and Ishbel's writhing bodies.

"But," the One's tone relaxed almost into geniality, "the curse can be destroyed. That is possible. All Maximilian and Ishbel need to do is to bring me the—"

"You will kill them," Isaiah said.

"Of course I will, but Elcho Falling shall remain inviolate. If they bring to me those three objects, then, yes, they die, as they would have me die, but I shall turn my back on Elcho Falling and return to DarkGlass Mountain. If they deliver to me their lives, and those objects which are most precious to them, then Elcho Falling and all the peoples of the northern kingdoms shall live. If they do not bring those objects to me, and if they try to save their own lives, then the curse remains, and all shall fail and fall into sorrow and ruin."

Again that casual hand wave over the pyramid, and within the space of a breath it vanished.

"I want you," said the One, "to take my message back to Maximilian and Ishbel. They are already doomed, but I will spare Elcho Falling and the lands and peoples north of the FarReach Mountains if they bring to me at Sakkuth that which I desire."

The One looked at Isaiah's face, and he very slowly smiled. "Ah, I can see your thoughts mirrored all over your desperate face, Isaiah. You think you can get to Maximilian and warn him in time, don't you? Warn him before he condemns Elcho Falling to my rule? But I am afraid, Isaiah, there is one other little disaster I need to tell you about."

Eleanon circled high above the column of slow-marching men. Armat was clearly visible, riding a horse at their head.

There was a horde of Lealfast in the sky, invisible save for that curious grayness they lent to the air. The men below had made no indication they realized the presence above them.

It was going to be a nightmare, but it was a nightmare that would free the Lealfast into their destiny.

Eleanon allowed himself a moment of hesitation to reflect on his decision, then, mind settled, he gave the order to attack.

CHAPTER THREE

Isembaard, and the Outlands

You're a powerful man, Isaiah," said the One. "A god. A being many thousands of years old." He was relaxed, almost happy. It was time to have his fun with Isaiah.

From the corner of his eye Isaiah saw Hereward blink out of her fugue of shock at that piece of information.

"How would you feel," continued the One, "if you lost that power, and became as any ordinary mortal? If you became as . . . Hereward is."

"The only means to remove my power is to kill me," Isaiah said.

"Not necessarily," said the One. "You can also relinquish that power of your own free will. That won't kill you." He paused. "Well, not physically."

"Destroy that curse," said Isaiah, "and I *will* agree to give up my power."

"I was thinking of something a little more challenging for you."

The One raised his finger, and Isaiah tensed, thinking he was going to draw another curse.

But at the One's signal there was a movement, and two Skraelings appeared out of nowhere behind Hereward. Isaiah started to rise, but found himself suddenly in the grip of two more Skraelings who had appeared behind him.

"You may not interfere," said the One.

Hereward was staring at Isaiah; she was hyperventilating, terrified. Each of the Skraelings had one clawed hand on a shoulder, the other gripping one of her arms.

She struggled, but the Skraelings held Hereward so tight she had no hope of escape.

Now the One nodded at one of the Skraelings, and it shifted its grip on her shoulder a little so that one taloned finger slid up her collarbone.

Then, without any warning, it sunk the talon deep into her neck so that blood spurted forth and flowed down her neck.

"Keep your power and she dies," said the One to Isaiah. "Relinquish your power and she lives."

Isaiah struggled against the two Skraelings who held him. He was a powerful man, but the Skraelings held him easily.

Hereward's chest and belly were now soaked in blood. She stared pleadingly at Isaiah, who still struggled futilely.

There were many people for whom Isaiah would not have hesitated.

Axis.

Maximilian.

Ishbel.

But Hereward? She was but just one woman, when already so many had died.

A kitchen steward.

A servant.

And Isaiah would need his power to travel quickly on his way back to Maximilian. Or to contact him, through power. To let him know that whatever else, a sexual or marital reconciliation with Ishbel was not a good idea . . . not in the current circumstances.

And it was going to happen, Isaiah knew that. Ishbel and Maximilian might currently be estranged, but Isaiah knew that it was only a matter of time before the inevitable occurred.

Gods, gods, if he had to walk north, then it might take him months.

"Hereward . . ." Isaiah said.

"Please," she whispered. The Skraeling's claw had now sunk deep into her neck and blood was gurgling out.

Isaiah could literally hear it pumping from her body.

"Not enough to kill her," said the One. "Not quite, not yet, but if you hesitate much longer, Isaiah, she is going to be so weakened she will be a serious hindrance to you on your way north to Maximilian and Ishbel."

No, thought Isaiah.

"Her life for your power," said the One. "Will you give it, Isaiah? Will you become a mere mortal, just for Hereward's pathetic little life?"

No, thought Isaiah.

"Will you agree to relinquish all your god abilities, Isaiah, for the life of a servant?"

No, thought Isaiah.

"Yes," he said.

The One laughed, and clapped his hands. "Yes!" he said, and suddenly a vast emptiness consumed Isaiah as all of his power drained away.

Gone.

"Good," said the One, and he waved back the Skraelings.

The instant Isaiah felt himself free, he sprang across to Hereward and clamped a hand down hard on her neck. Her blood was warm and thick, and Isaiah could feel the blood vessel pumping under his hand, but at least the flow of blood had stemmed.

"Feed the pretty kitty," said the One, and he reached over, scooped a finger through the coagulating blood on Hereward's breast, and held the finger out for the kitten to lick.

Everything went bad from the moment the first Lealfast arrow sped down from the sky.

Firstly, Armat completely disappeared. One heartbeat he was there, the next he was gone.

Secondly, the column of Isembaardian soldiers, apparently relaxed, unaware, and vulnerable, instantly swung large oblong shields from their backs and either raised them above their heads or to one side. Within moments each unit of soldiers was encased within the protection of their shields, which formed both a roof and walls about them.

The Lealfast arrows bounced away harmlessly.

Then a third and far more deadly surprise hit the Lealfast.

Arrows. Tens of thousands of them, fired from bowmen hidden in the rocks at the sides of the gully.

The entire force became visible as Lealfast started to fall from the sky.

Eleanon made certain he received at least one arrow—to a limb where a wound was not critical—then retreated, sick to his stomach at the slaughter.

It was for the best of the Lealfast Nation, he said to himself. *For the best.*

* * *

"I will take the book," the One said. "It belongs to me."

He rose, tucking the *Book of the Soulenai* under one arm, and regarded Isaiah and Hereward.

"I wish you joy in your journey," the One said. "Please don't forget the message."

He took a step away, then stopped and looked back. "Your journey north will be as uneventful as I can make it. The Skraelings will not bother you, but neither will you receive much aid. At least not while you are in Isembaard."

Again he paused. "Enjoy your mortality, Isaiah. I am sure Hereward is worth what you have lost."

And then he was gone, the red kitten gamboling along behind him.

Far to the north, Bingaleal had just lifted off in order to fly into the Salamaan Pass to check on the refugees streaming through, when he heard a shout from behind him.

It was one of the other Lealfast, flying toward Hairekeep.

Behind the Lealfast, perhaps three or four hundred paces distant, was a massive rolling wave of darkness that stretched hundreds of paces into the sky.

It moved at supernatural speed.

Then, twenty paces from Bingaleal, it stopped. One instant it was hurtling forward, the next instant it hung still in the air, towering above all before it.

Bingaleal took a deep breath. He gestured to the other Lealfast to stay where they were, then he flew forward slowly, dropping to the ground before the great wave as it hung in the air.

This close Bingaleal could see that it was made of tens of millions of tiny shards of black glass.

He stood watching.

Then, after a time, Bingaleal walked forward and stepped into the cloud.

"Isaiah!" Lister jerked his horse to a halt, not caring that Vorstus, and every soldier in the vicinity, was staring at him.

"Wait here," Lister snapped to Vorstus, then kicked his horse into a gallop to catch up with Maximilian near the head of the convoy.

Maximilian had already pulled his horse to one side, waiting for Lister. "You felt it," he said, as Lister pulled up.

"Isaiah is dead," Lister said.

"It might be that—"

"Isaiah is dead."

Maximilian lapsed into silence. His connection with both Isaiah and Lister was a deep, semiconscious thing. He could feel their presence, their life force, but little else about them.

Now his sense of Isaiah was gone. It had abruptly winked out of existence a few minutes ago.

He looked at Lister. He had avoided the man as much as possible since he'd joined the convoy, disliking and distrusting him.

Lister didn't feel any better to him now, either.

If only it had been Lister he'd sent south, not Isaiah!

"We need to talk, Maximilian," Lister said.

"If we must," Maximilian said.

CHAPTER FOUR

The Central Outlands

The first Axis knew of the disaster was when Lealfast began to drop out of the sky about him. Hundreds of them, thousands, all wounded to some degree, and many suffering horrendous injuries.

"What the . . ." he began, unable for the moment to continue as first his, then Zeboath's, horse shied at the sudden rain of bodies about them.

"Georgdi," Axis snapped, bringing his horse back under control, "get the men into defensive formation. Stars knows what is following behind this lot. Zeboath—"

"I'm moving," Zeboath said, in the next moment shouting to his assistants to get out the medical packs.

Axis sat his horse for the next minute, just watching the Lealfast land.

How had so many been injured?

What had happened? Had they flown into a storm of arrows?

"Eleanon!" he shouted, then with his power: *Eleanon!*

"Here," came a voice behind him, and Axis wheeled his horse, cursing as it stumbled over a wounded Lealfast.

Eleanon was standing awkwardly, clutching at one arm, which had a broken-off arrow embedded in its bicep. Blood stained his tunic and one of his legs.

"Armat," he began, then wavered a little on his feet, pale and shocked.

Axis jumped down and took two huge strides to reach Eleanon and bury his fist in the front of the Lealfast's tunic.

"What the fuck has happened?"

"Armat..."

"Armat? *Armat?* What did you do, Eleanon? Line up your entire fighting force against a wall so he could request his men to shoot at their leisure? Oh for the stars' sakes, look there...and there...stars, the *injuries!* Eleanon, *what the fuck happened?*"

Eleanon didn't reply. His expression closed down, as if he were withdrawing deep inside himself, and Axis assumed it was a result of his combined shock and humiliation.

"Shit," Axis muttered, pushing Eleanon to one side as he strode into the mayhem. He bent down to a Lealfast man who looked merely exhausted rather than wounded. "What happened? For the stars' sakes, *will someone tell me what happened?*"

"We came upon Armat leading a column of a few thousand men westward from Margalit," the man said, his voice weary and utterly devoid of emotion. "We thought we had them. Eleanon ordered an attack—"

"Did he scout first? Check for archers?"

"We just didn't think," the man said. "We flew in a group, straight in, and—"

Axis muttered something so obscene that finally the Lealfast man showed some emotion.

"Our bowmen and women set their arrows to the Isembaardian soldiers," the man said. "We thought that we could—"

"Will you stop telling me what you thought you *could* do, and just tell me *what* happened?"

"As soon as the first of our arrows rained down, the Isembaardians formed a protective turtle with their shields. Our arrows bounced off harmlessly."

And who would have guessed that? Axis thought, growing angrier by the moment. He and Maximilian had wondered about the Lealfast's experience... but this! An Icarii child could have commanded better. "And?" he said.

"Then Isembaardian bowmen, thousands of them, stood from their hiding places behind rocks to either side of the gully—"

Axis rubbed at his eyes with one hand. Armat had set his trap well. Had he known the Lealfast to be so gullible? Had that been what the earlier incident had been about?

"We were all in a group," said the Lealfast. "Largely invisible, although our bowmen had to return to their visible state in order to fire."

As Bingaleal had to do in order to stage the assassination on Isaiah, Axis thought. *And Armat had been there to see it.*

"Tens of thousands of arrows rained into us, StarMan. We . . . we just couldn't escape."

"You panicked," Axis said.

The Lealfast hesitated. "Yes," he said finally, hanging his head so he didn't have to look at Axis.

"How many dead?" said Axis. "How many left behind?"

Another longer, more awful hesitation.

"Maybe five or six thousand dead," said the man. "Maybe even more. I know some fell from the skies, dead from their wounds, on the flight back here. How many left? I don't know."

"Oh stars," Axis said. He sighed, rested his hand for a moment on the man's shoulder, then went in search of Georgdi.

Armat walked slowly through the killing field, his eyes cold, but a small smile curving his thin mouth.

It had been so easy.

A slaughter.

Would that all battles were like this.

"What think you, my friend?" said the softest of voices to one side, and Armat glanced at Ravenna's glamour.

"Elcho Falling will be ours within a week, if this," he waved a hand contemptuously over the fly-riddled corpses, "is all Maximilian Persimius can throw at us."

"Most of the Isembaardian soldiers have left him," Ravenna said. "They are marching to join you. They cannot be more than a few days away. Maximilian has his Emerald Guard, perhaps some four thousand— although they are no match for you—and some nine or ten thousand Isembaardians, including Ezekiel, who chose to stay with him. There are some Icarii as well. Nothing much. Maximilian's force is utterly insignificant compared to what you command. Maximilian cannot stand against you, Armat."

"Will we get to Elcho Falling before him?"

"Probably not. He is far enough ahead of you to get there first."

"He has the lighter force to move, too," Armat said, with some grim humor. "Well, if he gets to that mountain first then he will have the advantage of a good defensive position."

"But you can still . . ."

"Oh yes. I can 'still.' If his magic isn't too powerful."

That last was a question.

"Maximilian is weak. Once the line of Elcho Falling was very strong, too strong for either you or me, or us combined. But Maximilian has lost most of the knowledge of Elcho Falling. He has relatively little power. And he has a pitiful force to protect him. Elcho Falling waits for us to take it."

"And his wife, Ishbel? And Isaiah?"

"Isaiah is gone. Dead, I believe. And Ishbel . . . Ishbel is fatally flawed. Once Maximilian is dead then she will fail. Besides, if I get the chance to kill her before I leave Maximilian's train then I shall."

Not so insignificant, then, Armat thought, if Ravenna felt a need to kill her. But then, maybe it was merely Ravenna's petty jealous heart.

"There is but a little tidying up for us to do, Armat," Ravenna's glamour continued, "and then the mountain and all its power is ours. Axis?"

"He is not far away, according to your report. We can reach him by dawn tomorrow. Then he, too, will be dead. I have little time for useless legends. Tell me, how much longer will you spend haunting Maximilian's pitiful train? How much longer before you join me in the flesh rather than in glamour?"

"Soon, Armat. Soon I will be with you."

It had been several hours since the Lealfast returned, and the scene continued to be disastrous: there was only Zeboath and several assistants to offer any skilled aid to the wounded, and there were thousands upon thousands of wounded. Eleanon had commanded a force of some twenty-five thousand and had, so far as Axis could see, led the entire lot into disaster. Many would die without help, but there was nothing Axis could do about that. Axis had spent some time searching for Inardle. No one knew where she was, and Axis could not stop a growing sense that she must be lying dead back in Armat's killing field.

At least he had caught up with Georgdi again.

"Armat will be coming after us," said Axis.

"I most certainly would," said Georgdi, looking at the sea of wounded

Lealfast with incredulity. "By the gods, I couldn't think of an easier target. He'll be here to finish this lot off within what . . . how far distant is he?"

"The Lealfast who have been coherent enough tell me less than a day's march."

"Shit," said Georgdi.

"I'm tempted to mount up, Georgdi, and just leave this lot to their damned fate. Maximilian surely has little need of such as these."

Georgdi grunted. "Give the order, StarMan, and I'll be right behind you."

Axis caught his gaze, and smiled a little. "The only thing stopping me is that I wouldn't want my legend tarnished by such a despicable action."

"That's a shame, StarMan. All you want to do is run away and your damned reputation keeps you here. I'd be fuming, if it was me."

Now both were grinning.

"I suppose we'd best think of something to do," said Axis.

"I suppose."

"Well . . ." Axis sighed, losing his humor. *What to do?* There were, at best approximation, some eighteen or nineteen thousand Lealfast stretched over the dusty plain. Those who weren't physically wounded, like the Lealfast man Axis had talked to, were so emotionally traumatized and physically exhausted by what had happened that they were of little use.

Of the wounded, Axis thought that there were at least five thousand who were now incapable of flight. That they'd reached this far was miracle enough.

He looked back at Georgdi, thinking. Georgdi had some three hundred Outlander soldiers with him and under Axis' overall command. Axis had never meant this to be much more than a fast-moving force meant to locate the generals. If he had discovered them, then he would have preferred to move in with a force of less than twenty men to try and take one or more of the generals—he certainly would have never had enough men to try and fight an all-out pitched battle with their army.

The rest of the Outlander force which had returned from the devastation of the Central Kingdoms had largely been disbanded throughout the Outlands. They were exhausted after their campaign and their horrific journey to escape the Skraelings.

"How soon could you remobilize an Outlander army, Georgdi?" Axis said.

"What? To fight Armat? I'd not be able to send messengers out, let alone—"

"No. Not to aid this lot. There is no time . . . but I have a feeling Maximilian is going to need you, Georgdi. At Elcho Falling. Listen, this is what I want you to do . . . what I *ask* you to do. Forget the Lealfast. You don't have enough men with you to do more than protect a small number of them, and that's fairly pointless. No use risking good fighters for . . ."

He didn't have to go on. *For such as these.*

"What do you propose?" Georgdi said.

"Mobilize as many of your men as you can and get them to Elcho Falling—Serpent's Nest. I don't trust the Isembaardians with Maximilian, and—"

"By the stars! What has happened here?"

Axis turned around. BroadWing EvenBeat had just landed a few paces away, and was looking at the chaos incredulously. BroadWing had been a senior member in Axis' Strike Force, the highly skilled fighting unit among the Icarii, and Axis could only imagine what he was now thinking.

No, he didn't need to imagine. BroadWing would be thinking much the same as Axis.

"Eleanon led his people into a slaughter," said Axis. "He was stupid and unthinking, and I am too angry at the moment to allow myself to speak with him. For the moment the details will need to wait, BroadWing. I am too heartsick to go into them. What are you doing here? Did Maximilian send you?"

BroadWing gave a nod. "And with news possibly even worse than this." BroadWing waved a hand about him. "Insharah has led the vast majority of the Isembaardian force away from Maximilian to join with Armat, and—"

"Well, well," Axis said softly. "Insharah. I would not have thought that of him."

"There is worse, Axis. Maximilian and Lister suspect that Isaiah is dead."

Axis could not speak. He stood there, staring at BroadWing, and it was as if the entire sorry mass of the Lealfast had vanished into insignificance. *Isaiah? Dead?*

"I'm sorry," BroadWing said.

"What . . . how . . . what do they know?" said Axis, and BroadWing knew he wasn't referring to the Isembaardian defection.

"Maximilian and Lister have some connection to him," said BroadWing. "They said there was something very, very wrong, and both mentioned death with fear in their eyes."

"Oh gods..." Axis said, half turning away. If Isaiah was dead it was a disaster for Maximilian, but all Axis could think of for the moment was his own sense of loss. Isaiah was—*had been*—a valued friend, and Axis knew it would take him time to come to terms with his grief.

"He may *not* be dead," said BroadWing.

Axis gave an uncaring shrug. Maximilian would not have sent this news if he'd thought there was any real chance of Isaiah's continuing life.

How had Ishbel taken this? She may not have loved Isaiah as she did Maximilian, but she *had* loved him, and would grieve deeply for the man.

"Axis," Georgdi said softly. "We have a hundred thousand men or so coming our way. We're sandwiched between them and Armat."

Axis pulled himself out of his reverie. "Insharah...I knew he was frustrated, but I had not thought he would go this far. Maximilian did, though."

"Maximilian said Insharah told him the men had been plagued with nightmares of the deaths of their families," BroadWing said. "I think the dreams pushed them into outright rebellion."

"Ravenna," Axis muttered.

"Probably," said BroadWing, "but Maximilian doesn't seem bothered. He gave them permission to leave and waved them good-bye with a cheery smile."

Axis finally managed a small smile. "Well, that's Maximilian. I doubt this has surprised, or worried, him overmuch."

He looked about, thinking, then spoke again. "All right, this is what we are going to do. Georgdi, as I said, I want you to take the men you have here with you and mobilize whatever else you can and ride for Serpent's Nest to meet Maximilian there. Get clear of the mess here. I am certain that Armat and the other generals...BroadWing, you have no news of Lamiah and Kezial?"

BroadWing shook his head.

"I am certain Armat will ride for Elcho Falling," said Axis. "He is in league with Ravenna, and she will want Elcho Falling. BroadWing, go back to Maximilian and tell him what has happened here. Tell him the Lealfast are as useless as a throng of blind virgins . . . and that 'blind virgins' more than adequately describes their fighting ability. Oh, stars . . . what am I going to do with them?"

Axis stopped, thinking a moment. "BroadWing, eventually I am going to hand the damned Lealfast over to you. I know you are reforming the Strike Force from the Icarii flying in every day from the west and the Lealfast need to get some training. But not just yet. I'm going to send them away to lick their wounds for a while. Currently they're too shocked to be useful—or to be amenable to any instruction."

"And you, Axis?" Georgdi said as BroadWing nodded. "Are you going to get clear of 'the mess here'?"

"Leave me several horses and some men. Ten, at most. I will wait here for a while, do what I can for the Lealfast, then I will ride for Maximilian."

"Axis?" said Georgdi.

"Yes?"

"Make sure you *do* ride for Maximilian, eh?"

Eleanon had faded away when Axis talked to the Lealfast man, and now he crouched beside Inardle, lying injured on the ground.

She had been hurt badly, but not fatally.

"What happened back there, Eleanon?" she hissed at him, one wing sprawled awkwardly behind her as she doubled over her bleeding belly.

"I did what I thought was best," Eleanon said. "Are you badly hurt?"

"Yes," she said, "but give me an hour and I can—"

"Don't heal yourself!" Eleanon hissed. Like himself and Bingaleal, Inardle was one of the more highly trained in the ancient arts of the Magi, although she'd never reach the heights and skills of her two brood brothers. She could heal herself fairly easily now that she was out of immediate danger and could concentrate.

But Eleanon did not want Inardle to heal herself.

"This is the perfect opportunity," he said, a hand resting firmly on Inardle's uninjured shoulder. *"This,"* he waved his other hand down her bloodied body, "will bring you to Axis' bed. Now, listen to me, and do what I say . . ."

Inardle's expression hardened as he spoke, but eventually she nodded reluctantly, and Eleanon once more vanished into the night.

CHAPTER FIVE

On the Road to Serpent's Nest

Ishbel, I am sorry, but I am afraid that Isaiah is dead."
Ishbel stared at Maximilian, unable to believe he had actually said those words.

Maximilian glanced at Lister, standing to one side, before looking back to Ishbel. "We are not completely certain, but we cannot think what else has happened."

"There is no contact," said Lister. "Before, he and I... there was always awareness of each other's presence. Now—nothing."

Ishbel tore her eyes away from Lister and stared across the grasslands. Some part of her shocked mind noted that the snow had by now almost melted, and that spring could not be far distant. There would be new growth soon, and the plains would be green again.

And Isaiah was dead and would never see the fresh growth.

"Ishbel?" Maximilian said.

"I felt nothing," Ishbel said. "Nothing. How could I have felt *nothing?*"

"Ishbel," Lister said, "you didn't have the bond with him that Maximilian and I—"

"You have no idea of the bond I had with him!" Ishbel said. "He was a better man than you, Lister. Why could it not have been *you* who died?"

"Ishbel—" Maximilian said.

"I loved him once," said Ishbel. "I can't believe... oh gods..."

"I'm sorry," Maximilian said, and Ishbel saw that, indeed, he was very sorry and sympathized with her. It comforted her that he understood, and that he wasn't jealous of her grief.

"Axis will be upset," said Ishbel. "Axis loved him, too."

"I know," said Maximilian. "I have sent BroadWing. He should be there by now. Axis isn't that far distant for an Icarii."

They lapsed into silence, Lister looking a little impatient, Maximilian at ease with the quiet.

"There is something we need to discuss, Ishbel," Maximilian said eventually. "We'd agreed not to unravel the Weeper's soul until we were safe inside Elcho Falling."

Lister, who had been looking bored and slightly irritated with the silence, now looked sharply between Ishbel and Maximilian.

"But now . . ." Ishbel said.

"But now I think I need to know who and what the Weeper is."

"Too much has gone wrong for you," said Lister. "You need all the help you can get."

Ishbel had to look down at the ground and clench her hands to stop herself hitting the man.

Maximilian gave Lister a steady look, then looked back to Ishbel. "Ishbel, I hate to ask this . . ."

"When?" she said.

"Tonight," Maximilian said.

"Good," said Lister. "I can help, and certainly ensure Ishbel's safety. I—"

"I don't want you present," Maximilian said, then addressed Ishbel again before Lister could respond. "I know you wanted to be safe in Serpent's Nest, or perhaps Elcho Falling once it is raised, but I no longer want to wait. Something terrible took Isaiah, and I—" He stopped, glanced at Lister, then continued. "I need whatever aid I can get."

"Tonight, then," Ishbel said.

"He said, 'I need whatever aid I can get,'" Lister told Ravenna, "but not *my* aid! Nor yours."

Ravenna wrapped her arms around her shoulders. They were standing in the dusk, hidden in the long shadow of one of the tents, and the air was chilling rapidly. She wished she'd brought her cloak with her.

"I am the very last person Maximilian would want," she said, "while Ishbel was being heroic . . . and vulnerable. What do you think is in that bronze statue, Lister? Good, or bad?"

"I don't know," Lister said, frustration roughening his voice. "I don't know! It is powerful—it must be if it gave wings to StarDrifter and his wife . . . and if it kept half of Coroleas in petty enjoyments for thousands of years. But what? What connection to Maximilian and Elcho Falling?"

"It hated me," said Ravenna. "I could barely hold it without the damn thing hissing."

Lister finally laughed, soft and genuinely amused. "Then it must be a Persimius, my friend."

She shot him a dark look. "What if whatever is in there is Ishbel's dark conspirator? Could that be why it never liked me?"

Lister went very still, thinking.

"What should we do, Lister?" Ravenna said, quietly.

He continued to think, his eyes fixed on the distant horizon, his teeth working at an edge of his lower lip.

Eventually he put a hand on Ravenna's shoulder, pulling her close. "How powerful are you, Ravenna? And how badly *do* you want to save this land?"

CHAPTER SIX

Isembaard

Isaiah had torn a strip of cloth from Hereward's robe, twisted it around a pebble, then tied it across her neck and under one arm so that the pebble pressed down on the still-oozing vein.

He sat a few paces away, looking at her, wondering if he dared risk using a little of the water they had left to wash his hands.

He decided Hereward would need it more.

She looked as close to death as any could get without actually stepping over the threshold. She was white, her skin cold and clammy, and she was too weak to stand. Blood encrusted the upper portion of her body, from her chin to her waist and belly. She was shivering, her body trying its best to warm itself.

"I'm sorry," she whispered, as she had been whispering every so often these past hours since the One had vanished.

Isaiah had not responded to her once. He had attended her as best he could, and had then moved away to sit by himself.

Hereward did not blame him for isolating himself from her. She had known nothing of his true nature, and still knew little of it now save that he'd given up a great deal for her.

A woman he disliked.

Just to save her life.

A wave of nausea and dizziness threatened to overwhelm her, but Hereward fought it off.

"Isaiah," she said, clearing her throat to make her voice work properly.

He made no response.

"Isaiah, leave me. Get to Maximilian as fast as you may." She paused, fighting off another wave of dizziness. "I will just hold you back, and—"

He turned to her at that. "I have given away that which is most precious to me, beyond the gift of life itself, in order that you may live, and you say, 'Just walk away'? If I'd known you'd *wanted* to die then I would still have my own life intact!"

"I'm sorry."

"The One wanted to torment me. He wanted me to ruin myself for a woman for whom I cared nothing. The ultimate cruelty. If you had been Ishbel I would not have minded. But you—"

"Isaiah, I am *sorry!*"

"Stop telling me you are sorry! I never want to hear it again! *I* am the one who is sorry, Hereward."

Isaiah stopped, taking a deep breath.

"And now I *am* sorry," he said. "None of this is your fault. None of it. I apologize for what I just said to you, Hereward."

She was crying quietly, unable to look at him.

He hesitated, then rose, fetching a small flask of water they'd kept filled from the rapidly emptying barrels on the riverboat, and squatted down by Hereward.

"Drink something," he said. "You will be thirsty with all the blood you have lost."

He put the flask to her lips, and Hereward held it and took a sip.

Then she began to gulp as she realized how parched she was.

"That's enough," Isaiah said, taking back the flask. "You'll make yourself ill."

Hereward wiped her mouth, smearing it pink from the dried blood on the back of her hand. "Who are you, Isaiah? What is going on? What is *happening?*"

"It is a long and sad tale," he said, then sat down by her, checked the compress on her neck, and began to speak in a low tone.

CHAPTER SEVEN

The Central Outlands

A xis went in search of Inardle once BroadWing had left to fly back to Maximilian. He supposed there were other things he could have been doing, but none of them would have been much use, and he needed to find Inardle.

Very badly.

He was still furious at Eleanon's stupidity, and he thought that he might actually kill him if he'd left Inardle to die back at the ambush gully.

But in the end he found Inardle just before dusk, and Eleanon's life was spared.

She was huddled by herself a little distance from the main group of Leal-fast. Axis almost fell over her by accident as he was moving toward a section of the Lealfast he hadn't yet searched.

"Inardle!"

She was curled on the ground, wrapped about her belly, her wings askew behind her. Both her body and wing posture instantly told Axis she was hurt, and badly.

"Inardle." Axis crouched down, putting a hand on her shoulder, trying to roll her over.

She resisted a moment, then uncurled slightly.

Her arms, belly, and chest were covered with blood, but at least her eyes were bright.

"Where are you wounded?" Axis said.

Inardle moved a hand slightly, over her lower rib cage, and Axis pushed it gently to one side and lifted back the sodden material of her tunic.

There was a long, deep gash running from her lower rib cage across the top third of her belly.

"Anywhere else?" he said.

"One of my wings," Inardle said. Her voice was unnaturally calm, and Axis wondered if she was in shock. "I managed to get back here, but I do not think I can fly again for a while . . . my wing . . ."

Axis quickly checked her wing—a sword had sliced deep into its underside close to her back. He thought it was possible the blade had cut one or more tendons in the wing and that she had managed to get this far was a miracle. But at least it wasn't bleeding much, and was thus not fatal.

But the belly wound . . .

He rolled her very carefully onto her back, ignoring her soft cry of pain as her injured wing momentarily caught beneath her, and examined the wound over her belly more carefully.

"This needs to be stitched," he said, "and we need to pray the blade didn't slice open any of your internal organs."

He rocked back on his heels. "We have only one physician with us, and he has only two assistants. He won't have time to see you."

Axis looked up, called over one of the soldiers that Georgdi had left behind, and asked him to find Zeboath and beg a needle and thread from him.

"I have spent years in the battlefield," said Axis to Inardle, "and I didn't always have a physician with me. I have stitched more battle wounds than I care to remember. I may not do a pretty job, Inardle, but I can do something for you."

Axis realized suddenly that Inardle was silent. "Inardle?"

She gave a little nod of acknowledgment, but did not speak.

"Nothing in your chest hurts?" said Axis. "Your throat or upper back?"

"No," she said, finally, and Axis felt himself relax a very little. She cleared her throat. "Eleanon? Have you seen him?"

"Yes."

"Is he injured?"

"A little. Not enough."

"Eleanon—"

"Has murdered with carelessness thousands of your people, and injured everyone you can see about. There are thousands who have died, and who will die, Inardle." Axis paused. "He's had no battle experience at all, has he?"

Inardle turned her head away from Axis, and did not reply.

"Stars, I suspected it, and still I sent him into danger. I am a fool, Inardle." Axis paused, looking out over the mass of Lealfast spread over the plain. It was growing dim now, and the individual Lealfast were turning into indistinguishable lumps under the darkening sky. It was a complete disaster, with Armat on his way to turn it into a greater one.

"Inardle?"

She made no reply.

"Inardle, I know the Lealfast use the Star Dance in a manner I don't comprehend. The way you move invisibly through the air . . . the way Bingaleal vanished after his assassination attempt on Isaiah. Can you not do the same now? Everyone here is vulnerable. Armat is heading this way, he can't be far away now, and there are more soldiers—" *Many more. Thousands more.* "—moving down from the north. We need to get everyone to safety."

"When we are bloodied," Inardle said, lifting a bloodstained hand slightly, "we lose the ability to vanish into the air. We really can only travel invisibly when we are whole. We cannot fight in that state, and if we are wounded . . . then no. It is too powerful an enchantment to be worked when we are distracted with other matters."

Shit, Axis thought. "Inardle, can you call your brother here?"

"Yes, but—"

"Call Eleanon here. *Now.*"

"He didn't answer before, Axis, when I tried. That's why I asked you if—"

"Call him now, and let him know that I need to see him, and that you are badly wounded. Call him. *Now!*"

She closed her eyes, and Axis felt a little disturbance in the Star Dance about him.

Just then the soldier arrived back carrying a little pack.

"Zeboath said there is suturing equipment inside, as well as a poultice and some antiseptic swabs."

"At least there is someone around here I can rely on," Axis muttered as he unwrapped the pack, then looked back at the soldier. "Thank you ... I included you in that group of those I can rely on, if you didn't realize."

The soldier gave a small smile and a nod of acknowledgment.

"What is your name?" Axis asked.

"Raph, my lord."

"You are one of Georgdi's men, Raph?"

"Yes, my lord."

"Then no wonder I can rely on you," Axis said. He knew he was punishing the wrong person by pushing this point in front of Inardle, but right at this moment he was still too angry to care. He paused while he threaded a needle with catgut.

"Raph, Georgdi left some men with you ..."

"There are nine others, my lord."

Axis carefully pulled the thread through, then set the suture needle to one side. "Raph, I want you to collect the other men and ride from here. You know the Isembaardians are closing in on us."

"We will not leave you—"

"You damn well *will* leave me!" Axis said, then apologized for his tone. "Look, Raph, I am going to stay with the Lealfast. Armat will not kill me, I am too important a hostage, and, whatever else he might do, Armat will recognize that usefulness. But he *will* kill you, and don't give me any bravado about fighting to the last man. There is no need for you to die. Not for the Lealfast. Catch up with Georgdi, and tell him that I have stayed behind."

Raph gave a nod, then moved off.

"You must really hate us," said Inardle.

"I am very, very angry at you," said Axis. "Have *none* of you any sense?"

He pushed her hands away from her belly, and tore back the material of her tunic to expose the top portion of the wound. As he did so, he inadvertently exposed one of her breasts, and Inardle clutched her hands over her chest protectively.

Her gaucheness and modesty irritated Axis, and somewhat frustrated him. Hadn't she been Lister's lover? If so, she'd probably insisted they kept their clothes on for their beddings.

"Keep your hand out of my way," he said, pushing one of Inardle's hands away from the top of her wound, and ignoring her look of embarrassment. He swabbed away roughly at the blood about the wound, not caring that Inardle bit her lip in pain as he did so.

Frost encircled the wound, then ran a little way along one of her ribs.

Axis stopped, staring at it, then looking at Inardle in question.

"We frost, StarMan," she said, "when we are in pain, when we are delighted, or at the touch of a lover's hand." She paused. "That was caused by pain."

Axis' mouth twitched into a smile, which faded almost instantly as he wondered what it would be like making love to her and watching his fingers trail frost across her body.

There was the sound of a step behind him, and Axis jerked his mind away from images of Inardle's aroused and frosted body.

"Inardle!"

Eleanon bent down beside his sister. Someone had removed the arrowhead from his arm, and it was now roughly bandaged. "What are you doing?" he said to Axis.

"I am trying to help your sister," Axis said. "There was no one else about to aid her."

"I—" Eleanon began.

"Armat is close," said Axis. "I've sent the few remaining Outlander soldiers away. I will stay with the wounded, but I want you, Eleanon, to take every last one of the Lealfast who can fly and find somewhere you can lick your wounds and reflect on your stupidity. The lower Sky Peaks, perhaps. Eventually I want you to report to BroadWing EvenBeat, who commands the Strike Force with Maximilian Persimius, so he can teach you some warcraft. But not yet. You are useless to everyone at the moment. Heal your wounds, lose some of that blind arrogance of yours, and then you may prove of some use. Come back when you're prepared to learn, and not before."

"I—" Eleanon said again.

"You will take those Lealfast who can fly and you will *leave!*" Axis said. "I truly mean it when I say you are of no use here."

"Eleanon," Inardle said, "do as Axis says."

She locked eyes with Eleanon for an instant, and he gave a curt nod. He leaned down and gently kissed Inardle's cheek, then whispered into her ear: "Use this opportunity, sister."

Eleanon straightened. "The Sky Peaks," he said to Axis.

"And then to Maximilian at Elcho Falling, if you have managed to learn some sense," Axis said.

Eleanon gave a nod, stepping back.

Axis began to stitch Inardle's wound, not seeing Eleanon's small smile of satisfaction as he lifted into the air.

CHAPTER EIGHT

On the Road to Serpent's Nest

They gathered in Maximilian's command tent just after dusk: Ishbel, Maximilian, StarDrifter, Salome, Garth, Egalion, and BroadWing. Maximilian was worried for Ishbel's safety. They simply could not wait until they got to Serpent's Nest to free the Weeper, nor until they raised Elcho Falling.

But what would it do to Ishbel?

Maximilian was worried also about Ravenna. He hadn't seen her all day, and when he'd sent Garth to look for her earlier, Garth had returned with the news that he had not been able to find her.

What was she up to? Maximilian wished he'd had the forethought to ask Ravenna to return home to Escator well before this.

He looked at Egalion and raised his eyebrows.

Egalion gave a nod. *The tent is protected.*

Maximilian hoped that whatever, or whoever, the Weeper might yield, that it would be worth this risk.

"Are you certain you have no idea what, or who, the Weeper might hide?" Maximilian asked Salome.

Salome shifted a little, easing her back. She was very close to giving birth now, and StarDrifter had not wanted her to attend tonight because of the inherent danger, but Salome had insisted.

And whenever Salome insisted, she tended to get her way.

"We knew nothing of it," she said. "Trust me when I say I tried to unearth whatever information I could, thinking to unleash yet more of its powers. All I know, as all the dukes of Sidon ever knew, was that an extraordinarily powerful soul went into its making."

"A good soul," said Egalion, "or a wicked soul? I do not like that everyone seems to assume that the Weeper's soul will be benevolent."

"Thank you for that touch of negativity," StarDrifter muttered. "I am sure we all truly appreciate it."

"The Weeper has never done anything wicked, Egalion," Maximilian said. "Not since I have known it, and—" he raised his eyebrows at Salome.

"No. Never anything wicked," she said. "It tended to do anything we wished of it save harm to another." She gave a small smile. "Naturally the dukes of Sidon, as myself, thought that a terrible flaw, but we managed. It gave us protection and incredible riches, and we learned to ask no more of it."

Maximilian looked down at the bronze statue he had in his lap. It looked so innocuous, but it had been through such a journey to reach him and had been so desperate to reach him that surely, surely, its soul had *some* meaning.

"Ishbel?" Maximilian said. "Are you ready?"

"Yes," Ishbel said.

"Ishbel, be careful."

"I'm *ready*," she said, "but I am only going to try this the once, Maxel. If I can't do it this time, I do not think I could ever try again."

"If it gets too dangerous," Maximilian said, "then get out. We can live without whatever the Weeper might hide. Ishbel, I cannot live without you."

She took a deep breath at that, and locked eyes with him for a long moment. Then she gave a nod. "Give me the Weeper, Maxel."

Venetia walked through the night. She walked some fifty paces north of Maximilian's command tent, through the low brush and early spring turf, turning every so often to glance at the softly illuminated tent, looking at the shadows of the people inside moving against the canvas walls. The tent was ringed by armed men, but Venetia wondered what use they might be against whatever walked this night.

She could feel the pathways between the Land of Dreams and this world opening up, and power seeping across.

Ravenna.

Venetia wept, cursing her daughter. Why was Ravenna doing this? *Why?* Venetia wished she were home in her house in the marshes; instead, she was so far distant from the smell of the marsh that she could barely remember it.

What did she do here? What was the point of it? Why had she come?

"Why, Ravenna?" Venetia whispered. "Why this?"

She turned for her own tent, looking one more time at Maximilian's command tent.

Ishbel was starting her journey into the Weeper now.

Venetia knew beyond any doubt that she would never come out.

Not alive.

CHAPTER NINE

The Central Outlands

Eleanon had left, together with those Lealfast who could fly. Axis had no way of numbering them, but they had made a vast cloud as they lifted into the air and flew slowly northward.

But however vast that cloud had been, there were still many thousands left on the ground.

Axis had finished stitching Inardle's wound, and now helped her to her feet.

"There is no chance you can fly?" he said, desperately wanting her to get to safety somehow.

He knew the answer before she spoke. Inardle was so weak she could barely stand, and Axis had to support her to keep her upright.

"My wing is too stiff," she said. "Axis, you should go."

"I am going to be the only thing that might keep you alive," he said.

"The woman is right, Axis," said Zeboath, walking out of the night. "You should go. I've heard that Armat is close. There's no reason for you to stay."

"And you?" said Axis.

"There are wounded who need my attention," said Zeboath, "and—"

"Then I am staying," Axis said. He began to say something else, but then everyone stiffened at the sound of a horse's hooves. They relaxed, if only slightly, when Georgdi rode his horse into their range of vision.

"Oh, for the gods' sakes," Axis said. "What are you doing back?"

"I won't leave you," said Georgdi. "My men are riding for Serpent's Nest, and have orders to gather there along with those other of my men who can leave their families. But you thought that *I* would just ride away?"

"You're dead if you stay," Axis said.

Georgdi dismounted, patting his horse on the neck once he'd jumped to the ground. "I'm as dead as you are, Axis," he said, "which is to say not very much. We're both too valuable to Armat, as is Zeboath. No general, even in his most maddened moments, ever killed a physician."

Axis noted that Georgdi had left Inardle out of the list of those sure to be spared. He wasted a moment wondering if he'd ever felt this useless before. There were thousands upon thousands of Lealfast left, desperately wounded, and no means to protect them.

"You did the right thing, Axis," Georgdi said softly, watching the emotions play about Axis' face. "There was no point keeping soldiers here to fight. They would have died uselessly."

"Armat hates me," said Axis. "He will take it out on—" He couldn't finish.

"Listen," said Georgdi.

They stood, listening to the sounds around them: the soft voices of some Lealfast; someone crying in pain, very quietly; the footfalls of one of Zeboath's assistants as he moved from one Lealfast to another.

The sound, very low, of horses' bits.

Axis glanced at Georgdi's horse, now wandered away a few paces to graze.

The sound hadn't come from him, and the next moment Axis heard the sound again, louder this time.

Many horses.

"Armat," he said.

CHAPTER TEN

On the Road to Serpent's Nest

Ishbel spiraled down into darkness. She followed the route that the god priests had taken when first they'd torn the soul from the body of the living man and imprisoned it in the bronze statue.

She followed the trail of pain.

The pain Ishbel could steel herself against, even though it was frightful—*gods, what had the god priests done to this man?*—but it was the sense of despair that almost murdered her. This man, whoever he was, had somehow known from a very early age that this was his fate, and that he was destined to be abandoned.

The sense of abandonment; that was what was so frightful. This man had been abandoned in every sense. His parents had turned their backs on him. His brother, also. He'd been sent from his home—Serpent's Nest! He had come from Serpent's Nest!—to this fate, and no one had tried to save him, or had ever thought of him again.

No one had ever remembered him. He had been lost within the bronze, and no one, *no one*, had cared.

Ishbel moaned, and for the longest time it was as if she were trapped again in her parents' house, the rotting bodies of her family about her, and the bleak crowd outside, shouting at her to die, die soon, so that they might burn the house.

And turn their backs, and forget her.

Maximilian glanced at StarDrifter, who had shifted uncomfortably, then looked back to Ishbel. She sat cross-legged, the Weeper resting in her lap, her hands resting gently atop it. Her eyes were closed, her head very slightly thrown back, a wisp of her fair hair caught across one cheek. Maximilian wanted to reach out and tuck it behind an ear—it irritated him, that wisp of hair—but he did not want to break Ishbel's concentration.

She moaned, very softly, and Maximilian tensed. He looked at StarDrifter, who gave a slight shrug of his shoulders.

I don't know. I cannot tell.

Maximilian looked quickly at the rest of the group—everyone had their eyes locked on Ishbel—then looked back to Ishbel.

There were colors and textures about her now. Initially, Ishbel's journey had been through darkness, but after what had felt like endless pain and despair different emotions and sensations began to trickle in.

Fright.

The man had initially been overwhelmed by pain and despair, but he'd managed to conquer them, or at least set them partially to one side. But in doing that, he'd allowed other emotions to beset him.

Fright.

Not so much at what was happening to him, but at the thought that he'd not ever be able to endure. He'd believed that he wasn't strong enough, and that he would fail. He'd wept. The god priests had been torturing him, slowly and with infinite pleasure, and the man had wept. Not from the pain or the hatred that surrounded him, but from the thought that he'd not be able to endure.

He'd been sent to suffer this fate for a reason . . . it was not happenchance that the god priests had seized him, but someone . . . someone . . . His father! His father had sent him.

"Go and be destroyed," his father had said, "for it will serve my purpose well."

Ishbel wept.

His father had been the Lord of Elcho Falling.

Venetia sat alone in her tent. Like Ishbel she was cross-legged, her head thrown back a little, her eyes closed. Her chest rose and fell with shallow, rapid breaths and her pale skin gleamed with perspiration.

She was in a forest, following Ishbel down, deeper and deeper into the Weeper.

Into a forest of pain and despair and terror and such aching loneliness that Venetia could hardly bear it.

Ishbel did not know of it, but Venetia could feel another in that forest, trailing her to one side, all her attention fixed on Ishbel.

The colors were harsh and textured. They hid shapes, but Ishbel could not determine them. It was as if she were in a maze of sensation, and she could no longer decide which way she should go. The path had been clear, now it was muddled.

The god priests had left traps.

Ishbel was starting to sweat now, and was very, very pale. Her hands trembled slightly where they rested on the Weeper.

I don't like this, Maximilian thought. He wished he could follow Ishbel, but he did not have the knowledge or power to penetrate the Weeper.

He wished also that he hadn't asked Ishbel to do this. It was so dangerous, and Maximilian very suddenly and very painfully realized how deeply he cared for Ishbel.

"StarDrifter?" he said.

StarDrifter shook his head. "This is magic unknown to me, Maxel. I wish . . . oh stars, I wish I could help, but there is nothing I can do."

Now Maximilian looked to Garth.

"I can't touch her," Garth said. "I can't touch her with my hand or my Touch. Anything like that will disturb and distract and likely kill her."

"Hello, Ishbel," Ravenna said, and stepped through the colors to block Ishbel's path.

Ishbel stopped dead, forcing herself not to panic and to keep her focus.

"All I need do," said Ravenna, "is to break your concentration, and you're trapped here. Your soul, that is. The rest of you will die when your heart stops."

"Let me pass, Ravenna."

"No. I'm sorry, Ishbel. Under different circumstances I think I may have liked you. But you are so bad for Maxel, and for the land."

"Ravenna—"

"You can't attack me," said Ravenna. "I can see how intently you maintain your concentration just in conversation. You cannot accomplish anything more without losing the faint strands of connection back to your own body."

"Ravenna, I won't harm Maximilian! All I want is to help—"

"You mean well, Ishbel. I know you do. I am sorry, but the only way for you to help Maximilian is to die."

Then Ravenna leapt forward, catching Ishbel about the throat.

Venetia cried out, "Ravenna!"

She tried to move faster, move to where she could see the forms of Ishbel and Ravenna struggling deeper within the forest of memory and pain, but, oh, it was so hard to move, so hard, and Venetia struggled to maintain both her determination to reach Ishbel and Ravenna, and her hold on the life force of her body that lay slumped in its tent.

Ishbel closed her eyes. Ravenna had her by the throat and was strangling her, but Ishbel did nothing to throw off the woman. She focussed her entire being on holding her concentration, on her desperately fragile hold over the links which led back to her body, and on ignoring Ravenna as best she could.

That was difficult, given that Ravenna was sinking her fingers deeper and deeper into her throat.

Ishbel?

Ishbel jerked, her eyes opening.

Ishbel? Hold on just a moment, hang on to my voice. Help is coming.

It was the Weeper, or the soul which inhabited it, and Ishbel clung to the sound of his voice with all her strength. He kept talking, murmuring her name over and over, his voice forming a pathway of light deeper and deeper into the sorceries that bound him.

Ravenna tightened her grip, strengthening her efforts to either kill Ishbel or force the woman to lose her concentration and her hold on her physical body.

Then, unbelievably, Ravenna let go, staring over Ishbel's shoulder in amazement.

Venetia was there, fighting with everything she had to maintain her own concentration.

"Stop," she said to her daughter. "Are you mad, to so dishonor the marsh-lands and your mother?"

Ravenna was, for the moment, so shocked by her mother's appearance that she did nothing.

"Run," Venetia said to Ishbel. "Run now, and leave me with my daughter."

CHAPTER ELEVEN

The Central Outlands

A xis SunSoar. Where the glory now, eh?" Armat lifted a leg over the wither of his horse and slid to the ground.

All around Axis could hear columns of horsemen moving to surround the wounded Lealfast.

Armat came to stand directly before Axis, who was still supporting Inardle. Armat looked at her, then back at Axis.

"They're very pretty, Axis," Armat said, "but what in the world ever made you think they could fight? They have shamed you . . . or . . . is it that they are but a reflection of your own shameful lack of ability?"

Axis said nothing.

Again Armat slid his eyes back to Inardle. "They are pitiful. *Pathetic.*" He moved his eyes about the group. "Georgdi, and Zeboath. Is this all that is left?"

"You will not catch the others," said Georgdi.

"Was that a challenge?" Armat said, a smile of what appeared to be genuine amusement on his face. "I do not need to catch the others, Georgdi. Not just yet. Looks like there is work for me to do here. Why did you stay?"

"I would not leave the wounded," said Axis.

"Ah, he speaks," Armat said. "And so nobly. 'I would not leave the wounded.' Just this one, Axis," he nodded at Inardle, "or do you feel emotional toward the entire lot?"

"They are my responsibility," Axis said.

"Not for much longer," Armat said, and he lifted a hand to signal to his men.

"Stop!" said Axis. "For gods' sakes, Armat, these wounded are of no danger to you. They—"

"They are lying here dying in slow degrees," said Armat. "I am merely being efficient in hurrying them along a little. Even if I were not here, Axis, what could you do to aid them? Zeboath is a good man, but by the gods, even this lot might stretch his capabilities." He lifted his hand again, then brought it down in a swift movement.

Axis did not so much hear as sense the movement in the dark behind him. He thrust Inardle into Zeboath's arms, then took several steps toward where the mass of Lealfast were lying.

There were shapes moving through the darkness, bending down to the first ranks of the Lealfast.

"No!" Axis cried. "For the gods' sakes, stop this—"

Then there came a great blow to the back of his head, and the darkness consumed him.

CHAPTER TWELVE

On the Road to Serpent's Nest

Ishbel's body jerked, and her hands half raised.

Dark bruises appeared about her throat.

Ravenna. Maximilian almost panicked. He knew instantly what it was—Ravenna had managed to follow Ishbel deep into the Weeper—but he had no idea what to do. To touch Ishbel could be catastrophic.

StarDrifter had started forward, but Garth held him back.

"Don't touch her," Garth said. *"Don't touch her!"*

"Oh gods, Ishbel," Maximilian murmured. He was on one knee before her, one hand partly extended. *Ishbel...*

Ishbel's breath wheezed in her throat, and then, suddenly, just as Maximilian thought he could not bear it any longer, her entire body relaxed, her breathing grew easy, and the bruises about her throat, although they did not vanish entirely, became far less marked.

Maximilian's shoulders slumped in relief, and he allowed his hand to rest on Ishbel's knee, knowing instinctively that his touch would no longer disturb her.

"Maxel," Garth said, his voice tight. "Look at the Weeper."

It was icing over.

There was a battle going on behind her, but Ishbel ignored it. Any further distraction and she knew she'd lose her focus.

She followed the voice, now almost a soft litany in her mind—*Ishbel, Ishbel, Ishbel*—like a pathway. The sorceries still twisted about her, the pain and despair and terror still battered at her, but the man's voice tolled like a temple bell on a snowy night.

All she had to do was to concentrate on his voice.

Then, suddenly, horrifically, death seethed down behind her.

Maximilian cried out, jerking to one side as Ishbel's face and body spattered with blood.

In an instant Garth was at his side, one hand grabbing at Maximilian's shoulder. "It isn't her blood, Maxel. *It isn't her blood!*"

Maximilian forced himself to look at Ishbel, sure he would see her slack in death, despite what Garth had said.

But Ishbel wasn't dead. Instead, she wore a faint smile on her face.

Death surged up behind her, then as suddenly receded, and Ishbel was free. She fled down the path, following the light of the man's voice.

"Ishbel? You must be able to hear me audibly now. Can you see my hand?"

"Yes, yes, I can see it. Where is Ravenna?"

"Too far behind now to catch you."

"Venetia?"

"She is dead. I am sorry. Come, take my hand."

"She saved my life."

"Yes, she did. Ishbel. Come, come, take my hand."

Then, suddenly, there it was, and Ishbel reached out and took it in both of hers.

Everyone in Maximilian's command tent jumped and cried out in surprise as the bronze statue in Ishbel's hands suddenly exploded into thousands of tiny pieces.

Maximilian grabbed at Ishbel, pulling her head against his shoulder and shielding her face from the flying shards of metal. He closed his own eyes and turned his face aside, hoping everyone inside the tent would escape the flying shrapnel. Several of the shards caught one of his cheeks, causing some minor scratches, but when he opened his eyes again he saw that no one had suffered any serious injuries by the disintegrating bronze statue.

He blinked, using his free hand to brush some of the debris out of his hair, and looked about, expecting to see . . . well, someone *extra*.

There was no one.

Very carefully, Maximilian looked at Ishbel. She was breathing easily, but was not conscious. Garth raised an eyebrow at Maximilian, then laid a hand on one of hers at Maximilian's nod.

"She is all right, Maxel," Garth said. "For the moment she is in a deep sleep—a reaction against where she has been, and the effort it took. My guess is that she will sleep for several hours at least."

"Thank you," Maximilian said. "Salome, Garth, can you look after her for the moment?"

Then he rose, and left the tent.

CHAPTER THIRTEEN

On the Road to Serpent's Nest

W hat have you done?"
Ravenna turned about as Maximilian entered her tent. "You speak so harshly to me," she said.

Maximilian barely managed to keep his anger under control. *Gods, the nerve of the woman!* She stood so pale, her eyes so huge, her hand just so faintly trembling as it hung at her side, and all of it, he knew, was pretense.

"You tried to kill Ishbel," he said, coming to a halt and trying, largely unsuccessfully, to keep his hands from clenching at his sides.

"I tried to help you."

"You—"

"Maxel, please, listen to me! I know you love Ishbel, but—"

"Do you have any idea how *sick* I am of hearing this petty chorus?"

"You have seen the vision! Do you have any idea of how heartsick I am that you continue to ignore it?"

Maximilian half turned away, hands now on hips, smothering a curse.

"Ishbel loves you, but she will murder you, Maxel, and murder Elcho Falling. Nothing shall come of her but sorrow."

"What must I do to prise you out of my life?" Maximilian said, turning back to Ravenna. "What must I do to—"

He stopped, staring. His movement in turning back to Ravenna had altered his stance enough that he could now see beyond the chair that stood just behind Ravenna.

He could see a hand, and a pale arm, outstretched on the carpet.

He pushed past Ravenna, dropping on one knee beside Venetia.

Her skin was gray, clammy, and very cool.

She was dead, her throat torn apart by strong, cruel fingers, and he finally knew from where had come the blood that had spattered over Ishbel.

Maximilian laid a hand on Venetia's forehead, and closed his eyes for a moment. Then he stood and looked at Ravenna, the expression on his face making her take a step backward.

"You killed her," he said.

"Yes."

"Yes? *Yes?* Why?"

"She tried to aid Ishbel—"

"She was your mother! Your *mother!* And you *killed* her?"

Ravenna's eyes were wet, and a tear slid down one cheek. "I loved her, Maxel. But she tried to stop me from preventing Ishbel—"

Maximilian stepped forward and hit Ravenna so hard that her body jerked in a half circle and she fell to the floor.

He paused, waiting until Ravenna had raised herself on one elbow, staring at him in shock, then he reached down and hauled her to her feet.

"If you were not pregnant, Ravenna, I swear to the gods I would kill you right now! What can be worth the murder of your own mother, eh?"

"You have no idea what is coming, Maxel! I keep trying to warn you but—"

"Don't you *ever* call me that again! You are gone from my life, Ravenna. *Get out of this tent.* Get out of my company! Walk into the night, Ravenna, and never, *never* walk back into the light again in my presence!"

Ravenna just stared at him, too shocked by his words to speak.

He gave her a hard, painful shake. *"Get out of my life, Ravenna."*

"Why do this to me, Maximilian, when you have been my entire delight, and all my joy?"

"Oh, for all the gods' sakes, Ravenna. Go."

"I have ever stood ready at your hand, to—"

"Go!"

Ravenna pulled herself away from him. "You do a great wrong, Maximilian," she said softly. "You do *me* a great wrong, to cast me off with such discourtesy."

"Don't you ever speak to me of discourtesy, not when you just tried to murder my wife—"

Wife, she thought numbly. He called her his wife.

"—and took your mother's life when she tried to aid Ishbel!"

Maximilian stepped forward and shoved his hand against Ravenna's shoulder, hard enough to make her stumble back. "Get out of my life, Ravenna, and be grateful I leave you with yours."

Ravenna took a backward step to the tent flap, then another, then bent down and retrieved her cloak from the floor without shifting her eyes from Maximilian's face.

"I saved you from the Veins, Maximilian Persimius. I have waged life and land for you, and for *this* discourtesy? I do not think you worth the struggle, and so I shall save my efforts for your son."

With that she turned on her heel and was gone through the tent flap.

Maximilian stood for a few minutes once Ravenna had gone, trying to calm himself, trying to let go of his anger.

To kill your own mother. Gods, how deluded was Ravenna to do that?

Finally, calm enough that he had stopped shaking, Maximilian went back to Venetia's body, and knelt by it for a little while in prayer, feeling a profound guilt over her death.

In time, he rose, called for one of the Emerald Guard, and asked him to fetch help to prepare Venetia for burial, then went to see Ishbel.

Garth had moved her back to her own tent, where she was asleep in her bed.

When Maximilian entered, Garth moved over to him, motioning him to speak softly.

"Maxel?" Garth said. "What is wrong?"

"Is my face that bad?"

"*Maxel?*"

"Venetia is dead. Ravenna killed her. If Ishbel managed to survive her attempt to unwind the Weeper, then that was all Venetia's doing. Ravenna attacked Ishbel, and when Venetia tried to stop her, Ravenna killed her."

Garth stared, mouth agape.

"I'm sorry, Garth. I know you loved Ravenna."

"I loved Venetia, too. And Ravenna . . . she has not grown into the woman I expected. Maxel, what have you done with Ravenna?"

"I wanted to kill her. So badly. Garth, I was so angry, I thought it would kill me. I've never been that angry . . ."

Garth laid a hand on his friend's shoulder and Maximilian felt calmness radiate through him.

Maximilian sighed, allowing some of his anger and guilt to dissipate. "Ravenna is gone, Garth. I should have done it many days ago, but she is gone now. Where, I don't know and for the moment I don't care. I told her I never wanted to see her face again. I should have killed her, but I couldn't, not with the child . . ."

Garth wrapped both his arms about Maximilian and hugged him for a long moment. "I'm sorry," he said.

"Garth," Maximilian said, "I have been so stupid, I—"

"You haven't—"

"Everything is muddled because of my stupidity."

"Then everything will unmuddle itself. Maxel, I will take care of Venetia, all right? Go and sit with Ishbel."

"She is well?"

"Yes, just very tired. She needs her sleep, but it will do you good to sit with her, and it will do her good to see you when she wakes."

"Did she say anything about the Weeper?"

"She woke only briefly as I moved her back here, and she said only that she needed to speak to you."

"I wonder what happened. Could it have been worth Venetia's death?"

"No one will know until Ishbel wakes. Maxel, go sit with her."

Maximilian took one step toward Ishbel. Then he stopped and half turned. "Garth, will you ask Egalion to make damned sure that Ravenna is gone? Perhaps escort her a few leagues into the wilderness. I don't care. Just make sure she is gone."

"I will do that. Sit, Maxel, and rest."

Maximilian sighed again, then went to sit at Ishbel's bedside.

CHAPTER FOURTEEN

On the Road to Serpent's Nest

Lister paced up and down in the darkness beyond Maximilian's camp. Vorstus stood to one side, irritatingly calm.

"Where is she?" Lister muttered. "I need to know what happened."

"Maxel has abandoned me," Ravenna said, walking out of the night. "*That* is what has happened. He is blind to Ishbel's danger, and thinks *me* the greater one!"

Lister had to repress a smile at that last. "You're upset," he said.

"My mother is dead!" Ravenna said. "So, yes, I am upset!"

"And now your fair prince has abandoned you," Vorstus murmured. "After all you have done for him."

Ravenna gave Lister an irritated look. "We need to leave. I need to leave—Maxel will surely have his damned Emerald Guard out hunting me—and I want to know if you are coming with me."

Lister stared back at the camp, at Maximilian's command tent. "I have watched him so long, longed for him so long."

"He is set on a path of destruction," Ravenna said. "He cannot see past Ishbel, and she will murder him and this land. This," she laid her hand on her stomach, "is Elcho Falling's future now."

"Lister, we need to get the crown."

Lister turned a little so he could look toward Ishbel's tent. "Maximilian is in there with her at the moment," he said. "It would be too foolish to try for it now."

"You're afraid of him?" Ravenna said.

Now Lister's eyes slid back her way. "You're *not?* We can snatch it later, but for now . . ."

"For now," Ravenna said, "Armat. He is close. We can be with him within the day."

"I had hoped it would not come to this," Lister said.

"So did I," Ravenna said, a catch in her voice. "But now it has. Come."

Maximilian had been sitting with Ishbel for an hour when Egalion came in.

Maximilian motioned him to stay by the door, and himself moved to speak to him quietly.

"Ravenna?" Maximilian asked.

"We can't find her," Egalion said.

"Shit!"

"There is more bad news. Lister has gone, and Vorstus also."

"And how is that bad news?"

"Well, obviously Lister and Vorstus have gone with—"

"Yes, I know, Egalion. I was just making a bad jest." He rubbed a hand over tired eyes. "What else can go wrong, eh? Isaiah is dead, and his loss I do most deeply regret. Venetia is dead, murdered in the saving of Ishbel's life. Lister and Vorstus have taken up with Ravenna, believing her lies for whatever reason they choose. I worry about Axis, and what is happening with Armat." Maximilian looked at Ishbel. "And Ishbel . . . what happened? Did she free or destroy the Weeper?"

Now he turned his gaze back to Egalion. "Should I just go home, Egalion, and allow the entire world to destroy itself? I need to say this, my friend, but I have never been as low as I am at this moment. There is no brightness left, no hope."

"Perhaps when Ishbel wakes . . ."

Maximilian gave a soft laugh that was bereft of any humor. "Perhaps when Ishbel wakes she will compound my despair, Egalion. Perhaps Ravenna was right."

"No," Egalion said in a low tone, but fiercely. "Ravenna was not right. Look, Maxel, go back and wait by Ishbel's side. Rest, if you can. Perhaps tomorrow will bring—"

Maximilian gave Egalion a look of such cynicism that the man broke off.

"Perhaps," Maximilian said, then he turned his back on Egalion and went to Ishbel.

Despite his low spirits and the uncomfortable chair, Maximilian eventually drifted off into a doze. He woke, suddenly, when Ishbel whispered his name.

"Ishbel! Are you well?"

"Yes, just very tired. Maxel, what happened to Venetia?"

"She is dead. I'm sorry. Ravenna—"

"Ravenna killed her. Maxel, if it wasn't for Venetia . . ."

"What happened, Ishbel?"

Briefly Ishbel told him how Ravenna had attacked her, and how then Venetia had come to her rescue. "She saved my life, Maxel."

Maximilian squeezed her hand. "I know. Ishbel . . . Ravenna has gone. I said harsh words to her and struck her. I have never been so angry before."

Ishbel attempted a small smile. "Not even at me?"

"Not even at you. I found her, with Venetia's body. I just . . ."

Now it was Ishbel who squeezed Maximilian's hand.

"Venetia saved my life, Maxel. I will forever be grateful to her."

"Ishbel . . ."

She gave a small smile. "Do you want to know what happened? Did I free the Weeper?"

Maximilian was so terrified of her answer, and so completely unable to read her face, he could not frame the question.

"Maxel, we need to go into the Twisted Tower."

CHAPTER FIFTEEN

Inside the Twisted Tower

Maximilian was concerned Ishbel might not be strong enough to stand on her own, but she shook off his hand as they stood on the path that led to the Twisted Tower.

"I am well enough, Maxel. Just a little tired. Not yet bedridden."

"Ishbel—"

"Oh, for the gods' sakes, Maxel, stop worrying. I am no invalid. Come, we need to go inside the Twisted Tower."

With that Ishbel walked down the path, leaving Maximilian to follow.

At the door she paused, her hand on the knob. "Maximilian Persimius, I would like you to meet the man who has waited so long for you."

Then she opened the door.

Maximilian stared into the Twisted Tower.

A man stood just inside the first chamber, regarding Maximilian with an expression composed partly of happiness, partly of relief. He was very young, which surprised Maximilian, perhaps no more than nineteen or twenty, olive-skinned, dark-haired, and with a fine, aquiline face.

A face that Maxel recognized, if only because of the lines of suffering on it. Whoever this was, he'd suffered as much—*greater*—as had Maximilian.

The man smiled, just a little, and then he bowed in an elegant, courtly movement.

"Greetings, my Lord of Elcho Falling," he said. "My name is Josia Persimius. I am Keeper of the Twisted Tower."

"Greetings," Maximilian said, returning the bow. "You are Persimius?"

"Of the line of your ancestors, Maximilian," said Josia. "Will you step inside? We need to speak of so much."

The first thing Josia did once the door had closed behind Maximilian and Ishbel was to step forward and envelop Ishbel in a massive hug.

"Forgive me," he said, standing back but keeping one hand on Ishbel's shoulder, "but I doubt you will ever comprehend just how grateful I am to have finally escaped that cursed bronze statue! Thank you. *Thank* you."

Maximilian's eyes filmed with tears at the emotion in Josia's face and voice.

"I thought Ravenna would kill her," Josia said to Maximilian. "Ishbel was my only hope, she has ever been the only person with the training and power to free me, and I thought Ravenna would kill her. But then the woman Venetia came, and I am safe. Venetia is dead now, surely."

Maximilian nodded. "She gave her life to save Ishbel, and you," he said. "I never knew her well, and I cannot understand that she could have thought enough of me to sacrifice herself."

"I imagine that most who meet you come to love you within hours," Josia said.

"Not all," Maximilian said, carefully not looking at Ishbel.

Her mouth twitched.

"Well, then," said Josia, "perhaps we can fix that." He let Ishbel go, then looked about. "Where shall we sit? I have a long tale to tell and nowhere to tell it."

"There are many empty chambers above," Maximilian said. "We can sit in one of those."

"How *many* empty chambers?" said Josia.

"Well over half the tower is completely empty," said Maximilian.

Josia's face went expressionless. "Then I am here only just in time," he said, and led the way up the stairs.

They settled in the first completely bare chamber, sitting on the floor with backs against the walls, facing one another, Maximilian warmed by the fact that Ishbel sat slightly closer to him than she did to Josia.

"My name," Josia said, "is Josia Persimius. I am the son and younger brother of now long-dead Lords of Elcho Falling. I lived some two thousand eight hundred years ago at a time when the Lords of Elcho Falling were considering leaving the mountain and retiring to Escator. My father, Escretius, feared, however, that if the Lords of Elcho Falling abandoned Elcho Falling itself, then all the knowledge associated with it might fall into forgetfulness."

"And thus this?" Maximilian said, waving a hand about at the Twisted Tower.

"Yes," Josia said. "My father built it. My brother, Cooper, and I aided him."

"You *know* what these chambers should contain?" Ishbel said, getting the question out a moment before Maximilian.

Josia grinned at the expression on their faces. "All in good time. Let me tell the tale my way, for I have been composing it for twenty-eight hundred years, and I think I am owed the stage."

Maximilian inclined his head.

"My father worried that if too many generations should pass before the Lords reclaimed Elcho Falling," Josia continued, "then items might be forgotten. But I never imagined so much could have been lost." He sighed. "While my brother Cooper would wear the crown of Elcho Falling, my father asked me if I would shoulder the responsibility of remembering."

"Remembering?" Maximilian said.

"Remembering everything for every chamber." Josia said. "Yes. I can remember every object for every chamber."

Maximilian lowered his eyes in order to gather his composure. The worry about the empty chambers had eaten away at him for so long that he could not believe it could be rectified this easily.

"I can help you put the objects back, Maximilian," Josia said. "It is why I exist." He paused. "It is why I have suffered."

"Why is there so much suffering associated with Elcho Falling?" Maximilian said, very softly. "Why?"

"Because that is what built Elcho Falling," said Josia, "and that is what powers it."

He shifted a little, raising one knee and resting an arm across it.

"My father built the Twisted Tower, and populated it with the knowledge that every Lord of Elcho Falling would require. But then, as I said, my father worried that somehow the tower would degenerate and memories would be lost. My father was a pessimist."

Josia paused. "But a realist, also. Cooper would wear the crown of Elcho Falling after our father, but I would remember the knowledge for all the generations ahead.

"This required me to live for a great deal of time. While the Lords of Elcho Falling can wield much power, granting indefinite life to a son is not one of their greater skills."

"You father sent you to Coroleas, didn't he?" Ishbel said.

"Yes," Josia said.

"Gods damn Elcho Falling," Ishbel muttered, "for all the suffering it requires."

"He sent you to Coroleas as a god-offering?" said Maximilian. "So you could be slowly tortured into death and your soul encased in a bronze statue?"

Josia inclined his head. "How else could I, and all my memory, be kept alive, save inside one of the Coroleans' cursed bronze statues?"

Ishbel and Maximilian could not speak. They looked at each other, then back to Josia, Maximilian making a gesture that was part disbelief, part anger.

"And in answer to your unspoken queries," Josia said softly, "no, I was not happy about this fate, nor particularly willing."

"But you went, in any case?" Maximilian said.

"Would you rather I had not?" Josia said. "Look, it was needed, and I went. I suffered, and for the longest time I wept, but then one day StarDrifter came to Salome's chamber—ah, the things I had to witness under her companionship!—and said to me, 'I have come to take you home to the Lord of Elcho Falling,' and suddenly, again, I was happy. It has been a long imprisonment, Maximilian Persimius, but it gives me a little comfort to realize that my father was right, and that I am needed."

He gave a wry smile. "I do not think I could be as joyous had I arrived back to find the Twisted Tower as complete as the day I had left it."

"I could always throw a few more objects out the door, if that would lift your spirits even more," said Maximilian, and Josia laughed.

"You cannot leave here, can you?" Ishbel said.

"No," Josia said, "I have no physical body left. The Twisted Tower, in its own way, imprisons me as much as did the weeping bronze." He gave a little smile. "It is a happier prison, though."

"Well," said Maximilian, "I *am* glad to discover you, Josia. To be frank, I think the Twisted Tower a more serene world than that which exists beyond its walls. Are you aware of what has happened in these lands?"

"Yes. You are in a pickle, Maximilian."

"Then you shall need to help me."

Josia gave another slow smile. "Tell me, Maximilian—"

"Maxel, please."

"Maxel, then. Tell me, how far have you explored the tower?"

"I have climbed all the way to the top chamber. Everything above this chamber is empty."

"Yes. Ishbel, how far have you climbed?"

"No further than this chamber, Josia," she said. "I have been to the tower only rarely."

Josia nodded, as if digesting this information. "Maxel, how many times have you been to the top chamber?"

"Once, when I was a boy, and once since I have been a man." His eyes glinted with humor. "It is a long climb, and a depressing one."

"True enough," said Josia. He paused for a moment. "Maxel, have you ever looked out the window in the top chamber? It is, after all, the only level that has a window."

Maximilian opened his mouth, then hesitated. "No, I don't think so."

"Just as well," said Josia, "for if you had then you would have been dead."

Maximilian looked startled, but before he could comment, Josia continued.

"I know something of Ravenna's vision," he said. "Tell me, Maximilian Persimius, how much do you trust Ishbel? Is she worth Elcho Falling's betrayal and destruction?"

Maximilian looked directly at Ishbel as he answered. "I trust her completely, Josia, and I do not believe her to contain Elcho Falling's betrayal and destruction, whatever vision Ravenna summons."

Ishbel took a very deep breath as Maximilian spoke.

"Are you certain, Maximilian Persimius?" Josia said in a soft voice.

"Absolutely certain," said Maximilian, and Ishbel gave him a small smile.

They stayed within the Twisted Tower until dawn. Maximilian came back to consciousness slowly, still sitting in the chair by Ishbel. He struggled to sit upright, looking at her.

She was awake, watching him.

"Thank you," she said.

"For what?"

"For trusting me."

He gave a nod, not knowing how to respond.

Then she gave a little smile. "I am afraid I do not have a flower to hand for your payment this morning."

"Then I shall take my payment in other currency," Maximilian said, and leaned forward and kissed her.

He meant to keep it brief, but somehow he did not quite lift his mouth before the kiss deepened, and he was leaning down to the bed, and she had the fingers of one hand soft against his neck.

"My lord?"

Maximilian pulled back.

Serge had entered the tent. "BroadWing has returned," he said. "He needs to speak with you."

Maximilian sank into his chair in his tent. "I cannot believe it," he muttered.

"It was a slaughter, my lord," said BroadWing. "Axis was furious."

"And now Axis undoubtedly is in the hands of Armat because of those fools," Maximilian said, and muttered a curse. He paused. "Where are the Lealfast now?"

"Axis said they'd eventually come to me for some training, but for now he has sent them off to lick their wounds. They will be rejoining you once they've had time to think. It cannot be enough time for me."

Maximilian grunted. "I cannot for the life of me believe them capable of learning any skills. You shall need good luck and some inspiration, my friend, once they join you. Well, I for one don't want to see them just yet." He paused. "Damn them, BroadWing. I cannot afford to lose Axis for any reason, let alone their stupidity."

CHAPTER SIXTEEN

The Outlands

Eleanon did not lead the remainder of his fighters north into the Sky Peaks.

After they'd left Axis, Eleanon took the Lealfast a little way north, then turned everyone southeast instead, toward the FarReach Mountains and the Salamaan Pass.

What he had done sickened him. Eleanon had known it was more than likely Armat had set a trap, but he deliberately led his fighters into it. Eleanon knew his force could probably have defeated Armat had he approached with more circumspection and cunning, but had chosen instead to approach directly, incautiously.

Thousands had died, but they had not died needlessly.

Axis now thought Eleanon—and every other Lealfast—an utter fool. That meant that Axis and Maximilian would now severely underestimate Eleanon and his fighters.

Eleanon could use that.

The One could use that.

The disaster, and Axis' contemptuous dismissal of Eleanon, also meant that Eleanon was now not only free to rejoin the Lealfast Nation waiting in the FarReach Mountains, but free to seek out Bingaleal.

Something had happened in Isembaard. Bingaleal was now something "other" than what he had been less than a day earlier.

Something more powerful.

Had he communed with the One?

All of the Lealfast with Bingaleal had transformed—*evolved*—and Eleanon needed to know what had happened.

Quite desperately.

The final positive that had resulted from what might otherwise be construed as Eleanon's total madness was that Inardle was now with Axis. Her wounding was a piece of extraordinary luck, and Eleanon had used it to best advantage.

She would be in Axis' bed within days, surely, and would prove another weapon against Axis and Maximilian.

A *weapon*. Eleanon could feel what Bingaleal and the Lealfast with him had become, and he wanted it, badly. The One could give them salvation, not the weakness that currently walked as the Lord of Elcho Falling.

So Eleanon flew southeast, drawing behind him the Lealfast fighters, toward the Lealfast Nation, toward Bingaleal and the One, and toward outright treachery against the Lord of Elcho Falling.

CHAPTER SEVENTEEN

The Central Outlands, and Isembaard

Insharah pulled his horse to a halt. It was close to dawn, and there was just enough light to see the horsemen waiting for him ahead.

Forty or fifty men.

He motioned the eight men who rode with him to wait, then urged his horse forward. When he got to within four or five paces of the group ahead of him, he reined in.

"Who goes there?" he called out.

"Perhaps we wonder the same thing," said one man, now pushing his horse forward to meet Insharah. "Ah," he said as he rode up, "you are Insharah. What is this, have you been sent out to scout for the rebellious generals? Or have you deserted with a few of your friends?"

"Neither, Risdon," said Insharah, recognizing the man as one of Armat's leading commanders. "I bring the remainder of the army to Armat, to aid him in his quest to liberate Isembaard."

Risdon smiled, a brief glint of teeth in the dim light. "The entire army, Insharah?" He peered dramatically behind Insharah. "What, eight men only? That's all that's left? Did Maximilian eat the rest for his breakfast, then?"

"The rest follow an hour's ride behind," said Insharah. "I rode out ahead, as I knew Armat must be close."

"Why should Armat trust you?" said Risdon. "You are close friends with Axis, and thus too closely allied to Maximilian for Armat to greet you easily."

"I admire both men," said Insharah, "but my loyalties are to Isembaard."

"And to Armat," said Risdon softly. "You forgot that important little bit."

"And to Armat." Insharah pulled out his sword, making the men behind Risdon draw theirs as well.

Risdon continued to sit relaxed in the saddle.

Insharah rode forward a pace and held his sword out to Risdon, who accepted it only after a long moment.

"You will be watched," said Risdon. "You surely didn't expect to be welcomed with open arms into Armat's camp."

"I am Armat's man," said Insharah.

"We'll see," said Risdon.

Isaiah woke at dawn, stiff from a night spent on the ground. He sat up, stretching slowly to unbend his muscles, and looked at Hereward.

He would not have been surprised to discover her dead. She'd lost so much blood, and was so weak, that a night spent in the cold could easily have killed her.

But even though she was lying very still, Isaiah could make out the movement of her chest.

She breathed, at least.

Isaiah stood, stretching his back as he looked around. There was movement on the eastern horizon, now faintly stained with pink.

Skraelings probably, looking for food.

Food.

He and Hereward had very little left. Hereward had existed for days while she waited for him by living off supplies from the riverboat. But while the boat had been well stocked from the kitchens of Aqhat, most of the food had been spoiled in the horrific Skraeling attack—neither Hereward nor Isaiah felt much like eating grain sodden with clotted blood—and what remained was now almost exhausted. They would need food soon.

Isaiah looked once more at Hereward, then bent down, picked up his sword, and trotted off into the lightening landscape.

Two hours later Hereward stirred, then, with some difficulty, rolled over toward the fire.

Isaiah sat there, cooking something in a pot on the coals.

It smelt like meat, and Hereward's mouth watered.

"Isaiah?"

"How are you?" he asked.

"Alive," she said. "Just. Isaiah . . . what is that you're cooking?"

He grimaced. "Four Skraelings had run down an antelope to the north. I managed to chase them off . . . there are a few mouthfuls left. Not much, I am afraid, and not the choicest bits."

"It smells good, nonetheless." Hereward looked at Isaiah more carefully. "You're injured."

"Not badly. One of the Skraelings caught my arm with its claws. It will heal soon enough."

Hereward struggled to sit up, overbalancing slightly as she almost blacked out with the effort.

"Isaiah, please, go on without me. You can leave me here. You don't need me to hold you up."

"Such a tempting idea," Isaiah said, allowing a little humor to creep into his voice, "but I can't do that. You're all of my Tyranny I have left."

He was rewarded with a small smile.

"This is almost cooked," he said. "Do you want—"

"I would eat it raw!"

Isaiah smiled—that was her desperation for blood talking—and dished out some of the barely cooked meat into a bowl.

"Insharah," Armat said. "Risdon tells me that you have decided to join us."

Insharah paused just inside the door of the tent, and saluted with his clenched fist across his chest.

"I am loyal to Isembaard," he said.

"Well, that is as may be," said Armat, "but why are you *here?*"

"Because you, too, are for Isembaard."

Armat said nothing, watching Insharah carefully.

"I bring the remainder of the army," said Insharah, "save for some few thousands who decided to remain with Maximilian."

"So also Risdon informed me. Did you not kill Maximilian?"

Insharah blinked. "No. I . . . I asked his permission to leave his command so that—"

"Don't treat me like a fool, Insharah. Do you honestly want me to believe that Maximilian just waved you good-bye happily and with warmest best wishes?"

"He did not want to hold us against our will," Insharah said. "He knew how desperate we were to aid our families. He did, indeed, wish us well."

"But you didn't tell him that you were riding toward me."

"Not in so many words, my lord, but he must have realized we'd join up with you."

Armat turned away, pretending to toy with some maps on a table so that he could think.

Ravenna had let him know that Insharah and the army were on their way to join him. She'd told him that she'd interrupted their sleep with nightmares of the cruelty their families endured, and thus Armat was not in the least surprised to discover Insharah in his tent, and approximately two hundred thousand men within a few hours' distance, but he was surprised to hear of Maximilian's willingness to allow the army to go.

Maximilian was either smarter than Armat had given him credit for, or he was a complete fool.

Armat himself was not such a complete fool that he believed the latter option. Maximilian was up to something, but whatever that "something" was, Armat knew he would not discover it from Insharah, who was enough of a fool to think that there was anything left worth trying to save in Isembaard.

"Well then," Armat said, turning about with a genial smile on his face, "I shall admit myself glad to have your company again, Insharah, and that of the men you drag at your heels."

"When will we march for Isembaard?" Insharah said.

"When we are strong enough," said Armat. "There are more men yet to join us, and supplies to organize. Now, go find Risdon and get him to organize you some breakfast, and tents and horse lines for the men soon to arrive."

Insharah saluted again, and walked over to the door. He paused just as he was about to duck through and looked back to Armat.

"Axis SunSoar and Georgdi were in this area," he said, "together with a large force of Lealfast. Have you come across them?"

"I slaughtered them," said Armat. "They were fools. But lose that look of dismay, Insharah, for Axis still lives. At my pleasure." He paused. "They wanted to stop us, Insharah. They did not want us to go home to Isembaard."

"Axis—"

"Axis is none of your business. Now leave me."

CHAPTER EIGHTEEN

The Central Outlands and Isembaard

Axis woke only very slowly. His head throbbed with pain, and he didn't want to wake enough that he might actually move it.

Stars, why come back from death if he had to endure this level of pain again?

"Axis?"

That was Zeboath's voice. Axis decided to ignore it.

"Axis . . ."

Go away, Axis thought, not wanting to use his voice in case even that small amount of movement within his head increased the pain.

"I'm going to place a compress against the back of your head, Axis."

"Don't!" Axis whispered, then moaned as agony flared up the back of his skull.

He felt a hand on his shoulder, and then a cool wet cloth placed at the back of his neck.

The pain flared again, but then very, very slowly subsided.

"Axis," Zeboath said one more time, and Axis finally, and highly reluctantly, opened his eyes.

At first he saw nothing, and had a moment of panic as he thought his injury must have blinded him. But then his eyes grew accustomed to the darkness, and he saw that he, Zeboath, and two others were sitting in some kind of cellar . . . there was a faint glimmer of light above them from a shuttered window . . . or perhaps slatted wood.

Axis was sitting slouched against a wall, and he closed his eyes again as he slowly, and very painfully, tried to sit up a little straighter, accepting Zeboath's assistance without complaint.

Stars, he was weak!

"What happened," Axis said, squinting once more into the darkness. "Where am I? Who else is here?"

"We're in a pit," came Georgdi's voice, "somewhere in Armat's camp. So far as we can work out it is midmorning. It was last night that Armat captured us. You've been unconscious for most of the night."

"One of Armat's men hit you on the back of the head with the hilt of his sword," Zeboath said. "We thought at first he'd killed you."

"Death would have been less painful," Axis muttered. "Trust me, I've been there before. Who else is here?"

"I am," came Inardle's voice, and Axis looked in the direction of her voice and saw her crouched against a far wall.

"How are you?" Axis said.

"Stiff," she said. "Sore. Heartsick."

"Did Armat . . ." Axis couldn't finish.

"Armat killed all the Lealfast," said Zeboath. "My assistants he spared, but I do not know where they are."

Shit, Axis thought.

"So what do we do now, StarMan?" Georgdi asked, a little light sarcasm in his voice.

"Wait," said Axis. "We wait."

Isaiah and Hereward had eaten what little meat there was, Isaiah making sure that Hereward had the larger share.

"We cannot leave for a few days," Isaiah said. "You are too weak."

"Isaiah, I—"

"Please don't suggest that I leave you behind. I won't do it."

Hereward almost said she was sorry again, then decided Isaiah had probably heard that too much. She was both physically and emotionally numbed from all that had happened over the past day. She could barely move, and her upper body throbbed painfully where the Skraeling talon had penetrated. Her body and robe were encrusted with blood, and she wanted nothing more than to wash . . . but they didn't have enough water to spare, and what they did have they certainly couldn't afford to contaminate with dried blood.

It was ironic, she thought, that they camped on the banks of such a great river, and there was no water.

While her physical condition distressed her, what Isaiah had told her—as well as what the One had done with that pyramid—had shocked her as even the Skraeling attack on the riverboat had not.

Hereward simply could not comprehend that so much had been happening, and that so much had not been as it had appeared. She found it difficult to grasp the fact that what she'd believed to have been a secure life had in fact been so precarious.

And Isaiah had sat there on his throne and overseen the entire disaster.

Hereward tried to be angry with him, but she couldn't summon the energy. Breathing was more important for the moment.

"Hereward," Isaiah said, "I've said some things to you that were unnecessary. Words that were hard and cruel. I was wrong to do that. You are far more than 'just' the bastard daughter of a slave and servant within my palace."

He stopped for a moment, choosing his words carefully. "The book that hit you on the head has been missing for some two thousand years. It chose you to reveal itself to and it chose to involve you in . . . all of this." He waved a hand about as if indicating all of Isembaard's troubles. "You are far more than just Hereward the kitchen steward."

Hereward was so incensed she had to close her eyes briefly. Isaiah had to make her something *other* than a serving woman in order to feel comfortable? "Does that make you feel better about traveling with me, Isaiah?" she said.

He sighed softly, then rose and left the campfire.

Axis had shifted himself closer to Inardle. His head still throbbed painfully, but the pain was subsiding little by little, and he no longer felt nauseated or so weak.

"How are you feeling, Inardle?" he asked, his voice low in a somewhat futile attempt to keep their conversation private in their cramped conditions.

"My wound throbs," she said, "but it is well enough. Zeboath said you'd done a fine job in stitching."

"Zeboath is very kind. I fear you will be marked for life with the scar I have made for you. The wing?"

"It throbs, and is swollen. Zeboath says he will need to wait for the swelling to go down before he can examine it properly. Axis . . ." Her voice broke, and she paused to compose herself. "They all were killed. Every one of them. The screams . . ."

"Inardle—"

"They died—and in fear and agony. How can one man be so cruel, Axis? What drove Armat to it?"

"Necessities of war, perhaps," Georgdi answered, breaking their illusion of privacy. "Armat understands the Lealfast as his enemies, and there was little else for him to do with a field full of wounded Lealfast than to slaughter them. Armat would not waste valuable resources on trying to save them, Inardle, and he could not have left them alive at his back!"

"Would *you* have killed them?" Inardle said.

"I don't know," Georgdi said. "If I had been afraid enough of them, then yes, perhaps. Axis? Would you have left a few thousand injured Skraelings at your back?"

Axis silently cursed the man for the question. Did Georgdi not know that Inardle was half Skraeling? *No*, he answered himself. *He probably didn't.*

"No," said Axis, "I would not have left them at my back. I would have, and have in the past, ordered them put to death."

Inardle's entire body tightened at Axis' side, and he felt her pull away from him slightly.

"They were *injured*, Axis," Inardle hissed. "They were no threat to anyone!"

"Then they should not have been injured in the first instance," Axis snapped. "For the stars' sakes, Inardle, how could Eleanon have been so *witless*? He *led* them into slaughter!"

Inardle did not answer, but Axis could feel her trembling in anger.

"Axis is right," Georgdi said. "If so many died, then it is Eleanon's fault."

"Eleanon didn't—" Inardle began.

"Will you tell me what training the Lealfast *have* had?" Axis said. "I asked Eleanon and Bingaleal once, and they snapped at me something about being an elite force. Well, I think we can all dispense with that myth here and now, yes? What fighting experience have the Lealfast had, Inardle?"

She didn't answer.

"You have lived in the northern wastes for stars knows how many thousands of years," Axis said. "What enemies did you have there? Against whom did you *perfect*—" that word was laden with sarcasm "—the arts of war?"

"Did you fight the Skraelings?" Georgdi asked.

"We are unable to fight the Skraelings," Inardle said, very low.

"Why not?" Georgdi asked.

"Inardle, as all the Lealfast," Axis said, "is half Icarii and half Skraeling. The Lealfast are, apparently, unable to harm their blood kin."

Axis couldn't see either Georgdi, or Zeboath—who was keeping well out of this conversation—very well in this darkness, but he could sense their shock.

"We trained in the frozen wastes," Inardle said into the silence, her voice very quiet and now completely devoid of emotion.

"Against whom?" Axis said.

There was a silence.

"We shot at the snow rabbits," Inardle said, loathing having to paint herself and her fellows in such a ridiculous light. *Damn Eleanon!* "We used them to perfect our skills with the bow and arrow."

We shot at the snow rabbits? Axis was so appalled that he did not know how to respond.

"Then should we be faced with an invasion of devious rabbits," said Georgdi, "we can all rest easy knowing we have such skilled soldiers to hand."

Axis couldn't help himself. He laughed.

"I apologize, Inardle," Georgdi said, his own voice still riddled with amusement.

Axis supposed he should apologize, too, but he couldn't. He just sat there in the silence that followed Georgdi's apology, allowing his amusement to go some way to relieving some of his frustration and anger.

"Why did you stay, Axis?" Inardle said eventually. "You could have left at any time. There is no need for you to be here."

"I couldn't leave the Lealfast," Axis said. "No matter how angry I am at Eleanon, or at the entire situation in general, I just could not walk away from them."

"Unlike Eleanon," Georgdi said, "who lost no time in escaping."

"That is not fair!" Inardle said. "Axis commanded him to go."

"The only thing that is not fair at the moment," said Axis, "is that Georgdi and I are making you the focus of our anger and frustration. I think what we say about the Lealfast in general, and Eleanon in particular, is fair enough. I asked Georgdi to go, and he didn't. Eleanon went, not through any cowardice as such, but because he was so shocked by what had happened at the gully that he simply could not think. As a leader and a commander, Inardle, he has a great deal to learn."

"And you shall teach him, I suppose," she said.

"If ever I get out of here," Axis said, "then maybe. And if ever I think it worth the effort."

"Are *you* such a good commander?" she said. "*I* heard that the main reason you stayed was because of me. Zeboath told me while you were unconscious that you spent hours searching for me among the wounded."

Thank you so much, Zeboath, Axis thought.

"Surely it is a pitiful thing," Inardle continued, her voice hard and bitter now, "to risk so many men just for your concern for a half Skraeling?"

"I risked myself only," said Axis. "Zeboath and Georgdi remained, or returned, of their own free will. Perhaps they were fixated on you, too."

This was beginning to sound like a lovers' spat, Axis thought, becoming ever more uncomfortable and wishing he'd not allowed Inardle to needle him. *Damn* Zeboath!

"You should have left me," Inardle said.

"Trust me when I say I'm coming around to that conclusion myself," Axis shot back.

"Oh, peace," said Georgdi. "Listen for a moment." He paused so all could strain their ears, although Georgdi thought Axis and Inardle would spend the time fuming at each other. "There are men moving about above us," he continued. "Perhaps someone will be kind enough to remember us, and give us some breakfast."

CHAPTER NINETEEN

The Central Outlands

Maximilian pulled in his horse beside that of StarDrifter's, who was choosing to ride instead of fly this day to keep company with Salome, who was confined to the ground. He glanced at her as she rode five or six paces behind, chatting to one of the Emerald Guardsmen.

"Salome is continuing well?" Maximilian said.

"Yes," StarDrifter said, "she continues well. Impatient for this child to be born, as am I, but she is well. What do you want, Maximilian? There is no need to run through the list of social politenesses before you get down to business."

"I was actually concerned, StarDrifter."

"Yes, yes. What do you want?"

"I am also very concerned about Axis."

"And so am I," StarDrifter said. "I heard about the . . . the . . ." StarDrifter was so angry about what he'd heard of the Lealfast that he simply could not finish.

"Yes, well," said Maximilian. "Axis is currently caught between Armat moving west and Insharah moving east. I worry not so much about Insharah—"

"Traitor that he is," StarDrifter put in.

"—but about Armat, who has no love for Axis. I don't know where Georgdi is right now, nor where are his men, but I worry."

"BroadWing has been talking to me," said StarDrifter.

Maximilian smiled, moving his horse aside momentarily so it could avoid a great rut in the road. "Good," he said, "that was to be my next question. StarDrifter, I believe there are some three thousand Icarii now with this column."

"Just over," StarDrifter said.

"And," Maximilian said, "of those three thousand, BroadWing tells me he has five hundred who were once in Axis' Strike Force."

StarDrifter noted the careful distinction between the Strike Force that existed before Axis took over its command—which was weak and ineffectual—and the Strike Force under Axis' command, which was a highly skilled and deadly force.

"Easily," said StarDrifter. "Maybe a few more."

"BroadWing has them training to the north."

"Yes. What do you want, Maxel?"

"They are doing well?"

StarDrifter grunted. "Better than the Lealfast. *Maxel, what do you want?*"

"I may have a use for them. Can you contact BroadWing? Fast?"

StarDrifter's eyes twinkled. "Do the stars shine in the heavens? Maxel, they are yours. You do not need to ask my permission."

Maximilian gave a smile. "Call BroadWing to me, if you would, StarDrifter."

Ravenna pulled her horse to a halt, allowing the weary animal a long rein so it could stretch its neck and relax.

It had been a hard ride getting here, but get here they had.

"They're just ahead," Ravenna said to Lister and Vorstus, who had pulled their horses up beside hers. "Look, here comes a scouting party. My friends," she said, turning a little in the saddle so she could look them in the eye, "leave Armat to me. He is touchy, and somewhat difficult. I don't want to—"

"We know how to behave, Ravenna," Lister said, "but you also need to know that we must get what we want. Armat setting off on his own dangerous ambitious tangent is not what either Elcho Falling or this world needs."

"Then leave him to me," Ravenna said. "Please. I've managed him thus far."

"And you don't want us stepping onto your territory?" Vorstus said.

"*Leave him to me!*" Ravenna snapped.

"As your ladyship wishes," Vorstus said, kicking his horse forward, Lister immediately behind him.

A moment later Ravenna gathered up her reins and urged her horse after them.

Armat heard them enter, but amused himself by keeping them waiting a few moments while he shuffled useless bits of paper on the table.

Finally he turned about, gracing Ravenna with a very slight inclination of his head. "My Lady Ravenna," he said. "How good to see you in the flesh. Those apparitions were interesting, but somehow . . . unsatisfying."

"Just Ravenna," she said. "I make no claim to pretension."

"A marsh-witch," Armat said to the two men who stood just behind and to one side of Ravenna. "Did she tell you?"

"Ravenna is well known to us," said the more commanding of the two, a tall, spare man with an ascetic face.

"As you are not yet to me," said Armat. "Ravenna, if you please?"

"This is Lord Lister," said Ravenna, indicating the man who had just spoken. "He is a man of great power and knowledge, and shall be invaluable to us. He knows Maximilian well."

Armat raised his eyebrows, although he was not in the least impressed. "You can deliver to me Elcho Falling?" he said to Lister.

"I know Elcho Falling intimately," said Lister. "I lived there for a time and know its mysteries."

Armat beamed. "Than we might as well just murder Maximilian now and depend on our new friend for what we need!"

"We still need Maximilian to open the mountain," Ravenna said. "Don't be hasty, Armat."

"I shall delay a day or two, then," Armat said. He looked to Vorstus. "And you are . . . ?"

"I am Vorstus," he said, "Abbot of the Order of Persimius. I also know Maximilian well, for I have been an intimate of the Persimius family all his life."

"Maximilian has certainly chosen his friends well," said Armat, "if such cherished acquaintances *and* his lover stand here in my tent plotting his downfall. But enough of that. You look weary. Would you like some food and drink before we continue?"

Armat waved them toward a table on which was set food and decanters of warmed ale, and for a while there was nothing but banalities passed between them as Ravenna, Lister, and Vorstus ate.

"I must thank you," Armat said eventually, wiping his mouth with a napkin after sipping at a goblet of the warmed ale, "for sending me Insharah and his men. They shall come in useful."

"And weaken Maximilian," said Vorstus.

"Indeed," said Armat, rising from his chair and stretching a little as if he had a stiff back.

"But we must insist," said Lister, "that you do not attack Maximilian right now. We need him to—"

Armat was now walking about the table. "I shall attack whoever I damn well wish to, when I damn well want to," he said. "Just like this."

In a sudden brutal movement, he whipped a dagger out of his belt with one hand, gripped the back of Vorstus's neck with the other, and slid the dagger through Vorstus's throat. Armat held him as he struggled briefly, drowning in his own blood, then allowed the dying man to sag forward across the table.

"You will do well," Armat said very quietly as he wiped his dagger on the back of Vorstus's robe before sheathing it, "to remember that you are but my allies and my guests. You are not my lords, to command me as you will."

Then he looked at Ravenna, a query on his face. "Did I kill the right man of the two, Ravenna? I didn't dispatch the most useful, by any chance, did I?"

"There was no need—" Ravenna began.

"There was every need," Armat hissed. "*I* am your ruler, and you must not believe otherwise."

Ravenna glanced at Lister, then bowed her head.

"Lord Armat," she said.

"Good," Armat said, then looked at Lister.

Lister had been staring at Vorstus, but now he lifted his eyes to the general. "I shall not be so easily disposed of, Armat."

"Don't make it a challenge, Lister," Armat said.

We should allow him to think he is our better, Ravenna said into Lister's mind, and very reluctantly Lister inclined his head.

"Excellent," Armat said, pushing Vorstus's body to the floor and taking the man's chair. He poured another measure of ale into Vorstus's goblet and took a sip.

"Where are the other generals?" Ravenna said after a long moment of uncomfortable silence.

"Kezial commands sixty thousand men about Adab," said Armat. "He undoubtedly thinks he'd like to use them against me, but he knows that by now—if, as we all suspected, Maximilian's portion of the army deserted him for me—I would have well over three hundred thousand soldiers in the Central Outlands, and Kezial is not a stupid man. He will wait where he is for the time being."

"And Lamiah?" Ravenna said.

Armat fiddled with his goblet. "Lamiah was stationed close to the Salamaan Pass," he said after a moment. "I have not heard from him recently."

"Is he heading north?" Lister said.

Armat raised his eyes and looked at Lister. "You tell me."

"How many men does he have?" Ravenna said.

"I don't know," Armat said. "Probably at least thirty thousand . . . but he may have more."

"Isaiah commanded a huge army," said Ravenna. "Where are the others?"

"Isaiah led a convoy that included settlers and families as well as soldiers," said Armat. "The settlers have now largely dispersed themselves about the southern and eastern Outlands. Of soldiers he had close to five hundred thousand. The others? Stationed here and about, and some, I assume, chose to remain with Maximilian."

"Ten thousand at most," said Ravenna. "You command by far the greater portion of the five hundred thousand, Armat, but even taking into account the men Kezial and Lamiah control, there must be tens of thousands elsewhere."

"They are likely scattered," Armat snapped. "The Outlands is a large area. Besides, they have almost no command save for relatively junior officers. They will be no trouble."

Ravenna raised an eyebrow at that, but said no more on the matter.

"Axis," said Armat, making Ravenna jump.

Axis?

"He is currently sitting," Armat continued, "together with Georgdi, a physician, and a somewhat bedraggled Lealfast woman in a pit within my camp."

"What?" Ravenna said. "How?"

"How did the almighty Axis SunSoar manage to allow himself to be captured by such a poor commander as I?" Armat asked. "Sadly, far too easily. I am wondering what to do with him."

He leaned back in the chair, tilting it backward, and rested his booted feet on the table. "I have several options," Armat said, numbering them on his fingers. "I could keep him as a hostage to bargain with against Maximilian. I could parade him and use him to demoralize the few pitiful remnants of fighting men that remain with Maximilian. I could kill him as the pathetic wretch that he is. Which do you think?"

"He is a dangerous canker within your camp, Armat," Ravenna said.

"Kill him," said Lister. "He is dangerous, and no one knows his true motives. You can't afford to keep him alive."

"He is powerless," said Armat. "He has none of his magic."

No, Ravenna said to Lister. *Don't tell Armat that Axis has—*

"He has refound the Star Dance," said Lister. "Don't think you have some washed-up outdated military commander sitting in that pit, Armat. You have instead the greatest Enchanter the Icarii have ever known, and if he continues to sit in the pit, then that is because he wants to—because it suits his purpose. Kill him. He is far too dangerous to allow to live."

CHAPTER TWENTY

Armat's Camp, the Central Outlands

A xis," said Georgdi, "I don't like to mention this, but I've heard a rumor that you discovered your connection to the Star Dance a week or so past. I don't suppose you could, ah, shed a little light on our current predicament?"

Axis roused himself from the light doze he'd fallen into. "Georgdi, I am sorry. I had gotten too used to *not* being able to use the Star Dance."

A phrase of soft music ran among the four occupants of the pit, and the next moment a soft light illumed their surroundings.

Everyone blinked.

"I'm not so sure the light was a good idea," said Axis.

No one looked their best. They had all been treated roughly by Armat's men and were dirty and bruised. Inardle looked even worse: her abrasions and wounds were now surrounded by deep bruises, and Axis thought he could see some grazes and marks on her arms that hadn't been there previously. In the time he'd known her, Inardle had always looked immaculate— her clothes simple yet elegant, her hair carefully arranged to best advantage atop her head. Now her clothes were filthy and torn, and her hair half tumbled down her shoulders.

In this soft light it looked part silver, part rosy, and it reminded Axis a little of the pyramids the Lealfast had given Lister and Isaiah.

She looked very vulnerable, and very lovely, even through the bruises and grime.

Axis realized he was staring, and looked away.

"You can't use that power to aid us escape?" Zeboath said to Axis. He probably looked the best of the quartet, but even so his eyes were ringed with exhaustion and his skin was unnaturally pale.

Axis gave a little shake of his head. "While I have managed to reconnect to the Star Dance, it is in a different manner than previously. The Dance is all about me, but far more subtle than what I could hear when it thundered through the Star Gate. I am still learning to use it in this form, learning its nuances. I have nowhere near the power I had as StarMan—" he grinned "—even though that title is once again being bandied about, and only a tiny percentage of what I commanded as Star God. Inardle, no doubt, would sneer at my limited capabilities. The Enchanter cannot rescue you from this pit, Zeboath, but I hold out hope for the man."

"I do not sneer at you, Axis," Inardle said. "I could not have provided that light with my own command of the Star Dance." She paused, glancing at him with an awkward expression. "Thank you for the light. It is most welcome and more than comforting."

Axis felt a little ashamed of his anger toward her earlier; she was not to blame for Eleanon's stupidity.

"You use the Star Dance differently from Icarii Enchanters," he said to her. "Would you explain to me how?"

Inardle sat thinking for a little while, and Axis thought she struggled with the Lealfast's general tendency toward wrapping themselves in mystery in order to bolster their own importance.

Eventually, however, Inardle spoke.

"Before the Star Gate was destroyed," she said, "you used music to access the Star Dance. You literally heard the Star Dance, and thus your command over its power was vast. Now, I believe you access the Dance by vision, by 'reading' it in the fall of dust motes, the way a woman's skirt ruffles in the wind, the clouds in the sky."

"Yes," Axis said, "and in suddenly realizing we can *read* it, we realize the Star Dance is still all around us, and once again we allow it to filter through our bodies. It is a paler version of what once we heard, but it is still there."

"We are not so fortunate," said Inardle, moving ever deeper into her deception. "I, like all the Lealfast, need to literally *feel* the movement of the Star Dance—wind, usually. In here, in this windless pit, I am powerless.

Even when outside among the elements, our use of the Dance is limited. We could not, for example, do what you just did in providing light. Our abilities are largely centered on movement, on the ability to fly with the Dance through the air. It is pretty, and useful, but limited in scope. Possibly that is because . . ."

"Of your Skraeling blood," said Axis. "But then, I had a human mother and am only half Icarii, and that has not affected my ability to use the Star Dance. My wife, Azhure, is the same. She is exceptionally powerful, but also had a human mother."

"The Skraeling blood corrupts us," said Inardle. "It limits us."

"You are very ambivalent about your Skraeling heritage," said Axis.

"We want more than anything to escape it," Inardle said. She paused, then spoke again. "You asked once why we are so loyal to Maxel as Lord of Elcho Falling."

"You spun a pretty tale about legends and whispers, as I remember," Axis said.

"It was true enough, but there is more depth to it. We loathe our Skraeling blood, *loathe* it." She paused, her teeth gleaming in the low light. "Almost as much as we despise our Icarii heritage. We yearn for the day when we can be free of both Skraeling and Icarii blood and be pure Lealfast, not half-breeds. We want to *own* our heritage and our blood, not be indebted to two races who loathe us for the taint of the other.

"Those icy whispers told us that the only one who had enough power to manage this for us was the Lord of Elcho Falling. We have yearned for him, Axis. We thought him the one who could save us, offer us the salvation of our own identity, our own future. But . . ."

"But?" Axis said.

"But now we hear that Maximilian wields only a fraction of what the ancient Lords of Elcho Falling once commanded."

"Who told you that?" Axis said.

Inardle shrugged. "General camp gossip," she said. "Is it true?"

Now it was Axis who hesitated. "Yes."

Inardle sighed. "Then there is no hope for us, Axis. None. Who else can aid us, if not Maximilian?"

Axis didn't respond to that, and the group sat quietly for a while. They could hear the sounds of the encampment above them, horses moving, men talking and occasionally laughing, the clatter of cooks' pans and weapons being cleaned.

Axis found himself focusing on the clatter of cooks' pans, and the faint aroma of meat cooking, and tried to forget how hungry he was.

Some time passed, then everyone jumped as a grating noise came from above them.

Several of the large logs of wood rolled away and daylight flooded the pit.

A soldier leaned in: Risdon.

"Armat wants to see you, Axis."

CHAPTER TWENTY-ONE

Armat's Camp, the Central Outlands

Several soldiers jumped down into the pit, trampling on Georgdi's and Zeboath's legs, who were not quick enough to rise.

Axis cried out, grabbing at one of the soldiers, but the next instant was himself grabbed from behind and thrust against the crumbly earth wall of the pit as his hands were tied behind him.

"Get the woman, too," one of the guards snapped.

"For the stars' sakes," said Axis, "Armat can't need anything from—"

"Keep quiet," said the guard directly behind Axis, and put his hand into the center of Axis' back and pushed him into the wall again, so that Axis had to spit out dirt in order to keep breathing. "Keep that mouth shut or I'll take out my anger on the woman. Understand?"

Axis was fuming, but he kept quiet. He tried to make eye contact with Inardle, to reassure her, but she was not looking at him, and was the next moment lifted roughly in the air for a guard on the surface to haul upwards.

The man grabbed one of her wings, lifting her by that, and she cried out in pain.

Axis turned around, about to protest, but the guard hit him on the side of his jaw with the hilt of a dagger, and Axis sagged, rendered half insensible by the blow.

Rough hands grabbed him, too, and he was hauled up to the surface.

"Walk, damn it," said the guard, pushing Axis in the small of the back so that he stumbled forward. "Armat awaits."

Axis walked forward, concentrating on remaining upright, and thinking that if ever he met these guards with his hands unbound they would live to regret their treatment of Inardle.

They led Inardle and Axis—Inardle several paces forward so that Axis had no way of catching her eye—through the encampment toward a rust-red tent erected at the end of three long horse lines. Axis spent the time looking about, studying the encampment.

Armat had set up a tight camp, and Axis thought, more than grudgingly, that any general capable of this might well prove a formidable opponent on the battlefield.

A camp always reflected the quality of its leadership.

Axis kept his head high as they walked, although it galled him that many of these men would know him, and see him humiliated in this fashion, and he wondered if they gloated or were embarrassed.

Just before they reached Armat's tent, Axis saw Insharah standing ten or twelve paces away, partway behind a horse.

Axis sent him a cold look, then ducked inside the tent flap as the guard behind gave him a shove.

What he saw inside appalled him.

Armat standing in the center of the tent commanding attention, was nothing more or less than Axis had expected. But Lister? And *Ravenna?*

"Maximilian's suspicions were true, then," Axis said, staring at Ravenna. "You *are* a traitorous bitch, and once I had thought better of you." He turned his head to Lister, standing toward the back of the tent. "Your falseness, however, doesn't surprise me. I remember counseling Isaiah against you."

"Words of swaggering bravado," said Lister, "do nothing to bolster either your position or your reputation, Axis. I'd advise you to keep quiet and see if you can't reclaim some dignity."

That stung, and Axis felt his cheeks redden. "Where is your companion in treachery, Vorstus?" he said.

Lister said nothing, but his eyes slid to a large bloodstain on the carpet.

"Dead?" Axis said, incredulous.

Lister gave a small shrug of his shoulders. "Armat felt a lesson needed to be learned."

Stars! Axis looked away, toward Inardle, who was being held to one side.

Her rough treatment at the hands of the guards had pulled apart her attempts to stitch her clothing together, and her torn tunic had fallen away from her side, exposing her stitched wound and most of one breast.

Axis glanced at her face, knowing she would be humiliated. Besides himself, Armat, Lister, and Ravenna, there were four or five other soldiers within the tent, and Axis could see at least two of them grinning toward Inardle.

He looked again at Lister. The man had been Inardle's lover. Had he no feeling left for her? How could he allow this?

"I thought I'd have a few words with you, Axis SunSoar," Armat said, "before I have you killed. You are of little use to me, and Lister advises that we'd all rest a little easier with you dead than alive."

"And is this what you counseled, Ravenna?" Axis said, and she colored and turned her eyes away.

"You do not speak until I require it!" Armat said. He looked behind Axis. "Risdon . . . if you please."

Armat's second-in-command brushed roughly past Axis and walked over to Inardle. With three or four brutally rough movements, he tore away all her clothing, leaving her utterly naked before everyone within the tent.

She closed her eyes, and Axis saw her cringe within the guard's grip.

"I can, and will, do a great deal worse to her," Armat said, "if you do not cooperate, Axis."

"*Lister!*" Axis hissed. "For the gods' sakes! Have you no pity? She was your—"

Armat stepped forward and hit Axis across the face with his fist. Had it not been for the fact that the guard behind Axis still held his bound arms, Axis would have fallen over. As it was, his vision grayed for a moment, and he felt blood run down his chin and neck from a cut on his cheekbone.

"I have some questions you can answer, Axis," Armat said conversationally. "I am still going to kill you, but in answering them truthfully you can spare Inardle some indignities that I am certain Risdon would love—" the word rolled off Armat's tongue with a bleak lasciviousness "—to inflict upon her. Do you understand me?"

Axis shook his head, trying to clear his vision.

"Do you understand me, Axis?" Armat said, gesturing to Risdon, who grabbed at Inardle's breasts.

"Yes, I understand you!" Axis said. "Please, leave her alone."

A small smile filtered across Armat's face. "Good. Now, to details. What is the strength of the Icarii with Maximilian?"

Axis did not immediately answer, and Armat nodded to Risdon, who motioned the guard holding Inardle to step to one side. Risdon then stood behind Inardle, sliding his hands about her body and pulling her back against his own body.

One of his hands slid down her belly, toward the fine blond hair at her groin, as he simultaneously lowered his face, grabbing at her shoulder with his teeth. Inardle cried out, struggling uselessly against him.

"I am not sure of exact numbers," Axis ground out, unable to tear his eyes away from Inardle's humiliation, "but over the past weeks some two and a half, perhaps three thousand Icarii have joined my father—"

"StarDrifter SunSoar," Ravenna said, her voice calm, "now Talon of the Icarii."

"And are they just pretty drifters?" said Armat. "Or do they constitute some danger? How many Enchanters do they have among them? Although," Armat said, turning to address his remarks now to Ravenna, "I cannot think their magic very useful, if all Axis can do to save this petty creature is to mouth useless words."

Axis felt more angry, and more useless, than ever. Most of what he could do now with his power would be utterly useless against the weapons within this room. He might be able to save himself, but not Inardle.

He was also very wary of Ravenna, for he knew she commanded powerful skills that he had no doubt she would use against him.

"I believe Lister overestimated Axis' powers," Ravenna said. She caught Axis' eyes with that, and for an instant he wondered if she were more ally than enemy.

"Answer my questions, Axis," Armat said, holding out a hand as if to signal to Risdon again.

"There are forty or fifty Enchanters among the Icarii with Maximilian," Axis said. "We have only just rediscovered our power, and are learning to use it properly. We are not, as you have realized, at our best right now."

"All the more reason to kill him quickly, and any Enchanter we find," said Lister.

"I concur," said Armat. "But back to my little interrogation. What are the Icarii doing with Maximilian, Axis?"

"They are traveling with him to Elcho Falling," said Axis. "My father wants to reform the Icarii nation, and thought to use Elcho Falling as a base."

"Very pretty," Armat said. "Now tell me, Axis, why did Maximilian allow so many men to desert so willingly?"

"I doubt he had any damned choice."

Armat gave a little shrug. "I heard he waved them good-bye and wished them well. Why?"

"Maximilian is a man who does not hold others against their will."

"He must have something planned," Armat said.

"Then it must be subtle, and I do not think subtlety something you can grasp, Armat."

Armat gave Axis a cold look, then spun on his heel, and strode over to where Risdon still held Inardle. He grabbed Inardle out of the man's grasp and threw her to the floor.

Armat grabbed one of her wings, held it so that it spread out before him, then stamped down on it with all his strength.

Bones and tendons snapped, the sharp cracks and pops appalling in the confines of the tent, and Inardle screamed, writhing and twisting away from Armat, causing her wing yet more damage as he had not let it go.

"What is he planning?" Armat hissed.

"I don't know!" Axis shouted. "*I don't know!*"

"He doesn't know," said Lister.

"Fuck you," Armat said to Lister in a calm voice. He let Inardle go—Risdon immediately snatched her back into his grip, causing her to almost black out with the pain from her broken wing as he crushed it between their bodies—and strolled back toward Axis.

"How many of the Lealfast are left?" Armat asked.

"Does it matter?" Axis said. "They're damned useless, as you have proven."

Armat turned back toward Inardle.

"I have no way of estimating the dead," said Axis hurriedly, "but I sent some fifteen thousand flying off to lick their wounds. I think they are somewhere in the lower Sky Peaks. Most of them are in a state of shock or injury. They are useless."

"And that must be the first utterly truthful thing you've said to me since you came into this tent," Armat muttered.

"There was a force of some twenty thousand that went south into Isembaard to aid refugees," said Axis. "We don't know what happened to those. We *don't*, Armat. Isaiah was with them, and they have all, apparently, been killed by whatever it is that now controls Isembaard."

"A toddler with a reed could kill the Lealfast," said Armat. "If they are dead it doesn't signify that what waits in Isembaard is of any concern."

Fool, thought Axis, hoping that Armat was about to murder himself by ordering a march back south through the Salamaan Pass.

"Malat?" Armat said, surprising Axis with the question. "The state of the Central Kingdoms?"

"Malat has taken a small force to go back and see," Axis said. He glanced at Lister, knowing that Lister knew this information and that he couldn't lie. "While Pelemere was destroyed, as was much of the western parts of the Central Kingdoms, I believe the rest of the Kingdoms escaped fairly unscathed from the Skraeling invasion."

"So Malat could raise an army?" Armat said.

"Not enough to bother you," Axis said.

Armat grunted. "Perhaps." He turned and looked to Lister. "Has he told the truth?"

"Mostly," said Lister. "As he understands it."

"What are you doing, Lister?" Axis said. "Why turn on Maximilian like this? I had thought you'd dedicated your life to grooming him for Elcho Falling. And why allow such treatment of Inardle? She was your *lover!* Do you have no feeling for her at all?"

That was quite a speech, and Axis was sure that Armat would punish him for it, but Armat seemed unconcerned, and motioned to Lister to answer.

"Inardle is immaterial," said Lister. "There is too much at stake to waste energy on her." He looked at Inardle. "I am sorry, my dear. I was quite fond of you, but there is far more here than you can comprehend."

Lister looked back to Axis. "As there is much you do not know, nor comprehend. Ravenna and I are certain that Maximilian has been corrupted, and—"

"For stars' sakes, Lister—you cannot surely have been seduced by Ravenna's jealousy of Ishbel?"

"This goes far beyond Ishbel," Lister said quietly. "I liked her, too, as once I liked Inardle. But Ishbel needs to die if this land is to be saved. Maximilian cannot see that."

"You're going to march on Elcho Falling, aren't you?" Axis said. "Armat, have you told your men that? They were not happy to march to Elcho Falling with Maximilian while Isembaard was being eaten; they'll not do it for *you!*"

"Silence!" Armat shouted. "You have *no* idea of what this army will do for me!" He looked at the guards. "Take him back to the pit. We can haul him out later, with his friends, for an execution at my pleasure."

"Inardle—" Axis began.

"Inardle can live," said Armat. "For the time being. I am giving her to Risdon as a reward for his services."

The guards behind Axis grabbed at him, hauling him away toward the door.

Axis managed one brief glance at Inardle, and stumbled in horror at the expression in her eyes.

CHAPTER TWENTY-TWO

Armat's Camp, and Maximilian's Camp, the Central Outlands

They took Axis back to the pit, literally throwing him into it before re-sealing it with the great logs of wood.

"Axis!" Georgdi helped him to his feet. "Where's Inardle?"

"Armat . . ." Axis had to stop and bring his anger under control before he could continue. "Armat tortured her to get information from me, then gave her to Risdon to play with as he wanted."

"Shit!" Georgdi said. "What—"

"Ravenna and Lister have joined Armat and are aiding him to launch an attack on Elcho Falling."

"Ravenna I am not surprised at," Georgdi said, "but *Lister?*"

"Aye," Axis said. "Gods, Georgdi, Isaiah is dead, and Lister turned trai-tor. Maximilian has sore need of good and true friends."

"And us?" Zeboath said softly into the darkness. "Are we soon to join the list of Maximilian's once-friends?"

Axis hesitated, then spoke plainly. "He has ordered our execution—at a time of his choosing. No doubt he will let us linger here a while and fear. I am sorry, my friends."

"This is hardly your fault," Georgdi said. Then he grinned, his teeth a brief flash in the darkness. "We'll just have to fight this one out, Axis."

Axis could not find the heart to smile at the jest. "I fear the odds are a little against us, Georgdi."

He felt his way over to one of the earthen walls, too dispirited to work the enchantment for light, and sat down, back against the wall.

He stayed like that for hours, staring into the darkness, trying not to think and worry about Inardle, and failing utterly.

Maximilian had pushed the columns hard during the day, determined to reach Elcho Falling as fast as possible, but tonight, instead of resting, he went to Josia in the Twisted Tower. Ishbel did not come with him this time. Tonight, as Maximilian suspected every night for the foreseeable future, would be spent with Josia, learning the objects that had vanished.

"What did you mean about the top chamber?" Maximilian asked Josia as they climbed into the first of the chambers which had items missing. "You said that had I ever looked out the window I would have died."

"What exists out the window," said Josia, "requires a Lord of Elcho Falling to be at his full strength and power to view. We will work our way there gradually, item by item, chamber by chamber."

"Do you know what it is?"

"Yes."

"Not even a hint?"

Josia laughed. "Not even a hint, Maximilian. Tell me, you said you have been to the top chamber . . . yet you never looked out the window? Most people would, having climbed all that way. They would think a view recompense for the long climb. Why didn't you look?"

They had reached the chamber they would be working in tonight and Maximilian stopped, thinking. "I don't really know, Josia. I certainly looked at the window, and I remember taking a step toward it, but I always turned away." He shrugged. "I don't know."

"Then you either have good instincts or a good protector, Maximilian Persimius," said Josia. He leaned back against a wall, crossing his arms, and regarded Maximilian speculatively. "You love Ishbel, yet are not with her. Do you doubt her still?"

"No. I don't doubt her at all. I am sick of doubting her."

"Yet others plead with you to forsake her."

"Ravenna?"

Josia inclined his head. "And others, too, I suspect."

"I am sick to death of doubting her, Josia. That's all. I doubted her once, and look what a disordered mess we have found ourselves in."

"It would be better, for everyone, if you were husband and wife again."

Maximilian smiled. "At least *you* do not doubt her. But as to the husband and wife, Josia, that needs to be decided between Ishbel and me."

"Indeed." Josia straightened up. "I am going to take up six of your hours tonight, Maximilian. These are six hours when you should be sleeping, but we have little time and much to accomplish."

"I can doze well enough in the saddle."

"Good! Then see here, this space between the brass lantern and the egg cup. Can you imagine what should sit here?"

"Something tall and heavy, by the shape of the dust-free area and the scratches on the table surface."

"Yes. It is in fact a porcelain candlestick. See?"

As Josia spoke, Maximilian saw the air move slightly and a shadow grew in the space of the missing object.

"You need to realize it, not just accept what I say," Josia said softly, watching Maximilian keenly. "You need to understand not only what the object physically is, but what knowledge it represents."

"How can I know what knowledge it—"

"Look to the objects surrounding it: the lantern, the egg cup, the folded hessian cloth just behind it. You know the knowledge they represent?"

"Yes. They are all concerning the peak of Elcho Falling, and what it contains."

"And you know what that is."

"Yes."

Now it was Josia who smiled. "So tell me what knowledge this candlestick will contain."

Maximilian frowned. Surely Josia could just tell him? But then he realized that no, Josia couldn't "just tell him." Maximilian had to somehow "remember" it.

He concentrated, looking at the lantern, the egg cup, and the folded hessian cloth, and going over in his mind what knowledge they represented. They were all to do with the mystery at the top of Elcho Falling, and specifically how to access that mystery. Maximilian cast his gaze about the table, going over all the objects, looking for the missing blank in his knowledge of how to access the . . .

"The candlestick contains the knowledge of the location of the door to the peak of Elcho Falling," Maximilian said, and as he said the words the candlestick materialized in the space it had once occupied.

"Exactly!" Josia said. "Pick it up now, and learn what you need."

But Maximilian hesitated. "Josia, I could work that out because of the objects surrounding the candlestick. I could discover what blank I had in my knowledge. But so many chambers are utterly empty. There are no clues. How then can I—"

"By skill and cunning," said Josia. "But do not worry about it yet. By the time you reach the utterly empty chambers you shall have learned a few new talents. Now, pick up that candlestick and learn the location of the door to the mystery at the peak of Elcho Falling."

They worked for hours through the night, until Josia called a halt.

"You are tired, Maxel. Return to your bed, and sleep for a few hours."

They walked to the door, but before he left, Maximilian turned to Josia. "I have a request of you," he said. "A favor I would ask you grant me."

"Yes?" said Josia.

Axis supposed that he had slept a few hours, for when he heard his name being hissed through the gaps in the wooden logs which imprisoned them in the pit, he felt groggy and a little stupid, as if he had just woken.

"Axis!"

He blinked, trying to orientate himself.

"*Axis!*"

He rose to his feet, slipping a little on the damp floor. *Stars, he would end up crippled with rheumatism if he had to spend much longer in this hole!*

"Axis!"

"Insharah," Axis said softly. He stretched his back and legs, then jumped up, managing to slip his fingers through the cracks between the logs. He swung his legs up so that his feet pushed against one of the pit walls and, thus propped, firmed his grip on the logs.

"Axis, are you all right?"

Insharah sounded as though he was leaning over the logs, his mouth pressed close to the gap where Axis had his fingers.

"Oh well," Axis said, "apart from living under a death sentence, and a few scrapes and bruises, I'm perfectly well thank you. You?"

"Axis, I came to explain—"

"I don't want any explanation of why you deserted Maxel. I do assume, however, that you now live with peace and joy in your heart at discovering such a fine commander to serve."

Insharah didn't immediately respond. "Axis, we needed to aid our families and—"

"And you think the fuck Armat is going to do that for you? He is planning on making war on Maximilian at Elcho Falling, my once-reliable friend. Isembaard can go to hell for all he cares."

Now Insharah was completely silent.

"Look," Axis said, adjusting his grip with both legs and arms, all of which were beginning to ache. "I think Isembaard is lost anyway. Isaiah is dead, so we believe, and I think all the Lealfast that went south with him are dead as well. Isembaard is lost."

"Then I might as well stay with Armat. He is what I know."

"As you wish, Insharah, but there is war coming, and you are going to have to make a final choice. Maximilian or Armat."

"We'd choose *you*, StarMan."

"Oh, fine words, indeed, considering you will not lift a finger to aid me to escape!"

Again Insharah was silent, and Axis sighed. "I know you cannot aid me, Insharah. To do so would be to sign your own death warrant. But I ask you, how can you respect any man who thus imprisons me, and Zeboath, who is also your friend, and so brutalizes a woman? You have heard what happened in Armat's tent?"

Again silence, but Axis could swear that this time it was far more uncomfortable than previously.

"He tortured her, Insharah, having just murdered a few thousand of her wounded kin. How many of those did *you* murder, Insharah? How many did—"

"That's enough, Axis!"

"No, it isn't, damn it! Is any of this to your liking? If it was, you wouldn't be here trying to seek absolution." He paused. "Insharah, is Armat planning on executing Zeboath as well?"

A hesitation. "Yes."

"Ah, for the stars' sakes! Zeboath is a physician! Armat doesn't need a physician?"

"He doesn't trust him."

"Then the man is a fool as well as being a bully. What happened to Zeboath's assistants?"

"They were killed."

Axis heard Zeboath cry out softly below him, and then a movement, as if the physician had slid to the ground in his distress.

"Insharah, Armat has killed the defenseless and the innocent, and he has given a crippled women to Risdon to rape as he wants! *Tell me you respect this man!*"

Axis waited a few heartbeats. "Ah," he said softly, "your silence says it all, eh? Insharah, where has Risdon taken Inardle?"

"His tent is some fifty paces directly east of Armat's."

"How does the rest of the army feel about what Armat has done, Insharah?"

"Uneasy, which is why I am here talking to you now, and which is why I *can* talk to you now without your guards hauling me off to Armat. Axis, I am sorry, but I am afraid that I can do nothing. The world is chaos and I do not know which way to turn."

"Then dispel some of that chaos by aiding a woman in need, Insharah, if not myself, Zeboath, and Georgdi."

But there was no answer save the sound of a man rising and taking a step away.

"Insharah?"

The sound of steps stopped.

"Insharah, look after yourself and yours, but when the time comes, make the decision that is right."

There was no movement for several heartbeats, then the sound of steps resumed.

Axis jumped back down to the floor of the pit, rubbing his fingers.

"Do you think he will help?" Georgdi asked quietly.

"He agonizes within himself," said Axis, "and maybe one day he will turn against Armat . . . but not in time to save either our lives, or Inardle's."

CHAPTER TWENTY-THREE

Armat's Camp, the Central Outlands

More time passed. The three men sat against three different walls of the pit, not speaking, but not sleeping, either.

Axis shifted uneasily, unable to stop thinking about Inardle.

He hoped that Risdon would kill her sooner rather than later, and then hated himself for that thought.

He wondered if her body would frost when he raped her, and loathed himself for that reflection.

Eventually, through sheer determination to empty his mind, Axis slipped into another fitful doze. As he slipped deeper into unconsciousness, disconnected images began to flit across his mind until, finally . . .

"Axis?"

He blinked, then leapt to his feet, staring about.

"Axis, don't worry. We are in the Land of Dreams. I brought you here while you slept."

He turned around.

Ravenna stood there, wrapped in a cloak she hugged about herself. Her lovely face looked gaunt and pale.

"What do you want?" he said, his voice harsh.

"I needed to talk."

"Everyone seems to need to talk to me." Axis paused, again looking about. He seemed to be standing on a pathway in the middle of a marsh, mist drifting out of shadowy, ghostly trees to either side. He could hear the sharp plop, plop, plop of condensation dripping from their branches. "Where are we?"

"In the Land of Dreams. This is just glamour, Axis. I have not removed you physically from the pit."

She had huge power just to do this much, Axis thought. "I suppose you need to explain yourself to me as well," he said. "Guilt is keeping everyone awake tonight."

"Axis, I can save your life, but I need you to do something for me."

"And Georgdi's life? And Zeboath's? And Inardle's?"

"Inardle is already dead."

"*What?*"

"Perhaps not literally, not just yet, but she can't be saved now, Axis."

He turned and walked away from her at that point, standing a few paces distant, staring into the marshland.

She can't be saved now, Axis.

"I can save you, and Georgdi and Zeboath," Ravenna said, "but I need you to do something for me."

"No."

"Will you not hear what it is I want? Axis, *please . . .*"

He turned to face her. "I'll say again what I said in Armat's tent, Ravenna, you are a traitorous—"

"I have reason for what I do, Axis! Please, please, I beg you, *listen to me!*"

He stood still, silent, stony.

"Ishbel—" Ravenna began.

"Don't start on her," Axis said. "Everything you say is tainted by your jealousy."

"Everything I say is tainted by my *knowledge,* Axis." Ravenna was calmer now. "Ishbel the woman, I have nothing against. If she were not caught up in this nightmare then I would undoubtedly like her. She would make a good marsh witch."

Ravenna gave a tiny smile at the expression on Axis face. "Ah, that wasn't what you were expecting to hear, eh? But Ishbel as Maxel's lover or wife? No, then she becomes dangerous beyond knowing. Then she becomes this world's destroyer."

"Oh, for the stars' sakes, Ravenna—"

"If Ishbel continues to live then she will eventually destroy this world. I have seen this! But if Maximilian puts Ishbel to one side, or if—"

"If he kills her."

"Yes, if he kills her, then this world has a chance. But I fear he will never do this."

"What do you want *me* to do, Ravenna? Kill Ishbel for you?"

Again, that tiny, sad smile. "Would you? No, I thought not. I just need you to agree to talk to Maxel. Maybe from you . . ."

"He loves her, Ravenna. He won't listen to me."

"He is the lord of Elcho Falling first, Axis. The Lord of Elcho Falling might listen to you, even if Maxel won't. If he could just set her aside . . . I can hold Armat back for a while, give him time to think about it. But Axis, whatever else Maxel does, he can't take Ishbel back into his bed."

Axis gave a disbelieving laugh. "I can't tell him that!"

"Then you must ensure it!"

"I won't—"

"Axis, listen to me. Once I showed Maximilian a vision. It depicted Ishbel opening the doors of Elcho Falling to a nameless monster. A dark creature of great evil. Then, neither of us knew who that was. Recently, the vision changed, Axis. Very recently. Within the past day. Look, Axis." Ravenna flung one arm out toward the mists. "*Look.*"

Axis looked, and saw that the marshlands had vanished. He saw a roadway winding its serpentine path toward a distant mountain which gleamed with gold at its top set among the clouds.

Elcho Falling.

The road was littered with the bodies of men and horses. Icarii lay among the dead, and Emerald Guardsmen, and Axis could see Georgdi lying atop a heap of Outlanders to one side of the roadway.

"Look," said Ravenna.

An army now marched along the roadway toward Elcho Falling, pushing aside the bodies of the fallen as it went. The army consisted of creatures distorted into gruesome form, their eyes wide and starting—lost and hopeless.

At their head marched a man made of liquid glass, a tiny glowing golden pyramid pumping within his chest.

"This is what Ishbel shall call upon this land," Ravenna said.

The army marched its way to the doors of Elcho Falling, and Axis and Ravenna saw, as if they stood only feet away, the man of glass reach forth and pound his fist on the gates.

The gates shrieked, and opened, and Maximilian saw Ishbel crawl forth on her hands and knees, weeping.

The man of glass reached down to her, and lifted her left hand, and Maximilian saw gleaming on Ishbel's fourth finger the Queen's ring.

"You are the One," Ishbel whispered, "and you are the One I worship."

Then, suddenly, the vision winked and blurred, then vanished.

"Do you know who, what, that is?" Ravenna said.

"Visions can lie," he said.

"*Why will no one believe me?*" Ravenna cried, and it was her evident distress that finally earned some sympathy from Axis.

"What do you want me to do?" he said.

"Please, just talk to Maxel. Tell him that I love him, and that I am not trying to destroy him. Tell him that all I want is for him, and this land, to survive. But tell him also that I know Ishbel will be his undoing, as that of this land. Tell him . . ." She hesitated. "Tell him that is why I killed my mother, because—"

"*You killed Venetia?*"

"She tried to stop me, Axis. Do you think I wanted to do—"

Axis took a step back. "Stars, woman, you are crazed! You murdered *your own mother?*"

"Axis, please, will you tell Maxel what I have said? Will you tell him what I have seen? If you promise me, then it is your life, and Georgdi's and Ze-boath's. I can get you to safety."

The last thing Axis wanted to do was to bring news of this vision to Maxel.

On the other hand . . . if Ravenna could aid him escape . . .

"I will tell him, Ravenna. But he won't listen to me."

"All I need is for you to tell him what you have seen, Axis. Thank you."

CHAPTER TWENTY-FOUR

On the Road to Serpent's Nest

Ishbel? Will you ride with me a while?"

"Of course, Maxel."

She turned her horse after Maximilian, who was riding a little distance into the surrounding countryside.

"You look tired," she said as she reined in beside him.

They both pulled their horses back to a walk, ambling along twenty paces from the main part of the column.

"I spent most of last night with Josia," Maximilian said. "He left me enough time only for a few hours' sleep."

"And?"

He smiled. "So now there are a few more objects in the Twisted Tower, and a little more knowledge is gained."

"I'm glad."

"Ishbel, I asked Josia for a favor."

"Did he grant it?"

"I asked him to teach you as much as he could about the Twisted Tower, and the memories it contains. He agreed. Ishbel, I want you to know as much as I about Elcho Falling."

"Why?"

"Because I do not want it to just be me with this knowledge, Ishbel."

Ishbel took a deep breath, still staring at Maximilian. "Thank you," she said.

Maximilian gave a nod, but didn't say anything.

"When should I go?"

"I don't see any reason why we cannot work there together, Ishbel. The evenings and nights are the only time when we can spare the hours to slip away to the tower. I can work by myself a good deal of the time, while Josia works with you. If I need him I can call. With luck, you can catch up with me."

They talked for a while about the Twisted Tower, and the training both would undergo within its walls, then Ishbel changed the subject. "Garth told me something of what happened between you and Ravenna. I wish that Venetia had not had to give her own life to save mine."

"It is not your fault that Venetia is dead."

She shrugged.

"Ishbel, I am going to say something now, and I do not want you to either interrupt me or to spur your horse away from me. Can you just listen?"

She gave a nod.

"You and I, Ishbel . . . we met at the wrong time, and married at the wrong time. We both made some terrible mistakes, and said things that we both regret. I certainly regret what I said to you in the snow, when I denied you for Ravenna. No, Ishbel, hear me out, I beg you."

Maximilian paused to take a deep breath. "We would make a good marriage together now, I think. I *know* you said that there was no possibility of this, and that whatever was once between us was gone. Maybe so, and maybe that is a good thing. But what we could make between us now, Ishbel . . . I think that could be very good indeed.

"Just think about it. Please. Just think about it."

Ishbel stared at him, and Maximilian held her eyes for a long moment before he spurred his horse away.

That night they met within the Twisted Tower. There was a moment of awkwardness, then Ishbel relaxed and smiled, and the awkwardness passed.

They worked through the night with Josia, who spent most of his time with Ishbel. Three hours before dawn, he sent them back to their beds.

Alone in her tent, Ishbel dressed for bed, then sat on its edge, the Goblet of the Frogs in her hands. Holding it each night had become almost a ritual for her, strengthening her sense of peace.

Tonight, it wanted to chat.

Maximilian has asked you to marry him once more.

"How did you know that?" Ishbel asked.

Well, he was wearing his Persimius ring, and the ring told Serge's sword, which told Madarin's belt buckle when the two met for a game of dice at dusk. Then—

"Then the belt buckle told *you*," Ishbel muttered. "Am I to have no secrets?"

We all think it would be a good idea, the goblet said, and Ishbel sighed and put the goblet away. She was damned if she was going to marry a man simply because a ring, a sword, a belt buckle, and a goblet thought it a good idea.

CHAPTER TWENTY-FIVE

Isembaard

On the morning of the third day after the One had shown Isaiah the curse, and had caused Hereward to be so badly injured, Isaiah busied himself making final preparations for the journey back to Maximilian. Every day that he had spent waiting in their little camp by the river had galled him, but there was little he could do about it. Hereward had been in no condition to travel in the immediate days after she'd been injured, and even now Isaiah knew he was risking her life.

But he had to leave for the north. He had to.

Hereward could totter a few steps about the camp, but she was incapable of doing anything more. Isaiah couldn't leave her—to do so would be to make a mockery of relinquishing his power—but he knew he couldn't carry her, either.

So he spent the few days waiting for her to grow stronger either hunting out the occasional rabbit (and twice finding the remaining entrails and meaty bones of beasts that the Skraelings had eaten), or building a cart with which he could transport Hereward and what supplies they could take with them. He had found a small trolley on the riverboat, used for wheeling about casks of water and wine, and with its wheels and axle he had fashioned a small cart. With some canvas and ropes from the boat, he made a comfortable harness with which to pull it.

"When will we leave?" Hereward asked softly as Isaiah sat across the fire from her, sewing the last strap of the harness into place. She rarely spoke to him. This was not because of her guilt at what he had done for her and how she currently held him back, all of which she continued to feel keenly, but because she felt so out of place in his life. They had no common ground save that both had lived in the palace at Aqhat.

Even that divided rather than united them. He the Tyrant, she the serving woman; nothing in their lives had ever touched.

"Tomorrow morning," Isaiah said. He set the harness to one side, then stretched out his shoulders and neck.

Hereward glanced at the cart. Isaiah had already packed as much food as they had into it.

The bundle looked pathetically small.

"I can hunt as we move," Isaiah said, "and we'll be traveling close to the FarReach Mountains. There are a series of springs that dot the foothills. If we are lucky they'll still be running. The Skraelings don't like water and will have left them alone. They should be full of fish."

"Springs," Hereward said. "Water enough to bathe?"

Isaiah regarded her with genuine amusement. "Water enough to bathe," he said.

They lapsed into silence, and Isaiah looked north. It would take them months to reach Maximilian if they had to walk. He thought of how Maximilian and Ishbel had glanced at each other now and again in the days just before he left.

The curse was fixed.

For all he knew they had already sunk into its trap.

"Will we find anything at Sakkuth?" Hereward said, startling Isaiah out of his reverie.

"Sakkuth?" he said, wondering why that struck a chord deep within him. There was something about Sakkuth . . .

"To eat," Hereward said. "Or maybe we might even find a horse still stabled there."

"I doubt it," Isaiah said. "The Skraelings will have overrun the city. There'll be nothing left."

Sakkuth. The One had said that Maximilian and Ishbel needed to bring the Weeper, the Goblet of the Frogs, and the crown of Elcho Falling to Sakkuth.

Why didn't the One want them to deliver it to him at DarkGlass Mountain? Surely that was the heart of his power?

CHAPTER TWENTY-SIX

The FarReach Mountains

Eleanon led the Lealfast fighters into the FarReach Mountains two days after Axis' contemptuous dismissal of them. They flew into the mountains half a day's journey west of the Salamaan Pass where, forewarned by message, the entire Lealfast Nation was grouped waiting for him.

"Eleanon," said one of the elders, a man named Falayal. "What has happened? There have been rumors, and then your message." He looked about at the Lealfast fighters materializing on the walls of the deep canyon in which the Lealfast Nation had gathered. "Why so many injured? What has *happened?*"

Eleanon was exhausted, but he needed to speak without delay with Falayal, and then with the rest of the Lealfast. He wanted the Nation to hear of the "debacle" at the hands of Armat, and the reasons for it, from his mouth before they heard of it from any other.

"Matters have changed," he said. "In a way we could not have anticipated. The Lord of Elcho Falling might not be our only, or even best, hope of salvation after all, Falayal, my friend."

Falayal regarded Eleanon with concern. "Eleanon?"

His hand still on Falayal's shoulder, Eleanon turned to look over the mass of Lealfast below him.

"There is a new path open to us!" Eleanon shouted. He took a deep breath. "Listen," he said, his tone now lower but still perfectly audible, and spoke without pause for over an hour of the way of the One.

Much later that day, after he had rested and eaten, Eleanon lifted off once more, and flew further south.

Directly into Isembaard.

CHAPTER TWENTY-SEVEN

Armat's Camp, the Central Outlands

They came for Axis, Georgdi, and Zeboath toward dusk two days after Ravenna had spoken to Axis. In that time, the three men had been given no food and only the bare minimum of water. They were exhausted, cold and damp from the earth, and encrusted in filth. Axis had tried to rub away the dried blood from the cut on his cheekbone, but had, he thought, only made himself look worse.

"What a group of ruffians we are," he muttered to Georgdi as they stood, finally, gratefully, in the evening light as they waited for Zeboath to be hauled to the surface. "Please tell me I look better than you."

"I'm afraid I look far better," said Georgdi. He looked about. "Are you certain Ravenna will come to our aid?" he added, very quietly.

"No," said Axis, "I don't trust her at all. Virtually the last thing she said to me was how she'd needed to murder her own mother to aid her cause. Our deaths would be as nothing after that."

"Let's hope she harbors a secret passion for you," Georgdi said.

Axis grunted, more a warning that the guards had edged closer than any reply to what Georgdi had said.

Zeboath now emerged from the pit, blinking even in this dull light. He caught Axis' eyes, and Axis could see he was nervous.

And why not, he thought. *The man is as close to death as you can get without tipping over the edge.*

The guards manhandled them into a tight group, then marched them forward.

"The gallows are but five minutes' walk away," said one of them. "You can enjoy your last sunset on the way."

Ravenna sat with Armat in his tent. They were sharing a flask of wine, waiting for the guards to call them once the three men had been brought to the gallows.

Ravenna was very glad Lister was not with them.

Armat was distracted momentarily by a soldier delivering a whispered report, and she closed her eyes, visualizing Axis, Georgdi, and Zeboath being led toward the gallows.

Axis, she said.

Axis narrowed his eyes briefly, waited a moment, then took Georgdi's arm and gave it a brief squeeze. At Georgdi's look, Axis put a finger to his lips and nodded at Zeboath.

Georgdi understood, touching Zeboath's arm and nodding to Axis.

Axis tipped his head a little, then calmly walked to one side, slipping between the guards.

The guards did nothing.

Georgdi wasted one moment in an amazed glance, then pulled Zeboath out as well.

Once with Axis, they turned and looked back at the detail.

There marched the guards, surrounding Axis, Georgdi, and Zeboath, who walked apparently docilely in their midst.

A glamour, Axis said into Georgdi's and Zeboath's minds, not wanting to alert anyone to their presence by speaking aloud.

He led Georgdi and Zeboath toward a horse line a little distance away.

There are some horses saddled at the end of the line, Axis said. *Take them, and lead them quietly out of camp. No one will see them. When you get beyond camp, ride north, as fast as you can.*

You? Georgdi mouthed.

I am going for Inardle. I know this is a risk, but I will not leave her. Don't wait for me. Don't wait for me, Georgdi!

Georgdi gave him a hard look, then nodded, gesturing to Zeboath to follow him.

Zeboath paused briefly by Axis, giving him a look of deep concern, then he, too, was gone.

Axis sighed in relief.

Inardle.

He started to run for Risdon's tent. He didn't have long. The guards and the glamour they escorted were within a few minutes of the gallows, and the glamour would vanish the instant the ropes slid about the apparitions' necks.

Axis was lucky. There were only two soldiers anywhere near Risdon's tent—the others apparently having drifted toward the gallows. Axis paused just outside the tent flap, hearing movement inside. He wondered briefly what he would see when he entered, then he lifted the flap and ducked inside.

Risdon was standing by a camp bed, sliding his feet into boots as he buttoned his breeches. His shirt was lying to one side, ready to be donned.

Behind him, and beyond the bed, Axis could see a spread of blood-stained wing on the floor.

Risdon knew someone had entered the tent, but he could not immediately see Axis. He shouted a warning to the soldiers outside, simultaneously reaching for his scabbarded sword hanging from the back of a nearby chair. He had half drawn it when he felt a hand grab his wrist.

Then a great blow to his jaw made his vision gray.

Axis seized the sword as Risdon sagged back to the bed, then spun about, taking off the head of the first soldier who had rushed in. The second soldier, far more wary, hesitated just inside the entrance, eyes narrowed as they tracked a ghostly apparition as it took off his comrade's head, then came for him.

The soldier managed to trade just two blows with the apparition before he, too, fell dead to the floor.

Axis turned about, breathing deeply, knowing that his actions were wearing the glamour thin. Risdon had just struggled to his feet, but was still groggy, and offered no resistance when Axis seized his hair and forced him around the other side of the bed.

Inardle lay half on the floor, half huddled against the back canvas wall of the tent. Her face was bloodied and bruised, her breasts and abdomen worse. The stitched wound on her flank and abdomen was half open and oozing dark blood. Her broken wing, held awkwardly to one side, was swollen and covered with contusions; the swelling had spread down her left shoulder and arm.

She knew Axis' presence, and stared at him as he held Risdon over her.

"I wish I had more time to spend on this," Axis said, "but I fear Inardle and I have pressing business elsewhere. Risdon, take one more breath, and savor it, for it will be your last."

Axis waited for that one, terrified breath, and then he drew the blade of his sword across Risdon's neck and tossed the dying man to one side. He stuck the sword through his belt, then leaned down to Inardle.

"Can you walk?"

"I don't know." Her voice was harsh, very dry, and Axis had to strain to hear it.

He leaned down, and as gently as he could, but with as much speed as possible, lifted her by her right arm. He slid his other arm about her back as she inched her way upward, stopping at her cry of pain and as a sudden line of frost ran down one side of her body.

"Inardle . . ."

"Please, please, get me out of here, Axis. Whatever you do is going to hurt me, *just get me out of here.*"

Axis gritted his teeth and half dragged, half lifted Inardle toward the flap of the tent. She was a slender woman, but she was tall, and her wings heavy and awkward. Axis gave silent thanks to Isaiah and his war master for the intensive daily training over the past few months; without it, Axis doubted he could have managed this.

"There are horses outside," Axis said.

"I won't be able to ride."

"Then you'll ride with me. You still have some strength in that right arm?"

She nodded.

"Then you're going to need to grip with all your might, because I think we have a wild gallop ahead of us."

They were outside the tent by this time, and Axis glanced about. The attention of the entire camp was still on the gallows—he could see the guards now marching the apparitions up the steps—and Axis thanked whatever gods had arranged it that Risdon's tent was so close to the edge of the encampment.

There was a big bay stallion tethered by his reins to the back of the tent; Risdon's mount, no doubt. Axis propped Inardle up against a tent pole, tightened the stallion's girth—once more thanking the gods that he was already saddled—then lifted Inardle into the saddle.

Again she cried out as her broken wing caught for a moment between her body and Axis, but Axis ignored it. He untied the stallion, now dancing about in consternation at the wings which trailed down either side of its body, vaulted up behind Inardle, and turned the horse's head hard to one side as he kicked it into movement.

The stallion leapt straight into a gallop, and Inardle swayed alarmingly to one side and would have fallen had not Axis managed to grab her.

At the same time, Axis heard a cry behind him.

He didn't wait to hear what it was about, and dug his booted heels once more into the stallion's flanks.

The guards had informed Armat that the condemned men had mounted the gallows. Armat and Ravenna were almost at the gallows themselves when there came a cry from behind them.

Armat half turned to see, then whipped back to the gallows as the hangman shouted.

He had just slipped the noose about Axis' head when Axis had vanished.

Ravenna let out a tiny sigh, allowing the glamour to vanish completely. No need to keep it going now.

Run, Axis, run, she thought. *Run.*

Armat turned to her and grabbed her arm so painfully that she felt bruises form instantly.

"What have you done?" he said.

"Nothing, Armat," she snapped. "Think not to blame me for the fact you underestimated the StarMan!"

Axis managed, just, to turn the almost-out-of-control stallion in a vaguely northwesterly direction, then he gave it full rein and allowed it to gallop as hard as it wanted. It was a good horse, strong and fast, and he hoped that it would give him a precious few minutes' head start on the inevitable pursuit.

Gods knew what he'd do once—if—they caught up with him.

He had one arm wrapped tight about Inardle's waist—at least she seemed to have found her balance now—and had managed to get his feet into the stirrups, which had been flapping about, further frightening the horse, so that he could secure his own jolting position behind the saddle.

The arm he had about Inardle's waist was wet, and he knew the rest of the stiches on her wound must have broken open.

They rode without speaking for some minutes, Axis glancing behind him every so often, when Inardle gave a soft cry of warning.

Two riders had loomed up on their flank.

"Georgdi!" Axis cried.

"My friend," Georgdi called out as he and Zeboath pushed their horses to keep pace with Axis' maddened horse, "I am glad to see you! I wait most eagerly to hear your assurances that you escaped Armat's camp without the alarm being raised."

Axis sent Georgdi a dark look.

"Ah," said Georgdi, "good thing that Zeboath and I spent a precious few minutes cutting loose as many horse lines as we could manage, eh?"

A good thing indeed, Axis thought, but it would not buy them much time.

"Just ride," he shouted. "*Ride!*"

They could not continue at a flat-out gallop forever, and after a while Axis gathered in the reins of the stallion and pulled him back to a more controlled canter. Georgdi and Zeboath did the same.

"Georgdi," said Axis, "can you halt a moment, stand, and listen?"

Georgdi nodded, pulling his horse up as Axis and Zeboath rode on.

After a few minutes he caught his two companions.

"Many horsemen," Georgdi said. "At least a hundred. A few minutes behind us."

Axis felt his stomach turn over. *At least a hundred.* He looked at Georgdi and Zeboath. Only Georgdi had thought to find a weapon during their escape.

Two swords, against at least a hundred.

"It's full night now," said Georgdi. "We can take advantage of the darkness."

Axis looked at the ground. It was early spring, but there was still old, hard-packed snow in great patches on the ground.

Their horses' hoofprints were clearly visible, even in the night.

Georgdi saw the direction of Axis' eyes. "Ah," he said. "Then we'd best ride a bit faster, yes?"

"And look for a stream," said Axis. "We can lose our hoofprints in that."

They pushed their horses back into a gallop—all the horses responding only sluggishly—and Axis knew they would not be able to keep to this speed for long.

Shit!

StarMan?

Axis literally jerked backward on the horse, his arm inadvertently tightening about Inardle and making her cry out.

StarMan?

Who is this? he asked. It was an Enchanter, he knew, and one who had managed to rediscover the Star Dance, but who? And where? *Why?*

StarHeaven SpiralFlight came the response.

StarHeaven? Axis fought to remember the name. Ah, yes, StarHeaven was one of the Icarii who had joined with StarDrifter in recent weeks.

StarHeaven, where are you, and with whom?

I am with the Strike Force, StarMan.

The Strike Force! Stars, had his father sent them?

BroadWing leads us, StarHeaven continued. *We are in the spiral attack formation over those who pursue you. We—*

Listen to me, StarHeaven, and get this message to BroadWing before you do anything else. Do not, I repeat, do not kill any of the horsemen, but only their mounts! Give him that message now, StarHeaven. Now!

Yes, StarMan.

Axis pulled his horse up, signaling to Georgdi and Zeboath to do the same. "The Strike Force are overhead," he said.

"The what?" said Zeboath.

"Tencendor's legendary Icarii military force," said Georgdi, watching Axis keenly. "Axis, how many are there?"

"Wait," Axis murmured, concentrating as he looked upward into the night.

StarMan, StarHeaven said.

Yes?

BroadWing understands. We will aim only for the horses.

Good. How many are you, StarHeaven?

Five hundred, StarMan.

Axis grinned. Five hundred! *Then tell your Strike Leader not to hesitate, Star-Heaven.*

He felt her agreement, then he turned his horse slightly so that he faced the direction of the pursuing force.

StarHeaven, he said, *let me see through your eyes.*

Vision flooded Axis' mind. BroadWing led the Strike Force in a classic nighttime maneuver spiraling down toward their target from a great height, sliding silently through the air.

Armat's men would never hear them coming.

Axis could see them now—almost one hundred weaponed horsemen following a trail through the snow.

They had no idea of what approached.

StarHeaven, Axis said, *tell BroadWing to whisper to the men during the attack that their lives are spared through the goodwill of the StarMan, who bears them no grudge.*

I will tell him, StarHeaven replied.

Axis continued to watch through StarHeaven's eyes as the Strike Force continued their descent. Suddenly the leading wave of Icarii bowmen—at least fifty paces above the horsemen—let fly their arrows, immediately veering away and upward again. Then the next wave let fly their arrows, and veered away, and then the next wave.

Horses crumpled to the ground, throwing their riders several paces with the force and speed of their impact.

Two more waves followed, and then it was all over. Not a single horse was left alive, and men lay winded and moaning across the cold earth.

They would have had no idea what had hit them.

StarMan, StarHeaven said, *BroadWing says he will be with you in moments.*

Thank you, StarHeaven, Axis said, and finally allowed himself to relax.

"We've company," he said to his companions, and grinned.

[Part Four]

CHAPTER ONE

The Central Outlands

Axis dismounted, made sure that Inardle could balance herself, then handed the reins to Georgdi and walked a pace or two into the night.

BroadWing landed before him in a rush of wings and with a broad grin.

"By the stars!" BroadWing said. "That felt good!"

Axis laughed, embracing the birdman in a fierce hug. "We thank you, my friend. Without you . . ."

"Without me you would have been forced to some grand heroic action," BroadWing said. "I am sorry I stole your moment."

Axis couldn't keep the grin off his face. "I give you full permission to do so again, anytime you want, Strike Leader. Did my father send you?"

"Yes, but at Maximilian's instigation. And there's more good news, Axis. About five or six hours' ride to the north you will come across a contingent of the Emerald Guard, complete with supplies, food, medical equipment, and Garth Baxtor. You have heard of him? Yes? Well, Maximilian thought you might need the aid."

Axis gripped BroadWing's shoulder. "BroadWing, you are indeed the bearer of much good news. The Isembaardians?"

"Picking themselves up and brushing off the dirt," BroadWing said. "Before I left they'd started to trudge back to the encampment. It will take them several hours at least. I gave them your message, StarMan. I've stationed Icarii high above you. We'll keep watch while you ride to meet Garth and the Emerald Guard. No one will surprise you."

"Where's Maximilian?"

"Riding hard for Elcho Falling. Depending on how hard you want to travel, he will be four to six days ahead of you."

Axis glanced at Inardle. "More like six days, I think."

BroadWing looked at her as well. "One of the Lealfast?"

Axis nodded, and indicated to BroadWing to come with him. He led him over to Inardle, who sat on the horse watching BroadWing warily.

"This is Inardle," Axis said. "One of the nobility among the Lealfast. Inardle, this is Strike Leader BroadWing EvenBeat."

Axis wondered if BroadWing would say anything about the Lealfast debacle which had led to this rescue, but the birdman chose tact ahead of point scoring.

"My Lady Inardle," he said, and inclined his head. "You are injured."

"Badly," said Axis. "And Georgdi, Zeboath, and I worse the wear for our experiences. I think we will continue our ride, BroadWing. Inardle particularly can do with the comfort the Emerald Guard brings."

BroadWing turned away at that, but Inardle called softly to him. "Broad-Wing. Thank you."

BroadWing paused, nodded at Inardle in acknowledgment, then lifted into the sky.

"We ride," said Axis, and vaulted up behind Inardle once more.

It took them until dawn to meet the Emerald Guard. Inardle was almost insensible by that time, and the other three desperately weary. None of them had eaten for three days, all had been subject to deprivation, and Inardle to sustained torment and abuse.

Axis' shoulders sagged in relief when he saw the riders ahead of him on the lightening horizon. One of the Emerald Guardsmen called his column to a halt, then rode out to meet the four exhausted people.

"Greetings, StarMan," he said to Axis, who found the energy to wonder that now everyone, stranger as well as friend, was using that title. "My name is Clements, and I lead this contingent of the Emerald Guard. I have ordered them to make camp and set food to cook. BroadWing has sent word that you are not being pursued for the moment, so I suggest we wait out this day here, so that you may rest and receive what treatment you need."

"Thank you, Clements," Axis said. He nodded at the young man who had ridden after Clements and who was now pulling his horse to a halt. "Garth Baxtor, I assume."

"Indeed, StarMan," Clements said. He introduced Garth to Axis, then Axis introduced his own companions.

"And this is Zeboath," Axis said finally, "an Isembaardian physician of fine skill. He has been a valued companion of mine this past year."

Axis well knew Garth's reputation as a highly skilled physician who commanded the almost magical Touch, and he wanted Garth to know that Axis valued Zeboath as highly, if not more, than Garth's reputation.

Garth clearly took the hint. He smiled at Zeboath. "I have heard of the skill of the Isembaardian physicians," he said. "I am most pleased to meet you, physician Zeboath, and once you are rested and fed, look forward to picking your brains for new knowledge."

Zeboath grinned. "All I heard amid those words of welcome, Garth, were the words 'rested' and 'fed.' I am afraid my mind has clung to them exclusively." The humor died from his face. "Garth Baxtor, we have with us a most grievously injured woman. She needs your aid, as soon as you might."

Garth looked at Inardle, slumped in Axis' arms, noting the bruises and contusions, and the blood seeping down one leg from a wound on her abdomen. He pushed his horse forward and laid a very gentle hand on her cheek for a moment.

"Then I may need your assistance, Zeboath," he said, "before you have time for food and rest. I am sorry."

The Emerald Guard, comprising some forty men, had five wagons of equipment and supplies with them. Axis thought that Maximilian must have instructed them to prepare for any contingency.

But, oh stars, he was grateful to Maximilian for his forethought and care.

The guardsmen had fires started and food set out to cook by the time Axis and his group rode up. By the time they'd dismounted, and Axis had lifted Inardle down, Garth's medical bags were in evidence, a blanket was provided to cover Inardle's nakedness, and everyone was given a cup of ale to keep them going.

Axis couldn't believe their efficiency.

"Your cheek has been badly gashed," Garth said, tipping Axis' head to one side so he could see more clearly.

"It just needs a clean," Axis said.

"And perhaps some stitches," Garth said. "It will leave a scar, I am afraid."

Axis remembered once, long, long ago, someone had remarked to him that despite all the wars and battles he'd endured, and all the injuries, he'd never scarred. It was one of those times when he'd truly realized the depth of his gifts.

"It won't scar," Axis said. "Stitch it later, after you've seen to Inardle."

"What happened to her?" Garth said as they walked over to where one of the guardsmen had settled Inardle by a fire. Zeboath was kneeling by her, persuading her to drink something.

"The wound on her flank was caused by an Isembaardian sword, her broken wing by Armat's booted foot, and her various other contusions and bruises by Risdon, who—"

"I know," Garth said softly. "I felt it earlier, when I laid a hand to her cheek."

Axis halted just before they reached Inardle, putting a hand on Garth's arm and making him stop as well.

"You have the Touch," Axis said. "What did you feel?"

"She's a strong woman," said Garth. "Her injuries are very serious, but not life-threatening. More dangerous for her at the moment is the fact she's had almost nothing to eat or drink for some three days, and has had to endure a physically exhausting ride to escape. Her rape . . . I don't know. As ever in these matters, while her physical injuries will heal quickly, who knows what other scars this Risdon has left. Did you kill him?"

"Yes."

"In front of her?"

"Yes."

Garth gave a little smile. "Good. That may help. She needs to know he won't come after her again."

"But she *is* a strong woman?"

Garth paused, studying Axis closely. "You already know that, Axis."

"Garth, there is something else. One of the men who oversaw Inardle's torture and rape was Lister. He was Inardle's former lover."

"*Lister* is with Armat?"

"Aye."

Garth muttered a soft curse. "Then Vorstus must be with him as well."

"He was. Armat apparently murdered him to make a point to Ravenna and Lister."

"Ravenna is there, too." Garth rubbed at his forehead, looking devastated. "I think Maxel knew that, but still . . ." He drew in a deep breath. "And Lister, Inardle's former lover, stood there and allowed her abuse to happen? Let's hope Inardle chooses better in her future lovers, eh, Axis?"

Whatever Zeboath had given Inardle revived her a little, and Garth asked Axis to sit behind her and hold her propped up against his body so that Garth and Zeboath could examine her more easily.

Axis felt somewhat uncomfortable holding Inardle so close. He was very aware of her, and he was irritated at himself for feeling this way when they'd ridden for many hours in just as close contact and it hadn't bothered him at all.

Garth and Zeboath worked well together. One of the guardsmen had brought over several large bags of medical supplies, and Zeboath soon made himself at home sorting through their contents. Garth took some swabs soaked in an antiseptic fluid from Zeboath and wiped away the blood about the wound on Inardle's flank and abdomen, brushing away with an irritated hand the blanket Axis was trying to keep over her breasts.

"The stitching on this . . ." Garth said, obviously trying very hard to be diplomatic.

"Was very amateurish," said Zeboath.

"That's not what you said to me," Axis snapped.

"*Now* I am talking to a fellow professional," Zeboath said, grinning. He sobered, and addressed Garth again. "Axis did this. When the Lealfast fell down about us, there were so many . . . I had no time to attend to Inardle so Axis stitched her. In his defense, Garth, Inardle has since been through more wars. I doubt anyone's stitching could have held her together."

"Well," said Garth, now threading a needle, "we'll just have to keep her out of the wars again for the time being."

He bent closer to the wound, apologizing to Inardle as the needle slipped under the first layer of skin and muscle.

She jumped a little from the sting, and a line of frost ran up from her wound and vanished under the blanket covering her breasts.

Garth stopped, the stitch half completed, staring at the line of frost.

"It is her reaction to pain," Axis murmured.

"Ah," Garth said, and his face told what he was too diplomatic to express. *Fascinating.*

Axis could see that Garth and Zeboath would spend many hours over several mugs of ale discussing this phenomenon.

Garth managed to overcome his fascination long enough to stitch the wound, then he turned his attention to Inardle's left wing, spread out to Axis' side.

He hesitated before touching it, exchanging a glance with Zeboath.

"I'll mix something up for her," Zeboath said, then rose and busied himself among one of the medical packs.

"Zeboath is going to make you an elixir which will deaden the pain," Garth said to Inardle. "Even an examination of this will hurt, let alone any attempt we make to fix it."

"I don't really want—" Inardle began.

"You *will* take it," Garth said. "Among other things, it will help relax the muscles and tendons in the wing, and neither Zeboath or myself can do anything for you while the wing is so rigid."

Zeboath had returned, a small cup in his hand. Garth took it, and held it to Inardle's mouth.

"What are you doing to me?" she said. "There's more than just the mixture."

"I am infusing the elixir with a little added help, Inardle," Garth said. "It will help, not hurt."

"Please, Inardle," Axis murmured, and he felt her relax a little in his arms and accept the elixir.

While they waited for it to have an effect, Garth and Zeboath attended to some of Inardle's lesser wounds and bruises. One or two of the wounds needed a stitch, but most just needed a clean and, in the case of the bruises, a rub with an unguent and a gentle application of Garth's Touch.

"Most of these will have vanished within two days," Garth said, cleaning Inardle's face and running one of his fingers lightly over the bruising there.

"Your left arm, though, will take longer, perhaps a week, as its swelling is related to the severity of the break in your wing."

Inardle just tipped her head, as if she didn't care, but Axis felt her tense at the mention of her wing again.

It was more than possible that Inardle dreaded Garth and Zeboath splinting her wing, but Axis thought she was likely far more worried about whether or not she'd be able to fly again. In his former life Axis had known two Icarii who had been wing-crippled in accidents, and who could no longer fly.

Both had killed themselves within two years of their initial injuries.

Zeboath and Garth had now positioned themselves to either side of Inardle's broken wing.

It looked frightful—very swollen, crooked into an unnatural position, the bruising showing beneath the feathers as great spreading stains of black and red.

"How long ago did this happen?" Garth said.

"Four days," Axis said.

Garth winced, again sharing a glance with Zeboath.

"Please fix it," Inardle whispered, and Axis tightened his hold on her a little, leaning his face against the back of her hair. He wished, quite desperately, that he'd never verbally attacked her in the pit.

Zeboath helped support the wing while Garth ran his hand very gently over it. At one point he raised his face and locked eyes with Axis, and Axis knew the news was not going to be good.

"All the main supporting bones are broken," said Garth, "although fortunately they're broken cleanly. If they'd been smashed . . ."

"The tendons attaching muscle to bone are also torn, and very badly bruised. The swelling is bad and I am not sure I can do much while it is so extreme. The bones need to be set, but . . ."

"What happens if you delay?" Axis said.

"Setting the bones?" Garth said. "Well, they're already starting to heal themselves through calcification. Clots of blood, and bone tissue, have formed about all of the breaks—this will eventually resolve itself into new bone."

"So if you don't splint it now, the bones will start to set themselves into their current unnatural shape."

Garth nodded.

"I think that what Garth is trying to say," Zeboath said, "is that the wing can likely be healed reasonably successfully if the bones are splinted into their proper position. The tendons will heal by themselves once the bone has healed. But as the swelling now is so bad, that is going to be both terribly difficult and terribly painful. If we don't do it, then..."

"There's every chance Inardle won't fly again," Axis said.

"Set it now," Inardle said.

"It will hurt," Garth said, gently. "Very, very badly. What we gave you will not blot out the pain, and we have nothing else. Inardle, we are going to have to further injure the wing in order to set those bones, and I am terrified we will cripple you completely."

"Set it now," said Inardle. "I cannot bear the thought of not flying again."

Garth hesitated, exchanging yet another concerned look with Zeboath.

"Set it now," said Axis. "I know how my father felt without wings. Set it now."

Inardle twisted her head slightly to be able to look at him. "Thank you."

Garth looked at Axis and gave a very slight nod, and Axis tightened his hold about Inardle.

The physician stood up and asked Zeboath to hold out the wing as far as possible, then Garth stamped down on it with as much force as Armat once had.

CHAPTER TWO

Armat's Camp, the Central Outlands

"They escaped?" Armat stared at the soldier before him.

"We were attacked by a mighty force, my lord," the soldier stuttered. He was afraid for his life in bringing this news to the general.

As well he might be, Armat thought. "*What* mighty force," he hissed.

"A great winged army, my lord. There were thousands of them! They swept down from the heavens and—"

"Shot every one of your horses, but left you alive," Armat said. "What extraordinarily poor marksmanship, eh?"

"Such extraordinarily *good* marksmanship," Ravenna murmured to one side.

Armat wasted a moment giving the witch and Lister a hard stare.

"Were they the Lealfast?" Armat asked the soldier.

"No, my lord. They were . . . something else."

"The Icarii Strike Force," Ravenna said. "It could only have been them."

"And who the fuck," Armat said, his tone low and dangerous as he turned to Ravenna, "are the Icarii Strike Force?"

"They were legendary fighters among the Icarii," Ravenna said. "Led and trained by Axis SunSoar. I imagine that there were some members of the Strike Force among the Icarii refugees rejoining with Maximilian's column."

Armat was so angry he could not speak. He wanted to strike Ravenna, but was restrained by the fact that he thought he might kill her if he lost control that badly, and he had enough common sense left to know that he still needed her.

"You had not thought to mention them to me?" he finally ground out.

She gave a small shrug. "I had not realized they'd reformed, Armat. I had no idea . . . but it could only have been them if not the Lealfast."

Armat swore. He gestured to the soldier to leave, and the man almost stumbled in his haste to get out, grateful beyond measure that Armat's ill will was now directed at Ravenna and not at him.

"How many does Axis have?" Armat said. "A 'great winged army.' Thousands?"

"Probably only a handful," Ravenna said. "That soldier likely exaggerated. But they're undoubtedly good . . . and now they have their fabled commander back."

Armat's temper finally gained the upper hand. "Get out," he said. "*Get out!*"

Word spread rapidly along the Isembaardian camp.

Axis SunSoar had made his escape, and in legendary spectacular manner.

Soldiers murmured about the Strike Force, but most of all they murmured about the fact that Axis had spared every last man. He'd made certain they could not catch him, but he had chosen not to harm them.

When Insharah heard the news he lowered his face into a hand in sheer relief.

Then he felt shame that he had not helped.

CHAPTER THREE

The Central Outlands

Axis sat with Inardle in one of the supply wagons. It had been emptied of its supplies and its deck covered with many layers of canvas over which had been thrown blankets. Inardle lay with her broken wing stretched down the length of the wagon. It looked heavy and awkward in the splints Zeboath and Garth had applied, and almost twice as swollen as when they'd begun their work.

Inardle had fainted with Garth's first stamp on the wing, and Axis was glad. The repositioning and splinting had been a brutal affair, requiring both Zeboath's and Garth's full strength, as well as two guardsmen called in to help. Axis couldn't help them. He stayed holding Inardle as tightly as he could, murmuring her name occasionally into her hair, frightened both by the frost which encased her body as it reacted to the pain and by his own emotional reaction to it.

When had she come to matter so much?

Eventually Axis had been forced to close his eyes, burying his face in Inardle's hair. It hadn't helped; the sounds of screaming bones and tendons weren't any less if he couldn't see.

Now, thank God, it was over. Garth and Zeboath had looked haggard and utterly exhausted once it was done, collapsing onto the ground, unable to speak for long minutes.

But they had fixed the wing. Garth said that as long as the splints remained in place for the next few weeks, and the wing was kept as immobile as possible, there was every chance it would heal enough that Inardle could use it again.

"It might be a little crooked," Garth had said, "but if there is no infection, and if the bones heal cleanly, and if the tendons regrow, and if ... well. We can hope, and we can pray. Zeboath and I have done the best we can, Axis."

Axis had nodded, and thanked both of them.

She actually looked better, now, he thought, as he sat in the weak late-afternoon sun and watched her. Whatever Garth had done to her bruises had made a difference, even in the course of this day. Most had faded; the swelling about her face had virtually disappeared. She hadn't regained consciousness yet, and Axis wanted to be there when she did, if only because Zeboath told him she would need to drink something, and take some more of the pain-numbing elixir he'd mixed.

That was the only reason, he told himself, he'd not moved from her side all this day.

"Axis?"

Axis jumped a little, turning his head.

Georgdi had ridden his horse up to the side of the wagon.

"She looks frightful," Georgdi said. "Makes me glad I have never had wings."

Axis managed a weak smile. "StarDrifter wanted to give me my wings," he said. "I still have the wing buds, they've just never developed. But I said no. I'd have to agree with you, Georgdi. Wings are not worth the trouble."

"Not for their owners *or* their lovers," Georgdi said, and went on before Axis could speak. "Axis, I've slept and eaten, and I need to be on my way. I'm going to ride directly for Serpent's Nest, collecting what I may in terms of a military force as I go. I don't think there's any point in my diverting to meet up with Maximilian to pass the time of day. Tell him I'll meet him at the mountain."

Axis agreed. "Good luck, my friend," he said, holding out his hand. "I want to fight by your side again ... so make sure you get to Serpent's Nest safely."

Georgdi grinned and gripped Axis' hand for a long moment. "You'll be safe here?"

"BroadWing says there is, as yet, no pursuit from Armat's camp. No doubt his men are trying to explain why their horses were shot out from underneath them. We'll be safe here for the moment."

"Axis . . . why didn't you want any of the men to die?"

"Because I want them to remember, and to tell as many of their fellow soldiers within Armat's army as they may, that when I had the chance to kill them I did not. They'll know that is not something Armat would have done."

Georgdi nodded. "You'll stay with Inardle?"

Axis glanced at her. "For a day or two, until I know she's well on the way to recovery. Then I'll ride hard for Maxel, and leave the Emerald Guard to escort Inardle at an easier pace."

"Well then," said Georgdi, gathering up the reins of his horse, "may the gods grace you, Axis, and her."

She woke in the middle of that night, suddenly, with a great cry, leaping halfway into a sitting position.

Axis, who had been asleep himself, only just managed to restrain Inardle before she shifted—and damaged—her broken wing.

"Inardle. It was just a dream. It is gone now."

She was heaving in great breaths, obviously distressed. The blanket had fallen off her chest as she'd jerked upright, and now Axis started to tug it back into position, feeling embarrassed and awkward at his clumsy attempts.

Damn it. Had he ever been this self-conscious, even as a youth?

"Risdon . . ." she said. One of her hands had found his, and now clutched it tightly.

"Risdon is dead."

She continued to take deep breaths, staring into the night, then very gradually relaxed.

And immediately became aware of the pain in her wing. She turned to look, and gave a soft cry at the sight of it.

"Garth says it should heal well," Axis said.

"Axis . . ."

"Drink some of this, Inardle." He reached for the flask Zeboath had left, twisted off the cap with one hand, and put it to her lips.

She drank, a little reluctantly, but she drank.

"When the pain has subsided," Axis said, "you'll need to eat and drink something."

She nodded, her eyes looking up at the stars. "I didn't think you'd still be here."

"Look, Inardle, I am sorry for what I said to you in the pit. I was angry, but I had no right to—"

"You had every right to be angry, Axis. What happened in Armat's camp wasn't your fault."

Axis didn't speak for a long moment, and when he did so, it was with some hesitation. "Inardle, one of the enchantments I know and that I can work with great effect with the Star Dance available to me is a Song of Forgetting. I can erase your memory of what happened in Armat's camp."

"Everything?"

"Yes, everything. The enchantment is linked to location, so everything in the camp."

"What happened to me in Armat's tent?"

"Yes."

"What Risdon did?"

"Yes."

"The time in the pit?"

"Yes. Inardle, I can—"

"You coming to rescue me."

"Yes."

"Lister was my lover, you knew that?"

"Yes." Very soft, now.

"I didn't love him, Axis, but I liked and respected him immensely. I lived with him for years. We were friends as well as lovers, or so I thought."

"Inardle—"

"When I heard that you'd returned from the dead, I was consumed almost with hatred. We all hated you, Axis. The great arrogant StarMan. The magnificent war leader. Your elevation to god. Your hatred of the Skraelings."

That last was almost whispered.

"How could you be anything but a cruel, self-absorbed man?" she continued. "You would regard us with nothing but contempt."

She looked at him then, with the barest hint of a smile. "And regard us with contempt you have done, but perhaps we have deserved it. But for everything else we were wrong. Axis, you thought to rescue me when Lister couldn't be bothered, when he'd decided I got in the way of his ambitions. I know enough that you risked everything to do that—you risked your own life. You could have made an easy escape with Georgdi and Zeboath, but you did not choose that. Instead, you came for me."

She freed his hand, and reached up her own to touch his cheek briefly. "Thank you for rescuing me—you will never understand what I felt that instant I knew you were in the tent—and thank you for your offer of a Song of Forgetting.

"I will decline it, I think. Of everything that was agonizing and humiliating in Armat's camp, there was one shining moment I want to remember the rest of my life—that moment when I realized you'd come for me."

As she had done to him, now Axis reached out his fingers and softly touched her cheek.

A line of frost trailed where he ran his fingers, and he lifted his hand.

"I hurt you," he said. "I'm sorry."

"That wasn't pain, Axis," she said, very softly.

Axis remembered what she had told him while he was stitching her wound. *Pain, delight, and physical joy. Arousal.*

He tore his eyes away from hers, looking down at her body under its covering blanket (*Damn that blanket! Her prudishness wasn't Icarii. It must be her Skraeling blood*). He thought how good it would feel to lower his mouth to her breast. What would it be like, then, to taste that frost under his tongue?

He realized he was staring too long, and that his thoughts must be written all over his face.

He stood up, a little too quickly. "I'll send Garth or Zeboath over. You need to eat and drink."

Then Axis vaulted over the side of the wagon and walked away, forcing himself not to look back and cursing himself for such a stupid display. He found Zeboath and sent him to Inardle, telling him that she was awake and hungry.

Then he sought out Clements and told him that he wanted his (once Risdon's) horse saddled and ready at dawn the next day, together with two or three guardsmen.

Inardle didn't see Axis again that day. She'd recognized what he was thinking and feeling in that moment before he'd jumped out of the wagon and walked away, and knew that Eleanon would have crowed with delight if he had known of it.

She knew that she, too, should be pleased at Axis' feelings, but instead she felt confused.

She could not keep her distance from this man, nor pretend to herself that she was indifferent to him.

She'd had no idea that when he touched her, she would respond as she had.

Lister's touch had never caused her frost to rise.

She could hardly believe that Axis had risked so much for her in rescuing her from Risdon.

She could hardly believe how glad she had felt when he had come for her.

Inardle shifted a little on her makeshift bed in the wagon, wincing with the pain. What was she thinking? Axis would only ever cause her sorrow.

It was what he specialized in.

Her task was only to fall into his bed, and use him.

Not to fall in love with him.

The next morning, when she woke, Inardle resented the bitter pang of disappointment that Zeboath was by her side, and not Axis.

"Where is Axis?" she asked.

"He rode out an hour ago," said Zeboath. "He's gone to Maximilian. I'm sorry, Inardle, we'll catch up with him in a week or so."

"It is of no matter to me," Inardle said.

It was a long ride to catch up with Maximilian, and Axis spent it not talking to his three companions. Instead his thoughts were exclusively on one person.

His wife, Azhure.

CHAPTER FOUR

Isembaard

Eleanon walked forward, his feet crunching over the coarse sand and grit of the northern Isembaardian plains. To his left rose Hairekeep; to his right the desolate plains undulated westward toward the River Lhyl. Before him stood Bingaleal, with the twenty-five thousand Lealfast fighters he'd brought with him into Isembaard ranged behind him in ordered ranks.

They were all different. Their eyes as they watched him approach were sharper, their posture more still, their demeanor more confident than Eleanon had seen previously in any Lealfast.

They were stronger.

They were assured.

They were *whole*. No longer half-breeds of any manner, but *whole*.

Bingaleal took a few steps forward to meet Eleanon. They stopped a pace or two apart, Eleanon somewhat awkward, Bingaleal poised and confident.

"What do you here, Eleanon?" Bingaleal said.

"Come to see what has become of my brother," Eleanon replied. He hesitated, hating himself for it in the face of Bingaleal's self-possession. "I come on behalf of the Lealfast Nation, Bingaleal. Come to see what path it is you have chosen."

Bingaleal nodded, then swept a hand out behind and to one side of him. "Sit down, brother, and we shall talk."

As they sat cross-legged, the ranks of the Lealfast behind Bingaleal faded from view. They were still there, Eleanon could sense them, but to those only of ordinary vision it would have appeared that the two birdmen sat alone in the deserted plain outside Hairekeep.

"I have become Elcho Falling's enemy," Bingaleal said.

That shocked Eleanon. Not so much what Bingaleal had expressed, but the stark manner in which he had done so.

"Tell me," Eleanon said. "What has become of you, Bingaleal, and all our comrades?"

Bingaleal did not immediately reply. He drew in a deep breath, raising his eyes and focusing them in the far distance.

"I have entered into the One," he said eventually, softly. His eyes suddenly refocused, very sharply, on Eleanon.

"And where did that lead you?" Eleanon said, equally as soft.

"It led me into a promise," Bingaleal said. "It showed me a path toward a world of power and fulfilment. It showed me a clear path, Eleanon, step by step, toward what we have always lusted after. Our own future. Beholden to no one. Despised by no one."

"And the price?" Eleanon said.

"There is no price."

"There is always a price, brother." Eleanon sighed. "Bingaleal, I come before you today because I, as all our brothers and sisters, felt the change in you and those who came into Isembaard with you." He put his hand on his chest. "We feel it here. We felt it, and we yearn for it, and it was all I could do to stop the entire Nation following me down here . . . but there is still a little bit of me, Bingaleal, which remains cautious. What has the One offered you, what has he shown you, and what is the price he demands?"

"He has shown us a future free of our Skraeling blood, a future in which the Icarii kneel before us in humility, a future in which we no longer inhabit frozen wastes. The price? Only one price. The destruction of Elcho Falling and of its master."

"But Elcho Falling and its master is what we have dreamed of for millennia, Bingaleal."

Bingaleal smiled in genuine compassion. "Yet look to what the Lord of Elcho Falling has become, Eleanon. He cannot give us what we need. Not anymore. Now, brother, tell me. What do you here? Does Axis know where you are?"

Eleanon told Bingaleal what had happened—the slaughter at the hands of Armat, Axis' subsequent contemptuous dismissal of Eleanon, and the StarMan's belief that Eleanon and the remaining Lealfast fighters were sulking within the Sky Peaks, licking their wounds.

"Bingaleal, you have no idea what it cost me, to watch Lealfast fall from the sky, but—"

"But it has won for you Axis' disregard. I understand that and, while I grieve also for those Lealfast lost, I applaud your decision." A small smile curved about Bingaleal's face. "And so will the One, once he knows. You shall be our key into Elcho Falling, Eleanon. The One has constructed a curse with which to distract Isaiah, and shortly Maximilian and Ishbel, but it is largely meaningless. *You* shall be the One's key into Elcho Falling. You, Eleanon. You shall walk the One into Elcho Falling unseen while Maximilian and Isaiah and Axis fidget with worry about the curse."

Bingaleal chuckled. "You have no idea how easy this is going to be, brother."

CHAPTER FIVE

Isembaard

Isaiah and Hereward traveled relatively quickly given the circumstances of their journey. The cart worked well, although Hereward had to cling uncomfortably in order not to be catapulted out onto the uneven ground. They had little food with them, and even less water, and Isaiah pushed them hard in order to get to the first of the springs where both hoped they'd find food and water.

At least, Isaiah pushed himself hard. He woke Hereward well before dawn each day, giving her a little of their meager store of food and a sip or two of water, and then they were off, Isaiah striding resolutely forward into the predawn darkness, dragging the little cart behind him. He walked for many hours at a time, taking breaks only reluctantly, and then only when absolutely needed. Hereward thought he was pushing himself too hard, desperate to get to Maximilian Persimius before all was lost.

Hereward thought a great deal about Ishbel during the long days spent clinging to the cart as it jounced along. She'd seen the woman many times during her time at Aqhat, and had even served her luncheon on occasion. Ishbel had been the kind of woman that Hereward could only dream of being: beautiful, elegant, remote, and exuding a natural nobility that only those born into the aristocracy, and into power, could manage. Hereward had always felt like an awkward peasant around her.

Isaiah had adored her. It had been evident in his manner in her company, in his every glance and every gesture. It had been the gossip of the palace that he had finally fallen in love with a woman, and that a woman pregnant by another man.

Hereward thought Isaiah's efforts to reach Maximilian were probably in vain. She doubted that any man could resist Ishbel's allure for very long. Elcho Falling was likely already doomed.

She decided that life as a servant was much less problematical. Look where nobleness and power and purpose had brought Isaiah and Ishbel.

On the third day of their journey, about noon, they arrived at the first of the springs. It had been evident on the horizon for some two or three hours before they reached it, a green smudge of feathery palms and dense shrubbery, and Isaiah had doubled his efforts the moment he'd spotted it.

There was a wide track leading in through the vegetation and then, wonderfully, the sound and smell of water.

Isaiah almost ripped apart his canvas harness in his efforts to strip it off. He took two steps toward the water, stopped, then came back to help Hereward, struggling to rise from the cart.

He was grinning from ear to ear, and Hereward supposed she had as wide a smile on her own face. Isaiah carried her to the water and set her down on her feet, and then both of them stripped away their dirty clothing and waded in.

Isaiah checked to make sure Hereward was steady on her feet, then sank below the surface. Hereward took another two or three steps into deeper water, then did the same.

Oh gods, it felt wonderful. She scrubbed away at her body, wishing she had soap but not minding too much—just the blessed cool water was miracle enough.

"Mind the bandage about your throat," Isaiah said to her as she resurfaced. "I'll take it off for you in a moment . . . let it soak and it will come away easier."

Hereward nodded, lying back and allowing the water to wash over her body. She swore she could actually feel the sweat and dried blood lifting away from her skin in great layers.

She felt movement: Isaiah coming up behind her. He took her head in his hands and massaged her scalp, then ran his hands down her shoulders and raised her upright. Very gently he eased the bandage and compression pebble away from her neck.

"There's a huge scab over the wound," he said, his fingers moving over it gently.

"Can I do without the bandage now?" Hereward said, hoping she didn't have to put the filthy thing back on again.

He nodded. "Be careful not to knock the scab free, though. It must go right down to the torn vein."

His fingers moved from her shoulders down to her upper arms.

Hereward took a deep breath.

Very slowly Isaiah ran his fingers back up her arms, over her shoulders, and then down to the rise of her breasts.

"Are you remembering how you and Ishbel used to bathe in the Lhyl?" Hereward said.

Isaiah jerked his hands away.

"You must miss her," she said, very angry with him. Isaiah did not particularly like her, yet he could not resist trying to seduce her.

She supposed he had to find some use for her, now that he'd given up so much on her behalf.

"But think," she said, "if you manage to get to Maximilian in time, and he relinquishes Ishbel, then you can—"

Isaiah's left arm suddenly slid about her waist, pulling her tight against him.

Hereward opened her mouth to protest, now incensed at his behavior, but Isaiah clamped his right hand over her mouth.

"Quiet!" he hissed into her ear. Then: "Listen."

Hereward struggled against him for a moment, still furious at being held so tight. Then she forced herself to relax, and listen.

There was something in the shrubbery to the west.

Something moving.

Isaiah's hand and arm slid away from Hereward and he started to move very quietly back to the bank, where he'd left his sword.

The sound of movement became louder—cautious footfalls, and the scrape of a body against the bushes.

Hereward swallowed, suddenly scared. *Skraelings?* She glanced at Isaiah, wishing he had not moved out of the water.

The Skraelings did not like water; they'd be safe enough if they stayed away from the bank.

The noise of movement grew louder, and Hereward jerked her head toward the sounds.

They were very close now.

Isaiah was moving about the pool, his sword in one hand, his eyes intent on the shrubbery. Then, suddenly, he stopped, and a look of utter disbelief came over his face.

Hereward gasped in surprise.

A large, pure white stallion had moved to the edge of the pool, and was now watching Isaiah, ears laid back, eyes rolling, breath snorting nervously.

Isaiah's entire posture changed. He laid the sword on the ground, his every movement slow and reassuring, then began to talk to the horse in a combination of soothing words and tongue clicks.

The stallion relaxed, ears flickering forward, and he lowered his head to the water and took a sip.

Isaiah came closer, keeping up the soothing monotone of sounds.

Then he was next to the stallion, stroking him down, and the horse was relaxing against him, blowing droplets of water out of his nose, and nuzzling Isaiah's chest.

"He is missing his master," Isaiah said, glancing at Hereward as he rubbed the horse's ears. "And now we have a horse with which to travel. Thank the gods!"

"I cannot believe the Skraelings managed to leave that meal alone," Hereward said.

"He must have been hiding out close to the water," Isaiah said. "Perhaps standing in it whenever the Skraelings approached." He smiled, still rubbing the horse's ears. "He must be an intelligent fellow."

The horse proved a boon. Isaiah abandoned the cart and they rode the horse, carrying with them what little supplies they needed now that they had a string of springs from which to fish and water.

On the fifth day away from the River Lhyl, they passed to the north of Sakkuth.

"You don't want to go into the city?" Hereward said from her perch behind Isaiah on the horse.

Isaiah studied the city in the distance. It looked gray and still, its great turrets and spires empty of all life.

"What are you thinking?" Hereward asked softly.

"That the city is likely full of Skraelings," he said. "That they're all staring at us from behind walls and shutters. That while the city looks empty, there are a million eyes, fed and feasted on the former inhabitants, watching our every move."

Hereward shuddered, wrapping her arms about her chest as she looked away.

"We'd best keep moving," Isaiah said, and urged the horse forward.

CHAPTER SIX

Isembaard

Bingaleal gave a small smile. "You can see what I have become, Eleanon. You want it, too."

"I still harbor reservations about the One. Bingaleal, we have long known of the lore of the Magi, and of its power—"

"To touch Infinity!"

"Yes, to touch Infinity, but at what cost? With what danger? Who has managed it, eh, and emerged unscathed?"

"The One. The One *is* Infinity."

Eleanon did not reply. He sat thinking, staring at his hands folded before him. Bingaleal was *so* different. Eleanon could feel the power within him, feel the certainty and confidence in the direction he'd taken.

But Eleanon was not sure. He wanted it so badly, yet still that tiny, cautious voice sounded in his mind. *Surely the One would demand a price.*

"None," said Bingaleal, "save that we deliver to the One the citadel of Elcho Falling, and its master. I am no slave to the One, Eleanon. I am not his servant. This is a transaction only. The One can give me, *us*, what we have so long desired—freedom from both our Skraeling and Icarii blood— and for a single payment: Elcho Falling. He can give us our dignity and a future, Eleanon. Maximilian Persimius cannot do that. He is too weak."

"There may be a trap, Bingaleal. Why should the One be so generous?"

"Because we can aid each other. He can give us our hearts' desire. We can give him what he needs—the destruction of Elcho Falling."

"He can't do that himself?"

"Elcho Falling is still protected by ancient sorceries that even the One cannot penetrate. The One has cursed Maximilian and Ishbel—Isaiah is on his way north now, carrying news of the curse to Maximilian—which has a potential to win Elcho Falling for the One without so much as a finger lift of effort ... but even so, the One would like our aid, and is willing to pay handsomely for it."

Bingaleal sat back, considering Eleanon. "Would you like to speak with him yourself?"

Then he laughed at the expression on Eleanon's face. "He will not bite, nor ensorcel your soul, Eleanon. You shall not be enslaved."

"Do I have your promise?"

"Yes."

Eleanon reached out a hand, hesitating only slightly before he laid it on Bingaleal's arm.

He gave a breath of relief. "You are not enslaved, Bingaleal," he said. "I can feel it."

"I am only enhanced," said Bingaleal.

"Yes, I can feel that, too."

"Will you speak with the One?"

"Yes. Where?"

Bingaleal nodded toward Hairekeep. "There."

CHAPTER SEVEN

On the Road to Serpent's Nest

Maximilian and Ishbel spent six to seven hours each evening in the Twisted Tower with Josia. They used this time going through chamber after chamber, recovering lost objects and knowledge. Rediscovering objects Maximilian found increasingly easy, even in the virtually empty chambers, as he became more intuitive and more attuned to the Tower, but the lost sleep . . . that was growing more difficult. He'd told Josia that he could doze in the saddle, and yes, from time to time he managed that, but generally someone required his attention, and he got very little rest throughout the day. He managed two or three hours at the most from the time he returned from the Twisted Tower to when they broke camp in the early morning, but that was it.

Maximilian found himself lusting after a soft bed and an uninterrupted night.

On this morning he was riding only a short distance from Ishbel, and he pulled his horse back so that it fell into step beside hers. Apart from the occasional few minutes spent together in the Twisted Tower, they hadn't had much chance to talk over the past few days.

"You look dreadful," she said. "Exhausted."

"As always, your compliments warm my heart. Have you looked in the mirror yourself recently?"

Ishbel smiled, keeping her eyes on the road ahead. "Madarin keeps it hidden from me."

"You are doing well," Maximilian said. "Where are you now? The eighth level?"

"Ninth," said Ishbel, "as well you know." She paused. "Maxel... it is so exciting."

"What?"

"The learning, the discovering. I cannot wait to reach Elcho Falling, and to see you raise it into the skies."

Maximilian laughed. "You could do it yourself, almost."

"Where are you now?"

"In the fifty-third level. This one is more difficult, as it is virtually empty, but Josia shouts, and I fumble, and somehow we manage."

Ishbel smiled, knowing all too well how Josia could shout, and they rode a little distance in companionable silence.

"BroadWing sent one of the Strike Force back with messages," Maximilian said after a few minutes. "He arrived early this morning."

When Maximilian would have been snatching a few hours' sleep, Ishbel thought, and resented the Icarii man's intrusion. "What news?" she said. "Axis is safe?"

"Yes," Maximilian said, and Ishbel let her shoulders slump in relief. *Thank the gods.*

"He, Georgdi, and Zeboath were rescued from Armat's camp," Maximilian continued, "together with a Lealfast woman."

There was something in that last which made Ishbel glance sharply at him, but he did not say more about the woman.

"Axis sent news," Maximilian said.

"Yes?"

"Ravenna and Lister are with Armat."

Ishbel drew in a deep breath and studied his face carefully. "We suspected that."

"Yes, but still..."

But still it hurts, Ishbel thought. He may have cut her from his life now, but once Ravenna had meant a great deal to Maximilian.

"Lister's disloyalty turns my stomach," Ishbel said. "How many years has he manipulated people to get what he wants? And now he abandons all those manipulations to chase after another cause? Do you think he will give you your seventeen years back, Maxel?"

"Ishbel, I am not as upset as you seem to think that—"

"Well, you damn well should be."

He gave a small shrug.

"*Why* has Lister gone to Armat?" said Ishbel. "I can understand—just—Ravenna's blackened, jealous heart turning her loyalty, but Lister? Maxel, what is going on?"

He gave another shrug, and Ishbel repressed the urge to slap him. He knew, but he wouldn't tell her.

"Is this why you wanted me to start learning the tricks contained within the Twisted Tower?" Ishbel said.

"Partly," Maximilian said, "but also because it is your heritage as well."

"I cannot replace the Lord of Elcho Falling should he fall," Ishbel said.

He gave her a very small smile at that. "I do not intend to fall, Ishbel."

She sighed. "What do you think Armat is planning?"

"Axis thinks, and I agree, that he intends to lay siege to Elcho Falling. He wants it for himself. Gods alone know what Ravenna has promised him."

"Armat and his army are close, yes? Then why doesn't he attack now? We only have a relatively few thousand."

"Armat and Ravenna want to wait until we open Elcho Falling."

"They don't have the skills to do it themselves?"

Maximilian shook his head.

"Have you had any further news from the south, Maxel?"

"No."

He was very isolated, Ishbel thought. So much to bear, so much unknown, the whole burden to carry alone. She felt a great ache within herself, and knew that, whatever rationalizations she used to deny it, there was only one way to resolve that ache.

"Madarin's belt buckle," she said, "and Serge's sword think we should marry."

He looked at her, and she at him.

"I'll make a decision at Elcho Falling," she said, and something about him relaxed. He smiled, nodded, then pushed his horse forward, leaving Ishbel to ride on alone again.

CHAPTER EIGHT

Hairekeep, Isembaard

Eleanon paused a few steps inside the fortress. From outside, Hairekeep was a massive structure that soared high into the sky . . . but once inside the door it looked far smaller.

As if it was the interior of a different building entirely.

The space was very small (given the vast expanse of the exterior), almost intimate. There was a floor some fifteen paces square, and walls of golden glass, intricately carved, that rose in a pyramid shape to a point high above them.

"It is beautiful," Eleanon said. Then, remembering what he'd seen when he, Inardle, and Bingaleal had used the dark spire, "It is the heart of Dark-Glass Mountain."

"Yes," said Bingaleal, "it is a representation of the Infinity Chamber which powers DarkGlass Mountain and connects it to Infinity. And here, as in the Infinity Chamber," he nodded to the shadows at the back of the chamber, "is the One."

Eleanon tensed, but rapidly relaxed as he felt no threat from the figure which emerged from the darkness.

It was the size and representation of a man, save that his flesh appeared to be made of green glass. In the depths of his chest revolved a golden pyramid.

"You are the One," said Eleanon, and gave an elegant bow of his head.

"I am," said the One. "I am the One and I am Infinity. We spoke some weeks ago, when first I emerged into flesh." The One smiled, his teeth curiously transparent behind his glass lips. "Have you come to take final communion in the One? Have you come to learn what the ancient Magi forgot to teach the Lealfast?"

"Perhaps," Eleanon said, and the One laughed, a pleasant, rolling sound.

"And so also Bingaleal hesitated," the One said. "Until I showed him this."

He made a movement with his hand, and the back wall of the Infinity Chamber vanished. Eleanon found himself staring over a landscape of incredible beauty and power—a vast plain of emerald water, from which rose a magical citadel of such loveliness and power that he felt his knees weaken with need.

"Elcho Falling," said the One. "Your home, once I have done with it."

Eleanon stared, his knees growing even weaker. He could see birdmen and women flying about the citadel, and sense their joy and power.

They were Lealfast, not Icarii.

And they were whole. Not half of this and half of that, but whole and glorying in that wholeness.

They are at One with themselves, the One spoke inside Eleanon's mind.

Yes, Eleanon whispered.

This was not a future in which either the Skraelings or the Icarii had any place.

Moreover, Eleanon could sense truth in the vision. It was not a trick, not a sorcery constructed to fool him, but it was truth, and it was his future and the future of the Lealfast.

"You can do this," said Eleanon. "You would give this to us?"

"Yes, and yes," said the One. "I have no use for Elcho Falling save to remove any threat it harbors toward me."

"What threat?" Eleanon said.

"It and its lord seek to subdivide me," said the One, and now Eleanon could hear hate and anger in the One's voice.

"You want us to deliver to you Elcho Falling and Maximilian Persimius," said Eleanon.

"Yes," said the One. "I have cursed Maximilian Persimius, but you can be a more powerful friend to me than that curse can ever be. *You* will be my door into the citadel."

"I will be your key," Eleanon said softly.

"My key. Yes," said the One.

"Maximilian thinks we are loyal to him," said Eleanon.

The One smiled.

Eleanon locked eyes with Bingaleal, then took a deep breath, addressing the One. "I will put this to the Lealfast Nation," he said, "but they will agree. They know that Maximilian is weak and cannot deliver to us that which we desire more than anything."

"Wholeness," said the One. "Completeness. Your own dignity and destiny. Oneness."

"Yes," Eleanon said, and the One had to bite back his smile. *The Lealfast would be as malleable as Ravenna, and as had once been the Magi.*

"You may take this vision to your Nation with my blessing," said the One, "and as my promise to you."

Eleanon felt a peacefulness infuse his soul—and a certainty that he'd previously been denied.

It was hope, he realized. Destiny, even.

Once again he made his elegant bow to the One. "Thank you," he said.

CHAPTER NINE

On the Road to Serpent's Nest

A xis!" Maximilian leaned over the distance between their horses and clapped Axis on the shoulder. "You look exhausted!"

"A reflection of you, then," said Axis. He'd ridden for three days to catch up with Maximilian, who had obviously pushed his convoy harder than Axis had imagined.

Stars knew how long it would take Inardle to catch up.

But he was here, finally, and gladder than he had thought to see Maximilian again. "Thank you for sending the Strike Force," Axis said. "Without them . . ."

"You should thank your father for loaning them to me," Maximilian said.

"But you were the one to think of sending them, and for that you do have my thanks."

"And thus, I hope, your undying gratitude and intention to run yourself into the ground accomplishing whatever it is I might ask of you."

"Naturally!"

Both men turned their horses so they rode side by side at the rear of the convoy.

"But seriously," Axis said, "you look worn out."

"I have been spending each night in the Twisted Tower," said Maximilian, "learning from Josia who was once hidden within the Weeper. You heard how . . . ?"

"How Ishbel freed him, and suffered attack from Ravenna? How Ravenna murdered her mother? Not all the details, but I have the gist of it."

"Then the details can wait for the moment when we have more leisure, Axis," Maximilian said. "Tell me what you heard and saw in Armat's camp."

For the next hour Axis talked in a low tone, telling Maximilian what had happened from the moment the injured Lealfast started falling out of the sky around him to the time BroadWing's Strike Force had saved them. Maximilian listened in silence, not interrupting with any questions, keeping his eyes on the road ahead.

"Have you seen the Lealfast?" Axis asked.

"No. They must be truly licking their wounds somewhere."

"I think they will rejoin you at Elcho Falling," said Axis. "It will take time both for their wounds and egos to heal. I told Eleanon I didn't want him rejoining you until he was prepared to learn under BroadWing. Stars knows when that might be."

"Axis . . . why did Ravenna free you?"

"So that I might persuade you against Ishbel, Maxel. She said that she loves you, and that she is not trying to destroy you. She said that all she wants is for you and this land to survive. But she says that if you take Ishbel back to your bed then you will fail, and this land will become a wasteland. She showed me—"

"A vision?" Maximilian said sharply, looking at Axis once more.

"She showed me a wasteland, Maxel. It was a version of the same vision she must have shown you, but she said it was different. Maxel, instead of some nameless threat, the vision now very clearly shows that Ishbel aids the walking pyramid. According to the vision, it is DarkGlass Mountain to whom she will betray Elcho Falling. There, I have said what Ravenna wished."

Maximilian did not answer, and they rode a while without speaking.

"Maxel," Axis said eventually, "Ravenna seemed almost reasonable. And she *did* save me."

"Yet she murdered her mother."

"Yes," Axis said. "She murdered her mother." He paused. "Maxel, I do not believe this will have some happy, magical ending. Either Ishbel or Ravenna will prove your destruction, and this land's destruction."

Maximilian sighed. "Ah, thus speaketh the prophet of doom."

"Maxel, *listen* to me. One day you will have to put your sword through one of these women. Can you do it?"

CHAPTER TEN

Isembaard

Isaiah pulled the horse to a halt in the middle of the afternoon, when they were five or six days' journey from Hairekeep.

Hereward, who had been dozing against his back, jerked into wakefulness. "Isaiah?"

"Wait there," Isaiah said, swinging a leg over the stallion's withers and sliding to the ground.

Hereward slid off as well, one hand grabbing at the halter and rope that Isaiah had fashioned out of the harness he had made.

Someone was sitting cross-legged in the sand some twenty paces away, their head bent over the sword they were honing.

Isaiah was already walking toward the man, but Hereward did not follow.

Whatever waited there looked too dangerous.

Isaiah stopped several paces away.

"Bingaleal," he said, although he knew that the creature sitting on the ground before him was not in any manner the Lealfast he had known.

Bingaleal—or whatever he had become—looked up from his task. In features he looked as Isaiah remembered, but his eyes had been replaced with vivid emerald glass.

"Isaiah," Bingaleal said, then bent his head back to honing the sword.

"What do you want, Bingaleal?" Isaiah said.

Bingaleal's right hand moved down the blade of the sword, slowly and rhythmically, running the whetting stone over the cutting edge of the steel. It made a slow, whispering sound that grated on Isaiah's nerves.

"Bingaleal?" Isaiah said.

Bingaleal looked up again, and Isaiah heard Hereward's very soft gasp as she saw the creature's eyes.

"I have a message for you," said Bingaleal. "From the One."

"I grow sick of his messages," Isaiah said. "They prove a heavy burden."

Bingaleal grinned, and now Isaiah gasped in unison with Hereward.

Within Bingaleal's mouth there was nothing but blackness, and within that blackness, hands pressing forth in agony and terror.

"Take a good look at Hairekeep as you pass," Bingaleal said, "and know what awaits Elcho Falling should Maximilian think to ignore the One."

Then he rose, making Isaiah take an involuntary step back, and strode off into the distance.

When Isaiah returned to Hereward, she looked at him with worried eyes. "Who was that?" she said.

"Dismay and disaster," he replied.

CHAPTER ELEVEN

On the Road to Serpent's Nest

Axis went back to his tent. He knew that his father wanted to see him, but he was too tired to brave either StarDrifter or Salome and their happy, happy pregnancy.

He didn't want to be reminded of the family he'd lost.

Yysell, his body servant, was in the tent, setting out a tub of water and a cold meal on a table to one side. Axis thanked him, then waved him away.

He wanted to be alone.

As soon as the man had gone Axis stripped off his filthy clothing and sank into the hot tub. He scrubbed his body and hair, combing it out with his fingers, then lay back in the soapy water, thinking.

Not of what he and Maximilian had discussed, but of Inardle.

And Azhure.

He'd barely thought of anything else on the ride to rejoin Maximilian.

Since his return from death Axis had been tempted by women, but had never taken the opportunity to surrender to that temptation. He'd been attracted to Ishbel, and to a lesser extent Ravenna and Venetia, and there had been many opportunities from willing courtiers at Isaiah's palace of Aqhat whom he had waved away with a smile. But all these attractions and temptations had been intellectual. Axis had realized that he had the opportunity, and he had turned those opportunities over in his mind, but he never once came close to thinking, *Yes, I will take that woman.*

He had remained faithful to Azhure.

Then he had met Inardle.

The attraction had been there instantly and Axis had supposed that like all other temptations over the past two years he would mull it over in his mind, smile at the thought of succumbing, and then walk away. The attraction would fade.

Instead, it had grown stronger, and was overlaid with other emotions: irritation, anger, fear.

Irritation, anger, fear. Everything a man felt when he was falling in love, and fighting that love tooth and nail.

Love? Inardle?

A half Skraeling?

She was so very different from Azhure. Inardle was so very different from Faraday. She wasn't someone he had ever thought he'd be attracted to— damn it, she was half Skraeling!

Perhaps *that* was the attraction. The feared, forbidden fruit, packaged in such loveliness.

"Shit," Axis mumbled, rubbing a hand over his face, getting soap in his eyes, and trying his best to rid his mind of the image of the Skraeling mounting SummerStar.

What was he going to do? Should he remain faithful to a woman who was, to all intents and purposes, dead?

"What should I do, Azhure?" he murmured, but she didn't answer, and eventually Axis rose from the bath, sending water cascading over the floor of the tent, dried himself, and fell into bed.

It took him hours to get to sleep, but when he did, his mind was made up, if not utterly easy.

Azhure was dead, and Axis did not want to spend the rest of this new life yearning for what he had lost.

CHAPTER TWELVE

On the Road to Serpent's Nest

StarDrifter hugged his son as they met for breakfast in Maximilian's command tent. "I thought I might see you last night."

"I was exhausted, StarDrifter, and Maxel kept me talking until late in the night. Blame him. How's Salome?"

"Still sleeping," StarDrifter said, starting to fill his plate with the food servants had set out on a side table.

"There can't be long to go," Axis said, once more sitting down at the central table where he was already halfway through his own breakfast.

"A few weeks, we think," StarDrifter said, sitting next to Axis.

Axis looked at Maximilian at the head of the table. "And will it be an Elcho Falling birth, Maxel?"

Maximilian waggled a hand. *Who knows?* "If we continue at this pace we should be at Elcho Falling within two weeks. Whether or not I unwrap Serpent's Nest to reveal Elcho Falling immediately rather depends on what I find when I get there."

"Armat?" Axis said.

"Armat has broken camp," BroadWing said. He had arrived in camp very early that morning, together with most of the Strike Force, leaving only a few scouts to track both Armat and the Emerald Guard bringing Inardle, Zeboath, and Garth to rejoin Maximilian.

Axis nodded his thanks.

Egalion, captain of the Emerald Guard, was also present, together with Ishbel. Egalion had introduced himself to Axis when first the StarMan had entered, and the two men had spent several minutes in conversation, liking each other immediately, before anyone else had arrived in the tent. Ishbel had arrived only just before StarDrifter, had given Axis a hug of greeting and a kiss on his cheek, lectured him on getting into trouble, and had then sat down with a smile on her face and Maximilian's eyes watching her carefully.

Ezekiel, the single remaining Isembaardian general, was not present. Although Maxel trusted him, Ezekiel tended not to be included in the meetings of Maximilian's closest advisors.

"Armat is marching slowly northeast," BroadWing continued. "Not at a pace to catch us, nor on a line to intercept us."

Axis forked some more eggs into his mouth and then, having swallowed, looked between his father and Maximilian. "I need to thank you," he said. "The Strike Force saved my life."

"Maximilian asked me to send it," StarDrifter said. "Naturally, I had to consider the request carefully and at some length before I gave my consent."

Everyone laughed.

"I also need to thank and compliment BroadWing," Axis said. "An incompetent haggle of flighted bowmen—"

Everyone present knew he was referring to the Lealfast.

"—would only have exacerbated the danger to myself and my companions," Axis continued. "BroadWing, you commanded the Strike Force brilliantly, and if they responded in like manner, then it was because of the training you have given them over the past few weeks. You are an exceptional Strike Leader, my friend."

"That title should truly belong to you," BroadWing said.

Axis grinned. "Why is everyone trying to force ancient titles back onto my shoulders?" he said.

"Because you have shoulders broad enough to bear them," Maximilian said. "Axis, my friends, this is as good a time as any to talk some strategy. We have a massive army moving up behind us, determined to lay siege to Elcho Falling. We have between us some twenty thousand men: Icarii, Escatorian, and the Isembaardians who chose to stay with us. Axis, I talked with StarDrifter, Egalion, and BroadWing earlier today, and they concur with my decision to give you complete command of all the disparate elements of what forces I have at my disposal. I am not the brilliant war leader, you are. Take command."

Axis looked between StarDrifter, BroadWing, and Egalion. "You agree with this? StarDrifter, you are prepared to hand the Strike Force into my complete command, answerable only to me, and not to you?"

"It's yours, Axis," StarDrifter said.

A slow smile spread over Axis' face. *Command of the Strike Force again!*

"And you, Egalion," Axis said. "You are bound to Maximilian by strong obligations and bonds. You can accept my command?"

"If it means Maximilian's safety, yes," Egalion said. "If it means serving under the greatest legend this world has ever known, then yes again." He extended his hand over the table. "I am yours to command, Axis."

Axis shook his hand, his smile broadening even further, then leaned back to look about the table.

"Why do I suddenly feel so optimistic?" he said.

"Well, I don't feel optimistic," said Ishbel. "This is no reflection on you, Axis, but on the odds we face. It isn't just that Armat controls so many soldiers, hundreds of thousands to our pitiful twenty thousand, but that he also has Ravenna and Lister with him. Lister, particularly, is a powerful, powerful man. A god. And without Isaiah to counteract him . . ."

"I suppose we could hope that Armat puts a sword through Lister as he put a blade through Vorstus," Axis said. "But seriously, Ishbel, while I don't discount him, I am not terrified of him, either. He hasn't exercised the best judgment to this point, and actually is in a fair amount of danger in Armat's camp. I may have jested about Armat killing him, but it is a possibility. Lister will need to watch his step while he rides with Armat. And as for all those hundreds of thousands of men . . ."

"When we attacked the men who pursued Axis," BroadWing said, "Axis commanded us not to kill any of them, but merely their horses. He also commanded us to whisper to them that this was a message from the Star-Man."

Maximilian caught Axis' eyes and smiled.

"I was merely following your own strategy, Maxel," Axis said.

"Axis wants it known that those men survived by his grace," Maximilian said. "They'll not forget it. Likewise, I allowed Insharah to desert so readily and with good wishes. Neither he nor his men will forget that, either."

"I told Maxel this last night," Axis said, "but should share it with the rest of you now. I spoke briefly with Insharah while I was in Armat's camp. I think the man already harbors doubts. Maybe his men do, too."

"I hope that there will be enough doubts within Armat's force," Maximilian said, "that he cannot be sure of it. From what I know of Armat, he is not the most charismatic of generals. He leads through fear, not through skill. It is a weakness."

"The other generals?" Egalion said.

"Further south, I believe," Axis said. "They command the other half of the Isembaardian force between them. Considering their general tendency toward internal treachery and fighting, we could also hope that they distract Armat at some point."

"Can we ensure that happens?" Maximilian said.

"I'll look into it," Axis said. "Ishbel, may I have permission to talk to Madarin later today? He may have some useful ideas . . . and contacts."

"Of course," she said.

"And not to forget everyone's favorite assassins, Serge and Doyle," StarDrifter murmured. "They can both pass for Isembaardians if needed, and to think of the chaos they could cause . . ."

Axis grinned. "A suggestion taken, StarDrifter. But for now, and until we arrive at Elcho Falling and I can judge for myself what its defenses are like, I am going to concentrate on the Strike Force. BroadWing, you have . . . how many now?"

"Five hundred, StarMan."

Axis tapped his fingers on the table, thinking. "And how many more Icarii to join with you, StarDrifter?"

"Possibly another two thousand," StarDrifter said. "Icarii are still flying in from as far distant as Coroleas."

"So perhaps a few score more of former Strike Force members," Axis said. His fingers continued to tap slowly as he thought.

"Perhaps you can add the Lealfast eventually, Axis," Ishbel said.

"Perhaps," Axis said, without any conviction. "They are currently useless but they have talent and good skills with the bow and arrow. They lack any experience at all, which lack of experience they combine with a self-certainty in their own superiority. It is, I have to say it, the early Strike Force all over again."

"We were never quite that bad," BroadWing snapped.

"That's because you hid in the Icescarp Alps and didn't fight anyone," Axis retorted. "At least the Lealfast left their snowy safety and came looking for a fight."

"I had no idea you were their champion," Ishbel said.

"I watched as thousands of them were slaughtered in cold blood," said Axis. "I owe them something, and that something is a second chance, if they want it. I admit I have been their vicious detractor as well, but now . . . now, well, perhaps I see them in a different light."

Axis noticed that Maximilian was regarding him with a twinkle in his eye at that last, but he chose to ignore it. Stars alone knew what gossip BroadWing had been feeding him.

"We can't afford to ignore any potential military aid," Axis said. "And we should also remember that Georgdi will be meeting us at Elcho Falling with the forces he has mustered. From what I know of Georgdi, from my own experience and from what Malat told me, a single man of his is worth ten Isembaardians. I don't want anyone in this tent to discount what we have. I've faced worse odds than this before and won."

"A good point, Axis," Maximilian said. "Is there anything else to discuss? It is growing late, and we need to get on the road."

"Just one thing, Maxel," Axis said. "I want to send some Icarii south. We need to know what is happening."

"Not into Isembaard," Maximilian said, frozen in the act of rising.

"Not into Isembaard," said Axis, "but as far south as they dare."

Maximilian nodded. "Let's get moving," he said, and left the tent.

CHAPTER THIRTEEN

Hairekeep, Isembaard

Hereward sat behind Isaiah on the horse, swaying rhythmically to its gait. It had been over two weeks since the One had almost killed Hereward, and in that time she had recovered well. The scab on her neck had fallen off, and she had a shiny, pink, coin-shaped scar at the junction of neck and shoulder to remind her of just how close she had come to death.

Six days after they had talked to Bingaleal (or to whatever he had become) they had traveled closer to the fort of Hairekeep, which guarded the entrance to the Salamaan Pass. At first the countryside and road had appeared normal, but in the midafternoon of the fourth day since encountering Bingaleal the road they traveled turned to glass.

Both Isaiah and Hereward were appalled, and it made them wonder what they'd discover at Hairekeep.

There were far more Skraelings about, as well. They were traveling in large groups of fifty or more, in the same direction as Isaiah and Hereward, although they kept their distance.

Isaiah and Hereward, by silent mutual agreement, chose not to step onto the glass. Isaiah turned the horse off the road and traveled parallel to it. Every so often the sun glanced off the surface of the road, and they would think it flashed and grinned at them.

On the morning of the thirteenth day after they'd left the Lhyl, they drew close to Hairekeep. Isaiah was particularly tense, and kept glancing at Hereward to make sure she was close.

"At least I have a sword," he said.

"I would prefer ten thousand swordsmen at my back," Hereward replied, and Isaiah managed a brief laugh.

"Aye, ten thousand swordsmen would be much better. Hereward, keep close to my side, will you? I don't know what we will encounter ahead."

"I have no intention of straying, Isaiah."

Isaiah glanced over his shoulder, and they shared a brief smile. His dislike of Hereward had ebbed over the past weeks. He wasn't sure that he actually liked her, but he had grown used to her presence, and felt responsible for her.

An hour later Hairekeep rose in the distance, and as soon as he could see it clearly, Isaiah pulled the horse to a halt.

"What is it?" she said.

"The fort is different," he said. "You've not ever seen it before?"

"Servants didn't have much travel opportunity," she said. "We tended to be working too hard."

She earned herself a black look from Isaiah for that comment, but he didn't otherwise respond to it.

"Hairekeep should be a massive, rectangular sandstone tower," Isaiah said, "rising almost a hundred paces into the sky. This . . ."

This, thought Hereward, peering ahead, *wasn't exactly rectangular.*

Isaiah clicked his tongue at the horse and they rode closer, a little more warily now, senses alert for hidden dangers.

"Isaiah," Hereward said softly a few minutes later.

"I've seen them," he murmured.

Skraelings, tens upon tens of thousands of them, sitting in ordered ranks on the far side of the road, starting about fifty or sixty paces distant. They were hard to spot, because they were mere unmoving humps close to the ground, and their heads were lowered so that their silver orbs didn't catch the sun's rays.

"The One's invasion force," Isaiah muttered, and as one the Skraelings lifted their heads and their terrible orbs flared at Isaiah and Hereward.

"Walk on," Isaiah said to the horse, now skittering about in fear.

It got worse as they approached the fort. The ranks of Skraelings stretched back as far as either could see—there were likely millions waiting here.

And among them—rising now and again as if caught by the wind—were

Lealfast, or whatever they had turned into. There were thousands of them—Bingaleal's entire force.

"My fellows," said Bingaleal to Isaiah's and Hereward's other side, making them jump. He was walking parallel with them about five paces distant. "They are like me," he tapped his chest. "They have a heart of glass. A heart *devoted* to the glass." He grinned, showing the unearthly blackness behind his lips. "Axis SunSoar thinks to build a Strike Force again. But the One commands a Strike Force unlike anything Axis has ever had to deal with."

"The One is remarkably well informed," Isaiah said, keeping his eyes ahead as he and Hereward rode forward. He was tense now, worried not so much that Bingaleal would attack him (the One did, after all, need him to deliver a message), but that the stallion would panic and throw one or both of them. The horse was very tense, and Isaiah kept a close hold on his halter rope and a tight grip with his knees.

"The One is omniscient," Bingaleal said. "Look," he waved a hand ahead, "do you see?"

Isaiah took a deep breath of shock, and felt Hereward do the same behind him.

They were close enough to Hairekeep now to see it for what it had become. Not a huge block-of-sandstone fortress, but a twisting, writhing mass of darkness that rose to a peak in the sky like a distorted pyramid.

Faces and hands pressed against the darkness, desperate to escape.

"That's our larder," said Bingaleal. "That is what we feed on while waiting to invade, Isaiah. Your subjects. The ones you abandoned. We drag one out every so often and tear it open to eat. Would you like one now, for your supplies?"

Bingaleal watched Isaiah and Hereward ride past Hairekeep toward the Salamaan Pass.

Once they were out of sight, he resumed his normal appearance, then turned his head slightly.

Eleanon materialized beside him.

"Well?" said Bingaleal.

"The Nation has agreed," Eleanon said, then grinned at the delight on his brother's face. "We are all One."

"Yes," Bingaleal said. "We are all One."

"What was that face you showed Isaiah?" Eleanon said. He looked behind him, where the Lealfast were now lifting away from the Skraelings and vanishing into the air. "Why the disguise of horror?"

"It was what Isaiah expected to see," said Bingaleal, "and I did not want him to see me as I truly am. Isaiah needed to see a victim of the One, not an ally. What now for you, Eleanon?"

"For the moment I am keeping the fighters within the FarReach Mountains with the rest of the Nation," he said, "until Maximilian raises Elcho Falling, which is when Axis expects me to return, full of humbleness and contrition."

Bingaleal smiled. "Of course. But you are not remaining within the Far-Reach Mountains?"

Eleanon shook his head. "I want to see what is happening between Inardle and Axis," he said. "I want to see how well she is positioned. Inardle can work much good for us, brother, if Axis has become besotted with her."

"Be cautious with Inardle," said Bingaleal. "I do not trust her as once I did."

"She is a female," said Eleanon.

"And thus," Bingaleal said, "she has the potential to subdivide. She can never be a part of the One as can we."

"But she can still be useful," said Eleanon.

"She can still be useful," said Bingaleal, "but you should be cautious in sharing secrets with her, Eleanon. Go discover, then, if she has slid cold treachery between Axis StarMan's sheets."

When Eleanon had gone, Bingaleal turned to find a Skraeling standing just behind him.

Bingaleal jumped, wondering how much the Skraeling might have overheard.

"What do you want?" he snapped, annoyed at himself for being so obviously startled.

"To talk," said the Skraeling.

"What is there to talk about?" said Bingaleal. He looked behind the Skraeling at the army of Skraelings still massed across the plains behind Hairekeep, their front ranks only ten or twelve paces away.

Bingaleal felt the tiniest frisson of fear. There were millions of the creatures, all silent, all waiting, all staring at Bingaleal. In all the time he'd known the creatures they had been chilling, yes, but now . . . now they had a singularity of purpose about them, a steadiness of eye, that he found potentially terrifying.

With what had the One infused them? Purpose? Cunning? Knowledge? *Power?*

The Skraeling lifted its top lip and silently snarled. "We are your fathers," it said. "Have you forgot that?"

"We have long grown up and left the nest," Bingaleal said.

"You still owe us life," said the Skraeling.

"We owe you nothing," Bingaleal said, holding the Skraeling's eye.

"Who continued south to worship adoringly at the One's feet while you dithered in the FarReach Mountains, uncertain of who to support?" the Skraeling said. "Do you think that the One has not remarked upon that fact? That he has not noted well that it was *we* who came to him unhesitatingly? That it—"

"You fled south to slaver at the feet of Kanubai," Bingaleal said. "Not the One. Your allegiance turned with the swiftness of a treacherous wind. Do *you* not think the One has not noted *that?* Our decision was deliberate and considered. Yours was born on the back of your innate idiocy."

Something in the Skraeling's face stilled. "You think to despise us," it said softly. "You think to outwit us. You think to turn the One against us. No, no. You cannot do that. We were his first, and he will never forget that."

The Skraeling stared at Bingaleal a heartbeat longer, then he melted back into the mass of Skraelings.

Bingaleal looked at them for a long moment, needing to show them he was not cowed; then his mouth turned up in a slight sneer, and he lifted into the air.

The One sat cradled within the heart of the Infinity Chamber. His eyes were open, but they did not see the interior of the chamber; rather, they looked upon the ground outside Hairekeep where the Skraeling had just confronted Bingaleal.

The One smiled, then his eyes refocused within the chamber, and he picked up the red-haired adolescent cat, stroking its back and murmuring softly to it.

There was looming a great battle between the Lealfast and the Skraelings. The One wondered which he should allow to emerge victorious.

The Skraelings were so useful, but the Lealfast potentially more so.

The One sighed, and tickled the cat under its chin.

"It is time to move," he said. "We shall leave the *Book of the Soulenai* here."

CHAPTER FOURTEEN

On the Road to Serpent's Nest

Axis was riding with Maximilian and Ezekiel, discussing tactics that Armat might use in any possible siege of Elcho Falling. They had let their horses' reins lengthen, allowing their mounts the opportunity to relax back to a walk and stretch out their necks while the rest of the convoy moved past at a brisk trot.

"Siege engines?" Axis said.

"We use them as needed," Ezekiel said. "Expect them from Armat."

"Against a mountain?" Axis said, raising an eyebrow at Maximilian.

"Elcho Falling has its own defenses," Maximilian said. "I do not think siege engines will be of any concern . . . but it has been so long since Elcho Falling stood, and who can tell?"

"We should—" Axis began, then stopped as a soldier rode up.

"My lord," the man said, saluting Maximilian. "The contingent of the Emerald Guard with the physicians is rejoining the rear of the convoy."

Maximilian grinned and gathered up the reins of his horse. "Garth is back! Axis, keep the convoy moving, would you, while I—"

"Ezekiel can do that, surely," Axis said. "I'd prefer to come back with you, Maxel. I'd like to see—" *Inardle* "—Zeboath, and check that Inardle is well."

Maximilian gave him a guarded look, but nodded, and the two men turned their horses for the rear of the convoy.

* * *

She was riding a horse, which surprised Axis. He'd expected to see her still resting in a wagon, not sitting easy on the back of a rather large bay gelding watching him with wary eyes.

Inardle looked well, which also surprised Axis, who had somehow assumed her to remain swollen and bruised despite it being almost two weeks since she'd been injured. But her wing, while still splinted, was now back to its normal size, as was her left arm. All her bruises had vanished.

In fact, she looked rather lovely. Her hair was freshly washed and plaited into the elegant crown atop her head, and she was dressed in pale gray, almost silvery clothes: very slim, form-fitting trousers and a top of soft, almost gauzy fabric that wound simply about her breasts and left her shoulders and arms bare. Axis had no idea from where she'd managed to acquire the clothes. Did the Emerald Guard carry with them, as standard rations, gauzy silky textiles in case they should encounter a ball?

"Inardle," Maximilian said, giving her a nod of greeting, "perhaps we could talk later, once we have struck camp. Meet me in my command tent for a meal tonight." Then he looked past her. "Garth! Come, my friend, ride with me and tell me all your adventures."

Axis pulled his horse in beside Inardle's as Maximilian and Garth rode on ahead.

"You look very well," he said.

"Garth and Zeboath have given me great care," she said.

"The wing . . . it looks vastly improved."

"Yesterday Garth and Zeboath changed the splints. Now, at least, I can bend it."

"And . . . it is healing well?"

"No," Inardle said after a slight hesitation. "Two of the tendons have not been healing as well as they should."

"Will you be able to fly?"

"I don't know."

That would hurt, he knew. "But perhaps you can still travel through the air in your more magical guise."

"Not if I can't fly."

Stars, Axis thought, the Lealfast's command of the Star Dance was fragile indeed.

"Well," he said, "at least you ride a horse skillfully." That was no idle compliment. Inardle sat a horse with the natural ease and strength of a born horsewoman.

She didn't respond.

"Where in the world did you get those clothes?" Axis eventually asked as they merged with the back units of the main convoy.

Inardle turned her head and smiled at him. "Not all my command of the Star Dance is as fragile as you seem to think."

It was late afternoon, and Maximilian gave the command to make camp. Axis had been riding forward with one of the Isembaardian units, but now he rode back to find Inardle, who he'd left riding with the supply wagons.

"How much luggage have you managed to acquire in the past week?" Axis said with a hint of a grin. "Have you several trunks stuffed with garments as fine as that you wear now?"

"Just a small pack," Inardle said. "Garth and Zeboath have given me several jars of creams to rub into my wing."

"It still pains you."

"At times," she replied.

"Well, I'll get my body servant, Yysell, to put your pack into my tent for the time being, until we can arrange a sleeping place for you. You can wait there, too, if you like, until it is time to see Maximilian. Ah, here's Yysell now."

Axis spent the next two hours making sure the campsite was secure, setting guards about its perimeter, and receiving reports from several of the Strike Force about Armat's position.

The general was still well behind them, but close enough that a small force could attack, and Axis didn't want to take any chances with security.

It was just past dusk when he got to his own tent, a command tent almost as large as Maximilian's. There was the glow of a lamp inside, and a shadow as Yysell moved about, setting out fresh clothes and a hand basin and jug of water.

Axis lifted the tent flap and walked inside. Yysell turned from the side table and smiled, ducking his head in greeting, but it took Axis a moment longer to spot Inardle, who had seated herself on a stool in the shadows.

"Yysell has made you comfortable?" he asked her.

"Indeed," she said, "he has been very kind."

"Will you be eating here tonight, my lord?" Yysell said.

Axis shook his head. "We'll be eating with Maximilian."

Yysell bowed his head, and left.

"Did Yysell give you water to wash with?" Axis said as he shrugged off his jacket and then his shirt.

"Yes, thank you. Axis, can you arrange somewhere for me to sleep, please?"

"Yysell can hunt you out a small tent, if you like," Axis said, splashing water over his face and then his chest and shoulders. "I don't want you bedding down around the fires with the soldiers."

"Thank you. How far are we from Elcho Falling?"

"Possibly a week."

"And Eleanon? Have you news?"

"No. But I have heard of no disaster, so he and his fighters must be in the lower Sky Peaks."

She nodded, but didn't say anything, and Axis watched her carefully as he soaped his chest and arms.

Inardle had her eyes downcast, but she was still aware of his regard. She shifted on her stool, rearranging her wings self-consciously, then finally lifted her eyes as Axis started to towel himself dry.

"You didn't say good-bye to me," she said. "In the camp, when you left. I made you feel uncomfortable. I'm sorry."

Axis pulled on the fresh shirt Yysell had laid out for him, then the jacket. "It is time to go," he said. "Maximilian wants us in his command tent."

This was not going to be easy for her, Axis thought as they entered the tent. While she had met Ishbel and Maximilian before, she knew that their perception of her would be colored by Armat's catastrophic rout of the Lealfast.

It would have helped if Inardle had looked a little more demure, or perhaps less arrogant, but tonight she was all Lealfast and all pride, and very much on the defensive.

She also looked lovely in her silvery-gray fabrics with her crownlike silver hair and the gentle rim of frost about her eyelashes.

Axis instantly saw Ishbel and Salome raise their eyebrows.

It was going to be an interesting evening.

"Good," said Maximilian. "Everyone's here. Do you all know Inardle?"

Axis helped himself to a glass of wine and stood back, watching as Maximilian took Inardle's elbow and guided her amongst the small crowd, introducing her to those she had not yet met. The difference between her and the other Icarii present—StarDrifter, Salome, and BroadWing—was quite noticeable. Inardle was a little taller, slimmer, and almost ethereal beside them. She had an aura about her that whispered of the frozen wastes, and just sometimes, when she moved, she acquired a faint translucence.

She trailed glamour and mystery behind her.

The Icarii were generally regarded as extremely exotic by the non-winged races, but Inardle took that exoticness to far greater heights.

Axis couldn't take his eyes off her.

"StarDrifter is Talon of the Icarii," Maximilian said as he introduced her to him, "and Axis' father."

Inardle glanced at Axis as Maximilian said that, her only sign of nervousness thus far.

"StarDrifter," she said, inclining her head.

"We must talk sometime," StarDrifter said, his tone a little too cool, "about reintegrating the Lealfast back into the Icarii. It's time you came home."

"The Icarii are not our home," Inardle said. "We do not recognize your—"

"You cannot think yourself Skraeling, surely," StarDrifter said. Then, after a small, theatrically horrified pause, he added, "Do you?"

"StarDrifter," Axis said, giving his father a hard look, and stepping over to hand Inardle a glass of wine. "This really isn't the time."

"I do not blame your father for not thinking highly of me," Inardle said, setting the glass of wine to one side.

She turned slightly so she could look Maximilian in the eye. "My Lord of Elcho Falling, I must offer you my apologies for what happened when Eleanon—"

"You owe me no apologies," said Maximilian, "and you do not need to answer for Eleanon's error. Inardle, if your fellows have the same reserves of dignity and courage that you possess, then there may be hope for them yet." His mouth curved in a gentle smile. "Welcome to my table, Inardle. You appear to have impressed Axis," he sent an amused glance at Axis as he said this, "so now I look forward to being impressed as well. Will you sit on my right?"

Axis found it an intriguing meal. Maximilian was open and friendly enough with Inardle, as were Ishbel and Garth, but they were the only ones. StarDrifter verged on the openly hostile, Salome was not much better as she took her lead from StarDrifter, BroadWing ignored Inardle the entire evening, and Ezekiel clearly couldn't have given a damn about her and talked almost exclusively with Egalion, who was seated too far away from Inardle to do anything but give her an occasional intrigued glance.

It was an interesting reaction, Axis thought. The people who were most at ease with Inardle were those clearly less threatened by her . . . and they were the non-Icarii among the gathering. Axis had wondered what it might take for an Icarii to feel intimidated, and now he had his answer.

An Icarii who had evolved further.

And by mating with a Skraeling, no less.

Axis had his own problems with the Skraeling blood connection, but the more time he spent with Inardle the less it bothered him.

The meal progressed, the conversation meandering along inconsequential paths, until Maximilian settled back in his chair and turned the conversation to darker matters.

"Inardle, Axis tells me that Lister, along with Ravenna, is now with Armat."

"Yes."

"I do not know Lister well, although he has had a profound influence on my life," Maximilian said. "But you were once his lover, I believe. How do you understand his sudden defection to Armat?"

"Lister is a difficult man to know," Inardle said. "I shared his bed, but he was so secretive . . . I admired him greatly, and he was companionable, but there were depths to him that I never understood. His desertion into Armat's camp could mean anything. I just don't know, Maximilian, I am sorry."

"The Lealfast were his servants," Salome said.

"No," said Inardle, "we were not. We traveled with him because we felt that our ambitions coincided—to aid the Lord of Elcho Falling. Once we had a choice between Lister and Maximilian," she gave Maximilian a small smile, "then our association with Lister was over. Perhaps—"

She broke off suddenly, and looked down at the table.

"There was no excuse for Lister's desertion of you in Armat's camp," Maximilian said. Then, to cover the awkward silence, he leaned forward in his chair and addressed Axis.

"Will you find a duty for Inardle, Axis? She tells me she is mostly healed of her injuries now, save for her wing, and she surely can prove of some use to you."

"Inardle can serve as my second-in-command," Axis said. "My lieutenant."

All movement and sound ceased, and all eyes stared at Axis.

"I have overall command of disparate forces," Axis said, his tone as nonchalant as if he were discussing his breakfast order with Yysell, "and I need someone who can act as my eyes and ears, who can report back to me, who can convey my orders—"

"A kind of secretary," Salome said, with a somewhat condescending smile.

"—and who can give orders on my behalf, knowing my own wishes in any given situation where I can't be contacted," said Axis. "Inardle will need some instruction and guidance, but I think she can—"

"Stars, Axis!" StarDrifter said. "She'll order Maximilian's entire army into a massacre if she gets half a chance!"

"That was utterly uncalled for!" Axis snapped.

"StarMan," BroadWing began, his tone tight, half risen from his stool. "You cannot place the Strike Force in a position where they may need to take orders from—"

"A Lealfast?" said Axis. "You take them from me easily enough, and Inardle has the same amount of Icarii blood as myself."

"The Lealfast are utterly unknown to us!" BroadWing said, sinking back onto his stool and sending Inardle a cold look. "Who knows where their true loyalties lie? We cannot trust her, Axis."

"Trust is both earned and learned," Axis said. He was aware that no one knew much about the Lealfast, but trust had to start somewhere, and Inardle had endured enough over the past weeks for him to take that step. He was not overly surprised at the strength of BroadWing's reaction, but hoped Inardle's strengths would gain BroadWing's acceptance over time.

"I am not asking you to hand over your soul this very night, BroadWing,"

Axis continued, "but I do expect you, and Ezekiel, and Egalion, and even StarDrifter when it comes to military decisions, to respect what Inardle says as if I had said or ordered it. She will be my voice. Have I made myself clear?"

"StarMan," StarDrifter said, "you owe Inardle nothing, you were not responsible for what happened to her in Armat's camp, and you don't need to make recompense to her now. Not in this manner."

"Inardle," Axis said.

She was sitting in her chair, very still, very watchful, and Axis thought he could see both apprehension and excitement in her face.

There was no triumph there, and for that he was very grateful.

"Yes, StarMan?" she said.

"When BroadWing led the Strike Force in our rescue, he used a stratagem known as the spiral attack formation to rout the Isembaardians who pursued us. BroadWing, could you describe to Inardle how that works?"

BroadWing sent Axis a black look, but he complied, explaining to those at the table how the Strike Force used four waves of bowmen and women to attack the horsemen, spiraling silently down from the moonless sky.

"It was a flawless attack," Axis said. "Inardle, under what circumstances would you *not* use the spiral stratagem?"

Almost as one, all eyes swiveled back to Inardle.

"Not ever on the same men you had used it on before," she said.

"Why not?" said BroadWing.

"Because having suffered under it once," Inardle said, "they'd be expecting it again. And while the spiral formation is patently very effective when used with the advantage of surprise, given any other circumstances it might prove deadly to the Strike Force."

"How so?" said Axis.

"All the Icarii are packed relatively closely together. They'd be extremely vulnerable to attack from archers on the ground."

"As happened with the Lealfast in Armat's gully attack," BroadWing said.

"Yes," Inardle replied softly, holding BroadWing's gaze.

"She's got a good head on her shoulders, BroadWing," Axis said. "As do, I suspect, most of the Lealfast. She'll do."

BroadWing gave a slight shrug of his shoulders, but he dropped his eyes, and Axis knew that was as much of an agreement as he was likely to get from the man tonight.

But it was enough.

"Are you certain you want this?" Maximilian asked, very quietly.

"I am certain," Axis said, and Maximilian nodded.

"As you wish, then," he said, rising from the table. "And if you will all excuse me . . ."

Axis asked Inardle to wait for him in his tent, then sought out his father as he left Maximilian's tent.

"What are you doing with that woman, Axis?" StarDrifter said.

"I—"

"Have you no thought for Azhure? No sense of loyalty or love for her?"

Axis thought that was a bit much coming from a man who had spent his life cheating on Axis' own mother.

"She fascinates me," Axis said, "and she has great potential."

StarDrifter sneered.

"Stars, StarDrifter, what do you have against her?"

"She is *Skraeling!*"

"No, she's not," Axis snapped, "and she's not Icarii, either. You can't try to bring her under your control. You are not *her* Talon, as you are not the Lealfast's. Yes, the Lealfast are shitty warriors, but so also was the Strike Force when first I took command of it. Of all the sins of which the Lealfast might be accused, this must be one of the most easily amended. Get used to her, StarDrifter. Both she and her people will be around a little longer."

"And Azhure?" StarDrifter said, bringing the conversation back to the battlefield he wanted. "How will she feel, knowing you betray her with a *Skraeling?*"

"Azhure is dead," Axis said. "*Dead*, StarDrifter! I've had to come to terms with that, and so also must you. Yes, I want Inardle. I've watched you with Salome, and I yearn for the warmth and comfort of a woman by my side again. Inardle intrigues me as no other woman has since I came back from death. I'm not going to waste what there is of this life wallowing in guilt merely because I want a little of what once I had with Azhure."

"Then, by the stars, I hope you are not betraying every single one of us because you lust for that creature."

"I know what I am doing," Axis snarled, then strode off.

Axis paused for a few minutes before he reached his tent. He was still angry and emotional after the scene with his father, and didn't want to walk into the tent so wrought up that he ruined any chance he might have at broaching the distance between Inardle and himself.

He knew he should not have been surprised at StarDrifter's—or anyone else's—reaction. StarDrifter had been emotionally involved with Azhure himself, was very loyal to her, and was never going to react well to Axis becoming involved with someone else.

Especially not a someone as controversial as Inardle.

Half Skraeling, distant, unknowable, and already part of a military debacle, she was, indeed, a contentious choice for Axis' second-in-command.

He grinned to himself, calming down. Inardle was certainly much lovelier than his former second-in-command, and best friend, Belial. Belial had been so ... *un*controversial. Everyone had liked him, and had gotten on well with him.

Inardle ...

"Well," Axis murmured to himself, finally walking toward the tent, "it will be interesting, indeed."

Inardle was sitting on a stool by the brazier when Axis entered. She stood up, looking wary.

"Do you want the job?" Axis said. "Do you want some responsibility?"

"What makes you think I could do this? I can't—"

"Don't ever let me hear you say 'can't' again. You can—you just need training and experience."

"But why *me*? For the stars' sakes, Axis, Georgdi would be better, even Zeboath!"

Axis laughed. He gestured to Inardle to sit down again, and pulled up his own chair by the brazier. "Zeboath is a fine man, and everyone likes him. He would make a lousy second-in-command to me."

"And yet I would? How?"

"Because you have a much harder edge to you. People may not like you so much, but they will learn to respect you. I think also you can make decisions under pressure, and I need that."

Inardle stared at Axis. "How do you know you can trust me?"

"I will take the risk, Inardle. *Can* I trust you?"

"Of course." Inardle held his eyes with that, but it took all her willpower to do it. *Could he trust her? No. No. Never.*

"You will do well enough," he said. "It will be a duty you will ease into. I think you will enjoy it, and be challenged by it. I would never have offered it to you otherwise."

"You didn't offer it to me. You simply told everyone."

"True enough. Inardle, there's another reason I want you to take on this duty for me. It isn't the main reason, but it is significant. You're my bridge to the Lealfast, my bridge to understanding them, and them me, and each of us learning to trust each other. Somehow, whether they like it or not, the Lealfast are going to have to work with me, and with the Icarii, and with the Isembaardians and whatever forces Georgdi can summon. You and I are going to have to make that happen, Inardle."

Inardle needed more than anything to turn this conversation away from the subject of trust. "Axis, why didn't you say good-bye to me at the camp?"

He gave a short, uncomfortable laugh. "I wish you wouldn't keep asking me that question."

He took a deep breath, then looked her straight in the eye. "I am sure that Yysell has arranged something for you, but to be utterly frank I don't want you sleeping anywhere else other than in this tent. Will you stay with me, Inardle?"

"Is this why you want me to be your second-in—"

"No, damn it. But it *is* why I didn't say good-bye to you at the camp. I hadn't expected to want you this badly, Inardle. I hadn't expected to want you at all."

"You're not what I expected. I've said that to you."

Axis waited, his heart thudding uncomfortably, certain she would say no. She was so direct sometimes, and at other times so very reticent.

Inardle lifted her eyes and looked at him directly. "Am I a novelty, Axis? Is that why you want me to stay?"

"No. No novelty could make me feel as anxious as I feel right now."

Axis didn't know what to do. He wondered if Inardle was waiting for something, some words said, or some action.

Very hesitantly, he leaned over and kissed her. Just gently.

She didn't react for a moment, then she moved closer to him and kissed him more warmly.

"Very well," she murmured against his mouth. "I will stay, and we shall see."

CHAPTER FIFTEEN

On the Road to Serpent's Nest

Armat sat at the table, tapping his fingers slowly, pretending to read once again the report he'd just received from Kezial. He'd ingested its contents at first glance, but now he spent his time feigning deep interest in the report, simply to annoy (and hopefully worry) Ravenna and Lister, who sat silent and watchful.

They were also cold. Armat had set the table in the open air, just beyond his tent. He sat nonchalant in leather body armor over a sleeveless linen shirt and heavy breeches. Ravenna and Lister were both wrapped in cloaks and regarded him with stony, white faces.

Armat didn't trust them. He was certain one or both of them (and he suspected Ravenna before Lister) had been involved in Axis' escape and the debacle which followed. He had pretended to accept both their denials, but privately Armat wouldn't have trusted them with the breaking of a single egg, let alone his inner thoughts.

"What does Kezial report?" Lister said finally, and Armat dampened his smile. He'd known it would be Lister who would break first.

"He is well on his way," Armat said, carefully folding the single-page communication before laying it on the table to one side of the oil lamp. "He has consolidated all the troops from the central part of these godforsaken Outlands. Sixty-five thousand. They have made Margalit, and should now be well north of the city, marching on this Elcho Falling."

Armat paused, sighing theatrically and looking up, as if he sought salvation from the stars.

"There's more," Ravenna said, her breath frosting in the night air.

"Unfortunately, yes, there is more," Armat said, lacing his hands across his belly and allowing himself one more large sigh. "Kezial has heard word from Lamiah."

"Lamiah was at the Salamaan Pass, was he not?" Lister said.

"Aye," Armat said, "he was supposed to be guarding it. Well...apparently Lamiah has made the unilateral and singularly stupid decision to march back through the Pass and save what he can of Isembaard."

"No!" Lister said. "By the gods, has he no sense?"

"He has, from what Kezial reports," Armat said, tapping the folded report on the table, "fallen victim to his soldiers' delusions that somehow they can make a difference." He paused. "Lamiah is a fool. Isembaard is lost, from what you tell me."

Armat stopped, and looked keenly at Lister. "Isembaard *is* lost, yes?"

"I have told you all I know," Lister said. "I cannot know precisely the details, but I know that whatever has happened in Isembaard has destroyed Isaiah, and every single life within the nation. Armat, whatever was in that pyramid, whatever made it *live*, has now escaped and—"

"Yes, yes," Armat said, "you've told me all this before. I shall choose to believe you for the time being, and I suppose that I might as well assume Lamiah and the men he commands, all one hundred odd thousand of them, by the gods, are as good as dead?"

"They're dead the instant they set foot in Isembaard," Lister said.

"Well...at the least they won't be about to bother me," said Armat. "Lamiah was ever the fool."

"At least he'll die trying to save his own land," Ravenna said softly.

Armat shot her a sharp look. "Stupidity should never be admired, my lady."

"Loyalty is always—"

Armat guffawed loudly. "You are a fine one to talk so pretentiously of loyalty!" he said. "I assume that one day you will show me the same kind of loyalty you have shown your lover, and father of that child you carry?" He gestured at her belly.

Ravenna pulled the cloak even more tightly about herself. "I will not betray you, Armat."

"Of course you won't," he said, holding Ravenna's eyes with such a malevolent stare that she had to drop her own gaze away from his.

"So here we are," Armat said after an uncomfortable silence, "trailing after a ragtag army of about twenty thousand pitiful soldiers, with command of over three hundred thousand. I must tell you, my friends, the urge to order my massive force forward is almost overwhelming. We don't even need to fight. My army will simply trample whatever pathetic force Maximilian has into the gravel of the roadway. Even the Strike Force cannot dent three hundred thousand, surely."

"We can't—" Ravenna began.

"After all," said Armat, "what do I want with a mountain? Shall I mine it for gold? No, for I have no miners among my men. Should I till its soil? No, for its slopes shall be too steep. What on earth does a conqueror want with a mountain, Ravenna? I might as well—"

"It contains power and mystery beyond knowing," she said.

"I have power," Armat said, his voice low but infinitely powerful. "With Kezial's force I have almost four hundred thousand men under my command. This land is mine. I cannot think why I have not already declared myself Tyrant. And mystery? I have no use for mystery. It bores me."

"You need Elcho Falling's power to live," Lister said. "For all the gods' sakes, man—"

"Of which you continually inform me you are one," Armat said with a dismissive air.

"—whatever is in Isembaard *is not going to stay there!* It is going to see the north and it will eat everything—"

"Such melodrama," Armat said, now investigating the fingernails of one hand.

"Armat," said Ravenna, "stop playing the fool. If nothing else, there are a million Skraelings there. They're going to want to go home, eventually, and everything between Isembaard and the northern wastes is going to be—"

"I'm no fool," Armat said, leaning forward and abandoning the indifferent air, "but I don't trust you. I think you want the mountain for yourself and that baby," he nodded at her belly, "you carry. And I wouldn't be surprised if you want Maximilian as well. *I* think you're using me to get what you want from your pretty Maxel."

"Maximilian is set on the path to destruction," Lister said. "He cleaves to Ishbel, who will ruin him."

Armat had not taken his eyes from Ravenna. "Is that what you think?"

She nodded.

"Speak it!" Armat said.

"Maximilian is set on the path to destruction if he cleaves to Ishbel," Ravenna said, her voice steady. "She will ruin him."

"You're jealous," said Armat.

"For gods' sakes!" Ravenna said. "Stop toying with us, Armat. All we need is for Maximilian to resurrect Elcho Falling, and then . . . then . . ."

"Then we can kill him," Armat said.

"Indeed," said Lister.

"Yes?" said Armat, still looking at Ravenna.

"Then we can kill him," she said, her voice low.

"You're a nasty enough piece for any man to take to his bed, eh?" said Armat.

One of the lamps was still burning, flickering madly on the last few drops of oil as Axis lay on the bed, staring up at the shadows chasing each other across the canted roof of the tent. Inardle lay at his side and half across his body, warm and heavy, her injured wing lying across them like a soft blanket.

She was awake as well, moving very slightly every few minutes, one of her hands stroking occasionally on his chest. They hadn't spoken for over an hour, content just to lie.

Axis didn't think either of them would sleep. It would be nice to ascribe a romantic reason to this, but the brutal reality was that the narrow camp bed was uncomfortable for two people to share with any ease, let alone when one of them had a heavy and very large pair of wings. He thought the fact they had lain relatively unmoving for this length of time was close to being a miracle.

One of his hips and legs was paining him, however, and he knew he'd have to readjust his position soon.

"I'll ask Yysell in the morning if he can find something more accommodating," Axis said quietly. He slid an arm about Inardle's waist, holding her still, and turned over on his side so that they lay belly to belly and face to face. He was glad Inardle made no comment about Yysell finding them a more commodious bed. It meant she was prepared to stay.

"Better?" she said.

"My hip was on fire," he said, then kissed her softly.

"Lealfast make love in the sky and on the wind," she said. "We don't generally put up with this degree of discomfort."

He chuckled. "No wonder Armat's arrows caught you so unprepared."

Inardle's face went carefully expressionless as she tried to decide if she needed to be offended.

"It was a jest, Inardle."

"Well, then," she said.

"Well, then," he echoed, kissing her again, then once again, more deeply now.

Stars in heaven, Axis thought, *how had I left it so long before I made love to a woman again?*

And how, in stars' name, would he ever be able to make love to any woman *other* than Inardle after this night?

It had been extraordinary. On the one hand Inardle was extremely reserved—to the point of prudery at times, which drove Axis to the heights of frustration—yet her body clearly revealed just how much his touch affected her. She could feign diffidence all she liked, yet when he trailed his fingers down her body rivers of frost traced in their path. When he ran his tongue about her breast, and caught gently at her nipple with his teeth, he could feel a starburst of frost explode deep *inside* her flesh.

When he entered her, he could sense the waves of frosted pleasure wash through her with every stroke.

Her hand was running up and down his back now, and he hoped very much that she wanted to make love again.

"No one else makes my frost rise like you," she said, and Axis wondered how much that admission had cost her.

"Thank you," he said, meaning to thank her for far more than just that acknowledgment, and she smiled and moved against him and frost rimed her jawline where he ran his mouth.

Ravenna sat at the camp table for hours after Armat and Lister went to bed. She was cold to the bone, shivering now and again in sudden, painful bouts, but she knew she could not sleep, and could not bear the idea of being confined under canvas until the sun finally rose.

You're a nasty enough little piece for any man to take to his bed, eh?

That had hurt so deeply she could barely breathe for the pain. The last thing Ravenna wanted was to betray Maximilian, and to think of him dead... but she knew it had to be done if he could not be persuaded from Ishbel. She hoped quite desperately that somehow Axis had managed to convince Maximilian to stay away from Ishbel, but knew within her heart that he would not have been able to do so.

Maximilian would eventually take Ishbel back to his bed, if he had not done so already, and then they would curse this world to extinction.

Ravenna could feel whatever it was south of the FarReach Mountains. It was cold—in spirit, rather than flesh—and it was angry, and it had plotted revenge for thousands of years. It knew its enemies, had taken flesh from them, and if Maximilian thought that the battle with the beast was in the future then he was infinitely wrong.

The battle had already been fought, and lost.

Maximilian would need to die.

Ravenna closed her eyes, a single tear sliding down one cheek.

Maximilian would need to die.

Her hand slid over her belly. "You are this land's only hope, now," she whispered.

Elsewhere in Armat's camp three men sat, equally sleepless. They did not "sit" so much as hunch nervously under the canvas of a small tent, hoping that their two fellows standing guard outside would warn them of any danger approaching.

"Well, here's a fine thing," said Insharah, somewhat bitterly. "I remember someone saying to me, 'What in all the gods' names are we doing trudging along this slushy trail toward some mountain called Elcho Falling when our families are dying down south?' So we deserted Maximilian Persimius, and now... what? Why, we're trudging along the very same sludgy trail toward some mountain called—"

"Enough," said Rimmert. "How were we to know that Armat was going to abandon any concern for Isembaard, and for our families, to trail after Maximilian?"

Insharah looked between Rimmert and Olam. "If I was set on a path to Elcho Falling no matter what," he said, "I know which among Maximilian and Armat I'd prefer to serve."

"We made a mistake," Olam said. "Is that what you wanted to hear?"

Insharah sighed. "I've heard that Kezial is driving north as well, meaning to meet with Armat at this mountain called Elcho Falling."

"Lamiah?" asked Olam.

"Heading down south through the Salamaan Pass," Insharah said. "One of Armat's guards heard him talking about it to Ravenna and this man Lister."

"Then he, at least, can hold his head high," Rimmert said.

"Until it gets lopped off by whatever waits at the other end of the pass," said Insharah.

They sat in silence for a little while.

"What are we going to do?" Olam asked, eventually.

Axis finally rose just before dawn, hating to leave Inardle, who was finally sleeping, but so stiff and sore from the camp bed that he needed to stretch his back and limbs.

Yysell was already up and had a mug of tea ready for him.

Axis sipped it gratefully, stamping his feet in the frosty air and thinking that he vastly preferred the frost of Inardle's body to this biting ground ice, and talked quietly with Yysell about procuring a slightly more commodious bed.

Then, as Yysell moved off, he sent a quiet call out into the dawn.

StarHeaven.

She was with him within half an hour, apologizing for the delay.

"StarHeaven, Maximilian and I need some eyes and ears down south. We have no idea what is happening. Listen to me, StarHeaven, anywhere south of the northern approaches of the Salamaan Pass is off limits. You are *not* to enter the pass—whatever is down there is too dangerous—but if you could report to me directly from the northern exit of the pass, then you have no idea how grateful I will be. You have enough to power to reach me from that distance?"

"I think so, StarMan. I am growing better at filtering out the Star Dance from the ether every day."

Axis smiled. "Good. Take several companions—I've already discussed this with BroadWing."

Then, as StarHeaven was about to lift off, Axis added, "StarHeaven, do be careful. Good luck, and keep in touch."

Later that day, toward dusk, Isaiah and Hereward entered the Salamaan Pass from the south.

CHAPTER SIXTEEN

On the Road to Serpent's Nest

B roadWing?"

He turned about. "Inardle."

"BroadWing, I would like to learn about the Strike Force. What you did to save us when we were pursued by Armat's men . . . I have never seen anything like it. I would like to learn."

"I don't have much time, Inardle, and you can't fly. I can't afford to be earthbound right now."

"I'm sorry, I just wanted to learn something of tactics, and your history." *And I need to use your dislike of me to cement my hold over Axis.*

"From the gossip about camp, I'd have to say that you are sleeping with the man who can teach you far more than I."

Inardle managed to pale with embarrassment, hoping BroadWing would not see through the ruse. He was going to be easier to manipulate than she had thought.

Her stomach knotted with self-hatred at what she was doing, but she tried to ignore it as best she could.

"Get on your horse, Inardle," BroadWing said, "and rejoin the column. Surely Axis can find you something to do."

Now Inardle allowed her face to flame with humiliation. "Where is the Strike Force training?" she asked.

"In the air to the north," BroadWing replied. "Where I need to rejoin them."

"BroadWing, I would like to learn, and I would like to learn from you."

BroadWing half turned as if he were about to launch into the air, then paused, and looked back at Inardle. "Do you have any archery skills?"

"Yes. All the Lealfast train with the bow."

BroadWing stood considering Inardle silently for a long moment, then gave a nod, as if arriving at a decision.

"Some units of the Strike Force are practicing their archery close by today." Now he nodded in a northeasterly direction. "About fifteen minutes' ride that way. Why don't you join us, and we can see how skilled you are."

Camp had been pitched for about an hour, but Axis had still not seen Inardle. He'd not glimpsed her all day, but had not been worried as one of the Emerald Guardsmen told him he'd seen her speaking with BroadWing. Axis had assumed she'd spent the day with the Strike Force.

But he'd expected her back well before now.

"Yysell?" he said to his body servant. "Have you seen Inardle?"

"No, my lord," Yysell said, laying out fresh clothes for Axis across the newly acquired and far more commodious bed. Axis had no idea where Yysell had found it, but he was profoundly grateful. He didn't want to spend another night like the last.

He stripped off his dirty shirt and washed his face and upper body. "If you see her, tell her to come to dinner in Maximilian's command tent."

"Yes, my lord."

Axis dressed slowly, wondering where she was. Had she decided to leave Maximilian's column?

No, surely not. She would have said something.

Wouldn't she?

Stricken with doubts, and beginning to worry, Axis set off for Maximilian's tent.

BroadWing was already with Maximilian, together with StarDrifter, Egalion, Garth, and Ishbel.

Axis nodded a greeting to everyone, spoke briefly with Maximilian, then made for BroadWing.

"Have you seen Inardle?" he asked.

BroadWing raised an eyebrow. "You've lost your second-in-command?"

"Have you seen Inardle, BroadWing?"

"I saw her earlier in the day. She spent some time at archery practice with some of the units of the Strike Force, but left after a few hours. She couldn't keep up."

"Archery practice?" Axis said. "She's only just recovered from some terrible injuries. I would have thought that archery practice was the last thing she'd need. I'm not surprised she 'couldn't keep up.'"

"She insisted on taking part and I would think she was quite capable of making those decisions herself. Being your second-in-command and all."

Axis gave him a terse nod and turned away, more worried than ever. He was also angry at the birdman. Axis respected and liked BroadWing, but he thought the birdman was so set against Inardle that she could have shot Gorgrael out of the sky with a single arrow and he would still be contemptuous of her skills.

Perhaps, Axis mused, he should have been more circumspect in the manner in which he'd introduced Inardle as his lieutenant.

He circulated among the group as they shared wine before sitting down to dinner. He had a brief conversation with StarDrifter, mostly about Salome, who had gone to bed early as she was so tired, but extricated himself the moment StarDrifter asked, somewhat archly, where Inardle was.

He didn't want to get into an argument with his father about Inardle. Not tonight.

Axis was talking with Maximilian about the possibility of using several units of the Emerald Guard to scout the territory south of them when a movement at the door of the tent caught his eye.

It was Yysell. He had such a stricken look on his face that Axis immediately made his excuses to Maximilian, then joined Yysell outside the tent.

"Inardle has returned," Yysell said. "My lord, you need to see her. Now."

But Axis was already several paces away, jogging back to his tent.

She was sitting on the bed, face turned away from the door so that he could not immediately see it, clutching her left arm to her chest. The jar of liniment that she used to rub into aches in her shoulder and wing was lying smashed at her feet, the liniment dirtied and unusable among the dirt she'd tracked in on her boots.

She must have been trying to open the jar, desperate for pain relief, and had dropped it.

"Inardle?"

She turned her face even further away, her body visibly trembling, and, heart thudding in anxiety, Axis crouched down in front of her. *"Inardle?"*

She was crying, silently, her face white and drawn.

Axis stared at it a heartbeat, then looked at her left arm.

He saw the frost first, running the entire length of the arm.

Then he saw the bruises and contusions on her forearm.

Appalled and increasingly angry, Axis looked further up and saw her upper arm and shoulder. They were covered in patches of what he first thought were bruises, but which he realized were in fact layers of black frost over swellings and contusions.

He looked further back and saw that her wing was once more swollen, frost riming every single feather.

"Fetch Garth Baxtor!" Axis snapped at Yysell, who was out of the tent within a heartbeat.

Axis sat on the bed, took Inardle's chin in gentle fingers, and turned her face toward his.

She was in agony.

He had to close his eyes briefly in order to keep his anger in check. When it did explode, he wanted to be far distant from Inardle.

"How long did BroadWing keep you at archery practice?" Axis said.

"It wasn't his fault, Axis. He—"

"How long did BroadWing keep you at archery practice?"

"Until dusk," she whispered.

Axis cradled her gently against his body, hiding her face in his shoulder, not wanting Inardle to see his expression.

Until dusk?

"Garth will come," he said quietly. "He can help."

She was crying harder now, and Axis rocked her gently back and forth, wishing he could do something immediately to aid her pain. Stars, her broken left wing, as well as that shoulder and arm, must be in agony. Inardle would have used her barely healed flight muscles for archery, and to keep her at it hour after hour, *and without even the courtesy of an armguard if the condition of her left forearm was any indication* . . .

That had been deliberate.

BroadWing would have known the damage it would have caused.

Had he been amused, to watch her suffer while trying so hard to "keep up"?

"Axis?"

It was Garth, ducking inside the tent flap, and Axis was grateful to see he'd brought his medicine bag with him.

"BroadWing kept Inardle at archery practice for over ten hours today," Axis said. "Her shoulder . . . and wing . . ."

Garth met his eyes, gave a nod of understanding, then started to examine Inardle. He kept up a constant monologue of soothing words, persuading her to bend her arm, pausing whenever she cried out in pain. He ran gentle hands up and down the arm, then over the shoulder, then finally moved behind her to examine the wing.

At that point he caught Axis' eyes again, and this time there was anger in Garth's own eyes, as well as deep concern.

"The bones are still healing well," he said.

But, thought Axis.

Garth came about the bed and squatted in front of Inardle.

"Inardle, I am going to rub some liniment—"

"I broke the jar you gave me," she said. "I'm sorry, I should have been more—"

"Inardle, forget the broken jar," Garth said. "It doesn't matter. I will mix some more for you, and I will also mix a strong draught of analgesic, and you *will* drink it. Once that is down then I will massage the wing and shoulder. It will help the swelling to go down."

"It's the swelling that's doing the damage," Axis said, and Garth nodded. He moved over to his bag, took out several bottles, and combined their contents into a mug that Yysell held out.

Then Garth brought the mug over to Inardle, and sat on her other side. "Drink, Inardle," he said, and she drank without protesting, which made Axis realize just how much pain she was in.

"I'll be back in a few minutes," Garth said. "That analgesic mixture needs some time to take effect."

Axis nodded, and Garth rose and left, asking Yysell to come with him on some errand.

"I'm sorry," Inardle whispered once they had gone.

Axis said nothing, just holding her a little tighter and rocking her gently back and forth.

"Don't say anything to BroadWing," she said. "Please."

Axis closed his eyes again, unable to speak. That was not something he could promise.

"Axis," she said, now raising her face to look at him. "Please."

"He knew what he was doing, Inardle. These injuries are deliberate."

"I should have been able to keep up."

Stars, now *she* was talking about "keeping up." Had BroadWing taunted her with that all day, as she fell further and further behind while her shoulder and arm broke down?

"He is angry at me," Inardle said, "and I need to earn his respect. I—"

"Shush, Inardle. You need to earn no one's respect." Axis pulled her as tight as he dared, kissing her forehead and then her cheek. "Inardle," he said, "you amaze me."

Axis said that with such wonder, and such admiration, that Inardle started to cry again. Axis kissed away the tears and cuddled her close until Garth came back.

She was asleep now, exhausted by the archery practice, the pain and the emotion of the past day, and Garth and Axis stood just inside the doorway of the tent, talking in quiet tones.

"The wing was healing well," Garth said. "But after today . . . two of the major tendons in the wing are in danger of separating completely amid all the bruising and swelling. The stress Inardle put her arm and shoulder through—"

"The stress that BroadWing put her arm and shoulder through."

"Yes, well, what happened today has inflamed muscles and tendons very badly. The muscles will heal well enough, as most of the tendons, but there were two tendons in her wing that were under substantial strain anyway, and which had sustained considerable damage with Armat's initial attack. Axis, I don't like it. I think it is very possible that what happened today will cripple that wing. Inardle may never be able to fly again."

Axis stared at Garth, feeling his anger seething upward in great black waves.

"Will you sit with her until I get back?" he said.

"Yes."

"Good. When I get back, I may have more injured parties for you to work your skill on."

Then Axis strode through the door of the tent, and shouted to Yysell to saddle his horse.

CHAPTER SEVENTEEN

On the Road to Serpent's Nest

Axis pushed the horse into a gallop and headed slightly north of the camp. For what happened now he didn't want any accidental witnesses.

He was too angry.

Finally, he reined in the stallion, abruptly enough that the horse almost sank to the ground on its haunches, then swung it about in circles, calling out with his power.

StarDrifter! BroadWing! Now! Get here now!

He sent his anger seething out with the message.

They'd know well before they got here what they'd face.

It took them just over a quarter of an hour to join him, both arriving together, both circling warily before landing a few paces away.

Axis jumped off the horse, not caring that it cantered off into the darkness.

He tackled BroadWing first.

"What the fuck did you think you were doing?" he yelled, striding up to BroadWing and shoving him hard enough in the chest that the birdman staggered back a pace or two.

StarDrifter grabbed at Axis, but Axis snarled, flinging away StarDrifter's arm so that the Talon retreated a few paces.

Axis turned back to BroadWing. "You *knew* what you were doing to her! You didn't even have the grace to fit her out with an arm brace! What did you think when the blood started to run down her forearm, BroadWing? That she was being *weak?*"

"She refused to wear—" BroadWing began, but Axis hit him so hard that BroadWing tumbled over in the dirt.

"Axis," StarDrifter began.

"You wait your turn!" Axis snarled, and StarDrifter once again subsided.

Axis leaned down and hauled BroadWing up. "I have liked and respected you," he said, "but by the stars, I never thought I'd see you act this way!"

Then he turned to his father. "You knew about this. You were there."

That was sheer intuition on Axis' part. He didn't believe that BroadWing would have let matters get so out of hand without, at the least, some tacit support from his Talon.

"She said she was all right, Axis," StarDrifter said.

"For the stars' sakes, StarDrifter, what do you have against her? You accepted WolfStar's daughter in my bed, why not Inardle? Or is it that you suspect her to be somehow more beautiful than the Icarii? Somehow more powerful? Are you *jealous* of her?"

"The Lealfast are arrogant and untrustworthy—" StarDrifter began.

"And the Icarii are not? You two pathetic examples are *not?*" Axis took a breath, glaring between the two men. His hot anger was over; now it was as icy as the frost of pain that covered Inardle's body.

"The Lealfast's arrogance exists to cover uncertainty," Axis said. "The Icarii arrogance exists to cover . . . yet deeper and crueler arrogance."

"How is she, Axis?" BroadWing said. He had picked himself up from the ground and was rubbing at his jaw.

"Thank you for asking," Axis said. "She's almost certainly permanently crippled. The damage done to the tendons in her wing today will likely see her unable to fly again."

He stepped forward and gave his father a shove in the chest this time. "*You* know what it is like to be flightless, StarDrifter. How can you justify visiting that horror on another *merely through your petty small-mindedness?*"

"Don't forget who it was beat Azhure almost to death when he thought her a traitor!" StarDrifter shouted, shoving Axis back. "Don't you *dare* to lecture me!"

"And as I remember," Axis said, "you stood there then, too, and encouraged me, StarDrifter. You have a talent, it seems, for provoking unmerited cruelty in others."

"I think we have all said enough," BroadWing said, looking warily between Axis and StarDrifter, and wondering if the entire future of the Icarii was about to self-destruct in a battle between these two powerful Enchanters.

"If you resented my association with Inardle," Axis said quietly, "then you needed to approach *me* about it, beat *me* senseless, damn it, not a woman who over the past few weeks has been beaten, raped, and humiliated by half of the known world, so it feels to me. What the *fuck* has she done to deserve what you both did to her today?"

Finally BroadWing and StarDrifter dropped their eyes.

"When I first encountered the Strike Force," Axis said to BroadWing, "they were gaudy birdmen and women fluttering uselessly about the peaks of the Icescarp Alps. If they're something better than that now, then that is due to me."

Then Axis looked at his father. "When first I encountered the Icarii, StarDrifter, they were cowering within Talon Spike, full of hot words and arrogance but without a single iota of courage between them, without a single *wit* between them, to wing their way down from the icefields into the sun. If they've achieved something more than that, then that is due to me.

"I think the time has arrived," he continued, his voice even softer now, but still vibrating with anger, "to give something back. Generosity will do as a start."

Axis stared at the two birdmen before him, then he turned and walked away a few steps, whistling for his horse. When the stallion whinnied and trotted obediently out of the darkness, Axis gathered up the reins and swung into the saddle.

"Has it not struck you," he said to BroadWing and StarDrifter, keeping the horse on a tight rein as it circled restlessly, "that there was only one person on that archery field today who demonstrated leadership and courage, and it most certainly wasn't either of you."

Then he turned the stallion's head for camp, and booted his heels into its flanks.

Garth's head gave a final nod and he slipped into sleep, slouching comfortably in his chair.

As he did so, Inardle's eyes opened and she looked about the tent.

Yysell was nowhere to be seen, but there, toward the back wall . . .

The air moved and Eleanon materialized.

Inardle's eyes flew to Garth, and Eleanon gave a little shake of his head. "He will not wake," he said, walking over to the bed and crouching down beside it. "Tell me what has happened," he said. "Did Axis do this?"

"No!" Inardle said. "He . . ." She sighed, then, speaking softly and rapidly, told Eleanon what had happened, both in Armat's camp and since.

"You have done well," Eleanon said softly as she finished. "You have done what I asked."

"And look at the price I have paid for 'doing well,'" Inardle said, waving a hand at her wing.

"You know you are powerful enough to heal yourself with a crook of your finger. And you know also why you don't do it—because it binds Axis ever more tightly to you. He is such a fool."

Inardle dropped her eyes away from Eleanon. She could hardly bear the guilt she felt.

"You are in Axis' confidence?"

Inardle gave a small nod. "I told Axis we had little power."

"Ah, Inardle, you are worth your weight in jewels. You *have* done well. He suspects nothing?"

"No." Inardle lifted her eyes back to her brother. "I had to sit in a damp pit for days, Eleanon, and suffer rape, all for you."

"All for *us*, Inardle."

"All for us," she repeated dully. She took a breath. "Eleanon, you went south after Axis dismissed you, didn't you? What happened? Did you meet with Bingaleal? You are different—I can sense it about you. So different. The same difference I sense about Bingaleal."

"Yes. I am different. I have spoken with the One."

"Ah . . ." Inardle said on a breath.

"The One can give us what Maximilian is too weak to offer," said Eleanon. "The One can give us hope and dignity and freedom from both the Skraelings and the Icarii, Inardle. He can give us a home and a future. He can give us power. The Nation have accepted him, and we—"

Both their heads jerked toward the tent flap.

"Axis rides close," Inardle said.

"Yes. Listen, Inardle, continue with what you do. Draw Axis ever closer.

You will prove more than invaluable. I will rejoin you, suitably humble, when Elcho Falling rises, and bring my fighters with me. Watch for me. We will talk more then."

Eleanon leaned over, kissed Inardle on the mouth, and was gone.

Inardle kept her eyes closed and her body still, pretending sleep when Axis returned. She felt him bend down, kiss her forehead softly, then heard him settle in a chair close by the bed.

She listened to his breathing. It did not slow or deepen: he was staying awake, watching over her.

Inardle didn't know what to do. She felt trapped by a guilt that was growing deeper with every day, and that guilt had only been exacerbated by Eleanon's visit.

So much of what she had told Axis had been lies. The Lealfast were much more skilled fighters than she (and Eleanon) had led Axis to believe. They hadn't merely practiced on snow rabbits, but had trained extensively over the centuries with the Vilanders who lived close to the frozen wastes.

That was a lie Axis was sure to discover if ever he met any of the Vilander bowmen.

The Lealfast commanded much more power than what Inardle had told Axis. Their command of the Star Dance was much stronger, plus they had developed the learning and power the Magi had taught them so many millennia ago.

Many of the senior Lealfast were skilled in the power of the One. How in all the gods' names could she ever confess that to Axis now?

Yet the worst sin, and that which gave Inardle the most anxiety, was how coldly she had maneuvered herself into Axis' bed.

She could so easily have escaped Risdon and Armat.

But she hadn't. She allowed Armat to cripple her, and then Risdon to rape her, in order to make Axis feel responsible for her and to tie him the more closely to her.

Yes, Inardle had suffered in the doing, but she had chosen that suffering— and all in order to entrap Axis.

What would he do when he found out? Inardle couldn't bear the thought.

She would be the enemy. Not his lover. His enemy.

That made her feel cold inside, and desperate.

But what else was she now, save the enemy? If Eleanon and Bingaleal had committed themselves and the Lealfast Nation to the One, then she could be nothing else.

Inardle had the terrible feeling that Eleanon and Bingaleal had chosen the wrong way. Axis had told her that Maximilian was regaining the lost knowledge of the Twisted Tower. What if Maximilian Persimius *could* be what the Lealfast needed?

What if the One was nothing but danger?

Inardle didn't know what to do. She was not as committed to the way of the One in any case, for the One despised women for their ability to breed and thus to subdivide the One. No woman ever became a full Magi. She might command some of the Magi power, but no woman was ever initiated into the full mysteries.

But was there any purpose now to yearn for what might have been had she not committed herself to the path of deception? She could not even confess to Axis, for he would not believe a word she said to him once he discovered that everything she had told him was founded on lies.

She could not bear the thought that he would hate her.

Inardle began to cry, silently, and her weeping only grew stronger when Axis, concerned, came to her side and wrapped her in his arms.

CHAPTER EIGHTEEN

On the Road to Serpent's Nest

They stood under the stars, a pace apart, wrapped in cloaks. They did not look at each other, but instead both cast their eyes eastwards.

Toward Elcho Falling.

"There is trouble tonight about Inardle," Ishbel said.

"I think today StarDrifter and BroadWing overreached themselves," Maximilian said.

"She is a strange woman."

"No stranger than you, when first we met."

"She is very beautiful," Ishbel said. "Very ethereal. Very unknowable. I am not surprised Axis has taken her so close."

"He didn't win her any friends with the announcement that he was making her his lieutenant."

"Axis is isolating her. Inardle will never be a full part of the Lealfast again, nor of any other people. She has only one tribe now, and that tribe is Axis SunSoar."

"Then he is going to a great deal of trouble over her," Maximilian said. "She does not seem to be much like Azhure. Axis has talked to me of Azhure occasionally."

"I think the fact that she *isn't* anything like Azhure is the attraction, Maxel." Ishbel paused a little. "I will be more friendly to her. Perhaps ride with her during the day."

"I think Axis would like that, Ishbel. Thank you. I think you may find that you and Inardle are very much alike in some ways. You've each had a difficult journey at times."

"I was appalled to hear how Lister turned his back on her."

"Yes, I was, too."

They remained unspeaking for a little while, still not looking at each other, avoiding the two topics they needed to talk about: their marriage and Elcho Falling.

"How long," said Ishbel eventually, "before we arrive at the mountain?"

Maximilian turned his head to look at her directly. "Four or five days. We're moving faster than I'd hoped."

"Are you scared?"

Again he laughed softly. "Yes, but excited, too. You?"

"You have no idea, Maxel. It shall be so strange to see Aziel again, as all my old friends from the Coil. Maxel . . . do they know we're coming?"

"Yes. I sent two Icarii east a week or more ago."

Ishbel's mouth curved in a small smile. "Aziel will have been surprised to meet them, and yet somehow not. I think he knew, Maxel, that change was upon him. Would the Icarii have told him about Lister?"

"Yes."

Ishbel sighed. "Then he will be upset. What will he do, now that the Coil has no reason for its existence?"

"Move forward, as you have done. You are doing well in the Twisted Tower."

"Yes. I manage a different level each night now. Maxel, why did you want me to learn?"

"Because it doesn't hurt to have someone else know—"

"Maxel, please, why did you want me to learn?"

He turned to face her. "Because I wanted to share it with you, not only the Twisted Tower, but everything Elcho Falling is and can be."

Ishbel looked at him, feeling certain that there was a deeper reason, but she did not push him. Instead she smiled, and removed one hand from under her cloak.

In it she held a small bunch of wildflowers. "My payment, my lord, for traversing your territory."

He reached out his hand, enclosing hers within it, and pulled her closer. He leaned forward, and they kissed, very gently.

Then Ishbel pulled back, smiling a little, and walked away into the night.

CHAPTER NINETEEN

On the Road to Serpent's Nest

Inardle, you will need to use a sling."

She sat on the edge of the bed, using her right arm to clutch her left to her chest, and ignoring Yysell, who was trying to offer her an early morning cup of tea. Axis had been arguing with her for close to an hour, firstly about the fact that she wanted to ride a horse today and not rest in a wagon, and secondly about her refusal to wear the sling that Garth had left the previous night.

"You will do more damage to your shoulder and wing tendons if you let that damn arm dangle!"

She flashed Axis a sharp look at that. "I will not allow it to 'dangle.'"

"You don't have the strength to do anything else," Axis snapped. He sat in a chair and pulled on his boots, angry and concerned. Inardle had hardly slept last night. She'd woken crying after Axis had returned to the tent, and not gone back to sleep despite the analgesic Axis had virtually forced her to swallow. Her wing and upper left arm and shoulder were still swollen and thick with contusions, and her left forearm was bruised and scabbed where the string of the bow had snapped and scraped the skin and flesh. She looked exhausted, and her reluctance to stand meant she'd barely be able to sit a horse.

"At least drink the tea Yysell has made," Axis said. "He rose early to make that for you."

"Thank you," Inardle said to Yysell, and managed a smile for him as she finally took the mug. She winced as her left arm drooped, unsupported, and Axis managed to bite his tongue only just in time.

Stars, he was going to spend all day worrying about her.

"Inardle," he began, then stopped as StarDrifter drew back the doorflap and entered the tent.

Everyone inside—Axis, Inardle, and Yysell—stared.

Then Axis caught Yysell's eye, and tipped his head toward the door.

Yysell took the hint and left, edging his way about StarDrifter.

StarDrifter glanced at Axis, then picked up a stool that was sitting against the tent wall, walked over to Inardle, and sat down just before her.

Axis tensed, standing up from his chair, watchful.

"Inardle," StarDrifter said, looking directly at her. She met his eyes, but Axis could see that she was very, very wary.

"Axis talked to me last night," StarDrifter said, and now Inardle flashed a look of sheer anger at Axis.

"He said to me that on that archery field yesterday," StarDrifter continued, "there was only one person who demonstrated any courage and leadership, and that was you. Inardle, I am an arrogant man, a powerful Enchanter, an Icarii prince, and I am Talon over the Icarii nation—and what Axis said did not sit well with me. He was, however, right, and it was only my pride and arrogance which refused to allow me to accept that."

StarDrifter took a deep breath, then slid off the stool to kneel on one knee before Inardle. He bowed his head, then swept his wings out behind him in the traditional Icarii gesture of deference and respect.

Axis' mouth dropped open. A Talon, and particularly one as proud as StarDrifter, *never* bowed before anyone!

"Inardle," StarDrifter said, now raising his face to look directly at her, "what BroadWing and I did to you yesterday cannot be condoned. We were angry at Axis, yet it was you who felt the sting of our ill temper. That was inexcusable, and I have no right to ask you for forgiveness. Nothing I can say can ever take away the horror of what we did, and what you may have to suffer for it. Inardle Lealfast, you are an extraordinary woman, and one of great courage." He gave a little smile. "There are very few people who can bring an Icarii Talon to his knees before them—and this was not something Axis asked me to do."

He had to tell her that, Axis thought with an inward smile. *He had to let her know that this was his idea.*

"Inardle," StarDrifter continued, "you have an Icarii Talon at your feet, and while I cannot undo the damage I have done to you, I can say that the stars will fall from the sky and crumble into dust before I allow any harm to come to you again. I am your servant, Inardle Lealfast."

And with that he rose, sent a single glance toward his son, and left the tent.

Axis and Inardle looked at each other.

"I think I might wear the sling after all," said Inardle, and Axis laughed, walked over, and kissed her forehead.

"There are many things that I love about you, Inardle," he said, "but your magnificent diffidence rates among the highest."

CHAPTER TWENTY

The Salamaan Pass

Hereward and Isaiah had been in the Salamaan Pass a week. They were tired, hungry, dirty, and almost out of water.

The Skraelings had remained in Isembaard, and they'd needed to rely exclusively on what they carried with them. There were no leftovers from the creatures' hunting.

Neither had spoken to the other for at least three days. This was due in part to their fatigue, but also due to their mutual despondency. What they had seen at Hairekeep continued to eat away at their souls. Even the horse seemed to wallow in dejection, and walked along with his head drooping.

It was midafternoon, and both were half dozing atop the ambling horse. Hereward jerked awake as she almost toppled off the horse, then shaded her eyes and looked ahead.

"Isaiah?" Hereward said.

He paid no attention.

"Isaiah?" she said again, a little more loudly, and gave him a prod in the ribs.

He jumped. "What?"

"Look ahead, Isaiah. Look ahead."

Isaiah pulled the horse to a halt and shaded his eyes as Hereward had done.

His own mouth sagged.

* * *

Lamiah simply could not believe what he was seeing. One of his scouts had ridden up, gasping out the news that the Tyrant was riding a white stallion toward them from out of Isembaard, a woman with him.

None of that made any sense to Lamiah. Isaiah was far *behind* him, some-where in the northern Outlands.

So Lamiah had ridden forward, a small unit to escort him, and then had pulled up his horse in astonishment.

There sat Isaiah atop a somewhat bedraggled but otherwise handsome white stallion, a dark-haired woman sitting behind him and clinging to his shoulders

Both were dirty—Lamiah had not *ever* seen Isaiah in a state anything close to this—and looked drained and exhausted.

Very slowly Lamiah pushed his horse forward, waving at his escort to stay where they were.

"Isaiah?" he said, bringing his horse to a halt a few paces away from Isa-iah's stallion.

"The very same," Isaiah said. "And why is it I find General Lamiah, hav-ing deserted his command, leading a column of soldiers back into Isem-baard?"

"Someone has to save our people," Lamiah said.

"There is no one left to save," Isaiah said. "Hereward and myself and this horse are all that is left, Lamiah, and if you continue in the direction you are currently headed, then you will lead your men into a death so terrible that the thought of what I might do to you for your treachery will seem as naught."

Lamiah stared at him, then laughed in genuine amusement. "You look as though you need some food, Isaiah, and a drink if your hoarseness of voice is anything to go by. We will rest here for the night, and I will permit you to tell me your story."

Lamiah leaned back in his chair and stared at Isaiah. The story he'd just heard was . . . extraordinary.

And so infuriating that Lamiah did not think he could maintain his composure for much longer.

"Lamiah," Isaiah said, looking better now that he'd had an opportunity to wash off some of his grime and had eaten a meal, "what I need you to do is—"

"How *dare* you tell me what you need *me* to do!" Lamiah said. "You never once thought to mention to anyone that Isembaard was facing certain destruction? We could have evacuated the entire—"

"That is nonsense, Lamiah, and well you know it," Isaiah said. "If I had come out with any of this while we were still in Isembaard then we both know you and the other generals would have murdered me within twelve hours. I saved what I could, and I am now pleading with you to save what is left. You *cannot* continue into Isembaard!"

Lamiah did not respond. He looked past Isaiah to where the woman Hereward sat. She'd been quiet all afternoon and evening as first they'd shared a meal and then Isaiah had told his story. *She* was all that was left?

"Where are Kezial and Armat?" Isaiah asked.

"Waging war on Maximilian," Lamiah responded automatically, trying to think through what he should do.

Isaiah muttered a curse, and Lamiah looked at him at that.

"Did you honestly think we would support Maximilian?" Lamiah said.

"He's all that can save you now."

Lamiah grunted.

"Lamiah," said Isaiah, "you need to believe me. Maximilian is the only one who can—"

"Save us against what you have described? Why should I believe that? Is the One afraid of Maximilian?" Lamiah said.

"Yes."

Lamiah raised his eyes and looked at Isaiah. "What in the name of all gods are we going to do, Isaiah?"

[Part Five]

CHAPTER ONE

Serpent's Nest

Aziel drew the crimson hood of his robe over his head so that it shadowed his face, then picked up the reins and urged his horse forward.

The gelding managed to break into a slow amble, but Aziel didn't have
the heart to push it to any greater exertion.

Besides, it would allow him to savor his remaining few minutes at Serpent's Nest.

The horse strolled through the open gates and down the road that sloped
down to the plain. It was early morning, only an hour or so after dawn, and
the low light illuminated the surrounding countryside in a soft, rosy glow.

It caught at the spears and shields and stirrup irons of the army spread
out on the plains below Serpent's Nest. The army was arrayed in columns
and units, each clearly defined and well ordered, everyone horsed and weaponed. High above circled units of the Icarii Strike Force.

It was, Aziel thought as the horse made its unhurried way down the road,
a salutary lesson in the unpredictability of life and the foolishness of mor-
tals who thought to influence it. It was almost two years now since he had
farewelled Ishbel for her marriage to Maximilian, King of Escator. Now,
here she was again, probably one of the as yet tiny figures sitting their horses
in a group just ahead of the first units of the army. There was a winged man
standing slightly to one side of those three—his wings glinting gold now
and again as he moved in the sunlight—and Aziel supposed he commanded
the Icarii in the sky.

It was ironic, he thought. He'd sent Ishbel to marry this man, Maximilian, in the hope that it would prevent disaster befalling the Coil and Serpent's Nest. He'd promised her she would return, and that all would be well.

Ishbel had indeed returned, but Aziel doubted very much that all would be well. The Coil was disbanded, fallen into irrelevancy as their Serpent god revealed his true self and abandoned them, and Serpent's Nest was now to fall to Maximilian, no longer of Escator, but of Elcho Falling.

Ishbel had returned, but she'd brought the destruction of Aziel's life with her.

But, oh, he could not wait to see her face again. Aziel had sent a repressed, uncertain woman away to Maximilian, and he wondered now what he would find at her return.

The horse had by now ambled its way to the foot of the mountain road and had picked up its pace slightly as it saw the horsemen waiting a few minutes away.

Fool horse, thought Aziel. *Why rush away from the only home you have ever known?*

He swiveled about in the saddle at that, looking one last time on the place he'd called home for over thirty-five years. Tears filmed his eyes, and he blinked them away before he turned back and prepared to face the Lord of Elcho Falling.

Maximilian watched the crimson-cloaked man ride slowly toward him. Serpent's Nest rose behind him, a great blue-tinged granite massif that reached forever into the sky, and Maximilian found it difficult to keep his eyes on the man despite the fact that he'd spent most of the night standing, silent, studying the mountain.

But he needed to concentrate on Aziel at the moment. He was the last remnant of Ishbel's life as Archpriestess of the Coil, and Maximilian wondered how Ishbel was feeling. He glanced at her—she was pale, all her attention on the man riding toward them.

Maximilian looked back to Aziel. He was impatient to kick his horse up that rising road and actually enter the mountain—he'd been unable to eat this morning for his combined excitement and nerves—but Aziel deserved the respect of his attention, if only for the next few minutes.

Axis had eyes only for the mountain. He'd heard enough about Aziel to know that the man was not likely to be harboring a concealed weapon or any ill-intent toward Maximilian, so he felt free to study Serpent's Nest itself.

Serpent's Nest . . . Elcho Falling.

It was huge, easily as big as Talon Spike had been, and unusual in that it rose precipitously out of relatively flat plains. There were no foothills, no surrounding mountains.

Just this one great peak. Blue-hued and slab-faced, great granite cliffs and turrets projecting forever into the sky and backed, in the east, by a vast gray ocean rolling away into infinity.

The Mountain at the Edge of the World.

It reeked of magic. Axis could feel it stirring the hairs at the back of his neck and trailing soft fingers down his spine. It wasn't overt, but Axis had known magic much of his life, and had wielded enough of it, to be able to sense its presence.

Stars, he thought, *what will this place be like when Maximilian awakes the Elcho Falling within?*

He glanced above, and could see that the Icarii wheeling overhead had their eyes firmly fixed on the mountain.

He wondered if they thought the mountain would prove home for them.

Ishbel could scarcely contain her emotions. Aziel was close enough now that she could see every feature of his face. He'd aged, she thought, since last she'd seen him. His face was more lined, his eyes more pouched, and he wore an air of fatigue that generally only the very elderly shouldered.

His eyes were locked on her, and for the first time Ishbel realized that Aziel had loved her, probably since she'd been a girl, and that sending her away to another man must have been a nightmare for him.

What a fool I was then, she thought, and tried to smile for Aziel, and failed, miserably.

Josia stood in the top chamber of the Twisted Tower at the window. From his vantage point he could see Maximilian's combined forces arrayed before him, the pitiful figure of Aziel on his horse approaching them, and beyond that the rising bulk of Elcho Falling.

But Josia had no eyes for Maximilian and his forces, or for Aziel, or even for the mountain.

Instead his eyes were fixed on the rolling gray seas beyond.

Aziel pulled his horse to a stop a few paces from Maximilian's.

"Maximilian Persimius," Aziel said. "Welcome . . . I suppose."

That drew a small smile from Maximilian. "We have disturbed you from your home," he said. "I am sorry, Aziel. It was not my intent. There was no reason for the members of your Coil to have left. I am sure there would have been room within the mountain for all."

"That is kind of you," Aziel said, "but none of us could stay. Our god is gone, our purpose destroyed, and our lodgings are about to become the home of something much greater than we ever could have been."

"Aziel," Ishbel said, edging her horse a little closer to Maximilian's. "Stay, please. Don't go."

Aziel looked at her. Ishbel was almost unrecognizable from the woman he'd sent away. That woman had been repressed and unhappy, a complete naïf in the ways of the world and of her own heart. Now she looked very different. She affected clothes and a hairstyle that flattered and accentuated her natural beauty, and she held herself with both confidence and dignity.

Ishbel had grown up.

He realized he was staring, and he smiled for her, and inclined his head. "I can't stay, Ishbel. I am sorry. I do not think Maximilian can have his new home soiled by the remaining presence of members of the Coil."

"He will not mind!" Ishbel said.

Aziel looked back at Maximilian. *Yes, he would mind. Very much.*

"*I* will be staying," said Ishbel, "and if *I* stay, then I cannot see why—"

"You are so far removed from what you once were," said Aziel, "that no stain of the Coil remains about you. Ishbel, I need to go. Besides, I fancy seeing my home again."

"Aziel, the world is at war! Armies gather about us, and to the south—"

"Let him go, Ishbel," Maximilian said quietly.

She stared at Maximilian, her face stricken, but she fell silent, and eventually dropped her eyes to her hands gripping the reins of her horse.

"There are servants within the mountain," Aziel said, addressing Maximilian once more. "They are not associated with the Coil. We have made as much as possible comfortable for you, but we had few hands for the task, and there was no means possible to prepare chambers and beds for your entire force. I am afraid that while there will be space and chambers enough for them, they may have to make their own beds."

"I am grateful for what you have done, Aziel, thank you," Maximilian said.

Aziel looked at Axis. "You are Axis SunSoar, I believe?"

Maximilian apologized for not introducing Axis and StarDrifter, and made good his error.

"Such legends," Aziel said, smiling and nodding his head at both men. Then he addressed Ishbel once more.

"I loved you, Ishbel. I needed to say that. I love you still—all the more reason, I think, for Maximilian to want me gone." His eyes were twinkling merrily now. "Be happy, Ishbel, and don't revert to the woman you once were—too scared to take life in both hands . . . and too scared to love."

He gathered the reins of his horse. "Maximilian," he said, "the mountain is yours. Raise its ghosts, people its corridors with memory, and unwind its terror into the sky. And respect it, for without that, the mountain will murder you."

Without waiting for a response, Aziel pushed the dozing horse into a walk and turned its head for the road westward.

"Aziel!" Ishbel called, but she made no attempt to move to his side, and Aziel rode on through the ranks of silent armed horsemen, until eventually he reached empty road.

CHAPTER TWO

Serpent's Nest

As soon as Aziel had gone, Maximilian gave the order to enter the mountain, and for the next half an hour Axis concerned himself with moving the army forward. Inardle alternatively rode at his side or out to outlying units to relay his orders. Axis kept an eye on her, but was not worried about either her fitness or her reception. The Isembaardians and the Emerald Guard had never had a problem with her, and the Icarii had accepted her in the five days since StarDrifter had made his dramatic apology. It was a grudging acceptance, and overlaid with coolness, but at least Inardle and the Icarii had managed to get themselves to a point where they were prepared to consider the possibility of mutual regard if not outright friendship.

Inardle was also much better physically. She'd recovered well from the bruising and swelling of her arm and shoulder, although the wing still gave her, and Garth, some concern. Garth said the tendons were healing better than expected, but he was noncommittal when Axis pressed him privately about whether or not Inardle might fly again.

Maximilian and Ishbel rode ahead, and entered Serpent's Nest's first. Axis was some fifty or sixty paces behind them, and he and Inardle rode into Serpent's Nest together.

It was extraordinary.

Axis hadn't known quite what to expect. They'd had the opportunity to study Serpent's Nest for two days before actually arriving—it had appeared as a purple smudge on the horizon two dawns ago—and all he could make out of it was its massiveness . . . and the sense of magic that pervaded it.

Today, as they'd ridden to their meeting with Aziel, Axis had seen the road sloping its way up the lower part of the mountain to a set of two huge wooden gates, but not much else apart from the world of rock that extended skyward.

But once through the gates . . .

Axis' first impression was of a deeper sense of magic. The second was that he and Inardle had ridden into a forecourt that was already far too crowded. They pulled their horses over to a far side and sat looking around.

The gates led into a semicircular forecourt, its straight back wall being formed by the mountain itself. There were three large arched openings in this wall, and Axis spotted Egalion walking out of one of them. He called the captain of the Emerald Guard over.

"Egalion? What is beyond those arches?"

"Another court, much larger than this one," said Egalion. "And beyond that are gates and doors and archways leading to stables, kitchens, corridors . . . I don't know what else. It's huge. Ishbel is in the far court, trying to direct people and horses." He grinned. "She's losing her temper."

Axis chuckled. "I'll stay out of her way for the time being, then. Inardle, would you go and try to get some sense of where she's sending people? Of where are stables and dormitories, where halls and chambers? Of where people are actually *going*? We'll meet up again . . . ah, find us a chamber, would you, if you can dare Ishbel's temper? And send me word once you have one, and we can meet there once all this fuss has died down."

She nodded, riding her horse toward one of the archways leading to the court beyond. Axis watched her go, checking her wings and shoulder for any frost.

But there was none, and, satisfied that she was in no immediate discomfort, Axis looked back to Egalion.

"Can you send a unit of your Guard to assess the defenses, Egalion? So far as I can see, this is the only entrance to the mountain, but I need to be sure."

Egalion nodded, and strode off.

Axis went back to his silent study of the mountain as men and horses moved about him, and Icarii dropped down from the sky to land on wall tops and ridges.

It looked like a mountain at first glance. There appeared to be little above the structures of the forecourt and archways save slabs of rock.

But if he narrowed his eyes, Axis could almost see the structure beneath. The "mountain," the rock, was a falsehood.

Elcho Falling waited.

Axis jumped down from his horse, then led it through the confusion of the forecourt, under one of the arches, and into the even greater confusion of the inner courtyard.

It took five or six hours to sort everyone out. Axis saw Inardle from time to time, either talking with Ishbel or various commanders within the ranks of the Emerald Guard and the Isembaard contingent. She stopped at one point to confer with Ezekiel, and laughed at something he said, and Axis was glad that she was relaxed enough, and confident enough, to smile with the Isembaardian general.

The chaos of the inner courtyard gradually abated as various units were assigned, and then directed to, quarters within the mountain. Axis met Inardle briefly on the steps of the main staircase leading deeper into the mountain, where she gave him directions to a chamber she'd managed to obtain for them.

"What do you think?" he said to her, nodding about them.

"Of the mountain?"

"Yes."

She smiled again, transforming her face. "It's excited."

"*You're* excited, I think," he said, returning her smile.

"Yes, I am, but the mountain is as well. It knows Maximilian is here."

"Perhaps. Has everyone found quarters?"

"Yes. Aziel left servants here who have been scurrying about leading people to chambers and dormitories. Ishbel has been a help, too. Axis, the mountain is huge . . . there are doorways and corridors and vast chambers everywhere. What Maximilian brought with him today will take up only a hundredth of the space available, if that."

"I'm going to find Egalion, and then Maxel. Get some rest, Inardle. You are starting to look tired."

All her diffidence returned. "I'm not so tired."

"Get some rest, Inardle." Axis touched her cheek, then ran lightly down the stairs, calling out to Egalion, who was crossing a far corner of the court-yard.

Axis found Maximilian in the early evening in a massive space deep in the mountain. The chamber was floored in smooth buffed stone and had a great domed roof of roughly chiseled rock. When Axis entered, closing the door quietly behind him, Maximilian was standing in the center of the space, looking at a far wall where hung chains and ropes.

The floor just beneath the restraints was discolored.

Maximilian turned very slightly as he heard Axis walk up behind him. "It is very quiet here," he said. "Very peaceful. Very still."

"What is this place?" Axis asked.

"It is the Coil's Reading Room," said Maximilian. He nodded at the re-straints hanging from the wall. "That is where Ishbel caused her victims to be chained, and where she disemboweled them, and where they died in ag-ony while Lister pretended great wisdom and beneficence and spoke to her through the windings of their bowels."

Axis looked at Maximilian curiously, not sure how to respond.

"Oh, I have made my peace with Ishbel's past, Axis," Maximilian said. "I stand here and feel . . . slightly saddened, I think, that this is what Elcho Falling came to for so many hundreds of years."

"What will you do with it?" Axis said.

"Before I raise Elcho Falling," Maximilian said, "Ishbel will need to un-wind the taint of the Coil from the mountain. She will cleanse it, so that Elcho Falling can rise anew. This chamber, and anything that has any as-sociation with the Coil, will be destroyed."

"Where is Ishbel now?"

"Gone visiting her old haunts, I believe. Gone to sit in empty chambers and reflect."

Then Maximilian smiled, that sudden, unexpected expression which lit up his face. "But enough of the past. What has Egalion said?"

"About the defenses?"

Maximilian nodded. "And stores, and whatever it is we need to maintain a possible siege in this place—although unless Armat arrives within the next day or so I doubt Serpent's Nest will need to contend with a siege."

"Well, the news is mostly good. The only entrance into the mountain is via the gates we entered by, unless Armat wants to set his men to weeks of mountain climbing. The gates themselves can be shut, barred, and bolted, and each has a strong metal portcullis which can be lowered into position to reinforce it. The gate access to the inner courtyard likewise. The mountain is easily defensible—Armat would lose most of his men just trying to get them in the gates."

"So he'll need to talk us out with sweet words."

"*Very* sweet words."

"And stores?"

"Egalion says the mountain is extraordinary. The cellars and basements are packed with dry goods and salted and smoked meats and preserves. There are also wells deep under the mountain which will provide fresh drinking water for many months, if not years. Even the horses are well provided with hay and grain stores. I have no idea where Aziel would have—"

"The mountain provided them, Axis."

"Well, if it could do this as Serpent's Nest, then I can only expect that as Elcho Falling it will wrestle Armat to the ground for us, as well."

Maximilian laughed, the sound ringing through the cavernous chamber. "Don't get your hopes up, Axis."

"When will you raise Elcho Falling, Maxel?"

"In two or three days. I'm not going to waste time."

"BroadWing tells me that Armat is perhaps that distance behind us."

"Then he will get a good showing for his arrival, eh? Have you heard anything of Georgdi?"

"Yes. One of the Icarii scouts reported him two days to the south. He has perhaps twenty thousand men with him, Maxel, and, knowing the Outlanders, they'll be exceptional fighters. Stars alone knows where Georgdi found them—the man is extraordinary."

"Then pray he gets here before Armat, because I doubt Armat will be kind enough to just wave Georgdi's twenty thousand through the ranks of the besiegers."

"Have you heard anything about Eleanon and the Lealfast?" Axis said.

Maximilian nodded. "Eleanon contacted me briefly earlier today. He says he is bringing the Lealfast fighters in this evening."

Axis grunted.

"Be careful with Eleanon, Axis."

"What? I shouldn't hurt his feelings? I will be as careful as needed, Maxel, but I won't coddle him. He'll have to accept BroadWing's command, and somehow, *somehow*, they're going to have to be ready to fight within the week if Armat does what we expect. It isn't long enough to transform them into usefulness. Oh, don't look at me like that. I will be careful enough."

"Have you heard from StarHeaven, Axis? It has been a week, surely, since she left."

"Just occasional reports as she and her companions flew south. They should be in the area of the Salamaan Pass now." Axis paused, shifting a little uneasily on his feet. "I should hear from her soon."

"Let me know once you do, Axis. I do not like this silence from the south."

Axis nodded. "Do you need me anymore tonight?"

Maximilian smiled. "No. Go back to your Lealfast lover. Her wing . . . ?"

"Is healing, but we still do not know if she'll be able to fly again."

Maximilian nodded. "Good night then, Axis."

CHAPTER THREE

Serpent's Nest

Inardle stood at the balustrading on the balcony of the chamber she'd acquired for herself and Axis. It was very high up the mountain, and she stared below her, mesmerized by the space, the fall, the lift of the wind as it rose into the twilight. She shifted closer to the railing, sitting down on it, leaning out a little, spreading her wings, wondering if she dared heal herself for long enough so that she could snatch a few moments' flight into the—

Suddenly someone grabbed her arm and hauled her back to safety.

"Stars, Inardle! What were you *doing?*"

She pulled her arm from Axis' grasp. "I was safe. I wouldn't have fallen."

Axis was still staring at her, and Inardle realized how frightened he'd been. "I'm sorry."

"Your wing isn't stable enough to support you, Inardle."

"I know, Axis." The guilt was biting even deeper now. How could she tell Axis that she would have been fine, that it would have taken only a fraction of her power to heal her wing then and there so she could take to the skies? Inardle was very much afraid that she might have to allow herself to remain crippled, just to keep Axis at her side.

"Stars," he muttered, and turned away a little.

Inardle didn't know what to say. She was sorry he was angry with her, but she was also a little flattered that he *had* been that frightened. "I'll be more careful, Axis."

He took a deep breath, letting go his fear-driven anger, and nodded. "Has Garth seen your shoulder and wing since we've arrived?"

"Yes. He was here about an hour ago. He gave me a massage."

"Good for him. What did he say about the wing?"

"That neither he nor I would know for a week or more if it would heal enough for flight. How is Maximilian?"

Axis gave a little shrug. "He is well enough. He says he will raise Elcho Falling within two or thee days."

Something in his face softened as he regarded her. "Come to bed," he said, and Inardle smiled, relieved they had moved past the subject of her wing.

"How well you have made your new bed, sister."

Inardle gave a soft cry, waking from her light sleep with a jerk, trying to disentangle herself from an equally disoriented Axis.

"*Shit!*" she heard Axis mutter.

Eleanon, she said to her brother, keeping the communication blocked from Axis, *you have returned.*

We have a part to play here, sister, he said. *Remember it.*

Axis managed to sit up, swing his legs over the side of the bed, and draw the sheet over Inardle's nakedness all in the one smooth movement.

"Eleanon," he said, "do you take every open balcony door as an invitation?"

"I could sense my sister in here," Eleanon said. He was standing just inside the doorway, outlined in moonlight, and now he made his slow way inside as Axis rose and pulled on a pair of trousers. "I had no idea in what company I would find her." He paused. "Nor that I would find her so injured."

Axis had found a taper and used it to light a lamp, and he picked it up and moved closer to Eleanon. "Have you seen Maximilian?" he said.

"Not yet," said Eleanon. "I thought to greet my sister first. Inardle, what has happened to your wing? And your shoulder... it moves stiffly... who has beaten you? Axis?"

Stop it, Eleanon, Inardle said to him. *Don't toy with either me or him.*

"Eleanon," Inardle said. "You need to see Maximilian—"

"Has Axis got you so firmly under his command that now you echo his every word, sister?" Eleanon said. "Have you forgotten that you are Lealfast, and not Icarii, to fawn so at his feet?"

"That is enough, Eleanon," Axis snapped. "What the hell do you think you're doing? You are under Maximilian's ultimate command, and beneath that, under mine. And under me, had you thought to make some enquiries before you started to make yet a further fool of yourself, you would find yourself under Inardle's command as my lieutenant."

"My, my," Eleanon said softly, his eyes sliding to Inardle. "She has done well for herself, has she not."

Inardle met his eyes without a flinch.

Axis stopped himself from hitting Eleanon only by reminding himself that Inardle was present. "Get out of here, Eleanon. You need to see Maximilian. He is expecting you."

"As you and my sister were not," Eleanon said, now edging toward the balcony door.

"In the morning, you can report back to me," Axis said. "Now get out!"

Eleanon paused in the doorway. "Do you think the StarMan actually cares for you, Inardle? Do you think you are anything but a slight diversion before he reunites with his only lover, Azhure? He will break your heart."

With that, he was gone.

Axis turned back to Inardle. "I'm sorry."

Inardle was not sure what he was apologizing for. She gave a slight shrug. "It doesn't matter."

Axis sat down on the bed, studying her carefully. "What he said at the end about Azhure, does matter."

Inardle did not look at him. She didn't want to talk about Azhure. All she wanted to do now was think about Eleanon, and what his arrival meant.

Choices.

"We've become very good at making love," Axis said softly, "but not so good at talking. You asked me once, that night you first came to my bed, if you were a novelty to me. I meant it when I said no. Neither are you a replacement for a lost love, nor are you someone with whom I am merely marking time until, as Eleanon put it, I reunite with the only woman I have ever loved."

He gave a short laugh. "Azhure hasn't ever been the only woman I have loved, Inardle, and I wasn't always true to her. And she is dead, now, and I no longer so. We live in different worlds. I do not yearn for her, and—"

"Does she yearn for you, do you think?"

"Perhaps," Axis said, "but I cannot live my life here wondering what Azhure is thinking or doing. What I do here makes no difference to her, or to what she is feeling."

Inardle remembered all the stories she had heard of Axis. How he'd justified hurting both Faraday and Azhure by thinking he could have both. She thought of what Ishbel had told her about Salome a few days ago, when they'd broken their day's ride to share a meal of bread and cheese at noon, how Salome's grandmother had been a former and discarded lover of Axis' and StarDrifter's who had come to a terrible death because of their lack of care.

Axis, Inardle fully realized, could justify anything to himself at any point, if he wanted it badly enough.

As can I.

"I don't care about Azhure," she said, still not looking at Axis.

He slid over the bed to her, running soft fingers over her face, smoothing her tousled hair back over her forehead. "Yes, you do," he said. "And you shouldn't, Inardle, you shouldn't."

He kissed her jaw, running his mouth down to her neck.

Inardle shuddered, wishing that, just sometimes, she could control her reaction to him.

"I love the taste of your frost," he whispered, one of his hands now pushing the sheet away from her breasts.

So much for talking about Azhure, Inardle thought, *or about what we feel for each other, or mean each to the other.*

"Axis . . ." she said, trying to find the strength to push him away and the courage to finally speak some truth to him, but suddenly he sprang back from her anyway, and stared into the night.

"My brother has decided he wants to be born," he said.

There was no sleeping after that, nor lovemaking, nor talk of how they felt for each other, nor any revelations of truth. Axis pulled on his shirt and boots, and paced restlessly about the chamber before finally slumping into a chair.

Inardle sighed, as softly as she could, and rose, and washed and dressed as well.

"You don't want to go to StarDrifter?" she asked Axis finally as they sat in their respective chairs in opposite corners of the dimly lit chamber.

He shook his head. "StarDrifter is with Salome. There's just the two of them."

"No midwife?"

Another shake of Axis' head. "Salome needs no midwife. StarDrifter is all she needs, to sing out my brother."

A shiver ran down Inardle's spine. "You can sense what is happening?"

"Yes."

"And the birth is going well?"

"My brother is being born, yes. It is going well enough."

He was very much on edge, and Inardle wondered about it. "You've had brothers before."

He glanced at her then, very cool, and Inardle thought she might have gone too far.

"Two brothers," he said. "Borneheld and Gorgrael. Both of them brought their worlds, and mine, to ruin."

"I am sure this new brother will not—"

"Who knows what any of StarDrifter's sons will bring."

"Axis, what's wrong? Do you want me to leave?"

"No. I do not want you to leave, Inardle." He sighed, stretching out his legs. "I have been StarDrifter's only son, only *reputable* son for so long that perhaps I now find it hard to accept he has another."

It was a glib enough statement, and Inardle accepted it only because it was obvious that Axis did not want to elaborate on how he really felt.

She settled back in her chair as well.

Two or three hours passed.

It was close to dawn when Inardle woke with a start. She was stiff and sore from having slept in the chair, and for a moment was disoriented and uncertain of her surroundings.

Then she realized Axis was standing in the middle of the chamber, looking toward the door which led to the internal corridor.

It opened, and StarDrifter and Salome entered.

StarDrifter was carrying a blanket-wrapped bundle.

Inardle sat up warily in the chair. She was certain that whatever scene was to follow she should not be here, and glanced at the balcony door.

Don't, Axis whispered in her mind. *Stay. Don't fall.*

"Very well," Inardle murmured. She thought about standing, then decided that sitting unobtrusively in the chair was probably the best she could manage under the circumstances.

StarDrifter and Salome, who by now had advanced to where Axis stood, ignored her completely.

"Look," StarDrifter said softly, and held out the baby to Axis.

Axis hesitated, then took the child, balancing StarDancer in his arms before singing him a snatch of melody.

Inardle looked at Salome. She, like StarDrifter, was gazing at the child. She looked very weary, but also happy, and leaned in against StarDrifter as if he were the center of her world.

It brought sudden tears to Inardle's eyes, and she had to look down and brush them away.

"StarDancer," Axis said, then he turned around, held the baby out, and said, "Inardle?"

Inardle stared, unable to believe he would do this. She rose, managed to walk over, and took the child into her arms.

"You've not held a baby before," StarDrifter said.

"Not one as important as this," said Inardle, although StarDrifter was correct enough. She was terrified she was going to drop him and, worse, was unsettled by the knowing look in the boy's eyes. She supposed he was pretty enough, for a baby, but those deep blue eyes, fixed on hers . . .

Inardle—what secrets you hide!

It was StarDancer, and Inardle jerked, badly enough that Axis reached out and took the baby from her.

He caught her eyes as he did so, and she saw empathy there.

Gods, she thought, he has no idea at all.

"He is a beautiful boy," said Axis, handing him straight back to his father. "How joyous you must be."

That might have sounded better, thought Inardle, if Axis' voice had actually been somewhat happy instead of wooden.

StarDrifter gave his son a cryptic smile, then he and Salome said a quiet good night and left the chamber.

Neither Axis nor Inardle said anything for a long minute.

"So," Inardle said finally, desperate for *something* to say, "you have a brother."

"So," said Axis, turning away from her and walking over to the chair where was draped his jacket, "I have a brother."

CHAPTER FOUR

Serpent's Nest

Ishbel sat in the room that had been hers as archpriestess. It was dawn outside now, the light filtering through the shuttered windows, and Ishbel was cold and stiff from having sat virtually unmoving for eight or nine hours.

She had not slept in all that time.

Instead she had been remembering—her life as archpriestess, as a novice, and as the girl before Aziel had rescued her and brought her to Serpent's Nest. She remembered how the Serpent god had exhorted her to leave the mountain to marry an unknown and meaningless king on the other side of the continent, and how she had railed against that fate.

She remembered how she had clung to the promise that one day she would return home.

And here she was.

This room had been everything to Ishbel for all her years as archpriestess. Within its walls she had found peace and security, and forgetfulness from the horrors of her childhood. When she had left to go to Maximilian, Ishbel had visualized herself coming back to this room, over and over, flinging open the door and sinking down to the bed to bury her face in her beloved old pillow, finding peace and security once more.

To come home.

She had wanted to come home so much.

Ishbel had assumed that she would feel *something* when she reentered the room. Not the incandescent joy she'd once thought, but perhaps some lingering sweetness.

But there had been nothing.

The room had been a stranger to her. It was empty of everything—memories, emotion, meaning. Ishbel had lived over twelve years within this room, but she could barely remember any of it.

Everything had changed.

She became aware that it was a new day. Very slowly Ishbel rose from the chair, pausing now and again as a muscle twinged or a tendon creaked.

I am getting old, she thought, and was then consumed with sadness at that realization. *Not so old, surely, not yet.*

She walked to the twin windows, folding back the shutters and closing her eyes for a long moment to enjoy the flood of new-day sunlight on her face. Then, still at the windows, she looked to the west.

There was nothing on the horizon, but surely Armat couldn't be far away.

Armat and Ravenna.

Turning away from the window, Ishbel walked to a mirror hung on the opposite wall. Her hair had been neatly coiled about her head when she'd sat down, but at some point during the night the pins had loosened, and now hair hung in some disarray about her face. She smoothed the hair away, studying the new lines around her eyes and mouth.

Lines of strain, and experience, and pain and love.

Tears flooded her eyes, and she rubbed them away, then suddenly pulled all the pins from her hair and shook her head, the hair tumbling down around her shoulders and back.

Taking a deep breath, she leaned closer to the mirror, tilting her head so that the brightening sunlight illumed the crown of her head, then carefully parted the hair.

When she'd been archpriestess, Ishbel had done this several times a week at dawn. It had been a comfort to her, and a pride, and a reassurance.

It was not something she'd done at all since she'd left Serpent's Nest to marry Maximilian, and most certainly not whenever she'd been living with him as his wife.

She'd always been most careful about brushing her hair in Maximilian's presence.

Now she studied her scalp, frowning into the mirror, fingers parting the hair this way and that.

It was gone.

When Ishbel had been inducted into the Coil as a priestess, she had been marked with the sign of the Serpent: a coiled serpent rising to strike. But because the Great Serpent had told Aziel that one day Ishbel would be required to leave Serpent's Nest and live among ordinary people, they had marked her carefully so that the mark would not be observable.

When she was fifteen, Aziel had shaved Ishbel's head, and marked her entire scalp with the sign of the serpent.

Then her hair had gradually grown back, hiding the mark, although Ishbel could always see it when she'd parted her hair and looked.

But now it was gone. Faded away, just as the mark of the Manteceros had faded from Maximilian's biceps.

It was gone, and she was glad.

It was time to move on. The mark had gone, her former life was gone, and everything it had ever meant to her was gone.

There was only one place that was home now.

Rearranging her hair into a loose plait over one shoulder, Ishbel straightened her gown, then left the room, closing the door behind her.

She did not once look back as she walked down the corridor.

Ishbel went to the chamber Madarin had found for her, washed, dressed carefully in a fresh gown, and combed out her hair, redressing it in the long plait.

She went first to see Salome.

"I knew you'd had the baby," Ishbel said, sitting in a chair close by Salome, who was nursing the child. StarDrifter was leaning against the wall just to one side of Salome's chair, watching both his wife and the baby, and Ishbel was not even sure that he was aware she had entered the room.

Salome raised her eyes from her son and looked at Ishbel. "You can still have him, if you like."

Ishbel smiled, a little sadly, remembering the jest Salome had made that day they'd become friends. Ishbel had still been grieving over the loss of her daughter (*was still grieving over the loss of her daughter*) and Salome had pretended indifference to her own pregnancy and offered the baby to Ishbel.

"Maximilian might be suspicious," Ishbel said, carrying on the jest.

"You will have another baby, one day," said Salome. "I had Ezra, and had thought that ended my childbearing, but then my life ended and began anew, and with it came this baby."

"Do you think so?" Ishbel said softly, her eyes still on StarDancer, who had now finished his suckling and had turned his head to regard Ishbel.

Salome wiped her son's mouth. "I am certain so, Ishbel. Why, it would take less than an hour to walk up to Maximilian, and—"

"Didn't you give me this advice before?" Ishbel said.

"At least we are consistent," StarDrifter said, finally acknowledging Ishbel's presence. He leaned over Salome and lifted the child gently from her arms. "Look at my son, Ishbel. Is he not beautiful?"

"He is very beautiful indeed," said Ishbel. "And so aware."

"Would you like to hold him?" StarDrifter said.

"No," said Ishbel. "Do you mind?"

"I understand," said StarDrifter.

Ishbel left Salome and StarDrifter shortly after, and went in search of Maximilian. She found him in a large chamber that overlooked the inner courtyard and beyond, to the road that led west and up which Armat would approach. Axis, Egalion, BroadWing, and Ezekiel were with him, sharing some breakfast over charts spread on a large central table.

The men looked up as she entered, but she waved them into silence, indicating she would wait until they'd finished, then helped herself to tea and breakfast from a side table.

She sat herself down on a bench by a window, eating and drinking silently as the men continued their discussion.

"Eleanon arrived last night," Axis said.

"I saw him," Maximilian said. He paused, grinning a little wryly. "He was in an ill temper."

"Well," said Axis. "He'd just seen me. I'd shouted at him."

"He was upset about Inardle," said Maximilian.

"Eleanon is still upset about making an utter fool of himself with Armat," said Axis.

"Has he reported to you, BroadWing?" Maximilian asked, and Broad-Wing nodded.

"We have exchanged greetings, and a few cautious words," BroadWing said. "We agreed to meet again once I have done here."

Maximilian talked briefly about reawakening Elcho Falling in two days' time, then the meeting broke up, leaving Maximilian alone with Ishbel.

"You look tired," he said.

"I have been up all night, thinking."

"And?" Maximilian said.

"The Ishbel you married is well and truly dead, Maxel. The new one has decided she cannot wait for the rebirth of Elcho Falling."

CHAPTER FIVE

Serpent's Nest

Eleanon found BroadWing almost as soon as the Icarii birdman had left the meeting with Axis. BroadWing nodded at Eleanon, then indicated a doorway through to a public balcony which was for the moment empty of anyone else.

"It has been difficult, to return," said Eleanon. "It is not in my nature to ask for help, or accept that I might not be all that I could be."

BroadWing said nothing, regarding Eleanon with sharp eyes.

"My fighters, the twelve thousand I have left, wait close," said Eleanon, and BroadWing glanced out into the sky, seeing the grayish haze of the almost invisible Lealfast drifting through the sky at the base of a nearby cloud.

"They are yours," Eleanon said.

BroadWing brought his eyes back to the Lealfast man. He was still very unsure of Eleanon . . . but he had learned to respect Inardle, almost to like her, and he supposed that he could manage that with this one, too.

"I want them quartered with the Strike Force," said BroadWing. "I do not want separate forces, just one integral force. Do you see that balcony thirty paces higher and to the left?"

Eleanon glanced, then nodded.

"That leads into the Strike Force's lodgings," BroadWing said.

He paused significantly.

Eleanon looked at him, hesitated, then nodded. He lifted a hand and gestured into the sky.

A moment later the Lealfast fighters began to materialize in the air, banking their wings on an approach to the higher balcony.

"Good," said BroadWing. "I will address them shortly. From now on, you answer to me. The Lealfast fighters now are members of the Strike Force, and *I* am commander of the Strike Force. You no longer command the Lealfast fighters."

"Of course," said Eleanon.

"You are being more cooperative than I'd thought," BroadWing said.

"You have no idea how guilty I feel about what happened when I led the Lealfast into Armat's trap," Eleanon said. "I have lain sleepless over it. I need to make amends—not to you or Axis, or even Maximilian—but to the Lealfast who survived that nightmare. They have great potential, Broad-Wing. They will learn quickly and without murmur. As will I. BroadWing," Eleanon hesitated, then went on, "it has been a long road to admit to myself just how skilled the Strike Force is. I can learn from you, I want to learn from you . . . everything you have to teach me. My loyalty is to you, and then to Maximilian Persimius and Elcho Falling."

BroadWing relaxed. There had not been a false note in that speech. He rested a hand on Eleanon's shoulder. "We will start this afternoon," he said, "and I shall show you how the Strike Force will defend Elcho Falling against whatever that damned glass pyramid can throw against it."

CHAPTER SIX

Salamaan Pass, and Serpent's Nest

StarHeaven, closely accompanied by her three Icarii companions, banked her wings to prevent further descent, and hovered in astonishment a hundred paces above the northern entrance to the Salamaan Pass.

A large army was winding its way out of the Pass, moving north.

"They're Isembaardians," said BrokenFlight, one of StarHeaven's companions.

"Yes," said StarHeaven, "and look who is riding at their head! Is it Isaiah? I have not seen him before."

"It looks like it," said BrokenFlight, "but it can't be. He's dead."

"Apparently not," StarHeaven murmured. She thought for a minute, deciding what to do. "BrokenFlight, you and the others stay here. I need someone to report back to Axis if I don't come back."

"StarHeaven," said SureSong, another of the Icarii, "that may not be Isaiah. It may be a phantasm."

"I know," StarHeaven said softly, then began her descent.

Isaiah pulled his stallion to a halt, almost unable to believe that an Icarii woman was spiraling down from the sky.

Thank the gods!

"And pray to the gods that she is an Enchanter," Isaiah muttered. "Please, please, let her be an Enchanter."

And please, please, let it be in time.

"Who is it?" Lamiah said, pulling his horse in beside Isaiah's.

"One of the Icarii," said Isaiah. "At last we'll get some news . . . and hope we can get some news out. Take your hand off your sword, Lamiah. She means no harm."

Lamiah hesitated, then did as Isaiah asked. In the four days since he'd met Isaiah coming out of Isembaard, Lamiah had to all intents and purposes handed command of the one-hundred-thousand-strong army back to Isaiah. There had been no overt discussion of this, but Isaiah had taken command upon himself, and Lamiah had just allowed it.

It had, in the end, been the easiest thing to do. The first time that Isaiah had issued a command to Lamiah's men in front of Lamiah, Lamiah had opened his mouth to protest . . . and then closed it as Isaiah had sent him a hard look.

It had been the easiest thing to do, allowing Isaiah control, and no one in the chain of command had questioned it.

Now Lamiah looked curiously at the winged woman who had landed some distance away and was approaching Isaiah and Lamiah cautiously.

"Who are you?" the woman asked Isaiah as she stopped three or four paces away from his horse.

"Isaiah," he said, "Tyrant of a wasteland."

"You're dead," the woman said.

"Lessened," said Isaiah, "but not dead. You are . . . ?"

"StarHeaven," she said. "Isaiah—"

"StarHeaven," Isaiah said, "thank the gods, an Enchanter. Listen to me, please. I have a story to tell you and a message I need to get to Maximilian as soon as I can. Are you able to do that for me?"

"I can get a message to Axis, and through him to Maximilian," said StarHeaven. "I can do that fairly quickly."

Isaiah dismounted from the horse. "Lamiah," he said, "can you continue the march north? I'll rejoin you in an hour or two. I need to tell StarHeaven what I know."

Lamiah nodded and, as Isaiah moved StarHeaven to one side, waved the column forward.

"StarHeaven," Isaiah said as soon as they were safely out of the way. "How long is it since you have been with Maximilian's column?"

"A week, perhaps."

"And when you left, had Maximilian and Ishbel renewed their marriage?"

"No," she said, "they are close, but something still makes them hesitate." She shrugged. "No Icarii would act that way."

Isaiah almost sagged in relief. "StarHeaven, listen closely, for I have a tale to tell that you need to get back to Maximilian's ears as soon as you can."

"I want to show you something," Ishbel said to Maximilian, who now sat on the bench beside her, and she unwound her plait and loosened her hair.

"I was marked," she said, "and you ran your hands over it many times, but never saw it or intuited it."

"Your scalp," he said.

"You knew?"

Maximilian laughed. "Well, the fact that you are talking about your hidden mark while shaking your hair loose gave me a hint."

"Oh, well, yes. Look."

Maximilian hesitated, then took Ishbel's bowed head in gentle hands, parting the hair. "I can't see anything."

"No." Ishbel lifted her head and Maximilian lowered his hands. "I looked this morning," she continued, "for the first time since I left Serpent's Nest, and it is gone."

Maximilian sat silent, looking at her.

"I sat in the room I'd had as archpriestess, Maxel. Sat there all night. I had yearned for that room so much, yearned to come home."

"I know," he said softly.

"But . . . last night . . . there was nothing left there for me. It was empty." She paused. "What I had once been was gone. Empty."

"I know you'd wanted to see how you felt when you came back here."

"I was sure I would feel *something*. Sadness. Regret. Sweetness, perhaps. But there was nothing at all. Just emptiness." Another pause. "And when I realized that, Maxel, I grew fearful."

Again he sat silent, regarding her.

"I thought that perhaps I had left it too long. That I had missed the bridge that would lead from the life I had lost to—"

Maximilian leaned forward and kissed her, very gently. "Be my wife, Ishbel."

"I've been so angry at you, Maxel, and so scared of you. I am still scared."

"Of what?"

"I am terrified of once more ruining a marriage with you. I don't think I can survive again the pain we caused each other the last time."

"No one can guarantee anything, Ishbel. We can simply do our best."

"No secrets?"

"No. So confess to me whatever remaining secrets you have kept hidden, Ishbel."

"I stole my mother's favorite brooch when I was five," said Ishbel. "I hid it in the flour jar."

Maximilian smiled. "I can live with that."

"This is proving easier than I expected."

"That is because we are making a more honest start this time."

Ishbel took a deep breath, and nodded. "I have loved you for so long, Maxel."

"And I you, and we both needed to say that, very badly." Maximilian took her face between his hands, and kissed her again, very gently.

"What now?" Ishbel said, when he drew back.

StarHeaven had gone utterly white. She stared at Isaiah, unwilling to believe what he had told her.

"I don't need you to believe it," Isaiah said. "I just need you to pass it on to Axis and from him to Maximilian. *Can you do that?*"

She nodded, her eyes huge.

"Now?"

Again StarHeaven nodded. "I need somewhere quiet. Somewhere..."

"Oh for gods' sakes," said Isaiah. He waved his arm at the three Icarii he could see overhead, and they slowly, and with obvious uncertainty, spiraled down to him.

"Get her somewhere safe and quiet," Isaiah said to them when they'd landed. "And when she's done, get back to me."

Axis was walking with Egalion and Clements by the front gates to Serpent's Nest, checking the portcullis.

"Although why we bother," Egalion said as they stood back, watching a group of five soldiers lower the metal gate up and down, "I don't know. Maximilian says he will raise Elcho Falling the day after tomorrow, and what will become of all this," he waved a hand at the gates and the forecourt, "I have no idea."

"I doubt it will be substantially different," said Axis. "Just . . . different."

"Well," said Clements, "that's helpful. But I would have thought that . . . *Axis?* What's wrong?"

Axis had gone very pale, and had literally swayed on his feet for a moment.

Egalion grabbed at his elbow, steadying him. "Axis?"

"It is StarHeaven," Axis said. "Reporting back . . ."

Egalion kept his hand on Axis' arm, but he and Clements stayed silent for five or six long minutes as Axis listened to what StarHeaven said in his mind.

"What is it, Axis?" Egalion said as Axis finally blinked and came out of his fugue.

"Trouble," Axis said, and he pulled his arm from Egalion's grip and sprinted for the inner courtyard.

He found them where he'd left them, in the chamber where Maximilian had held his morning conference.

Unfortunately, they were not *quite* as he'd left them. A flush-cheeked Ishbel was sitting in a chair, braiding her loosened hair. When she saw Axis she gave him a part secretive, part self-satisfied smile, then dropped her eyes.

Maximilian was standing by a chair, lifting up his jacket and sliding an arm through one sleeve.

Axis stared at the jacket . . . had Maximilian been wearing that earlier . . . or not?

Oh stars . . .

"Axis?" Maximilian said. "Is there something the matter?"

"I need to speak with you," Axis said.

"What is it?" Maximilian said.

Axis hesitated, and Ishbel finished with her plait and rose. "I think he wants to speak with you alone, Maxel." She walked past Axis to the door, giving him another enigmatic smile.

"I'll see you tonight, Maxel," she said, and left the room.

Axis waited until the door closed.

"Maxel," he said, "Isaiah is alive."

CHAPTER SEVEN

Serpent's Nest

Maximilian paused in the middle of buttoning his jacket. "*What?*" "Isaiah is alive. I've just heard from StarHeaven. Maxel, had you made love with Ishbel before I arrived?"

This time Maximilian just stared at Axis.

"Maxel, I have reason to ask—the news from Isaiah is appalling, and it involves Ishbel. Do you remember Ravenna's vision?"

Maximilian finally pulled on his jacket with an angry jerk. "Oh for all the gods' sakes, don't tell me *Isaiah* has turned against Ishbel now! Has *he* started having visions as well? I have had enough of people telling me she will be my peril."

He paused. "Isaiah is alive . . . how? Axis, sit down, please, and tell me, in order, starting with the fact that Isaiah is alive, what you know."

Axis pulled out a chair from the central table. "Isaiah is alive. He met with what he believes to be the fleshly representation of DarkGlass Mountain—Isaiah said it was a man made of glass—who calls himself the One. The One stripped Isaiah of his powers, which is what you and Lister felt and you interpreted as his death. I believe there is a lengthy tale here to be told, but StarHeaven only gave me the absolute basics, because she, or Isaiah through her, wanted me to pass to you as fast as possible the One's message to you."

Maximilian was still standing. "And that is?"

"The One has constructed a curse. Isaiah stresses that it is not a possibility, but a reality."

"Very well. What is this curse?"

Axis took a deep breath. "This curse is powered by the fact that whatever form of flesh the One has assumed thus far was accomplished through the death of your and Ishbel's daughter. Her blood—"

"Yes, yes, get on with it."

"If you, Maximilian Persimius, slide the Queen of Elcho Falling's ring onto Ishbel's finger, if you bear her down to your bed, then so shall sorrow and despair envelop Elcho Falling and all it contains. The moment you marry yourself to Ishbel again, by consummation of ring and body, then so shall the One become Elcho Falling's lord. And when he arrives at the gates of Elcho Falling, so shall Ishbel crawl forth and surrender to him all the power and might of the citadel of Elcho Falling. It is what Ravenna saw in her vision, Maxel. You can do nothing to prevent this. The moment you wed Ishbel again, your fate, as the fate of all the lands and peoples above the Far-Reach Mountains, is sealed. You and they shall be wedded to the One, who controls the power of Infinity."

Maximilian's face was expressionless as he stared at Axis. "And this curse is a reality."

"Yes. Unless . . ."

"Unless . . . ?"

"To save Elcho Falling, the land and its peoples, you and Ishbel must present yourselves to the One at Sakkuth and deliver to him the Weeper—"

"Well, that's a small impossibility now, isn't it?"

"—the crown of Elcho Falling and the Goblet of the Frogs. You—"

"The goblet of the what?"

Now it was Axis' turn to stare at Maximilian. Hadn't either Isaiah or Ishbel told him about the goblet? "Maxel, you will need to ask Ishbel about the goblet. It is something that Isaiah brought north with him from Isembaard. It is just a goblet, Maxel—"

"*Just* a goblet, yet the fate of Elcho Falling depends on its deliverance to this One?"

"Maxel, this is hard enough for me as it is. Please let me finish."

Maximilian continued to stare at Axis with an expressionless face.

"If you deliver yourselves, the Weeper, the crown, and the goblet to the

One, then you and Ishbel will die, but he will spare Elcho Falling and the lands above the FarReach Mountains. Maxel, is this not what Ravenna was trying to warn you about?"

Maximilian sent Axis such a dark look that Axis found it difficult to ask what he needed. "Maxel, *have* you reconsummated your marriage to Ishbel?"

"No. Ishbel and I have not bedded for at least a year."

"Thank the stars!"

"Don't you *dare* say that to me!"

"Maxel—"

"Ishbel and I have made our peace, Axis. The day I raise Elcho Falling is the day we resume our vows."

"Maxel, the One did everything to try and ensure Isaiah did not get this message to you in time. He stripped Isaiah of his power, and Isaiah has had to walk across vast distances, although fortunately he found a horse left to run wild in the wilderness and managed to come faster than the One had intended. That he then came across StarHeaven was sheer luck. Don't discard that luck! Maxel, this curse is a reality. If you lie with Ishbel then there is nothing you can do to avoid the destruction of this entire land save—"

"Taking ourselves down to Sakkuth with the Weeper, the crown, and this goblet of which you speak. Yes. I heard you the first time. I assume this is what the One wants, otherwise why tell me about this curse? Why not just curse me and let me drift unknowing to my fate?"

"That is how Isaiah understands it. The One wants you and Ishbel in Sakkuth, with the items. You may not have the Weeper, Maxel, but perhaps you can hand to the One the keys to the Twisted Tower."

Maximilian shot Axis yet another black look.

"The One," Axis continued, "assumed that Isaiah would not get the message to you in time. Maxel, you can now avoid the curse. Very simply. Don't slide that ring onto Ishbel's finger. Don't sleep with her."

Maximilian leaned forward a little, sighed, and rubbed at his forehead with one hand. "Axis, if the One has gone to these lengths, then he is vulnerable."

"Perhaps he just wants to make sure."

"So, what happens if, as you suggest and Ravenna wants, I discard Ishbel completely, renege on any and all promises I have made to her, set her to one side, and refuse to attend the One in Sakkuth?"

"Then Isaiah says the One will invade. He has a huge unnatural army—Isaiah has not gone into details but I am assuming it is whatever those millions of Skraelings have become—with which he will swamp this land while you are distracted by Armat. Maxel, frankly I prefer the second option—dealing with an invasion from the south—rather than—"

"Destroying all my hopes by making Ishbel my wife. So, according to Isaiah, I face certain destruction via a curse which the One assumed Isaiah would not tell me about in time anyway, or I avoid the curse and suffer probable defeat via a war of attrition with the unnatural armies of the One."

"I say again, Maxel, that I prefer the second option. We need to deal with Armat, and then we need to prepare to face the armies of the One. There is better news which StarHeaven told me briefly. Isaiah is moving north with Lamiah and one hundred and fifty thousand men. He is bringing an army with him, Maxel."

"What for? To keep me from Ishbel's bed?"

"Maxel—"

"Go away and leave me, Axis. I want to think."

The moment Axis had closed the door behind him, Maximilian stood and began pacing about the room. He was furious: with Axis, with Isaiah, and with Ishbel, who had apparently kept secret an object important enough that the One had tied it to his curse.

Was the entire world conspiring to keep him and Ishbel apart?

The curse made no sense to Maximilian. Why had the One told him about it? If Maximilian had the ability to visit such a curse on his enemy, a curse which would *ensure* his enemy's defeat, then the very last thing he would do would be to send him warning of its existence, perhaps *in time to avoid it*. Maximilian wasn't sure that the One had assumed that Isaiah would *not* be in time. Everything seemed too . . . clumsy.

There had been too much "luck" on Isaiah's part to get the news of the curse to Maximilian.

In time to prevent it.

"Shit," Maximilian muttered, then he strode to the door.

"Ishbel?"

She turned from the window where she'd been looking for evidence of Armat's imminent arrival. "Maxel? I hadn't expected you before this afternoon. I thought you'd be spending the day with Josia."

"What is the Goblet of the Frogs?"

The smile faded from her face. "Who told you—"

"Who told me doesn't matter. What is it?"

"I was going to give it to you at your crowning, Maximilian. It was to be a gift. A surprise."

"So surprise me now."

She gave him a steady look, then walked over to her pack in the corner of the chamber, retrieved from it a package, and came back to stand before him.

"My ancestress Tirzah made this for Boaz, the man she loved." Ishbel slowly unwrapped the goblet, then held it out to Maximilian. "And thus I give it to you, Maxel, as a gift of love."

He took it in his hands, turning it about very slowly. "It is astounding."

"Yes," Ishbel said, watching his face carefully. "It is. Tell me, Maxel, does it speak to you?"

He raised his eyes to hers . . . and she knew what he must be hearing. *Hold her, soothe her, touch her, love her.*

"It tells me," he said, "to commit myself unto destruction."

Ishbel blanched. "What has Axis said to you?"

Maximilian sighed. "Ishbel, will you give me the crown, too, please."

Her face was stricken now. "I thought you wanted me to—"

"I need it only for tonight, Ishbel. Please give it to me, and then wait up for me. I will come and see you, very late, and then I will bring both the goblet and the crown back to you. Ishbel, trust me for the next twelve hours. Please."

"What did Axis tell you?"

"Ishbel, I need you not to talk to Axis for the moment. I want you to wait here until I come back."

He gave her his marvelous smile then, and her eyes filled with tears at its warmth. "I love you, Ishbel, but I need to be very, very sure about something, and for that I need both the crown and the goblet for the day. Will you trust me?"

"Yes," she said.

"Trust me, Ishbel, just a little longer."

CHAPTER EIGHT

Serpent's Nest

Maximilian went back to his chamber, and told Serge and Doyle, who stood outside, that he did not want to be disturbed.

"Not under any circumstance," he said. "I don't care if Armat himself comes storming up those steps, I must not be disturbed."

Then he went inside, placed the satchel with the crown in it, and the re-wrapped goblet, on a table under a window, and then sat down in a chair, staring at both satchel and wrapped bundle, thinking.

After a long while he closed his eyes, and his body relaxed.

Maximilian had gone to speak with Josia in the Twisted Tower.

Maximilian roused at dusk. He came back to awareness slowly, blinking and rubbing at his face, then stretching out his arms. He rose slowly, washed his face and hands, and wandered over to the window to look out as he dried them.

Finally he looked down at the table. He unwrapped the goblet first, setting it back on the table. He wrapped his hand in the cloth Ishbel had used to wrap the goblet, then used his covered hand to draw the crown out of the satchel.

He did not want to touch it until he used it to awaken Elcho Falling.

The crown was almost utterly enveloped in blackness now, with only an occasional glint of the three twisted golden bands.

Elcho Falling was very, very close, and for a moment Maximilian heard the pounding of the waves.

"Not yet," he whispered.

He looked out the window again.

The sun was now halfway beneath the horizon.

He had only a few minutes.

Maximilian withdrew the queen's ring from the inner pocket of his jacket, placed it on the table, then took off his own ring, placing that next to its mate.

He glanced out the window again.

There was now only the barest rim of light above the horizon.

The crown sat in the center of the table. Maximilian moved the other objects until the goblet sat behind the crown, and the two rings to either side.

Then, just as the sun finally sank below the horizon, Maximilian placed his right hand flat on the table before the crown and spoke a similar incantation to the one Isaiah had used to pull Axis from the Otherworld.

The chamber dimmed.

Maximilian stood straight, lifted his hand from the table, and turned to face the center of the chamber.

Instead of looking at the wall and door across the chamber, he looked into a long, dim corridor that seemed to stretch into infinity.

There were two figures in its distance, and Maximilian waited as they approached. From time to time the figures faded from view, as if obscured by time or difficulty, but they always reappeared, walking steadily forward.

Eventually they were close enough for Maximilian to make out their features.

The older man had dark brown hair and deep blue eyes: Maximilian's eyes. The younger man was much darker, his long black hair queued at the back of his neck, his hawkish face dominated by intense black eyes.

Even so, his face held a resemblance to that of the older man.

Both of the men wore long robes of a pale material, with outer robes of more colorful and heavier fabric.

They stopped just before they would have stepped from the corridor into the chamber, and then both simultaneously bowed.

"My Lord of Elcho Falling," said the older man.

Maximilian returned the bow. "Avaldamon," he said to the older man, then he looked at the other. "Boaz."

"Threshold has awoken," Boaz said.

"Yes," Maximilian said.

"I should have destroyed it completely," Boaz said.

"Indeed," said Maximilian, "but what was not done was not done, and now I need your advice."

He outlined briefly for the two men what he knew of the pyramid and its use of Kanubai. "Now a glass man walks forth, calling himself the One—"

Boaz made a soft expostulation at that.

"—and threatens me with destruction. Boaz, what is the One?"

"The One was what the Magi worshipped, my lord," Boaz said. "We were addicted to numbers and calculations, and took heart in their predictability. The One—the number one—is both birth and death within itself, for it is the number from which all other numbers and forms are born and into which they all eventually collapse and die. The One is both Creation and Doom in single expression and form."

"And this is what now strides forth to confront me?"

"No," said Avaldamon, "we don't believe so."

"What, then?" said Maximilian.

"We used the pyramid to touch Infinity," said Boaz. He glanced at his father, then looked back at Maximilian. "My lord, I think that the One *is* Infinity, or at the least draws almost completely on its power. He is a fearful foe."

Maximilian nodded, thinking for a moment. "You know of Ishbel?"

Both men smiled. "Yes," said Boaz, "she is our direct descendant, born of the line of Tirzah's and my eldest daughter."

"Everyone fears her," Maximilian said.

"Save you," said Boaz, "and for that I thank you."

"Everyone warns me against her," said Maximilian.

"Including the One," said Avaldamon.

Maximilian nodded.

"We cannot stay much longer," said Avaldamon. "Already we feel the tug on our souls of the Otherworld. What do you need to know from us, Maximilian, Lord of Elcho Falling?"

"I do not know the question," said Maximilian, "else I *would* ask it."

The three men looked at each other a long moment, then Avaldamon and Boaz simultaneously looked over their shoulders and took a step back.

"You and Tirzah had three children," Maximilian said to Boaz, holding out a hand as if he had the power to hold them back indefinitely. "Why is it that only your eldest daughter's line carried power? Why did only that line carry the weight of Elcho Falling within it?"

Boaz frowned, then the frown cleared and he gave a small smile. "Maximilian, Tirzah was pregnant with our eldest daughter when we did our battle with Threshold."

Maximilian's shoulders visibly relaxed. "Thank you," he said. "That was what I needed to know."

Boaz's smile widened a little. "Maximilian, let me say one other thing to you. When all looks at its bleakest, and you think there is nothing left, and no action worth taking, ask Josia in what manner he died. There shall lie your salvation." Boaz's smile faded, but his eyes remained warm. "The Persimius do not forget their own."

Then, quite suddenly, Boaz and Avaldamon were gone.

CHAPTER NINE

Serpent's Nest

She heard his step at the door, heard him pass a quiet word with Mada-rin, then slowly rose from her chair as the door opened.

She'd spent the past ten or so hours in the state of fear and anger she'd thought to have left behind her.

Why could nothing ever run smoothly for her and Maximilian?

And why, oh why, hadn't she thought to give Maximilian the Goblet of the Frogs earlier?

"Ishbel?"

"Over here, Maxel."

"I can afford lamps to light the chambers, you know."

"I'm sorry. I didn't think." Ishbel fumbled for the flint and lit a lamp on a side table.

He stood just inside the door, looking very tired, the satchel under one arm and the wrapped goblet in the other hand.

She almost couldn't believe he'd brought them back.

"Can we talk a little?" he said.

Ishbel nodded. She didn't know if she should offer him a seat, sit herself, or take the crown and goblet from him.

Maximilian decided for her by setting the objects on a table and walking over to her. Taking one of her hands, he interlaced their fingers.

"Isaiah is alive," he said, then smiled a little at the shock on Ishbel's face.

"But . . ." she said.

"He met with the fleshly embodiment of DarkGlass Mountain, a somewhat flashy glass man who calls himself the One. In order to either impress me or Isaiah, the One stripped Isaiah of his power, which is what Lister and I felt. We'd assumed that meant he was dead. But no. Isaiah is at this moment marching at the head of an army well over one hundred thousand strong—some weeks to the south of us, unfortunately, but nonetheless on his way. What say you to that, Ishbel?"

Everything about Maximilian radiated serenity and warmth, and that reassured Ishbel as nothing else might have done.

"I say that I am glad he is alive, but that I also find it very hard to think on Isaiah when you stand here so close."

"Isaiah brings some grim news, which is what Axis had to tell me today, and which is why I needed the crown and the goblet tonight."

"What did you use them for? What grim news?"

"To contact the dead. Ishbel, there are some things from the news that Isaiah sent, and some things that I did tonight, that for the moment I don't want to tell you. But I need you to trust me. I will tell you, but not right now."

"Why not?"

"Because I am terrified that you will panic and run out the door."

He was pulling her closer now, holding her hand so that the back of his hand rested against her sternum, and their conjoined hands were the only things separating their bodies. "Will you trust me, Ishbel?"

"Yes."

"Axis may not be very friendly toward you for a few days. Ignore him. Trust me."

Peace radiated out from him, enveloping her in tranquility. Ishbel wondered if this was just his own magnetism, or if he were using some sorcery he'd learned within the higher levels of the Twisted Tower.

"It doesn't matter," she said.

He leaned forward and kissed her, very softly.

"Will you stay with me?" she murmured.

"Not tonight," he said. "The day after tomorrow you and I will do what is needed to waken Elcho Falling, and I will put the crown of Elcho Falling to my brow, and that night . . . well, that will be a night of great power, Ishbel, and a fitting night to make a marriage between you and me that will, this time, stand the test of discord."

"But Axis will not be pleased."

"No. And you may hear Isaiah scream even from his vast distance. Trust me, Ishbel."

"I trust you, Maxel."

"There will be a storm about us, for some time. Can you accept that?"

"Yes."

He smiled, holding her eyes with his own, and pressed the back of his hand a little more firmly against her sternum. "I find all my strength," he said, "in the beat of your heart."

Then he kissed her again, and was gone.

CHAPTER TEN

Serpent's Nest

"Tomorrow, Elcho Falling," Eleanon said softly, leaning against the rock wall of Serpent's Nest. They were high in the mountain, having followed stairwells and corridors that lay under centuries of dust. Eleanon was sure that not even Ishbel could find them here tonight.

"Tomorrow, Elcho Falling," Inardle said. She had her eyes focused far out into the Infinity Sea.

Eleanon reached out a hand and touched her cheek softly. "Do you mind being with Axis?"

"No," she said.

"Do you love him?"

Inardle did not answer.

"Do not love him, Inardle. Surely you could not have fallen for his corrupt charms. He yearns for Azhure, and—"

"Do not lecture me, Eleanon!"

Eleanon remained silent, studying Inardle. "You are Lealfast first and foremost, my love," he said eventually.

"I have as much Icarii blood in me as Axis."

"You are *Lealfast*, Inardle, *not* Icarii! I can see now it was a mistake to send you to Axis."

"What?" she said, turning her face to him. "You think it a mistake to have me so close to Axis, and thus to Maximilian? Do you think it a mistake that I now sit in on their close counsel, and if I am not there, then I hear it from Axis' mouth later? Do you think it a mistake that Ishbel now thinks to befriend me, and that—"

Eleanon held up his hands in surrender. "Peace, Inardle! Ah, you had me worried there. I had thought you so besotted with Axis that you preferred him to me."

"It has been a long time since we have been lovers, Eleanon."

"But we can be again, yes, when this is all done?"

She shrugged.

"And when all *is* done, Elcho Falling will be ours, and we shall control our own destiny. We shall be whole, Inardle. Not half and half. Whole. The One has promised this."

"You believe him?"

"Yes. I had my doubts, but yes, now I believe him."

"And what price does the One demand for this, Eleanon?"

"Elcho Falling. Its master."

"Everyone wants Elcho Falling," she said quietly, then sighed. "And so, shall you commit your grand treachery against Maximilian tomorrow, Eleanon?"

"No. I—*we*—shall wait. We both learn all we can about Elcho Falling and its magics. We learn how Maximilian and Axis plan to defend it." Eleanon gave a short laugh. "Already BroadWing is taking me into his confidence, and Axis will tell you whatever you ask him. Are you with us, Inardle?"

"Of course, Eleanon."

He nodded. "Have you heard about the curse the One placed on Maximilian? Has Axis told you?"

"Yes. It seems . . . cumbersome."

"As it is meant to be. It is to keep Maximilian occupied only, like giving a child a puzzle to keep him quiet while the adults play games elsewhere."

"And we are to play the games."

Eleanon laughed. "Of course! We shall be the ones to deliver Elcho Falling, and Maximilian, and Axis and all the cursed Icarii to the One, earning for ourselves, in the doing, a home and a future."

Inardle stayed for a long time after Eleanon had left, staring out over the ocean, wondering where she could go from here.

There didn't seem a single safe place left for her.

CHAPTER ELEVEN

Serpent's Nest

Is everyone out?" Maximilian asked Axis as they stood in the inner courtyard.

"Yes, the last horseman left an hour ago."

"Everyone has taken possessions? Everything they need?"

"Yes, but we could not take much in the way of stores."

"No matter. Elcho Falling will provide."

Axis shifted on his feet. He held the reins of his horse, and his unease
communicated itself to the stallion, which began to toss its head and pull on
the reins.

"Armat is not far distant," Axis said. "Perhaps six hours. Eight at the
most. Maximilian, we are vulnerable outside the mountain. We—"

"Cannot stay inside it, Axis. Where are the mounted men positioned?"

"About a mile back down the road."

"The Icarii, the Strike Force, and the Lealfast?"

"On the ground, slightly to the north of the mounted men. Maxel, they
do not like to be kept to the ground. *I* would like at least a few scouts in the
air with Armat this close."

"The air will be too dangerous for them. They stay on the ground. Make
sure they understand this, Axis."

Axis nodded. "Georgdi is moving in with his twenty thousand, Maxel.
The last I heard he was an hour away."

Maximilian smiled. "Then he will be here for the entertainment. Twenty
thousand, eh? The man is a miracle."

Axis let his shoulders loosen a little. Maximilian was obviously relaxed—in fact, this was the most unconcerned Axis thought he'd ever seen him.

"How do you feel?" Axis asked. "The rise of Elcho Falling was something you tried to deny for a long time, and it will be a terrible burden, yet you seem so . . ."

"At peace with myself, Axis, finally. When I first realized that I would be the one to raise Elcho Falling . . . it was a bleak moment. I did not think I could manage it, or be able to wear the crown without failing."

"But now?"

"But now . . . now with Josia's aid I have virtually rebuilt the Twisted Tower, and together with Ishbel—"

"Ishbel? Maxel, you know you can't—"

"Axis, listen to me. I will do what I need to in order to ensure the survival of Elcho Falling and of the land. You can advise me, but in the end it is I who will wear the crown of Elcho Falling, and you will need to abide by my decisions." He gave a small smile to take some of the sting out of his tone and words. "I spent seventeen years crawling about in the blackness, Axis. I have learned some devious means to achieve the end I want."

Axis regarded him a long moment, then he finally gave a nod. "Have you told Ishbel what Isaiah has said?"

"No, and I ask that you don't, either. Ever since she was first named as my bride, she has had, at various times, the entire world set against her. She needs what friends and friendship she can, Axis. I don't want her to know Isaiah's words. Not just yet. She deserves a little peace herself. Don't upset it for her."

That was a clear warning, Axis thought, and some of his unease returned. What was Maximilian planning to do?

"We cannot spend the day chatting," Maximilian said, his smile widening just a little, "however pleasant that may be. Ride out to my army, Axis, and station yourself at its head. Ishbel and I will be with you within the hour."

He opened the door to the Reading Room and walked inside. Ishbel was standing in its center, and she gave him a small smile as he entered.

She looked lovely, dressed in a gown of soft, clinging fabric that shimmered turquoise and ivory and silver. Her hair had been loosely dressed with a web of pearls and diamonds wound through its waves.

Maximilian walked over, took her hand, and kissed it. "I asked you to dress as a queen," he said softly, "and you have given me instead the moon and stars."

She laughed. "All this courtly speak, Maxel! Is this what I must listen to henceforth?"

"I can assure you, my lady," Maximilian said very softly, his eyes holding hers, "that I will find much better uses for my mouth later tonight."

She flushed, and he grinned and let her hand go. "Are we ready to raise Elcho Falling, my lady?"

"Aye," she said. "Shall I start the cleansing?"

He nodded, and Ishbel looked about, taking a deep breath. "It seems so strange, this mountain so empty of everything but you and me. I can feel its sadness, and yet . . ."

"You can feel it waiting."

She nodded, then bent down and picked up a bundle of dried sage-bush twigs. "Wait by the door," she said, and Maximilian moved out of her way.

Ishbel lit one end of the bundle of twigs. Once it was smoking well, she began a slow, complex dance that started in the center of the Reading Room and gradually wound its way through the entire space. As she danced—very slow, very elegant—she moved the bundle of smoking twigs out at arm's length, raised it up to shoulder height, then slowly downward in an arc until she almost swept the floor with its burning embers, and then up again.

Maximilian leaned against the door frame, watching her. Ishbel was unwinding the memory and influence of the Coil from the mountain, and when she was done here, she would do the same dance at the main doors that led into the mountain, and then again at the front gates in order to remove the memory and presence of anyone who had entered the mountain since the last time a Lord of Elcho Falling had set foot within.

Maximilian thought he could stand here and watch Ishbel forever. She was so absorbed in what she did that she looked as if she had entirely forgotten his presence.

You have a somewhat unexpected offer of a bride, Vorstus had said to him so long ago, *but there is a complication. She is offered to you by the Coil within Serpent's Nest.*

Ishbel was now dancing in the far quadrant of the room, the smoke drifting up from the smoldering twigs to writhe about the domed ceiling. Now and again she scraped the burning ends of the twigs against both floor and wall, leaving curious scorch marks where they had trailed.

The Lady Ishbel is not as virtuous as you had hoped, Maxel, Garth had said to him.

She will bring you nothing but sorrow, Maxel, Ravenna had said.

And, so recently, both Isaiah and Axis warning him against her.

What is it, Maximilian thought, watching Ishbel as she drew closer to him, *that makes people fear you so?*

He was going to start something today that might well see the destruction of his world. And, once started, he could not walk away from it. It would be a stormy path indeed for the next year, but Maximilian hoped that he and Ishbel would weather it.

If not . . .

He was her only ally, Maximilian realized. He needed to be her rock, or else she could not endure what awaited them.

Ishbel came to a halt in front of him. Her eyes were downcast to the bundle of twigs she held in her hand, and for a moment she stayed entirely still.

Then with her free hand she plucked one twig from the bundle and cast it into the center of the Reading Room.

Instantly the walls and floor began to smolder.

Maximilian straightened hastily as the door frame grew warm.

"We need to leave, Maxel," Ishbel said.

Ishbel repeated the same dance by the main doors and then by the front gates. At the doors, as she finished her dance, she tossed in a single smoldering twig, and instantly all the corridors and passages leading back into the mountain began to burn.

As she finished the dance at the front gates, Ishbel tossed the remaining bundle of twigs forward and high into the air, throwing them through the gates so that they scattered far and wide as they fell.

Smoke and tongues of flame began to rise and flicker from every crevice in the mountain.

"Come build me a bed for our marriage tonight," Ishbel said, looking at Maximilian with such directness and intensity that he would, at her word, have utterly abandoned any attempt to raise Elcho Falling to take her there in the dust before the burning mountain.

"The flames are reflected in your eyes," he said.

"As they are in yours."

"Do you have the crown and the goblet?"

"Do you doubt me? Come, my lord, build me a chamber for our marriage."

He gave a small smile, and held out his hand, and together they walked down the road, the burning mountain at their backs, to where Axis and Maximilian's army waited.

Far distant, many hours' ride away, Ravenna pulled her horse to a halt and stared at the mountain on the horizon.

Smoke was rising from its peak and, as she looked, flickering lights, flames, began to work their way up the rocky face of the mountain toward its peak.

"What is happening?" she asked Lister as he reined in his horse beside hers.

"It is beginning," he said. "Maximilian is raising Elcho Falling."

CHAPTER TWELVE

Elcho Falling

A xis sat his horse, staring beyond Maximilian and Ishbel to the mountain. It was burning as fiercely as if it had been made of wood.

"What a wonderful beacon for Armat."

Axis glanced to his left to where Georgdi sat his horse. He'd arrived at
the head of his twenty thousand only half an hour before, just as the first
wisps of smoke had started to appear about Serpent's Nest. He looked tired,
but otherwise well, and his eyes gleamed mischievously. He said he'd seen
the smoke from Armat's campfires the previous night and had marched
through the night himself to ensure he got here in time.

There had been barely enough time to get Georgdi's men into position,
and to tell him what news there was, before Maximilian and Ishbel had
started on their way down the road.

Axis glanced about him to make sure that everyone else was in position.
Maximilian had asked that Axis, Inardle, StarDrifter, Georgdi, Egalion,
and Ezekiel all be positioned at the front of the ranks.

"What's he going to do?" said Georgdi as Maximilian and Ishbel drew
close.

"I have no idea at all," Axis said, his eyes fixed on Maximilian's and Ishbel's conjoined hands.

Maximilian saw Georgdi sitting just behind Axis, and gave him a nod.
Words could come later. He and Ishbel came to a halt some ten paces before Axis, who was at the head of the group of commanders. Behind the

commanders ranged Maximilian's army: Escatorians, Isembaardians, Icarii, and Lealfast, all standing in ordered rank and slightly distanced each from the other.

"Ishbel," Maximilian murmured, and she nodded, stepping away from him to one side.

"Axis," Maximilian said, walking closer to him. "Your sword, if you will."

Axis unsheathed it and handed it to Maximilian hilt first. Maximilian nodded his thanks, walked back ten paces to where he had originally halted, looked briefly at the burning mountain, then used the sword to draw three intersecting circles, large enough that he could stand in their center without touching any of the circles. He dug them deep into the ground, so that each circle became almost a mini-trench half a finger deep.

Then he walked back up the road three or four paces, and drew a straight, deep line back down to the intersecting circles.

"Your sword," he said, handing it back to Axis, who took and sheathed it wordlessly.

Maximilian walked toward Ishbel.

"My lady," he said softly.

Ishbel took a deep breath.

"First," she said, "a gift from the past that we may together weld a future."

Axis frowned at her phraseology, and hoped it was merely metaphorical.

Ishbel went down on one knee on the dusty road as she spoke, holding out her cupped hands.

Axis gasped, as did everyone else who could see.

As Ishbel bowed her head before Maximilian, the Goblet of the Frogs had appeared within her cupped hands.

"I had a vision of presenting you this goblet, my lord," Ishbel murmured, only for Maximilian's ears, "that night we first lay together."

He took the goblet from her, running his fingers over her hands as he did so, then held it up so that it caught the flickering light of the flames.

It flashed emerald and amber, and the frogs about its sides capered and leaped.

"It is an object of great magic," Maximilian said, then turned back to the waiting commanders.

He went to StarDrifter first. "Talon," he said, "may I have a feather from your wing?"

StarDrifter's eyes widened a little, but he gave a nod. "You may have a feather from my wing, my lord," he said.

Maxel reached out one hand and ran his fingers gently over the curve of one of StarDrifter's folded wings. When he withdrew it, he held a white and gold feather between two of his fingers.

Maximilian dropped it into the goblet, resting his hand over the mouth of the goblet for a moment, head bowed.

Then he moved to Ezekiel, sitting his horse just to one side of StarDrifter. "General," Maximilian said, "I see you wear a chain-mail tunic made of the finest rings of steel. May I have one of those rings?"

Ezekiel bowed his head. "Of course, my lord," and Maximilian reached out and ran his fingers over the skirt of the tunic as it lay over Ezekiel's thigh, and, as he withdrew the hand, a steel ring glinted between two of his fingers.

Maximilian dropped that into the goblet as well, resting his hand atop it a moment as he concentrated, then moved on.

From Egalion, Maximilian took a thread of his emerald tunic, and from Georgdi, a hair from his horse's mane. Each of these went, in turn, into the Goblet of the Frogs.

Then Maximilian came to where Inardle sat her horse, to Axis' right.

"I want nothing from you, Inardle," Maximilian said, "save your passion."

And with that he ran his fingers lightly down the wrist of Inardle's left hand where it rested on her leg, and then over the back of her hand and down her fingers.

She drew in a sharp breath, and frost rose where Maximilian had run his fingers.

Maximilian sent Axis an amused glance, then scooped up the frost on the tip of a finger and flicked it into the goblet.

"Thank you, my lady," Maximilian murmured to the now somewhat flushed Inardle once he had pressed his hand over the mouth of the goblet.

Then he turned to Axis. "From you, StarMan," he said, "I require something a little different. A snatch of Song, if you please. Something that relates specifically to the Star Dance."

Axis frowned, then a fragment of music filled the air. Maxel raised a hand, sweeping it through the air between them, clenching the music in his fist, and depositing it into the goblet.

"What was that song, Axis?" he asked.

"The Song of the Star Gate," Axis said. "We would sing it to teach Icarii children the wonders of the Star Gate and of the Star Dance which filtered through the gate."

"Thank you," Maximilian said, then turned away before a clearly perplexed Axis could ask anything of him.

He walked back to the three intertwined circles and stood in their center, placing the goblet carefully in front of his feet. He raised his head and looked for a long moment at the burning mountain rearing high above them, then turned his head and addressed the assembled mass behind him. His voice was low, but very clear, and it carried to every last soldier or bird-man and woman.

"What happens next," Maximilian said, "may appear to be catastrophic, but it will not harm you. *Nothing that happens will harm you.* Be still, and assured. Ishbel," he said, now looking to where she stood to one side and in front of him, "the crown of Elcho Falling, if you please."

She took a deep breath, then crossed her hands over her chest, bowing her head and closing her eyes.

When she lifted her head, and lifted her hands outward, they held a great writhing mass of darkness.

The crown of Elcho Falling, the three entwined bands of gold almost utterly hidden.

Maximilian reached out his hands, hesitated, then gripped the crown.

Instantly, cracks fissured up the mountain from its base, allowing great gouts of smoke and flame to spurt into the air.

"Stars!" Axis muttered, wishing that Maximilian had asked him to position the army even further back. He looked at those around him. Most people were staring at the mountain, their faces reflecting varying degrees of concern or fear.

Axis looked back to Maximilian.

Maximilian now held the crown before him, just in front of his face. He took a deep breath, then blew, and all the darkness about the crown was carried away, dissipating into the air as it went.

Now Maximilian held the crown in all its glorious simplicity. He raised it above his head . . . then let it drop.

The movement was so unexpected that Axis jumped. He expected the crown to hit Maximilian's head and bounce off into the dust, but instead it fell onto the top of Maximilian's head . . . then appeared to expand so that it slid down over his head, then expanded more to slide over his shoulders, then down his body, his legs, and expanded just enough that it fell into the three circles of intertwined trenches at his feet, filling them completely.

Now Maximilian stood in the center of three entwined circles of gold. He reached down for the goblet, lifted it up to chest height, and tipped it over the straight line that connected to the gold circles.

Emerald water poured forth, then fizzled into the dirt trench.

For a moment, nothing, then something in the distance made Axis look up, and he gave a cry of fear, echoing the cries about him.

Behind the burning mountain, the Infinity Sea had risen in a towering wave, higher even than the mountain, and was crashing down toward them with a roar that became deafening as it neared.

Behind him, Axis heard men and horses panic.

Before him, he saw Maximilian put an arm about Ishbel as she stepped into the circle.

CHAPTER THIRTEEN

Elcho Falling

The next instant Axis felt himself enveloped in a great wash of water. He felt as if he were tumbling over and over, and as if huge boulders—the remnants of Serpent's Nest—tumbled beside him, and yet he was also aware that he was not actually moving. He could feel his horse tight and tense beneath him, panicked but too terrified to move, and if he turned his head he could *see* the water so far above his head that the light was only a tiny emerald circle far above, and he could *feel* the mass of rock and debris grinding through the water ... and yet ...

There is no danger, Maximilian said in his mind, and Axis could feel his voice echo through everyone enclosed in this sorcery. *There is no danger.*

Then ... Axis blinked, and the enveloping sea was gone.

He blinked again, his vision clearing, and saw that while he still sat his horse, and that Inardle still sat hers beside him, and everyone else appeared as they should be, they sat those horses in an entirely different landscape.

The mountain was gone. There was not a single rock remaining.

In its place shimmered a vast expanse of turquoise water, rippling slightly as if it had just settled after a great turbulence.

Axis gazed around in wonder. The water extended as far as he could see—his horse, as all the other horses, and all those on foot, stood in the shallow water which reached partway up hoof and boot.

Ahead, Maximilian and Ishbel stood, arms loosely about each other's waist.

Maximilian turned slightly, enough to see the group of commanders.

"Wait," he said.

Axis looked about, more carefully this time, making sure that everyone was all right. Inardle looked shaken, but she nodded as she met his eyes. StarDrifter looked both shaken and very, very wary, an expression Axis supposed mirrored his own.

"What—" StarDrifter began, and stopped, staring ahead, his mouth open.

Axis turned back to the front.

"Oh stars . . ." he murmured.

In the distance, over the area of water where Serpent's Nest had once stood, three colossal twists of emerald water were winding up into the sky. They wound up and up, enclosing a space the height and breadth of Serpent's Nest, until, far, far into the sky, their three heads met.

For a moment, nothing.

Then Axis heard a heavy rhythmic whisper, as if somewhere a god swung his ax through the air again and again, or as if a massive windmill spun its sails over and over in the wind.

Thrum.

Thrum.

Thrum.

Axis could feel it through his entire body.

There was a movement at his side. Inardle, nudging her horse closer, and reaching out her hand.

Axis took it, squeezed it gently, and looked back to the twists of water rearing into the sky.

There was a glint of gold where the three twists met just below the few white clouds that dotted the sky. The sun caught the gold now and again, and Axis narrowed his eyes, knowing he had seen that same effect very recently . . .

The crown of Elcho Falling had glinted gold through the darkness that wreathed it when Ishbel had handed it to Maximilian!

"Inardle," Axis murmured, almost not believing what he was seeing as, very, very gently, the crown of Elcho Falling appeared in the sky at the very summit of the three twists of water, its three golden bands spinning about each other slowly, slowly, slowly, thrumming as they cut through the air. The crown had now grown to a vast size, and as the sun caught at it, it sent shimmering shafts of golden light scattering about the entire country.

Axis had never seen anything like it. Not the Star Gate, not Talon Spike, not the Temple of the Stars.

He wanted to check what was happening behind him in the army, but couldn't tear his eyes away from the spinning crown so high in the sky.

No wonder Maximilian had asked that all the bird peoples remain on the ground. Up close, those massive twisting rings would be deadly, and Axis had no doubt that they radiated sorcery.

"Axis!" Inardle said. *"Axis!"*

He couldn't reply. He was stunned Inardle had even managed to get those two words out.

Very suddenly, a mountain—no, no, not a mountain, a citadel!—started to fall from the spinning crown. The great twists of water merged, and from their very peak, where it passed through the spinning crown, spires and turrets and arches and windows started to appear, as if they were being poured out of a heavenly vessel. It happened in less than six heartbeats, so fast that Axis could barely comprehend what he was seeing.

Silence.

It felt to Axis as if the entire world was staring, unable to move or make a sound, at the wonder that rose from the shallow, shimmering lake of water.

For all he knew the entire world *could* see it, for Elcho Falling would surely be visible eight to ten days' ride away.

It was a citadel of enormous size and of extraordinary construction. It rose from the surface of the lake as emerald and turquoise and silver water, forming walls and arches and columns. About a third of the way into the sky the water slowly turned to crystal, and then a little higher to stone of a bright turquoise set off with traceries of gleaming ivory. At the very peak of the citadel, far, far into the sky, the three bands of the crown of Elcho Falling continued their slow sweep through the air.

It was so big, and so beautiful, that Axis could barely comprehend it. He'd thought Serpent's Nest a massive mountain, but it was as nothing compared to this. This . . . this could swallow nations, if it wanted.

"Elcho Falling," said Maximilian, now turned slightly so he could look behind him, "is not a castle, nor is it a mountain. Elcho Falling is a world within itself."

He gave a very slight smile, as if waiting for something.

Axis tore his eyes away from Elcho Falling to frown slightly at Maximilian, wondering why he had paused, then Axis jerked and groaned, along with every other Icarii and Lealfast present, as abruptly the Star Dance thundered out over the land.

"Elcho Falling," said Maximilian, his quiet voice carrying into every mind, "is also a gateway, which is why we have armies and ambitions converging upon it."

And soon it will be ours, sister, Eleanon said in Inardle's mind, and she let Axis' hand drop away.

Six or seven hours away Armat, together with Ravenna and Lister and his entire army, sat their horses and stared.

From their distance Elcho Falling was clearly visible.

"It is . . ." Armat began. "It is . . ."

Ravenna was crying, silent tears that streamed down her cheeks. "It is extraordinary," she said, "and the most magical thing that any of us will see, in this lifetime or in any to come."

"I want it," said Armat. Indeed he wanted it. He wanted it so badly that it took all of his strength not to dig his spurs into his horse and gallop headlong toward it. He'd always held his doubts about what Ravenna and Lister had told him about Elcho Falling . . . but, if anything, they had considerably understated its beauty . . . and power.

Armat was not a magical man, but he knew that Elcho Falling was of such power that the man who commanded the citadel could command the world.

"I want it," he said again.

CHAPTER FOURTEEN

Elcho Falling

Everything was happening at once. Axis was literally stunned by the intensity of the Star Dance flooding his existence—had he ever felt it this deeply before, or was Elcho Falling a gateway of such power that *no one*, perhaps not even WolfStar, had felt the Dance to this extent?

StarDrifter had stumbled the distance between them, putting a hand on Axis' thigh and then turning as someone landed beside them. It was Eleanon—Axis supposed that the Lealfast, who had only ever before felt the barest of glimmers of the Star Dance, must now be overwhelmed—and StarDrifter reached out to him, placing a hand on his shoulder, and the two birdmen leaned close for a brief word, their shared amazement making them momentary friends.

Axis looked at Inardle. She was staring at Elcho Falling, her face white, her eyes brilliant.

There were stars dancing in them.

"Maximilian . . ." StarDrifter said, and there was such hunger in his voice that Axis almost cried out.

"Yes," said Maximilian, and Axis wondered what had been asked, and what authorized, and was about to ask when suddenly there was a great sound and wind, and this time Axis did cry out, for every one of the Icarii and the Lealfast had lifted into the sky and for a moment there was nothing but the beating of wings and the rush of air.

Axis dragged his eyes away from the spectacle and looked again at Inardle. This time there was agony in her face as she stared desperately at the Icarii and Lealfast now circling high overhead.

Axis looked at Maximilian. "I had no idea," he said. "Why didn't you say something?"

"Would you have believed me?" said Maximilian. "Besides, I had no idea myself how intact Elcho Falling remained. It has been buried so long."

"Maxel, why were there no myths of this? Stars, news of this should have entered the folklore of the entire world!"

"Everything was buried when Elcho Falling closed down," Maximilian said, "even the memory of it."

Then he smiled. "Come. Shall we enter?"

There were two horses held in reserve for Maximilian and Ishbel, and once they had mounted they led the nonflighted army across the shallow waters toward the citadel.

"There is actually deep water to either side of the causeway," Maximilian said to Axis, pointing as they rode. "The causeway is only some ten paces wide. Anyone who stepped beyond it would be lost."

"How can we make our way to and fro," said Axis, "if you are not with us as guide?"

"Once Elcho Falling recognizes you as a friend—and that happens the moment you enter the citadel with my permission—you will always find your way without effort."

"Armat? Will this keep him at a distance?"

Maximilian shook his head. "Armat has Ravenna with him, and she well knows the ways and paths of mystery. She can guide him, and his army, across these waters."

"And once inside Elcho Falling?"

Maximilian gave a small smile. "Ah, once inside Elcho Falling it would be a different matter."

They rode in silence after that, Axis alternately studying the citadel rising before them and looking up to see the Icarii and Lealfast circling overhead (some, he was aghast to see, actually flying between the massive moving bands of gold) or basking in the Star Dance as it radiated out of Elcho Falling.

He thought about what Maximilian had taken from each of the commanders present—the song he had requested from Axis was clearly designed to align Elcho Falling with the Star Dance, but the other objects?

"Think back," Maximilian said softly as their horses stepped onto the incline that led to a massive arch which appeared to be made of solid water and which formed the entry into Elcho Falling, "to that moment when you first felt the Star Dance. StarDrifter was beside you, and then . . ."

"Then Eleanon landed," Axis said, thinking back. The moment when he'd first heard the Star Dance had been so overwhelming that everything about it was a jumble of images, and he had to sort through them to make any sense of what had happened in those first, remarkable moments. "Eleanon landed . . . and . . . oh stars, he and my father . . ."

Eleanon and StarDrifter had leaned close, smiling, sharing a word.

Previously, they'd been barely able to maintain any civility toward each other.

"Even Elcho Falling cannot heal all the rifts between them," said Maximilian, "but it can make a beginning. The rest is up to them."

Then Maximilian nodded at the archway.

"Elcho Falling," he said, and then they were through.

Axis could not speak for some time. From the road that rose from the water up to the great arch, they rode into a vast chamber of hundreds of columns supporting a high fan-vaulted ceiling. Everything, from the floor to the columns to the fan vaulting itself, appeared to be made of luminescent turquoise water. There were lights glowing gold through the chamber, hanging within the columns at the point at which the columns curved out into the vaulting.

Light shimmered everywhere, glistening through and off water, striking stars into the vaulted ceiling and ripples into the flooring.

Despite the appearance of walking on water, his horse's hooves sounded as if they struck solid ground with each hoof-fall, and as they passed one of the columns Axis reached out a hand to touch it.

It looked like flowing water, but it felt solid and cool to the touch.

He swiveled in the saddle, looking about and behind him.

All the horsemen were spread throughout the chamber as they continued to ride deeper into it. There was Egalion, and Garth, and there Inardle, there a score of men that Axis recognized, and every last one of them had a look of stupefied wonder on their faces. Even Ishbel, who Axis thought may have had some idea of what to expect, looked very much as though she might not be able to speak for some time.

"Maxel . . ." Axis murmured, turning forward once again in the saddle.

Maximilian nodded. "I can almost understand," he said, "why the last of the Lords of Elcho Falling to live here decided to close it down. All this beauty must have been heartbreaking."

"And Escator was better?" Axis said.

Maximilian gave a soft laugh. "No. Escator was not 'better.' But it was, I think, sometimes a little more comforting."

They continued to ride deeper and deeper into the chamber.

"If someone entered Elcho Falling without my permission, whether tacit or spoken," said Maximilian, "they would find it very hard to ever leave this initial chamber. They would lose themselves in it, and eventually sink into despair in their efforts to battle free. This is the first of Elcho Falling's defenses."

"It is big enough to take all of our army," said Axis.

"It is always big enough to take whatever is needed," Maximilian said. Then he nodded ahead. "Look."

A wide staircase had come into view. It curved upward and upward in a spiral that reminded Axis of the spirals of water that had initially risen from the water after the destruction of Serpent's Nest.

Light glimmered under each stair rise—not enough to distract, but just enough to light the way.

Maxel reined in his horse and dismounted, then moved to help Ishbel to dismount.

"Where do we go?" said Axis. "Where shall we stable the horses? What—"

He stopped.

From each column stepped forth men—at least that was Axis' first impression, although his second thought was that he was not sure *what* they were. They looked like tall, slim men clad in simple breeches and jerkins, but on closer inspection they were somehow . . . not.

"They are Elcho Falling's servants," Maximilian said, "and they will show all, men and beasts, to their quarters. Spend tonight exploring Elcho Falling, Axis, and discovering its wonders. Speak with me tomorrow."

Axis turned to say something to Maximilian.

But he and Ishbel were gone.

CHAPTER FIFTEEN

Elcho Falling

They rose higher and higher into Elcho Falling, first via the main staircase, then via alternate secondary stairwells. Maximilian led the way, holding Ishbel's hand. They did not speak, but occasionally Maximilian would turn his head and give Ishbel such a look that she began to wish, fairly desperately, that they would arrive at their destination shortly.

"Maxel?" she eventually said, pulling his hand so that they stopped halfway up one stairwell that had as its outer barrier a virtually translucent wall of stone. Beyond was the sky, and the occasional flash of a wing as either an Icarii or Lealfast tumbled by.

The sound of the slowly turning crown was far louder here, and Ishbel could hear it thrumming through her entire body.

"It isn't far," Maximilian said. "Come, Ishbel, see what kind of marriage chamber I have created for you. It is my gift. I asked Josia not to show you this trick during your lessons."

"Are we going to climb all the way to the top?" Ishbel said, and Maximilian smiled at the tone of her voice.

"In a manner of speaking," he said. "Come now, it isn't far."

He tugged at her hand, and they ascended another three or four twists of the stairwell until, quite suddenly, they came to a blank wall of apparently solid, cream-colored stone.

Maximilian pulled Ishbel close to him, their linked hands raised to chest height so that they were the only things that separated their bodies. Once again he pressed the back of his hand against Ishbel's sternum. "All of my strength," he said softly, "in the beat of your heart."

Then he moved their hands against the stone of the wall.

"My name is Maximilian Persimius," he said, "Lord of Elcho Falling. This is my lady, Ishbel Brunelle Persimius. Allow us entry, if you will."

And suddenly the wall was no more, and there was another staircase rising before them.

"This one will not take long," said Maximilian, pulling Ishbel close enough that he could kiss her briefly but with some considerable passion. He led her toward the stairs, and as soon as they were past the space where the wall had been, Ishbel heard a soft sound and she looked back.

The wall had once more returned into place.

"It will always move for us," Maximilian said, "but for no one else. Where this stairwell leads, Ishbel, is for you and me only."

He led her up the stairs, still holding her hand, and within moments they emerged into a circular chamber that brought Ishbel to a complete halt.

"Don't fear," Maximilian said, then he gave a soft laugh. "It is spectacular, though, isn't it?"

They were at the very top of Elcho Falling in a circular chamber that appeared to have no roof or walls at all. It was as if they stood on a platform high in the sky. It was dusk now—*how long had they been climbing?* Ishbel wondered—and outside, amid the early stars in the violet sky, she could see Lealfast and Icarii continuing their tumble of joy through the air and between the great bands of the crown, still in their slow, sweeping dance through the sky.

Thrum.

Thrum.

Thrum.

Ishbel could not hear the movement so much as feel it. The bands were very close, just beyond the edge of the large platform, and she thought their movement and vibration might have been disturbing . . . but, no. That deep, gentle thrumming was as comforting as a heartbeat.

She looked up again. An Icarii had tumbled very close to their chamber.

"They cannot see us," said Maximilian, "and I can, if you wish, close off our view of them." He paused, stroking the back of her hand with his thumb. "I'm sure they'll get tired, or hungry, and go to roost soon."

He gave a gentle tug on her hand, and Ishbel walked a little further into the chamber. It was simply but elegantly furnished—luxuriously upholstered daybeds and chairs, low tables and gleaming sideboards and chests, and a bed, modestly made with cream linens in the very heart of the chamber.

He saw her eyes light on the bed and pulled her very close. "Do you want me to close off the view of the night sky?" he murmured.

"No. Leave it."

They kissed, moving slowly against each other in the initial steps of a long, loving dance. Maximilian slid his hands into her hair, and shook out all the pins of pearls and diamonds, allowing the waves of her fair hair to cascade over her shoulders and back.

She pulled back a little from him. "You have a ring of mine, I believe."

"Are you sure you want it back? I remember how terrified you were of it that first time I slid it on your finger."

"I want it back, Maxel."

"Shall I make you beg?"

She laughed, sliding her hands inside his jacket, unbuttoning his shirt. "Shall I look for it myself?"

"That could be amusing."

They kissed again, far more fervently, moving ever closer to the bed.

Then Maximilian took a step back, laughing a little shakily. "The ring, Ishbel." He removed the ruby and emerald ring from the inner pocket of his jacket, then, completely sober, he took Ishbel's right hand, interlacing their fingers, the ring sandwiched between their palms.

Hello, Ishbel, the ring said. *There is a decision that needs to be made.*

"Maxel?" Ishbel said.

"Ishbel, I need to tell you now what Isaiah has told me."

"You choose your moments very carefully, don't you, Maxel?"

"When Isaiah was with the One, in his presence the One made a curse. Before the One stripped Isaiah of his power, he allowed Isaiah to see that the curse was a reality—not a threat, not a maybe, but a reality. It exists, and needs only two simple actions to become unbreakable. Because of the blood link from our daughter to the One, he is closely linked to us, and that is what gave him the power to create this—"

"*What* curse, Maxel?"

Maximilian squeezed his hand slightly, pressing the ring deeper into

Ishbel's palm. "The One has cursed this ring, Ishbel, and you and I and Elcho Falling with it. If I slip this ring on your finger, wedding you to me, if we sleep together, thus consummating the marriage, then so also I marry the One to Elcho Falling. Its fate is his fate. Destroy him, and I destroy Elcho Falling. It also means that should the One come marching up to the front arch of Elcho Falling, then Elcho Falling will surrender itself to him."

Ishbel's eyes widened. "It is the vision that Ravenna saw!"

She tried to lean away and pull her hand from Maximilian's, but he held her tight against him, and gripped her hand with his.

"Don't," he said. "Please, please, hear me out. Trust me."

"This curse cannot be undone?"

"No."

"And Isaiah is certain it *is* a reality? It *has* been made?"

"Yes."

"Maxel, we can't marry if—"

"*Listen to me, Ishbel.* Do you think we stand a chance with all that confronts us if we stay *apart?*" He took a deep breath. "Ishbel, I think the One fears us—"

"Thus he has so neatly cursed us." She gave a short, humorless laugh. "How can he fear us now? We can do nothing against him—at least not if you slip that ring on my finger, Maxel."

"The One constructed the curse in Isaiah's presence to torment him and, eventually, us. He wanted to crow his victory. He wanted us to weep, knowing he had won. He stripped Isaiah of his power so that Isaiah had to crawl through Isembaard and then through the Salamaan Pass in a desperate attempt to reach us *before*—" again Maximilian pressed the ring into Ishbel's flesh "—I slipped this ring on your finger and bore you down to my bed. Isaiah was always sure he would be too late . . . but by a miracle he found a horse to speed his journey, and then by another miracle he discovered Lamiah, and then, another miracle, the Enchanter StarHeaven, who got a message to Axis . . . just in time."

"Then we must take the chance that has been given us, Maxel."

"Indeed we must, Ishbel. I will slip this ring on your finger as soon as you say I might."

"*Maxel?* But that would mean—"

He laughed, kissing her mouth to stop her words. "Ishbel, think about it. Think about how carefully staged all this was. The One waits until he falls over Isaiah to create this curse, allows Isaiah to recognize its reality while Isaiah still has power to understand it, *then* strips Isaiah of his power and sends him on a long wander into despair in a futile attempt to get a message to me before I put this ring on your finger. But, lo! A miracle! Isaiah finds a horse that the Skraelings had somehow managed not to eat, then he rides it all the way through Skraeling-infested territory, still without it being eaten, and, lo, Isaiah manages to get the message to me *just in time!*"

Ishbel's mouth curved in a small smile. "Ah."

"Ah, indeed, my beautiful love. *I* think that the One is desperate that I do *not* slip this ring on your finger. I think that the very last thing he wants is you and I, united, and bound to him ... what if that does not curse us, but gives us power? He is giving us a reason not to marry, because that is what he fears more than anything else. Yes, the curse exists ... but what if it is a curse against the One, not us? He made sure we were warned, Ishbel. He made absolutely certain that we learned of the message in time."

"You think that the curse can work *for* us, not against us?"

"Yes. The One is terrified of us united, because somehow—I do not know the full intricacies of this yet—we are all three tightly bound."

"You are asking me, *us*, to take a huge risk."

"Yes. I know."

"The One's curse corresponds to Ravenna's vision, Maxel."

"And where did that vision come from, eh?"

"What if it was *true?*"

"The One has been doing all he can to make me set you aside, Ishbel."

She was quiet a moment, thinking. "Could we unwind this curse?"

"I don't know. It's probable that we can't. We'll know more when Isaiah arrives."

"But in the meantime ..."

"We can do what we want more than anything, and which the One desperately hopes we don't. I slip this ring on your finger, and we marry."

"Axis knows about this curse?"

"Yes."

"He'll be furious."

"He's not in this chamber, right here and now. Ishbel, I don't want to talk about Axis."

"I'm trying to hedge for time while I think."

"Ishbel, the One fears us. I think he fears you far more than me, but more than that he fears us united. He doesn't want us to marry."

"So you keep saying, but that could be just desperate hope. Why would the One fear me?"

"Because of your heritage. Because of your direct blood link back to the time when Boaz and Tirzah defeated the pyramid but failed to destroy it. Tirzah was pregnant with your ancestress during that battle. I think that there is something, some lesson or some power, that the growing baby imbibed about the pyramid, or from it, that has been passed down through her line to you."

He paused. "Besides, Ishbel, do you honestly think we're stronger apart than together?"

She smiled, and he knew he had her. "No."

He held her close, again pressing their hands together around the ring. "Do you trust me?"

"Yes. Utterly."

"Do you want to be my wife, the Lady of Elcho Falling?"

She smiled again. "Absolutely."

"Will you wear this ring? Ishbel, in asking you this, I am asking you to jump off a cliff blindly. As you said, it is a huge risk, and I have no idea how to play this curse. I do not know how to keep the One out of Elcho Falling if he appears at our gates. I do not know how—"

Ishbel put the fingers of her free hand over his mouth. "Yes," she said, "I will wear your ring."

Then she leaned back, taking her hand from his mouth and held it out, spearing her fingers, for the ring.

He grinned. "Not just yet."

He removed his hand from hers, taking the ring, and placed it on the bed. Then he came back to Ishbel and gently tipped her face up. "Look."

It was full night now, and the night was blanketed in stars. All the Icarii and Lealfast had gone.

The vast rings of the crown rotated slowly, appearing almost as if they caught some of the stars in their golden orbits.

"Tonight is a night of great power," Maximilian murmured, kissing Ishbel's neck and slowly unfastening her gown. "It is a good night to make a marriage."

"And a good night to make a curse," Ishbel said.

Maximilian slid the gown from her shoulders, running his hands over her breasts. "It is a good night to make an alliance," he said, "and to make love."

"It is a good night," Ishbel said, stepping out of her gown and moving into Maximilian's arms, "to come home."

They lay naked on the bed, touching, kissing, not talking.

The Queen's ring lay to one side of them, its gems glinting gold from time to time as, outside, the bands of the crown drifted lazily by.

Thrum.

Thrum.

Thrum.

They kissed, moving more urgently against each other now, and finally Maximilian reached over and picked up the ring.

He ran his hand down her outstretched arm, using the ring to caress her skin, his other hand in her hair, holding her head still so that he could kiss her once more.

"I prefer this night to that when first you put this ring to my finger," she said, finally moving her mouth away from his.

He smiled, moving his body against hers, running the ring down over her hand. Their eyes met, his again asking the question.

"Yes," she said, "I will wear your ring. Let us make this marriage, Maxel, here and now, in this chamber that you have made for me, and on this night of power. Let us make this curse, and let it give *us* power."

Maximilian shifted the ring so that it sat poised at the end of her finger. He took a deep breath, hesitant in this final moment, and she smiled for him, and moved her hand so that the ring slid down to the base of her finger.

"See," she said, "it is done."

"It is done," Maximilian whispered, and raised himself up and slid inside her body.

The One looked up from where he stood just outside Hairekeep. Behind and stretching far to the west ranged the Skraeling army.

They were crouched low, ready, awaiting a single command.

Their eyes stared north, unblinking.

"So," the One said, "it is done." He took a deep breath. "If that is the way you want it, my Lord of Elcho Falling, then that is the way it shall be. It is of no matter to me."

To one side the red tabby cat rose from the ground, stretched, then wound about the One's legs.

The One sighed, concentrated, then spoke a single word.

Eleanon.

He waited, and nodded in satisfaction as Eleanon responded in his mind.

We begin soon, the One said. *Be ready.*

He glanced up into the night sky.

Bingaleal? the One said. *Are you ready?*

Ready to kill, Bingaleal said, and the One smiled, and nodded.

"Soon," he whispered. "Soon."

They spent that night in the bed under the stars and the slow sweep of the crown of Elcho Falling, talking, touching, and making love. They spoke of their separate lives with each other: Ishbel's time alone in the house of her parents with their corpses, her life at Serpent's Nest, the men she had sent to the grave when she'd slit open their bellies; Maximilian talked of his childhood and training and his father's tutelage, of the black despair of the seventeen years in the Veins, and of his years as a resurrected king, marking time until he met Ishbel.

They talked of their daughter eventually, Ishbel weeping a little, Maximilian kissing the faint marks left by her pregnancy on her belly.

"Salome wanted me to hold her newborn son," Ishbel said to Maximilian, cuddling as close to him as she could. "I couldn't do it. She knew why."

"Perhaps we should have another child."

"Should we? After, perhaps, all this is done."

"And we in our dotage? Why don't we leave it to fate, Ishbel, and accept whatever happens?"

"I fear having another baby, Maxel."

"Because of what we have done tonight? Married each other and the One to Elcho Falling?"

"Only partly. I fear losing another child. I don't think I could survive it."

He moved her hand so that its back lay against his sternum. "In the beat of my heart," he said.

Her mouth curved in a small smile. "I shall find my strength."

In the morning, when they rose, it was to see a dark stain of men and horses across the western horizon.

They stood together at the edge of the platform, watching silently.

"Armat," Maximilian murmured.

"Within that army," Ishbel said, "Armat is not your true enemy."

[Part Six]

CHAPTER ONE

Elcho Falling

Axis stood on a large balcony that faced west. It jutted out from Elcho Falling's outer walls about a third of the way up the citadel: high enough to give him a good view, but not so high that he lost detail. He was tired and irritable. He'd barely slept last night, staying up late to ensure that everyone was settled (and making sure he knew where everyone was), talking with Georgdi, Egalion, and BroadWing, and then spending time with Inardle until dawn. That time with Inardle had not been all talk, but had also included an hourlong soak in the huge hot pool they'd found in one of the chambers of their suite.

Suite—not chamber. Elcho Falling's servants had led Axis and Inardle to a seven-chambered suite which catered to their every whim. Every one of the chambers was massive—ten to fifteen paces high with domed ceilings, and with vast glossy stone floors which reminded Axis of the beautiful floor of Isaiah's Sun Chamber at the palace of Aqhat. Both he and Inardle had stood and stared at the final chamber which contained a large circular steaming pool. They simply looked at it, then at each other, then stripped off their clothes and sank beneath the water. It had done wonders for Inardle's wing, although she still appeared tense. Axis had asked her what was wrong, but she'd just smiled and kissed him and said everything about Elcho Falling was so overwhelming.

She was with him now, along with BroadWing, Eleanon, Georgdi, Ezekiel, and Egalion. Behind them was a large commodious chamber that would serve well as a command center for the citadel. It had everything that

Axis or any of the other commanders could need, including maps and charts in drawers set either under the tables or in chests stacked against the walls. There were even bedchambers opening off the main chamber, for when an officer could not bear to be too far away from his command.

So far as Axis could work out, Elcho Falling somehow provided whatever was needed.

"They arrived some two or three hours after midnight," BroadWing said. "Since then they have been busy establishing camp, with a few small scouting parties circling the land around the edge of Elcho Falling's lake."

"Looking for a bridge, no doubt," said Eleanon.

Axis glanced at him. The Lealfast man had lost a great deal of his edginess since Maximilian had raised Elcho Falling, and he and BroadWing were standing together in a manner that was almost companionable. When Axis and Inardle had arrived in the chamber this morning they'd been perched on the balcony balustrading, discussing some of the Strike Force's tactics with only a minimum of tension.

It was not just Eleanon and BroadWing. Everyone appeared much more at ease with the others. Even Ezekiel, who had kept his distance from the other commanders previously, was clearly a member of the group rather than an orbiting and distant moon.

Whatever Maximilian had done with the Goblet of the Frogs besides raise Elcho Falling, it had been one of the more remarkable pieces of sorcery that Axis had ever seen worked.

He talked with BroadWing for a few more minutes, then looked up when there was a movement above him.

StarDrifter.

"How is my brother?" Axis said once StarDrifter had landed and greeted everyone.

StarDrifter grinned. "Axis, I swear I do not know how I can bear to wait until he is grown. He is going to be a magnificent son."

Axis managed a smile, just, then everyone turned as Maximilian and Ishbel entered the room behind them.

Axis looked instantly to Ishbel's left hand, but she had it hidden in the drapery of her skirts, and he couldn't see if she wore the ring or not. He tried to catch her eye, but she avoided it as she and Maximilian walked over to the balustrade.

"What do you know?" Maximilian said to Axis.

Axis sent one more glance Ishbel's way, but her left hand was still out of sight. "As you can see, Armat has established camp. He has supply lines stretching south and east. Georgdi told me last night that Kezial is a few days away, moving north from Margalit with between eighty to one hundred thousand men—he left some thirty thousand guarding Margalit. Broad-Wing reports this morning that they are even closer than Georgdi thought, perhaps thirty-six hours away."

"And Armat's army?" Maximilian said.

Axis hesitated, wondering what Maximilian wanted to know. "The camp is well established and ordered. There is no sign of internal insubordination."

"Do you know where Insharah has his quarters?" Maximilian said.

Axis looked at BroadWing, who stepped forward.

"Insharah has his encampment in that quarter," BroadWing said, pointing. "You might just be able to see his pennant, the blue one there, with the red tip."

"I can see it," Maximilian said. He smiled as Ishbel came close, pointing out the tent to her. "It is distant from Armat's tent."

"Don't read too much into it," said Axis. "If Insharah was going to make a move, I would have expected it by now."

"Perhaps," said Maximilian.

Axis leaned against the balustrading, folded his arms, and looked at Maximilian. "What now? What do you want me to do about Armat?"

Maximilian looked out over Armat's encampment, thinking. "We have the advantage," he said after a moment or two. "Armat cannot enter Elcho Falling, and his siege engines can do little damage to the citadel. We have the advantage of a flighted army as well as a horsed one. Elcho Falling will never run short of food, or supplies. A siege will do little to damage us, save force us to rely on our own skills for entertainment."

"And the One?" said Axis.

"I want to wait for Isaiah," said Maximilian. "How long before he can join us?"

"He'll never get through Armat," said Axis. "He has a quarter of the men of Kezial and Armat combined."

"*If* Kezial and Armat combine," Maximilian said.

"You are relying a great deal on the hope that the Isembaardians will shatter due to their internal rivalries," Axis said quietly.

"I am relying on history," Maximilian said, a little sharply. "Axis, can you contact Isaiah through StarHeaven again? Find out where he is, how long it will take him to reach Elcho Falling. Also station members of the Strike Force as well as Lealfast down south. I want to know if, *when*, something follows Isaiah through the Salamaan Pass."

At that moment the wind caught at Ishbel's hair, and she lifted her hand to brush it out of her eyes.

Axis went cold at the sight of the ring on her finger, and he looked back at Maximilian.

"I pray to the stars you know what you are doing," Axis said, then turned on his heel and walked away.

"*Axis!*" Maximilian said.

Axis came to a halt, but did not turn around.

"A word, if you please," Maximilian said, catching the eye of the others present and tilting his head.

A moment later the balcony was deserted save for Maximilian, Ishbel, and Axis.

"I know what I do," Maximilian said, and Axis turned round.

"What is worth risking——" he began.

"It is worth everything," Maximilian said, "but yes, I agree it is a risk."

"And you agreed?" Axis said to Ishbel.

She gave a small smile. "Not at first, but Maxel was very persuasive."

"This," Maximilian said, lifting Ishbel's hand so that the ring glinted in the sun, "is what the One did not want me to do. Yes, it binds him to Elcho Falling. I believe what Isaiah says about the curse. I believe in its reality. The One *is* bound to Elcho Falling. Elcho Falling will grant him entry the moment he walks up to its front archway. But . . . somewhere in all of this is something that the One fears greatly: Ishbel and I, united in marriage."

Maximilian told Axis what he'd told Ishbel the night before: that he believed the One had carefully staged Isaiah's miraculous achievement in getting the message to Maximilian in time to prevent the ring going on Ishbel's finger.

"And yet you have no idea *how* to prevent the One becoming Lord of Elcho Falling," Axis said. "If he takes this citadel, if he takes *you*, then——"

"Then I need to do all I can to prevent it," Maximilian said. "Axis, I think the answer to all this lies back in Isembaard. It lies somewhere close to DarkGlass Mountain itself. I need to talk to Isaiah, very badly, because I think he has the key. I need, like Ishbel, to finish my training within the Twisted Tower. I—"

"Ishbel is learning the Twisted Tower?" Axis said.

"She is not who we need to fear," Maximilian said, "no matter what you have been told."

Axis shook his head, looking away for a few minutes as he thought.

"I'll say it again, Maxel," he said eventually, "I pray to the stars you know what you are doing."

"Are you still with me, Axis?"

Axis again gave a small shake of his head. "You don't make it easy for me."

Maximilian smiled. "But . . ."

"But I suppose someone has to look after you."

"Thank you, Axis," Ishbel said softly.

CHAPTER TWO

Elcho Falling

Axis spent the day with his commanders, organizing the defenses of Elcho Falling as best he could, and gathering as much information as possible about Armat's force.

"But Maximilian said that Armat's forces could not enter Elcho Falling," Inardle said to him at one point after he'd spent an hour with her, BroadWing and Eleanon discussing flighted tactics against the Isembaardian army.

"Perhaps," Axis said, "and perhaps not. I need to plan for the eventuality."

They were sitting in their apartments eating a light lunch. Inardle poured a glass of weak ale and slid it across the table toward Axis. "None of your winged command will prove useful if the Isembaardians get *inside* Elcho Falling."

Axis sighed, turning the glass in idle circles on the tabletop. "I know. I want to talk to Georgdi, Egalion, and Ezekiel this afternoon about stationing men on the lower reaches of Elcho Falling. If Armat's men *did* get inside, we'd still have the advantage."

He stopped, his eyes still on the glass as he kept turning it.

"But . . ." said Inardle.

"But," said Axis, "Armat has so many men. He'd lose thousands, but Armat can afford to do that." Again he paused, still watching the glass. "And he has Lister. Maximilian hasn't considered him. Lister knows Elcho Falling, and knows too many of its secrets."

He raised his eyes, looking at Inardle. "What do you think of him, Inardle? How much does he know?"

"Too much, Axis. Too much."

"There is always a traitor somewhere, Inardle. It is always the way."

She froze, but Axis appeared to have made the remark without any underlying meaning, and so she nodded and changed the subject.

Eleanon moved deep within Elcho Falling. The citadel extended far underground, and he spiraled down stairwells for what seemed like hours until he could go no further.

The levels above had mainly been storerooms, but here, at the very core of the citadel, was nothing but a bare and somewhat dusty space with a smooth rock floor that extended so deep into shadows that Eleanon could not see any end to it.

He stood, turning every so often so he could stare into a different part of this cold, lonely chamber, scrying out with his power to see if there was anyone else in the area.

He did not use the power of the Star Dance, but that of the Magi, which Eleanon thought only Maximilian might recognize, and likely not even he.

He was safe enough for the moment.

There was no one else here.

Eleanon's chest rose in a long, deep breath, then he held out his hands before him and muttered an incantation.

The air shifted above his hands, and then appeared the dark corkscrewed spire that Eleanon, Bingaleal, and Inardle had originally used to contact the One many weeks previously.

It was a dark, twisted thing of great power—the most powerful of the spires that the ancient Lealfast had created with the aid of the Magi.

Eleanon held it for a long moment, then he set it down in the center of the rock floor, turned his back, and left.

"Axis! *Axis!*"

He woke grudgingly, tired after a long day spent organizing and worrying.

"Axis!"

He rolled over, unwilling to wake up.

Then he felt Inardle put her mouth right against his ear. "Someone is inside Elcho Falling," she hissed, and Axis almost knocked her over as he sprang upright.

"How do you know?" he said.

"I have felt the movement in the Star Dance," she said, "and in the eddying of the air as it flows up through Elcho Falling. There is an intrusion in the vaulted chambers that lead from the entrance arch, moving toward the great stairwell."

Axis was by now half dressed and pulling on his boots. "Wake Egalion, and BroadWing, and—"

She was already gone, and Axis didn't bother with his shirt, grabbing his sword belt and buckling it about his hips.

"Shit," he muttered as he ran for the door.

Axis almost slid down one of the final curves of the staircase as it wound to an end in the series of vaulted chambers that ran back from the entrance arch. He took several more steps down, then slowed, uncertain.

Everything appeared as it should. There was a pair of the Emerald Guard, standing sentry at one of the curves where Egalion had stationed them. Axis glanced up, seeing sentries further up the staircase and standing on internal balconies that overlooked the great stairwell.

They were watchful, but relaxed, and not a little curious as to why a half-unclothed Axis was sliding down the staircase in a state close to panic.

"StarMan?" one of the sentries near him said.

"There is something wrong," Axis said. "You can't feel it?"

The two sentries just down from him exchanged a glance, then shook their heads. "All is quiet, StarMan," one of them said.

"There is something wrong," Axis said, walking down the stairs more carefully now. He passed the two sentries, then glanced behind him as he heard more steps.

Egalion, and forty or fifty of the Emerald Guard, dressed and weaponed as if they'd been standing ready.

Axis looked back down the stairs. The hairs on the back of his neck were rising. *Something* was wrong, but he couldn't see anything, or otherwise recognize what it might be.

He stepped down a little further.

And, suddenly, there was a disturbance in the air before him.

Ravenna stepped out of the air, and behind her too many Isembaardian soldiers to count.

Stars! Axis thought, taking several steps back up the staircase as he turned to shout orders to Egalion.

"Wait," said Ravenna, "we have not come to fight or to harm."

Axis turned around. He didn't say anything, just looked at the soldiers that kept materializing out of the air. *Ravenna's trick.*

But how had she got them inside the entrance arch?

"Is Maximilian about?" Ravenna said.

"Yes," said a voice, "Maximilian is about."

Axis glanced over his shoulder. Maximilian was stepping past Egalion.

"What do you here, Ravenna?" he said as he came to stand beside Axis.

"Come to talk to you," said Ravenna, "and to demonstrate this." She turned a little, just enough to indicate the mass of soldiers behind her.

Axis glanced between Maximilian and Ravenna. Both appeared very calm, but he thought he could see traces of tension about Maximilian's eyes.

So much for Elcho Falling not allowing Armat's army entrance, Axis thought. If this was the point Ravenna had come to make, then she had made it very well indeed. He caught Egalion's eye, and the man gave a slight nod and began to make his way up the stairwell to get reinforcements.

"How are you, Maxel?" Ravenna said, folding her hands in front of her stomach. She looked very calm and very certain of herself, and the way she'd folded her hands before her tightened the fabric of her gown over her belly, emphasizing her pregnancy.

"You have not come this way and in this manner," Maximilian said, "to exchange banalities. What do you want, Ravenna?"

"You have seen how easily I gained entry," said Ravenna. "This time I brought a thousand men. Next time I might bring one hundred thousand. Have I made my point sufficiently?"

"Very efficiently," said Maximilian. "What have you come to say to me, Ravenna?"

"We need to talk, Maxel. We need to parley. Armat and I are prepared to offer you . . . a compromise, if you like."

"Say it here."

"No. I want to speak to you alone. Just you and me, Maxel, as once it was."

"It was never just you and me," Maximilian said.

"Then it should have been," she said, very quietly. "Come speak with me privately, Maxel. Please. Hear what I have to say." She paused. "Maxel, we need to talk about our child, and I will not do that with all these swords surrounding us."

"You were the one to bring the swords, Ravenna."

"Maxel, please." She hesitated. "Do not cast me off discourteously. Do not make me beg."

Something in Maximilian's face altered at that last. "Where do you want to meet, Ravenna?"

"Maxel—" Axis said, but Maximilian put a hand on his shoulder.

"It is all right, Axis," he murmured. Then, in a louder voice, "Ravenna?"

"Meet me in the Land of Dreams," Ravenna said. "You are skilled enough to find the way, and you know it will be safe there for both of us. Meet me in the Land of Dreams, tomorrow night."

Then, before Maximilian could answer, she turned around, and all the soldiers with her, and walked down the stairwell and back into the vaulted chamber.

"Follow them, and make sure they depart," Axis said to the sentries.

Then he looked to Maximilian. "How did they get in, Maxel?"

"The baby," Maximilian said. "Elcho Falling recognized the baby."

"As your child?"

"As the heir to Elcho Falling," Maximilian said.

"You can't do it."

Axis was with Maximilian, Ishbel, Egalion, and Garth in a chamber high in Elcho Falling.

"Maxel," Axis said, "you *can't* do it. It is too dangerous."

"She won't hurt me," Maximilian said.

Axis looked at Garth.

"I don't think she will, either," Garth said. "Ravenna has done many things I can't condone, but she would never stoop to harming Maxel."

"For all the stars' sakes," Axis said, "she allied herself with Armat! She was prepared to threaten you tonight with invasion! *She killed her own mother!* What *won't* she stoop to?"

"I agree with Axis," Ishbel said. "You can't trust her, Maxel. She wants Elcho Falling for herself and her child."

"If Ravenna wanted Elcho Falling for herself and her child," Maximilian said, "then she wouldn't be parleying. She would have simply led Armat and his two-hundred-thousand-odd men inside the arch this night and most of us would be dead by now. Axis, did you have defenses in place to repel that kind of intrusion?"

Axis shook his head. "Defenses would have been in place by tomorrow night, but even then . . ."

Maximilian grunted. "She could have had us all," he said, "but she didn't take the opportunity. She wants to talk, and I think I should hear what she has to say. For all I know she wants to negotiate with me against Armat."

"Maxel," Axis, Ishbel, and Egalion said as one.

Maximilian waved a hand, dismissing their objections.

"You should have known Elcho Falling would recognize the child," Axis said quietly.

"I had not thought," Maximilian said.

"Don't go," Ishbel said.

"I must," he said.

CHAPTER THREE

Land of Dreams and Elcho Falling

R avenna?"

Maximilian moved through the Land of Dreams carefully. He walked down a damp gravel path. To either side of him were mist-shrouded marshes, studded with gray-green trees draped in moss that reached twiggy fingers through the tendrils of mist to tweak at Maximilian's hair as he passed.

"Ravenna?"

He wondered if the Lord of Dreams was about, but he couldn't sense him. No doubt he'd want to avoid Ravenna.

"Ravenna."

She appeared ten or so paces before him on the path, emerging slowly from the mist as if she glided on ice.

"Maxel." She halted, and Maximilian thought she looked weary and low of spirit.

"What do you want of me, Ravenna?"

"You must know. I want you to acknowledge this baby as your heir. No, wait, please. Let me finish. This is your son, Maxel. Your heir. Elcho Falling knows it, why can't *you* acknowledge it?"

He didn't answer her.

She sighed, moving her shoulders as if trying to loosen them from tension. "Maxel, the only dispute between us is Ishbel. I have said enough to you that you know how I feel. Ishbel will murder you and this land. And know you know *why*. Isaiah has sent word to you that—"

"You know that?"

"Yes. Lister could overhear the communication between Axis and Star-Heaven."

Maximilian's face tightened, and he looked away from her.

Ravenna took a half step toward him. "Ishbel will *murder* this land if you put that ring on her—"

"*Ishbel* won't, you fool! It is the One who carries destruction at his heels!"

"I know you love her, Maxel, but you need to rid yourself of Ishbel in order to save Elcho Falling, and to save the land. You can allow neither to fall to the bleakness that approaches."

"Ravenna, all you want is power, and you use any argument you can to seize it."

"It is not power, my love, but you that I want. I love you, I am here, ready at your hand, for whatever you want. I have waged war for you, Maxel. All for you. Do not cast me off again."

"I am tired of this, Ravenna. Too tired. If there is nothing else you want save but to slander Ishbel, then go."

"Do not put the ring to her finger, Maxel. Your very life depends on that."

"It is too late, Ravenna. I slid that ring to her finger the night before last."

Ravenna went white, her gray eyes glistening madly. "No! Tell me you did not—"

"I have made my choice, my lady. Ishbel is my choice, and my wife. I choose her before you, and in defiance of the One."

"*No!*"

"Too late," said a new voice, and Armat stepped out of the mist at the side of the path, and, as Maximilian started back in alarm, brought down his sword in a murderous arc, slicing Maximilian open from chest to groin.

There was a sudden, horrifying spurt of blood, and then Maximilian vanished from the Land of Dreams.

Armat rested the sword on the ground, staring at the pool of blood on the pathway.

"I needed a second stroke," he said.

"It does not matter," Ravenna said, her voice and face wooden. "That was a death blow. If not in the first instant, within the next ten minutes."

Then she turned and walked back down the path, leaving Armat leaning on his sword, staring at the blood soaking into the gravel.

Axis was sitting in a chair in one of the bedchambers that ran off the main command chamber. He watched Maximilian insensible in his own chair partway across the room. Ishbel sat close to him; Egalion and Garth stood further back in the chamber.

Everyone's eyes were on Maximilian.

He'd been largely still as he traveled the Land of Dreams, although Axis had seen the muscles in Maximilian's face tighten and clench as if he spoke, or reacted to something said to him.

Everyone was tense, no one wanting Maximilian exposed to this danger.

Then, in an instant so horrific that Axis knew he'd never forget it, Maximilian's body exploded. Blood and tissue erupted in a great arc from the front of his body, and he jerked out of the chair and slid to the floor.

For an instant everyone looked, then, as Garth, Axis, and Egalion all made for Maximilian, Ishbel turned on them.

"Garth stays," she snapped. "Everyone else out. *Now!*"

They obeyed her.

There was nothing else to be done.

Both Axis and Egalion had enough experience to know a death blow when they saw one.

CHAPTER FOUR

Elcho Falling

S hit," Axis said. Then again. "*Shit!*"

He looked at Egalion. The man was ashen.

"We'll need to move fast," Axis said, speaking in a low but urgent voice.

They needed to move fast, yes, but giving Egalion something to do would break him out of his fugue faster than anything else.

"Ravenna and Armat will know Maximilian is dead," Axis continued. "It is just past midnight...Egalion, we can expect an attack before dawn. There will be nothing to prevent them now. Get Georgdi and Ezekiel, and get every damned soldier you can find and station them either in the vaulted chamber entrance or in the balconies lining the great stairwell. Remember how Ravenna got those thousand men in previously. Damn it, she likely has enough power to shroud Armat's entire army. Egalion?"

"Yes," he said. "Yes."

"*Move!*" Axis said, and Egalion stared at him a heartbeat longer before running for the door.

StarDrifter, Axis called. *BroadWing.*

In the ten minutes or so it took for them to reach him, Axis paced the chamber, looking every now and again at the closed door to the chamber holding Maximilian, Ishbel, and Garth.

Maximilian would be dead by now. Stars, he'd been eviscerated. That had not been just blood erupting from his belly wound.

Axis closed his eyes for a moment, fighting to forget what he'd just witnessed.

Shit! If only he had the power to turn back time and prevent Maximilian walking into Ravenna's trap.

"Axis?" StarDrifter and BroadWing arrived together, folding their wings as they walked in the balcony door.

"Maximilian has been killed," Axis said.

StarDrifter and BroadWing just stared at Axis, utterly shocked.

"Ravenna trapped him. She likely had Armat lying in wait in the Land of Dreams," Axis said. "We can expect an attack from Armat within hours. BroadWing, I will need you to get both the Strike Force and the Lealfast into the air. Report *any* movement you see in Armat's camp."

BroadWing nodded, turning for the balcony.

"BroadWing?" Axis said, and the Strike Force commander turned back.

"Be careful," Axis said. "I distrust Ravenna's sorceries."

BroadWing nodded, saluted Axis with a clenched hand across his chest, then was gone.

"Ishbel?" StarDrifter said.

"Still in with what remains of Maxel. I have no idea what she can do apart from grieve. Stars, StarDrifter, he was virtually sliced in two."

StarDrifter put a hand on his son's shoulder. "What can I do, Axis?"

Axis took a deep breath. "At the moment the only thing we have in our favor is that we have the Star Dance back in full measure." He gave a small, humorless smile. "At least we are Enchanters again, StarDrifter. I suspect Ravenna will use that trick she used last night to gain entry for her hordes. They'll come disguised with sorceries, and we'll need somehow to either negate those sorceries, or somehow combat them."

For some minutes they conferred quietly, discussing ways in which they could use the Star Dance and their own powers to protect Elcho Falling.

"It might be possible—" StarDrifter said, and both men looked up as Inardle, Egalion, and Georgdi strode in the door. Inardle came straight to Axis, and he gave her a quick hug, using it to comfort himself as much as her.

"Maximilian *is* dead?" Georgdi said, and Axis noted the pain in the man's eyes.

"I'm sorry," he said.

Georgdi's face tightened, but he gave a nod. "My men have taken up position within the vaulted chamber," he said. "Egalion has stationed the Emerald Guard up the main stairwell."

"Good," Axis said. "The Strike Force and Lealfast are in the air. We should get *some* warning of an attack, even if Armat's entire army vanish into a sorcerous gloom. I'm taking command for the moment. We can discuss later an orderly succession. I can't have—"

"There will be no need for such action," Ishbel said, closing the door to Maximilian's death chamber behind her.

Everyone was so shocked by her appearance they could not answer immediately. Ishbel was literally covered in blood. It had soaked and dried into so much of her skirts that they were as stiff as wooden boards, and made walking difficult. Her hands and arms up to her elbows were covered in thick, dried blood, and Axis tried very hard not to imagine where she'd had those hands and arms. Blood had also spattered over her face and through her hair, and soaked in great patches through the material over her breasts.

Thus walks the Archpriestess of the Coil after one of her slaughters, Axis thought, then felt ashamed at the ungenerosity of his thoughts.

Ishbel moved a little closer, and Axis felt everyone else tense, as if they wanted to take a few steps back. *Stars, she* stank *of Maximilian's blood—and worse.*

She raised both her hands before her, and everyone looked at them.

"See," she said softly, "I wear both rings of Persimius now. My marriage ring and that which Maximilian once wore. There is no need for you to assume command, Axis SunSoar. I *am* Persimius," her tone hardened slightly, "and I *am* the Lady of Elcho Falling, and can travel the Twisted Tower as well as once could my husband. What was once Maximilian's is now mine." She paused. "That includes your loyalty."

There was absolute silence as everyone stared at Ishbel.

She moved her hand, just a little, just enough so that the lamplight caught at the few unbloodied jewels of the rings on her hands. "I *am* Persimius. I *am* the Lady of Elcho Falling, and I *do* command your loyalty."

Axis stared at her, fixated by the frightful sight of her standing there, commanding his loyalty.

"And you have it, my lady," Georgdi said, falling to one knee before Ishbel.

She lowered her right hand to him, which carried on its fourth finger Maximilian's ring, and Georgdi kissed it.

An instant later, Egalion was also on his knee before her, kissing the ring.

Axis felt nauseated at the thought of the taste of Maximilian's blood in his mouth.

Georgdi and Egalion stepped back, and Ishbel moved a little closer to Axis and StarDrifter.

At this close distance, Axis' stomach turned at the stench of Maximilian's death, and he had to swallow to prevent himself gagging.

"You gave your loyalty to Maximilian," Ishbel said, holding Axis' gaze. "Will you now give it to me?"

"Ishbel—" Axis began.

"I command everything that Maximilian once commanded," said Ishbel, "and that includes you."

Her gaze was absolutely relentless, and Axis had the sudden thought that she'd prove a far better commander than Maximilian might have done. She had the strength and the stomach for it, he realized, and she might hold Elcho Falling together, where without her it would fall apart.

"You have it," Axis said.

"You don't wish to kiss the ring?" Ishbel said, and her mouth twitched, just slightly. Axis realized it wasn't humor so much as recognition of her current state.

"Perhaps later," Axis said, and Ishbel gave a nod.

"That is good enough for me," she said. "StarDrifter?"

"You have my loyalty," he said, "and that of the Strike Force."

"Inardle?" Ishbel said.

"And mine, and that of the Lealfast," Inardle said, and she had no hesitation in stepping forward and kissing the ring.

"You think Armat will attack now Maximilian is dead?" Ishbel said to Axis.

"Within a few hours," Axis said. "If I were him I would not waste this opportunity. He must think Elcho Falling in disarray."

"Well," said Ishbel, "bloodied, if not in disarray," and Axis once again marveled at how calm and self-controlled she was.

"You have plans for a defense?" she asked.

"Yes," Axis said, but as he began to explain them to Ishbel she interrupted him.

"No need," she said. "I shall defend Elcho Falling."

Before anyone could ask a question, Ishbel turned and walked toward the door that led deeper into Elcho Falling.

She vanished from sight before she reached it.

CHAPTER FIVE

Armat's Encampment

Armat finished his discussion with his leading commander, then dismissed the man.

As soon as the commander had left the tent, Armat looked between Lister and Ravenna. "I will need the cover of your sorceries to get the men inside Elcho Falling," he said. "Axis will certainly expect me to attack, and he has the defensive advantage. You can do it?"

Both Lister and Ravenna nodded, although Ravenna looked less certain of it.

"You have not the stomach for the fight?" Armat asked her. "Has your lover's death distressed you so greatly that—"

"I loved him!" Ravenna said. "Allow me a little room for grief, if you please."

"There is no time nor room for grief if you want your son to have that for which you slaughtered his father," Armat said.

"Then I am ready," Ravenna said. "I will not quail, Armat."

Armat grunted, exchanging a meaningful look with Lister.

Insharah sat in his tent, staring at the sword lying on the bed before him. The entire camp was alive with movement as men readied themselves for an attack upon the citadel of Elcho Falling.

But Insharah could barely breathe, let alone equip himself for the action.

Ravenna and Armat had trapped Maximilian, and murdered him. Armat had called his senior commanders, including Insharah, into his tent the instant he'd returned from the murder, informing them that Maximilian was dead and that Elcho Falling was theirs for the taking. Then he'd sent them away to rouse the army.

Insharah had, instead, come back to his tent, where he had sunk down on his bunk, unable to stir his command for anything. Rimmert had come in, asking questions about what had to be done, and Insharah had sent him on his way with some vague assurances that he'd be out shortly.

But Insharah did not think he'd be able to walk out of this tent, shortly or even lately, and take part in an attack on Elcho Falling.

Insharah thought he could have borne Maximilian's death if it had come accidentally, or nobly. But to be murdered by your lover, who carried your child? And in such a hateful and duplicitous way? For a man who had only ever done good, and that nobly?

All the doubts that had been growing inside Insharah for weeks now coalesced into a sudden, shining determination.

He picked up the sword and tossed it deep into the tent.

"I can't do it," he said.

"Good," said a voice from the dark depths of the tent, and Insharah started up in fear—then fell to his knees in terror as a nightmarish vision walked out of the depths of the tent carrying his sword.

"I seem to be spending tonight collecting loyalties," said Ishbel. "Do I have yours, Insharah?"

"How many can you conceal within your sorcery?" Armat asked Ravenna. He was fully armored and weaponed, and shifted from foot to foot in ill-concealed eagerness. Armat had been blooded that night, and now he wanted more.

"Enough," she said. "I don't have a precise number for you, Armat. Enough. That will have to do."

"No need to snap, my lady," Armat said. "Am I not about to deliver to you that for which you have lusted?"

"Am *I* not about to deliver to you that for which *you* have lusted?" Ravenna snapped. "Don't condescend to me, Armat."

"Oh, for all the gods' sakes," Lister said, "stop fighting like children. Another few hours and we will all have what we want. Power, and a chance to secure this land against that which approaches from—"

He stopped, suddenly very alert, and looked about the interior of the tent.

"What is it?" Armat said, drawing his sword.

"Someone—" Lister began, then drew in a deep breath of shock as power enveloped everyone in the tent. "Someone," he said again, his voice now hoarse with a combination of anger, fear, and surprise, "is using the Persimius gloom."

Before any among Armat, Ravenna, or Lister could move, or summon any sorcery of their own, the blood-soaked Ishbel appeared in their very midst. She spun on her heel as she materialized, flinging one hand out from the goblet she held in her other, scattering blood over the other three.

"I invoke the right of the dark-shrouded widow," she hissed, "given to me by Elcho Falling, to speak uninterrupted against the murderers of the Lord of Elcho Falling."

Armat and Lister both tried to speak, but found themselves unable to so much as open their mouths, while Ravenna struggled uselessly to summon any of her own power.

"You are all bound for the moment," said Ishbel. She looked at each of them, circling slowly, staring coldly at them. "If you had not planned or participated in Maxel's murder, then you would still be able to speak and move. What I have just spoken is a sorcery of justice." She gave a soft, harsh laugh. "Your immobility condemns you, all three."

She indicated a spot toward the door of the tent, and all three of her captives found their eyes drawn to it.

Insharah stood there, holding his sword.

"Behold," Ishbel said. "My witness."

Then she stepped close to Armat. "Yours was the sword," she said, and gave his chest a slight push, sending him toppling askew into the chair just behind him.

"I curse you," Ishbel continued, her voice low and powerful, "to live out what remains of your life as a puppet. You shall not move of your own accord, nor shall you ever speak, save to move to the wishes and to mouth the words of your puppetmaster. His name is Insharah."

"You will tell the Lady of Elcho Falling," said Insharah, "how grateful you are that your life has been spared."

Armat's eyes rolled frantically, but he could not halt the words issuing from his mouth. "I am most grateful to the Lady of Elcho Falling that my life has been spared."

Ishbel gave a cold smile, and looked at Insharah. "My lord, can you hold this for me for the moment?" She held out the goblet she carried in one of her hands, and Insharah took it in his.

Then Ishbel turned to Lister. "What can I say to you, Lister? For twenty years, *more*, I adored you and thought you omnipotent and blessed. I murdered men at your pleasure, and married a man at your whim. But your whim is capricious, is it not? You withdrew your love from me, as also from my husband, whom I had come to love. Thus I withdraw my love from you, Lister, and condemn you to the fate of the hundreds you sent to my knife."

Lister's eyes bulged, but he could not move, nor use any of his power against her.

Ishbel lifted her right hand, and every eye in the tent was drawn to the glinting blade that curved out from her first and second fingers.

"Die in the manner of my husband," Ishbel said, and the blade arced through the air, and in the next instant Lister's belly exploded, sending blood and organs cascading down his legs to the floor.

Fresh blood besmirched Ishbel's face, but she did not blink. She brought the blade down once more, and then yet again, as Lister tried to clutch his bowels back into his body, separating every single organ in his abdominal and pelvic cavity from their supports and sending them sliding through his frantic fingers to the floor.

Lister lifted his face, just enough to stare one long moment into Ishbel's implacable eyes, then he toppled over, the sound of his body hitting the pile of his entrails a frightful, sickening wet thud.

Ishbel ignored him. She looked to Insharah, and he handed back to her the goblet.

Then Ishbel turned to Ravenna. "You tried once to murder me, and then you murdered your mother, and you murdered my husband, who was your lover, and whom you professed to love. You carry his child. Shall you murder that one day, too, when the whim strikes you? Is no one safe from your ambition?"

She sighed, and held up the goblet. "See here, Ravenna. This is the Goblet of the Frogs. Is it not beauteous? It was made by my ancestress, and is a thing of great power. But on this vile night, its power is of no use to me. It is but a goblet, and it is what it contains which is of interest."

Ishbel dipped her free hand into the goblet, and when she withdrew it, her fingers were slick with blood.

"It contains the blood of my murdered husband, Ravenna," Ishbel said. "Imagine this blood's power, when presented to its murderer."

Ishbel flicked her hand suddenly, and even despite the enchantment that bound Ravenna, the woman managed to flinch.

Blood flew through the air to a point just above Ravenna's head. There it coalesced into one large globule and then, horribly, into a travesty of the twisting rings of the crown of Elcho Falling, the slowly turning bands now made of clotted blood rather than gold.

"This bloodied crown is my revenge on you, Ravenna," Ishbel said quietly, "and I use it not as Ishbel, Lady of Elcho Falling, but as the midwife of sorrow which you have always believed me to be."

She paused, taking a deep breath. "The first ring I use to curse you and to cut you off from the Land of Dreams."

One of the bloodied bands slipped free from its two companions, sliding down over Ravenna's body as once the true crown had slipped over Maximilian's body.

"Never more shall you walk the Land of Dreams," said Ishbel, "and never more shall you use its power for any means, fair or foul."

Tears slid down Ravenna's face. Her body twitched as if she fought to struggle free, but Ishbel's enchantment kept her bound.

"The second ring," said Ishbel, "I use to cut your child free from Elcho Falling. No longer Maximilian's heir, no longer his blood, he shall never be able to enter Elcho Falling again without the citadel recognizing him only as the murderer of the Lord of Elcho Falling."

The second ring slid down over Ravenna's body, and her mouth opened in a silent scream.

"The third ring," Ishbel said as the final ring began its descent over Ravenna, "I use to cut you completely from any society or land. No man, no people, and no country shall ever love or offer you safe harbor again, Ravenna. Go now. I free you from the enchantment that I used to bind you. Go now from this tent and from this land. Go and bear your child in agony and sorrow, and weep that you have so thoughtlessly murdered those who loved you."

Ravenna collapsed to her knees as Ishbel's power set her free, then managed to get back to her feet.

"You have made yourself a bad enemy—" she hissed, but Ishbel cut her off with a laugh of genuine amusement.

"A worse enemy than what I have in you already? Go now, Ravenna. I am not interested in what useless words you think to fling my way. If it was not for that child you, too, would be dead. Go. *Go!*"

Ravenna sent Ishbel one last, hate-filled look, then she stumbled from the tent.

Insharah waited a moment until he heard her footsteps fade, then he walked over to Ishbel and took her elbow as she sagged in exhaustion.

"My lady," he murmured.

"Take your puppet," said Ishbel, "and use him to establish your control over this army."

"And then?"

"Then do with it what you think best."

Insharah gave her a steady look. "My lady, you forget how well I know you." He glanced at Armat, and when he spoke again he kept his voice very low. "I am assuming, Ishbel, that you healed Maximilian as well as once you healed Madarin."

CHAPTER SIX

Elcho Falling

Axis, StarDrifter, and Inardle were still within the command room when Ishbel returned. She came through the door, and gave them a cool look.

"There will be no attack," she said.

Then, without waiting for a response, Ishbel entered Maximilian's death chamber and closed the door behind her.

Garth sat five or six paces away from the daybed that held Maximilian's body. He could not look away from it. In the past few hours it had cooled and mottled into the terrible gray and blue of death, its flesh cold and slightly clammy. Maximilian lay on his back, a bloodied sheet pulled up to his chest.

His face was slack, all expression wiped from it when his life had expired.

The door opened and Ishbel entered, startling Garth.

"Did Madarin bring water?" she asked, and Garth nodded at the large urn and basin set on a side table.

"Ishbel?" he said.

"Later," Ishbel said, and walked over to the table. She stripped off her blood-stiffened clothes, dropping them to the floor before kicking them to one side.

Garth stared, unable to look away. The blood which had soaked through her clothes had dried in crusty drifts all down Ishbel's body, and she wrung out a washcloth and scrubbed her flesh until it glowed. Then she shook out her hair, and poured water through it, soaping it thoroughly before rinsing and toweling it dry.

Then, as if oblivious to Garth's presence, she walked over to Maximilian on his day bed, lifted the sheet, and slid in beside him.

"He is so cold," she murmured.

Garth opened his mouth to say something, then realized Ishbel did not expect a reply.

She snuggled in close to Maximilian's corpse, her body against his, one arm sliding under his body so that her arms enclosed him.

She lay her face on his shoulder and clasped her hands about his chest.

Then, rhythmically, Ishbel's hands began to beat gently against Maximilian's sternum.

"I shall find all my strength," she said, "in the beat of your heart."

Ishbel walked into the Twisted Tower. Josia stood just inside the door, his face lined with desperation.

"You have little time," he said.

"I have time enough," Ishbel replied, turning for the stairs.

She walked up them unhurriedly, her naked body gleaming in the warm light, and Josia's eyes followed her until she disappeared from view.

For the next few minutes he listened to the soft footfalls of her steps as they climbed upward.

"Hurry!" he whispered.

Maximilian stood naked before the open window on the very top level. One foot rested on the windowsill, and his body leaned very slightly toward the opening.

His eyes were fixated on what lay beyond, his face awash with a soft green light that pulsated through the window.

Ishbel stepped into the chamber, pausing for a moment as she caught sight of Maximilian. Then she walked over to him, keeping her eyes averted from the view through the window, and stood behind him, pressing her body the length of his, her face resting between his shoulder blades, her eyes closed.

She slid her arms under his and clasped her hands gently together against his chest.

Then they began to beat slowly, rhythmically, against his sternum.

"Maxel?" she said. "Come home, please."

He didn't respond.

She kissed the cold skin between his shoulder blades. "Come home, Maxel."

She pressed herself even more strongly against his back. "Can you feel the beat of my heart, Maxel? Do you remember what you said?"

He didn't move, but Ishbel sensed something deep within him shift.

"Every beat of my heart, Maxel, is your strength. Come home, Maxel, come home."

He shivered, and Ishbel felt a sudden jerk beneath her hands as they pressed against his chest.

Her eyes filled with tears. "Maxel, come home, *please.*"

He relaxed against her, and she had to take a deep breath and hold it to control her emotion.

Then she unclasped her hands, and began to run them very gently over his body.

Wherever they passed, so the scars left by his time in the Veins vanished.

"Let them fly through the window, Maxel," she murmured. "Let both the scars and nightmares go into death. You don't need them anymore."

"Am *I* dead?" Maximilian said.

"No," she said, kissing the skin between his shoulder blades more strongly now. "*No.*"

Maximilian took a deep breath, his first, and lifted his foot from the windowsill and placed it on the floor.

"Come home, Maxel," Ishbel said, and he sighed and turned into her arms.

Garth started in amazement. Maximilian's body, mottled with death, suddenly flushed a rosy pink.

All the scars that had marked his body faded, then vanished.

Maximilian's eyes flew open. They stared at the ceiling of the chamber, then he turned his head and saw Garth.

Garth saw recognition in Maximilian's gaze, but Maximilian did not say anything. Instead he stretched his body very gently, then smiled suddenly as he realized Ishbel's presence beside him.

He rolled over, wrapping her in his arms.

Garth's eyes gleamed with tears. He rose and left the chamber, quietly closing the door behind him.

Epilogue

Go! whispered the One, and all along the southern foothills of the Far-Reach Mountains, from Hairekeep to the River Lhyl, millions of Skraelings darted forth, rushing into the gullies and crevices of the mountains.

By morning they would be through the mountain range and into the realm of the Lord of Elcho Falling.

Atop the peaks of the mountains danced the Lealfast Nation, almost a quarter million of them, holding torches gleefully into the night so that the Skraelings had both light and guidance, and singing with glee as below them silver-orbed horror seethed through the mountain passes.

Salamaan Pass was so thick with Skraelings they hid the ground completely.

Go! whispered the One, and in Elcho Falling Eleanon and his twelve thousand fighters picked up their weapons and dissolved into invisibility.

A moment later they were dispersing throughout the citadel, seeking out the units of the Strike Force and the Emerald Guard and the Outlander fighters, an unseen cloud of silent death.

Go! whispered the One, and in the Twisted Tower Josia frowned at the scratching at the door.

He opened it, and stared bemused at the red tabby cat that entered and began to wind its way about his ankles.

EPILOGUE

And now I! whispered the One, and deep in the heart of Elcho Falling Elea-non's dark spire glowed once, twice, then flared violently.

When the glaring light died, it was to reveal the green form of the One standing in the heart of the citadel.

The One looked about, flexed his shoulders as if he were working out a slight stiffness, then walked toward the staircase that led upward.

Infinity had come to claim Elcho Falling, and death its inhabitants.

The *Book of the Soulenai* lay in the center of the Infinity Chamber in the heart of DarkGlass Mountain, where the One had left it. As the One set foot on the first rise of the staircase in Elcho Falling, so the cover of the book opened slowly.

The rat, who had hidden in the book for so long, slowly emerged and moved away several paces.

It sat down, staring intently at the *Book of the Soulenai*.

The book burst into flames, very suddenly, and as it did so, the rat began to scream.

Glossary

Alaric: a nation in the extreme north.

Aqhat, Palace of: the home of Isaiah, Tyrant of Isembaard.

Armat: one of Isaiah of Isembaard's generals.

Avaldamon: father to Boaz.

Axis: *see* SunSoar, Axis.

Aziel: archpriest of the Order of the Coil.

Baxtor, Garth: a physician who employs the Touch (the ability to determine sickness through touch). Garth was primarily responsible for freeing Maximilian Persimius from the Veins eight years before this tale begins.

Bingaleal: one of the Lealfast.

Boaz: ancestor of Ishbel and Mage of the One. Husband of Tirzah.

Book of the Soulenai: an ancient book which once belonged to Boaz.

BroadWing EvenBeat: an Icarii, and friend of Maximilian Persimius.

Central Kingdoms: a loose coalition of the states of Hosea, Pelemere, and Kyros.

Coil, Order of the: an order that lives in Serpent's Nest. They worship the Great Serpent and use the bowels of living men to foretell the future.

Coroleas: a continent to the west, renowned for the immorality and cruelty of its peoples.

DarkGlass Mountain: an ancient pyramid originally built to provide a pathway into Infinity. Once it was known as Threshold.

Doyle: a member of the Emerald Guard and former assassin.

Egalion: captain of the Emerald Guard, and friend to Maximilian Persimius.

Elcho Falling: a magical and mysterious citadel of legend.

Eleanon: one of the Lealfast.

Emerald Guard, the: Maximilian Persimius' personal guard, composed of former prisoners of the Veins.

Escator: a poor kingdom on the coast of the Widowmaker Sea. It is ruled by Maximilian Persimius.

Ezekiel: Isaiah of Isembaard's most senior general.

Falayal: a Lealfast elder.

First, the: the top caste of Corolean society comprising the Forty-four Hundred Families. The First commands virtually all of the wealth and power within Coroleas.

Forty-four Hundred Families: *see* the First.

Georgdi, Chief Alm: general of the Outlander forces.

Gershadi: a nation in the extreme north.

Goblet of the Frogs: an ancient magical goblet created by Tirzah.

Hairekeep: a fortress standing at the southern entrance to the Salamaan Pass.

Heddiah: a servant within the kitchens of the Palace of Aqhat.

Hereward: Kitchen Steward of the Palace of Aqhat in Isembaard.

Hosea: one of the kingdoms which form the Central Kingdoms.

Icarii: a mystical race of winged people who once lived in the mountains of Tencendor. The Enchanters among them wielded the Star Dance to produce powerful enchantments. Now, a scattered remnant from the destruction of Tencendor live about the Central Kingdoms.

Inardle: one of the Lealfast.

Ingruit: a servant within the kitchens of the Palace of Aqhat.

Insharah: captain of a band of Isembaardian soldiers. Friend of Axis SunSoar.

Isaiah: Tyrant of Isembaard.

Isembaard, Tyranny of: a massive empire below the FarReach Mountains, currently ruled by Isaiah.

Jequial: a servant within the kitchens of the palace of Aqhat.

Kanubai: an ancient enemy of the Lords of Elcho Falling.

Kezial: one of Isaiah of Isembaard's generals.

Kyros: a city state within the loose alliance of the Central Kingdoms. It is ruled by King Malat.

Lamiah: one of Isaiah of Isembaard's generals.

Lealfast: an Icarii-like race of the frozen north.

Lixel, Baron: a trusted baron of Maximilian Persimius, currently ruling Escator in Maximilian's absence.

Madarin: an Isembaardian soldier.

Malat: King of Kyros.

Margalit: the major city of the Outlands, and Ishbel Brunelle's childhood home.

Maximilian Persimius: *see* Persimius, Maximilian.

Morfah: one of Isaiah of Isembaard's generals. Now dead.

Odella: a servant within the kitchens of the Palace of Aqhat.

One, the: DarkGlass Mountain incarnate in flesh.

Outlands, the: a province to the far east, renowned for its wild nomadic culture.

Pelemere: a city state within the loose alliance of the Central Kingdoms.

Persimius Brunelle, Lady Ishbel: orphan from Margalit, raised to be Archpriestess of the Order of the Coil, and former wife of Maximilian Persimius.

Persimius, Maximilian: King of Escator. Maximilian endured seventeen years in the gloam mines as a youth and young man when his cousin Cavor seized the throne.

Ravenna: a marsh witch-woman who patrols the borderlands between this world and the Land of Dreams. Her mother is Venetia.

Risdon: second-in-command to the Isembaardian general, Armat.

Sakkuth: capital of the Tyranny of Isembaard.

Salamaan Pass: a great pass which is the only easy access through the Far-Reach Mountains into Isembaard.

Second, the: the Thirty-eight Thousand Families who comprise the second caste within Corolean society. The Second is comprised mostly of the educated intelligentsia, traders, and minor landowners.

Serge: a member of the Emerald Guard and former assassin.

Serpent's Nest: a great mountain on the coast of the Outlands.

Skraelings: wraithlike creatures inhabiting the ice and snowbound wastes of the far north.

Star Dance: Enchanters among the Icarii wielded the music of the stars (the music made as the stars move about the heavens, and which the Icarii called the Star Dance) in order to create powerful enchantments. The

Star Dance is no longer available to those Icarii remaining alive as the Star Gate, which filtered the Star Dance through to them from the heavens, was destroyed during the final Tencendor wars.

Star Gate: a magical portal which once existed in Tencendor, the Star Gate filtered the magic of the Star Dance, which the Icarii enchanters used to create their enchantments. Demons destroyed the Star Gate during the final wars of Tencendor.

StarWeb: an Icarii, and lover to Maximilian Persimius.

SunSoar, Axis: formerly a hero from Tencendor and a member of the Icarii race, Axis once reigned over Tencendor as its StarMan before relinquishing power to his son Caelum. Axis died five years ago during the destruction of Tencendor.

SunSoar, Salome: former Duchess of Sidon in Coroleas, now wife of StarDrifter SunSoar.

SunSoar, StarDrifter: Axis' father, and a powerful Icarii prince and Enchanter.

Tencendor: a continent which once lay in the western region of the Widowmaker Sea. It was lost five years before this tale begins in a catastrophic war with demons.

Third, the: the third caste within Corolean society, mostly comprising workers.

Thirty-eight Thousand Second Families: *see* the Second.

Tirzah: ancestor of Ishbel and wife of Boaz.

Twisted Tower, the: a palace of memories.

Veins, the: the gloam mines of Escator where Maximilian Persimius was imprisoned for seventeen years.

Venetia: a marsh witch-woman who patrols the borderlands between this world and the Land of Dreams. Ravenna is her daughter.

Viland: a nation in the extreme north. The Vilanders often have trouble with Skraelings.

Vorstus: abbot of the Order of Persimius, Vorstus aided Garth Baxtor and Ravenna in freeing Maximilian Persimius from the Veins eight years before this tale begins.

Weeper, the: a strange but immensely powerful Corolean bronze deity.

Yysell: Axis SunSoar's body servant.

Zeboath: Isembaardian physician.